BROTHERS AND WARRIORS

Patriots of the American Revolution Series

Book One

©2016

Geoff Baggett

Cocked Hat Publishing

ISBN: 0997383305
ISBN 13: 9780997383300

Dedicated to My Editorial Team

To my beautiful, perfect wife and lifelong companion, Kim Baggett. She is a saint. She knew full well that I was a lifelong nerd when she married me. She puts up with a lot.

To my best friend and SAR Compatriot, Steve Mallory. His knowledge, expertise in weaponry, timeless witticisms, and constructive criticisms made this project a reality.

To Debbie Mallory, another saint. She is a constant and steadfast provider of encouragement and enthusiasm.

PART I

The Perishing of Peace

1

WARS AND RUMORS OF WARS

Sunday was John's favorite day. No plowing, no hoeing, no fencing, no work ... period. It was the only day of the week that he, his older brother, James, and younger brother, William, could do what they wanted to do, with just a few exceptions. On this particular Sunday morning, John packed a load of shot into his Papa's Pennsylvania Fowler and headed out squirrel hunting. He had a couple of hours to enjoy all to himself before church. He knew that he could have four or five of the critters felled and cleaned before service.

Of course, there remained a few chores that could not be avoided. The milk-cows, Sylvia and Barthenia, had to be relieved of their swollen burden like on any other ordinary day. Water had to be hauled up from the spring. All the livestock had to be fed. He and William had started on all of those daily chores right after sunup. And there was absolutely no getting out of the Sunday Church meeting. The Hamilton boys were fine Scotch-Irish Presbyterians, just like their Papa. Plus, they would never disappoint their mother by not making their weekly appearance at the meeting house.

John decided to fix a quick breakfast before heading out to the woods. The oldest brother of the clan, James, had already fried up a generous plate full of middlin' meat while the younger John and

William had been taking care of the livestock. The tasty pork grease still lay warm and fragrant in the deep cast-iron skillet perched on top of the tiny oak wood table beside the hearth. James had eaten his fill of the smoky meat along with some dried apples and hot tea. James loved his tea, sweetened with copious amounts of honey. Neither John nor William had ever developed a taste for it.

John elected to fry up some hot corn cakes to go with his meat. He pulled a pile of glowing hot coals out of the fireplace onto the hearth and placed the rack and skillet over them to heat up the grease. He then measured out a generous heap of corn meal into a wooden mixing bowl. He carefully poured a few ounces of the fresh, frothy, warm cow's milk into the corn meal to reach the right thickness and then mixed a simple batter. He tossed in a hearty pinch of black pepper.

Once the grease was sizzling and popping he carefully poured small puddles of the thick mixture, spacing perfectly round corn cakes in the yellow grease. The skillet hissed as the moisture of the milk rapidly boiled out and released steam into the chilly room. As soon as bubbles began to appear on top of the puddles he flipped them over, exposing their golden brown undersides to the air.

Within a matter of minutes he filled a hickory platter with about twenty of the crunchy treats. Young William walked in just as he was finishing, smiling at the site of hot corn cakes for breakfast. Slapping five of them onto his plate, he grabbed a handful of the middlin' and a jug of sorghum and sat down at the table. William grabbed his own plate and loaded it up. They ate ravenously with both hands, alternately dipping their greasy corn cakes in the sweet, syrupy sorghum and popping chunks of the smoky middlin' into their mouths. Both boys washed their breakfast down with rich, fresh milk.

John spewed tiny specks of corn when he broke the silence with a question, "William, what are you plannin' to do before meetin'?"

"I gotta mend my white breeches. Mama would just die if I showed up with 'em torn wide open like they are now. I gotta to clean this house, too. You and James make a frightful mess when you cook."

"You don't much seem to mind eatin'," John shot back.

"I ain't complainin', Johnny, just makin' what they call an 'observation.'"

His belly full, he grabbed his wide-brimmed hunting hat, lead pouch, hunting bag, and powder horn and headed out the door of the cabin. His older brother, James, was sitting beside the door carefully sawing thin wafers off of an antler to make buttons for the new buckskin breeches he was making. He shot a glance at John.

"Johnny, don't you make me late for service!"

"Promise I won't," he shouted over his shoulder. "I'm just goin' to fetch a few squirrels for supper down in the hickory hole. I'll be back in an hour or so."

"Just make sure you are. I'd best not have to come and fetch ya, or them squirrels won't be the only thing gittin' skint this mornin'!"

So off he traipsed into the woods in search of a tasty supper. A half-hour later he had four squirrels in his soft buckskin hunting bag, two of them dropped with one shot! He would have fun telling that story later at church.

Yes … there could be no doubt … Sundays were always the best of days.

But it was on Sundays, as glorious as they were, that John missed his Papa the most. He missed seeing him placing that enormous King James Bible in the wagon seat beside him for the ride to the meeting house. And if he was feeling particularly rowdy or engaged in one of his all-too-common theological tiffs with a fellow deacon, he would also tote his *Westminster Confession of Faith*. John missed him sitting by the fireplace on Sunday nights reading Ambrose's *Prima, Media, et Ultima* or Russell's *Seven Sermons*. He remembered fondly how his Papa always seemed to smile and never, ever, uttered a harsh word.

John ran his fingers along the heavy steel barrel of his father's Fowler, custom-made by Martin Fry back in York County, Pennsylvania. It was one of the few things he owned that had belonged to his father. He took off his straw hat and laid it on the ground beside him, leaned his head back against the hickory tree he was squatting beside, and closed his eyes. He tried to picture Papa's face and remember his voice. But it was becoming more and more difficult.

Beyond his Sunday memories there wasn't much that John could recall about his father. He had some tiny remembrances ... cutting logs for the cabin, fishing in Coddle Creek, and sitting in Papa's lap to read his hornbook. His father had been gone for so long, and those memories were distant and faded. It was hard to believe that it had been eight years now. John was only seven years old when his father died.

It had been a warm spell in February of 1772, about two years after Hugh Hamilton had led his family out of York County southward through the Shenandoah Valley and the dense woodlands of central Virginia and North Carolina to settle in the frontier county of Mecklenburg. The local men had taken advantage of the abnormally mild weather to help a neighbor, Ephraim Farr, get a new roof on his wind-damaged barn. That day Hugh took a nasty fall off of a rather rickety ladder. One of his neighbors volunteered to walk home with him, but about a quarter-mile from the cabin Hugh insisted that the neighbor turn back so that he wouldn't be caught in the woods at night, with the Cherokees making such trouble as they were known to do.

Hugh Hamilton never made it home. The next morning another neighbor, Thomas Bottoms, found him dead beside a spring, not one hundred yards from where his escort had left him the evening before. They buried him on a small rise near the Rocky River, about a quarter mile from his cabin home.

It seemed like the entire community turned out to pay their respects to this godly, honest man. And for the people of Mecklenburg County, most of whom were a wicked, filthy, backwoods bunch, Hugh Hamilton had been a man of some means. Unlike his barefoot and illiterate neighbors, he owned one hundred and ninety acres of land, and had several horses and cows. He even owned his own wagon, one of only a handful in the entire region, and a major investment. His wardrobe sported a French jac coat, several stylish weskits, and even a beautiful dark blue greatcoat … something unheard of for most men in the area. There was also a rumor that he was sitting on a sum of Spanish silver and French gold coin when he died.

So it came as no surprise that the newly-widowed Margaret Hamilton, a beautiful young woman of twenty-nine years, rapidly became the object of affection of several eligible bachelors along the Rocky River. All were eager to marry into the property and farm of Hugh Hamilton, especially since it was a spread that came with four growing boys to serve as current and future farm hands.

But it was the widower Ephraim Farr, owner of the barn and ladder that killed Hugh Hamilton, who won the prize. He courted the hardest. He was an old friend of the family, having traveled south from Pennsylvania with the Hamiltons shortly after the death of his first wife. And to top it all off and really close the deal, he paid off the outstanding mortgage on one hundred and ninety acres of Hugh Hamilton's land.

Since the North Carolina frontier was no place for a woman on her own with four small boys, and she was somewhat beholden to his "generosity," she rapidly consented to a marriage. She moved her four boys to the Farr farm, already occupied by Ephriam's daughter and three sons by his first wife. Eleven months later Margaret gave birth to her first little Farr, and she had been steadily birthing Farrs ever since.

It didn't take long for James and John, the older of the Hamilton boys, to figure out that they were going to be sucking hind teat at the Farr homestead. While their mama and baby Hugh moved into the cabin with all the rest of the Farrs, James, John, and William had to sleep in Ephraim's old cave house. It was his original dwelling on his land after moving to North Carolina, basically a log room built onto the front of a small cave in a hillside along Coddle Creek. He and his kids only lived there for their first six months or so after settling in the North Carolina woods while he worked on his new cabin. Since then it had served as a root cellar and storage for salt and other supplies.

So James, John, and William threw down their pallets right there amongst the beets and taters and made do as best they could. The cave was cold, the mud fireplace in the log addition drew pretty poorly, and the joint between the rock face and the timber leaked something fierce, but the boys made the best of their new home. They raked huge piles of dry leaves from the surrounding forest and hauled them in to cover the rock floor of the cave where they slept. They made a layer that was every bit of one foot deep. Their step-father was at least cordial enough to give them a huge, plush black bear hide to place on top of their leaf-pile "mattress." About a week after they moved in James shot another bear, which insured the boys a thick winter bear blanket ... something they would need in a few months.

The Hamilton boys took most of their meals outside on the porch or under the trees, either alone or with Farr's occasional hired hands. There were only rare occasions when they were allowed in the family cabin. In general, they weren't welcome there. Farr didn't want them. It broke their mother's heart, but she always made sure the boys were well-fed and clothed. They worked hard on the Farr farm ... as hard as boys age twelve, nine, and six could work ... and their mother saw to it that they received some book learning. But they were, for all practical purposes, pretty much on their own and raising themselves.

Such was their existence for six years, until early last year, when James turned eighteen years old. He went to Ephriam and demanded some land for his own. He wanted off the Farr farm, and he was taking his brothers John and William with him. First came a flood of their mother's tears, and then her feminine wiles kicked in. She bargained, pleaded, manipulated, and cajoled her husband, generally making his life unbearable and unlivable in a blustery storm of female emotion, until he relented and agreed to give the boys their father's land, but for a price. On January 30, 1779, he mortgaged Hugh Hamilton's original one hundred and ninety acres to James, John, and William Hamilton for the hefty price of one hundred Spanish dollars, to be paid back at a rate of fifty cents per month over twenty years. It was an enormous sum for three boys age eighteen, fifteen, and twelve ... especially with the War with King George going on. But they took the offer. Anything to get off of the Farr farm.

Amazingly, the boys were making a go of it. They moved their meager belongings back into the cabin that their father had built for them. At last they were back home. They grew a decent crop of corn their first season. They sold furs and brain-tanned deer hides to a trader who came through Charlotte every couple of months. James and John hired themselves out a couple of times for odd jobs on near-by farms to earn just a little extra money. Their mama pitched in, too, skimming a little flour, sugar, and coffee from the Farr family supply and gifting it to her boys.

It helped that their step-father was often hurting for extra labor, as well. He had begun to dig and purify salt from a lick on his farm. The local Commissioner of Mecklenburg County had contracted with him to provide salt for the militia as well as shipment to the Continental Army. It was hard work, but it paid well. Not in cash to the Hamilton boys, of course, but in "forgiveness" of their monthly debt payment. So the boys, on several occasions, were able to trade a few days of labor for their monthly payment on the farm.

Thus far the salt operation and sale of corn were the only connection the Hamilton boys had to the war. The local militia, of which James was a part, met and drilled about once a month. John also attended muster whenever James would let him. They occasionally fielded patrols to keep an eye out for Tory activity. But there wasn't much of that in Mecklenburg County.

Ever since the Mecklenburg resolves in 1775, the county had been a hotbed of independence and Patriot sentiment, a so-called, "Hornet's Nest," and the local residents lived up to their stinging moniker. The Presbyterians of Mecklenburg County were more than happy to cast off the yoke of King George and the Church of England. It galled them that they had to hire one of the king's vicars in order to have what the British would consider a "legal" marriage.

But politics, kings, and wars, on this beautiful Sunday, might as well have been a million miles away. Yes, General Clinton had invaded South Carolina by sea and put Charlestown under siege last month, but up until now the whole "official" war had basically been fought up in the north. And surely it would not come to sleepy little Mecklenburg County, North Carolina. Local folk were more concerned about wandering bands of renegade Cherokees or the occasional Creek Indian hunting party than they were Tories or Redcoats.

John, awash with memories and lulled by the comfort of the warm May morning, was just on the verge of dozing off against the tree when he heard a limb crash to his left. It was the din of a careless squirrel jumping from one tree to another. John scanned until he caught a glimpse of the little critter, cocked his Fowler, and aimed about a foot in front of it as it ran down the limb toward the trunk of the hickory tree. The loud report of the gun and the cloud of white smoke were followed by the dull thud of the lifeless squirrel hitting the hillside.

Five squirrels would make a fine supper for him and his brothers. Smiling with satisfaction, he scooped up the squirrel by the tail as he trudged up the hill toward the cabin. He knew that he barely had time to clean all the critters and get them soaking in salt-water before leaving for church.

Once back at the cabin William helped him make quick work of the squirrels while James hitched the horse to their small work wagon. Then all three of them washed up to make themselves presentable for church ... and for mama. They each donned their newest dark linen breeches and fine white shirts, all made by the loving hands of their mother. James and William wore beautiful yellow-gold weskits that matched the shiny buckles on their shoes. John preferred his emerald green weskit with matching socks. Green had always been his favorite color.

James grabbed his hunting rifle, pouch, and horn from beside the stone fireplace and headed for the door. William shot a wide-eyed glance at John.

"Mama ain't gonna be none too happy to see you totin' that there rifle into church," John cautioned.

For as long as he could remember, church meetings and guns did not mix in the Hamilton family. On Sunday they left them at home. No exceptions. Papa had never carried a weapon to church. He insisted that on the Sabbath they would rely on the sovereignty of God to protect them, not gunpowder and lead. He believed that God was surely capable enough to protect them for one-half mile of civilized road in a county populated by friends. Mama carried the sentiment into her new marriage and family.

"Mama just might snatch it and club you over the head with it, James!" quipped young William, cackling at the thought of their tiny mother disciplining his big brother.

"I ain't takin' it into church you numbskulls. I'll stow it under the straw in the wagon, just to be cautious. I'm in the militia. And this war is only two hunnert miles away at Charlestown. You never know when Redcoats might come a ridin' right through Charlotte and up into this holler. Maybe even on the Sabbath. So I say better safe than sorry. You boys need to grab your guns, too, and hide 'em with mine."

John and William looked at each other, nodded, and obediently grabbed their weapons. John took his father's Fowler from its place of honor over the fireplace. William fetched his shorter-barreled sea-service Brown Bess from under his bed. All three headed out to the wagon wearing their finest fur-felt cocked hats. James carefully concealed their weapons and equipment under the loose straw, then the boys headed off down the road toward the Poplar Tent Presbyterian Church.

Organized under a poplar tree in 1751 by the Rev. John Thompson, the church quickly graduated from an open-air meeting to a tent meeting. When the people of the church began to seek out a name for their congregation, legend says that someone supposedly threw a cup of water on top of the tent and exclaimed, "Let's call it Poplar Tent Church!" And the name stuck. Of course, the tent had grown over the years. Some folk wanted to erect a permanent wood structure, but the traditionalists all loved their old tent. So the tent remained.

As the boys rounded the bend leading up to the grove of poplar trees that towered over the tent they noticed a somewhat larger than usual crowd gathered around the meeting place. Kids were playing quietly, Sabbath-style, in the glade just downhill from the church tent. The ladies were, undoubtedly, inside the tent quietly talking and preparing for worship. Several men milled about in small groups around horses, mules, and wagons, talking reverently. Some were a bit more animated in their speech while others stared and nodded in reflection. Clearly politics and war were heavy upon their minds.

Ephraim Farr looked up from one of the groups and nodded at the boys as they pulled up in their small, humble wagon. James courteously, if not warmly, returned the nod. John paid little attention to the men-folk as he searched the glade for boys his age. Spotting his friend, Jacob Newman, and several other teenage boys sitting on and around a stump near the edge of the woods, John jumped from the wagon before it had even stopped moving. He walked deliberately toward the young men of his age-set.

A soft, feminine voice broke his concentration on his group of friends. "Oh, my, that is one handsome outfit you're a wearin', Johnny Hamilton."

It was Mary Skillington, a plain, pleasant fourteen-year-old who made no secret about her undying affections for John Hamilton. Though she was not unpleasant, John thought that she was a bit underdeveloped, lanky, and awkward. Her overabundance of freckles and slightly toothy grin made him cringe on the inside. He tried not to exhibit any of the awkward discomfort and displeasure he was feeling at the moment.

"Why thank you for noticin', Mary," he responded, rather coolly. "My mama taught me to wear only my very best in the worship and service of our Lord. You are most kind."

"Oh, you would look handsome in just about anything, Johnny." She grinned her toothy grin. Sensing the discomfort, she tried to change the subject. "Everyone is actin' so queer, sittin' around in little packs just a talkin'. What do you think all of the jabber is about?"

"Oh, I'm quite certain it's the war and the Redcoats. They're knockin' on the door of Charlestown, ya know."

"I reckon you're right ..." Her words trailed off into a disquieting silence.

John, not wanting to continue the conversation, spoke abruptly, "Mary, if you'll be excusin' me, I need to talk to the other boys for a bit."

Mary, crestfallen by the perceived rejection, just nodded in response, and turned quickly to walk back over to the area where the preteen girls were gathered, all of them whispering, giggling, and pointing toward the exchange between Mary and John.

John rolled his eyes and walked on, nodding to his peers and he knelt beside them. Jacob slapped him on the shoulder and quipped, "Nice of you to finally join us, John. We figgered you two was pickin' out a weddin' date, mebbe."

The boys chuckled.

Daniel Pippin, with a thick Irish brogue, followed, "Or perhaps you two were discussing some prospective names for your firstborn."

The boys laughed rather raucously, but quieted quickly upon several stern looks from the men's area.

"That'll be nuff of that, fellers. I got my Fowler in the wagon and I ain't skeert to use it."

Shocked, wide eyes glanced between John and the wagon, but he quickly broke the silence with a quick wink and a smile.

"What's all the high level talkin' going on here at church, today?" queried John. "Seems a bit odd ... and quiet ... all at the same time."

"It's this danged war," Jacob replied. "Ever since the Redcoats landed down at Charlestown and put it under the cannon and gun, people been gettin' jumpy. It's just a little too close fer comfort, ya know? Word is those folk are havin' a rough go of it down there, but nobody knows fer sure. We ain't heerd nothing for near on a week now. The safety committee sent a rider down that way on Monday, but they ain't heered nuthin' yet. Folks is gettin' a bit jumpy."

John nodded. "James is one of the jumpy ones, for sure. He made me and William pack our guns for the trip to church this mornin'. Said you never know when the militia might get called up or trouble might show up. I thought he was over-reactin' just a bit, but now I reckon not."

"No, I bet you can find a gun on every horse and in every wagon on this Sabbath day," Jacob confirmed. "Never thought I would see the day that good Presbyterian folk would trust the persuadin' power of lead over the sovereignty of the Almighty." He grinned. All of the boys did.

"Better safe than sorry, ain't that what folks say?" John commented. Quiet nods of affirmation flowed around the small circle of young men.

The slow movement of men toward the tent signaled that it was time for church to begin. The kids quickly followed their fathers' example and began walking toward the open flap of the tent. Just as the men started to enter a gunshot over the hill toward the south broke the silence of the holy migration. Everyone spun around to look. Some of the men made a quiet dash for their wagons and horses, in case weapons were needed. Soon the gallop of a horse could clearly be heard, and it was approaching quickly.

A rider topped the hill on the road to Charlotte. John recognized the rider immediately. It was Daniel Overton, an ensign in the local militia.

Jacob pointed up the hill and yelled, "It's Mr. Overton, back from Charlestown!"

Women were spilling out of the church tent just as the young soldier rode up, his horse soaked and streaked with lather, tongue hanging out and dehydrated. One of the teenage boys appeared almost instantly with two buckets of water. Ensign Overton drank thirstily from one while the boy held the other under the muzzle of the poor horse. Overton poured some water over his dusty face and then poured the remainder over his horse's neck.

The church people were as thirsty for news as that horse was for her water. Seeing the query in their eyes, Overton dumped a bucket of shocking news on them.

"Charlestown has fell." That's all he said. Succinct. Rapid. To the point.

"When?" shouted one of the men.

"On Friday. I've been ridin' two days straight just to get here. Ran two other horses to ground. Confiscated this one early this mornin'. I saw the white flag go up and everthin' on Friday. Lincoln surrendered his entire command. Over 5,000 men."

The congregation gasped.

"How many British?" asked another.

"I ain't sure. But it was a powerful lot of 'em. One feller who was there in the woods with me said he heerd it was over 12,000 of em."

"12,000!" exclaimed one of the women. "So many!"

"That's why I'm here. Col. Irwin let me rest a spell, then sent me straight on out to spread the word. The militia's bein' called up. All men sixteen and older. No muster date yet. Just git yer 'fairs in order and git yer gear ready for when the call comes. And it's a comin', gents. Because them Redcoats didn't come to just set up house in Charlestown."

2

VOLUNTEERS

The call-up did not come as early as everyone expected. Patriot spies in South Carolina kept a relatively constant stream of news about British movements flowing northward. It seemed that their main goal was to solidify their gains around Charlestown and slowly begin their pacification of the outlying areas.

There were scant few Tories in Mecklenburg County, but stories began to circulate about British sympathizers from South Carolina making forays across the border. Supposedly a few homes had been burned. It was reported by some that men loyal to the Patriot cause were snatched from their beds in the dark of night, never to be heard from again. But no one could ever seem to give the exact name of those men or where they lived, so the rumors didn't take much root. There were, however, reliable reports about Tories becoming more active in some North Carolina counties to the northwest and just across the border in South Carolina.

For the first week after the fall of Charlestown most people stayed pretty close to home. Women and children stayed indoors. The men worked their fields, tended their livestock, and operated as normally as possible. The one exception was that men and boys of a reasonable age were armed at all times. Muskets and rifles were kept within constant reach.

But after the initial spasms of fear waned, people began to wander a little further from home and in pretty short order the normal flow of life and commerce resumed. By the following Sunday life seemingly returned to normal, including the Sunday routine of attending church meeting.

It was at that first Sunday meeting after the fall of Charlestown that the war hit a little closer to home. The shock came in the form of a message delivered by a kindly looking gentleman that the Hamilton boys had never seen before. Immediately after the opening prayer Elder William Scott announced that they had a guest and invited the man to stand and speak. The man appeared somber.

"Brothers and sisters, I am Thomas Crawford, of the Waxhaws Presbyterian Church, just across the border in South Carolina. It is with a heavy heart that I come before you today. This past Thursday evening ruffians with sympathies to King George forced their way into the home of Mr. Edward McClelland … a fine, hard-working, God-fearing man of our faith. According to his precious wife, they demanded payment for his so-called traitorous sons, two of whom were captured and imprisoned at Charlestown. When he informed them that he neither had any money to give, nor the inclination to give any to thieves in the night, the Tories dragged him into the woods beside his barn and hung him. In cold blood, they murdered an unarmed man."

The congregation was visibly shaken. Several of the women wept. Men murmured in a mixture of anger and fear. John looked at his brother, James, and saw him clenching his fists and pounding them on his knees. His temples were pulsating.

Crawford continued, "I come to this congregation today to beg its kindness and generosity in a spirit of Christian charity to offer relief to Brother McClelland's poor widow. She is now alone with five children in her charge, with no help possible from her two grown sons, now suffering in the British gaol in Charlestown. Waxhaws church has dispatched envoys to our sister congregations throughout the region. They sent me hither to ask whatever support you might offer to this destitute woman, be it foodstuffs, supplies, funds, or labor on her farm. We entreat you to open your hearts and pantries and be a blessing to this woman." Turning to the elder, he concluded, "Elder Scott, I am most grateful for this opportunity to speak to you and your congregation. I trust that God's will shall be revealed and obeyed."

Clearly finished with his speech, the visiting church leader turned very slowly and deliberately and sat down on the front-row bench.

Elder Scott rose in his place to speak, "Brother Crawford, we are grateful for your presence today and for bringing this dire need to our attention. Our hearts are broken for the widow McClelland and her family. Obviously, this is a need that demands our utmost attention. We will commit the matter to prayer today, and so that it might provide the way for a greater opportunity for deliberate generosity, we will gather again here as a church late on Tuesday afternoon, the day after tomorrow, one hour before sundown, for the sole purposes of prayer and giving. On that evening we will pray for our brethren and collect the offering that God wills for us to share with this family."

Nods and murmurs of affirmation pulsated throughout the tent.

The Elder continued, "Once the offering is collected, we will dispatch men on Wednesday morning to deliver such gifts as we receive. All we need right now are men to volunteer for this humanitarian mission. Gentlemen, who will hearken to the call of the Word of God and answer, 'Here am I, send me?'"

Silence ensued. As the good Elder scanned the room he met the expectant eyes of the women and the downcast stares of the men. Few seemed to be willing to make eye contact. Clearly, none of them had any desire, whatsoever, to leave their homes and families with the cloud of war's uncertainty hanging over the entire land. But in a matter of moments John felt a sudden movement beside him as his brother, James, rose to his feet.

"Elder, if the church is agreeable, it would be an honor for myself and my brothers Johnny and William to take those supplies and gifts on Wednesday. We're at a good stoppin' point at our farm, so's we can afford a few days away. It might take a full day or day and a half with a loaded wagon, then maybe we could help out on the McClelland place for a couple of days, worship with the good folk at the Waxhaws church on the Lord's Day, then head back home on that afternoon. We should be able to make it back some time on Monday evenin', Lord willin'. "

"Here, here!" came a shout from the back, followed by a chorus of, "Amens," that was pretty raucous for a Presbyterian gathering.

Mr. Scott replied, "James, we are humbled by you boys' offer, and we gratefully accept. Brother Crawford, does such an arrangement seem agreeable to you?"

Thomas Crawford stood and replied, "It does, indeed, sir. We will prepare for their arrival and have lodging arranged at the McClelland farm. I stand humbled and most grateful."

John didn't remember much after that exchange. His mind was awash with visions of travel and adventure. Other than his early childhood in Pennsylvania, he had never been outside of Mecklenburg County, and here he was, headed into the Tory-infested backwoods of South Carolina. Sure, it was just barely across the border, but it was in South Carolina! The war was there! He shivered with excitement.

After the church gathering it took the boys a full half-hour just to get back to their wagon and start heading for home. The short walk was cluttered with interruption. The men shook their hands and slapped their backs. The women doted over them and promised to help "fix them up right" for such a journey. The teenage boys glared at John through a green fog of jealousy. The girls swooned, especially Mary Skillington. John thought that her face might split wide open if she smiled any wider and batted her eyes at him any harder. But, at long last, they finally made it to the wagon and began slowly rolling toward home. They all felt pretty satisfied with themselves ... even young William, who still didn't quite understand what he had been volunteered to do. Nevertheless, the pride was contagious.

Monday and Tuesday were filled with a flurry of activity. Even though, as James shared at church, they were in a bit of a quiet lull on the farm, there were still the basic chores to attend to. All of their crops were in the ground, and the corn had been chopped and weeded just that past week. But there was livestock to tend, fences to mend, and everyday mundane tasks to accomplish.

Visitors appeared at the farm almost hourly to drop off items for the collection. James had not thought of such a possibility, but after the first couple of unexpected visitors, he set aside some room in the barn to make a stack of goods. Clearly, not everyone was planning to attend the Tuesday evening prayer meeting, but it seemed like most of the local folk still wanted to help through giving.

By late on Tuesday there was a considerable pile of corn, syrup, salt, bedding, and deer hides. There were bags of corn meal and flour, small kegs of lard, jugs and jars of sundry food items, some smoked hams, sides of middlin' meat, along with several boxes and bundles of unknown items wrapped in colored cloth or brown paper. Several items of old, outgrown, and discarded clothing for children began to collect in a separate pile. A few visitors handed James money for the destitute family, but not many of them did so, and in the end it did not amount to much. He accumulated a humble collection of copper and silver coins minted in various nations throughout Europe, but mostly British coppers and little slivers and pie-cut pieces of Spanish milled dollars.

Their neighbors also brought a few items for the boys, themselves. These were mainly gifts of dried beef and venison, nuts, and dried fruit for the journey. James was dumbfounded when his step-father appeared late on Tuesday and delivered not only a basket of food from their mother, but also three horns full of powder and an ample supply of lead and patches for all of their weapons. He was touched by the gift ... but he still didn't care one bit for Ephraim Farr.

The boys loaded up and headed for the church tent as the hour drew nigh for the planned meeting. As James suspected, there were not many people present for the called meeting. Perhaps half of the membership was in attendance. But those who did come brought similar gifts to those dropped off earlier in the week. Their supply of goods was doubled and their money supply tripled. After all of the gifts were loaded in the wagon the members gathered around the Hamilton boys and blessed them with a prayer. The boys hurried home to prepare themselves for the next day's journey.

It took them two hours by candle and lamplight to load the wagon and get everything covered with canvas. It was way past their normal bedtime when they all tumbled into their corn shuck beds. They planned to rise early for the journey, but John didn't care. He was so excited that he had serious doubts as to whether he could sleep at all. He eventually drifted off, dreaming about the exotic wilderness of South Carolina and the marauding Redcoats that were sure to be there.

He awakened as his bed shook beneath him. James stood over his bed in the darkness, holding a beeswax candle in his hand, and vigorously kicking the leg of his corn shuck bed.

"I'm awake, James! Stop yer kickin!"

Wednesday had arrived. Finally, an adventure!

John jumped up quickly from his bed and pulled on his breeches. As he stretched his wool socks across his feet he noticed a cream-colored mass stretched across the chair beside his bed. The mixture of pre-dawn darkness and cloudy eyes from sleep made it difficult for him to see the mysterious object on the chair. He reached out and his hands touched soft buckskin. Along the side he felt a row of rough-cut buttons, most likely wafers of antler.

"What's this, James?" he queried.

"Aw, I had a cut of that buckskin leather left over and thought I would make you some new leggings," he replied. "Them old gray wool ones of yours are worn plumb out. I measured them off of your other set and made 'em to strap on nice and tight with them antler buttons. I hope you like 'em. A man settin' off into the wilderness needs a good set of leggings."

John's eyes swelled a bit, almost to the point of tears. James had given him a man-sized gift. These were garments that he had spent untold hours preparing, cutting, and sewing. John didn't know what to say. So he plainly and simply responded, "Much obliged, James. I'll wear 'em proud."

He partially buttoned his soft, supple new leggings and pulled them up over his socks until they reached just above the cuff of his breeches. They were sized perfectly, hitting right at the knee. James equipped them properly with a leather strap on the outside hips that would tie off on his belt and insure that the leggings would not sag and gather. Finally, John slipped on his black buckle shoes and secured the bottom three buttons on the outside of the leggings. A thick piece of leather slipped perfectly under the arch in front of his heel and secured to the bottom button. The fit was perfect. The buckskin was soft and thick. It was one of the nicest gifts that John had ever received from anyone.

As John finished getting dressed, William also began to stir in his cot on the other side of the cabin. James had been a little less violent in his efforts to wake the lad. John went over and helped his little brother get dressed and gather his personal bag and gear.

The Hamilton boys wolfed down a cold breakfast of biscuits and salt pork, washed down with tepid milk. James had milked their cow and fed the chickens for the final time before their trip. His younger Farr half-brothers were responsible for the twice-daily milking, livestock feeding, and gathering of eggs while they were gone. James hitched the horses while John and William filled their three wooden canteens and four large beeswax-sealed gourds with fresh water and stashed them in the few available nooks and hollows that were still available in the wagon. Finally, they all loaded and primed their flintlocks and climbed up onto the seat of the wagon just as the dull glow of the sunrise began to creep over the eastern ridge. James pointed the team southward toward Charlotte and their great adventure began.

The seven-mile journey southwest into Charlotte passed relatively quickly. It was a trip that they had made together many times. The sun was well up and bright and the main thoroughfare was bustling with life when the boys passed through town. The smell of fresh-baked bread and smoky middlin' and ham wafted from the windows of several taverns. John even caught a whiff of fresh coffee. He hated tea, but loved coffee. William begged James to stop so they could get a little something hot to eat, but James denied his request. He wanted to push on and get as close to their destination as possible before dark.

Once through Charlotte they set off due south into the Waxhaws. A couple of hours later they stopped along a small creek to eat and rest the horses. The boys shared a picnic of fried chicken that their mother had packed for the trip, cold fried potatoes and onions, biscuits with elderberry jelly, and fried apple pies. They washed the hearty meal down with cool spring water from home. After their dinner James smoked his clay pipe while the younger boys caught a quick nap in the shade. About a half-hour later James roused them from their slumber.

"Get up, boys. We need to move on. We ain't gonna get there tonight, but we need to move on as far as we can."

"How far you think we've got to go, James?" questioned William.

"I figger it's about another fifteen or sixteen miles, give or take. We've covered about nine since we left home this mornin'. We've got good road and a pretty light load, all things considered. We're already into South Carolina. I reckon we're makin' pretty good time."

"Do you think there are any Redcoats close by?" queried John.

"Naw. Tain't no Redcoats way up here. There might be some egg-suckin' Tory scum hereabouts and lookin' for trouble, though. We'd best be on our guard. Since there's still good road ahead William can drive the rig whilst you and me keep watch, Johnny. Make sure your pan still has a charge and keep your horn and measure close by."

"It'll be slow going if we get into a shootin' fight and have to be measuring powder straight out the horn," John responded.

"True. I reckon we should have rolled us a few cartridges before we left home. Don't know why I didn't think of that," mused James.

John slapped his hands on his knees, "Well, why don't we go ahead and roll a few now. We have some paper on a couple of these packages. You said we ain't gonna get there tonight, anyways. We would go ahead and prepare ourselves proper, even if it means a little longer trip in the mornin'."

James rubbed his chin and pondered, "I reckon you're right. Johnny, fetch us some good paper and our shootin' bags, and let's roll ten or twelve loads apiece."

John climbed up on the side of the wagon and found a parcel in the pile that was wrapped in brown paper. There weren't many such packages, since paper was such a rarity and sold for a premium on the frontier. He unwrapped the contents of the parcel, two well-worn but cleaned and pressed boys' shirts, and returned them to the wagon. Grabbing the paper and their three leather bags, he returned to the shade beside the creek.

Each of the boys reached into their leather bags and took out a small dowel stick that they used for rolling cartridges. They each rolled a tightly packed paper tube with a round ball at the tip of the dowel.

John asked, "Buck, too?"

"Prob'ly a good idea," James responded.

So the boys each added an additional three pellets of large buckshot to the end of their cartridges. They tied the bullet end closed with thread, removed the dowel, and then twisted and tied the tube just below the round ball. Each of them repeated the process ten times, rolling ten perfect cartridge tubes.

Next, they took out their powder measures and measured out 100 grains of powder, pouring it into each tube. The final step was crimping and folding the end with the powder. When they were done each of the Hamilton boys had ten fight-ready cartridges. They carefully placed the paper rolls into their bags. James and John had prepared loads for their .54 caliber smooth bore rifles. William had heftier .69 caliber loads for his stubby Brown Bess sea service musket that James had gotten for him in a trade the previous winter.

The process took about an hour, so it was mid-afternoon when the Hamilton boys got back on the road. James rode with rifle at the ready and sat on the seat beside William. John made himself a small nest in the back of the wagon and kept watch to the rear. But much to his chagrin, the remainder of their travel that afternoon was uneventful. They encountered local farm inhabitants, mostly children on foot, and the occasional rider. No one gave them any trouble, although they did encounter one particularly nosy older gentleman on a mule, a fellow with an unintelligible Scottish brogue named Mr. McCloud, who seemed a bit too interested in their wagonload of cargo. But he soon tired of James' vague answers and went about his own business. William kept the wagon going at a steady pace, stopping just once to water the horses in a shallow roadside pond.

Four hours after their extended lunch break, with about another six miles still to travel, sundown was imminent. They broke out of the thick Carolina forest into a wide area of grassland. Such meadows were not uncommon in the area. They were usually not very large, but these glades in the hills made beautiful homesteads and provided fertile land for farming. This particular oasis in the woods, for whatever reason, had not been settled as of yet.

"It'll be dark in an hour," warned John.

"Yep, this looks like as good a place as any to make camp for the night. Head yonder way, William," James urged, pointing to their left.

James had spotted a secure place to camp about a hundred yards to their east. It was a thick patch of pine trees on the edge of the glade, positioned along a small creek. There was a slight rise between the road and the trees, making only the top two-thirds of the trees visible from the road. William guided the team across the open grazing land toward the pines. As they neared the spot James realized that it was, indeed, a perfect campsite.

The pines backed up against a sharp outcropping of steep rock on the far side of the creek. Their camp would be protected from intruders from the rear, and with the hill blocking the view from the road, it would be safe enough for them to make a small fire.

James jumped from the wagon as William halted the team at the edge of the glade. He stepped off a few yards into the woods and scouted the site, returning quickly.

"Right here, William. Point the horses yonder way and line up the wagon across here, right at the edge of the trees," James instructed. "We'll drop a canvas over the far side to help block the light from our fire. We can sleep under the wagon."

William clicked at the horses and pulled the reins to the right, turning the wagon out in the glade into a big circle, then bringing it back around parallel with the trees. He parked the rig at the edge of the pines, placing its frame between the campsite and the road.

James watered the team in the creek and tethered them at the edge of the tall grass to graze. He then struck out walking into the woods, saying that he was going to, "scout the place out and make sure there weren't any surprises." He was also looking for a little fresh game for supper.

John and William started preparing the camp. The first order of business was to clear out the pine needles to make a clear spot and dig a hole for a cooking fire. Placing the fire a foot deep in the ground would help conceal the light of the flames. John dug the fire hole while William kicked and pushed mounds of soft, dry pine needles underneath the wagon for bedding under their sleeping blankets. Afterward they teamed up to loosen the canvas cover from the wagon and drape it down on the far side of the rig toward the road.

Both boys jumped when a single shot rang out somewhere to their south.

"That was pretty close," whispered William.

"Yeah, just a couple hundred yards. Don't worry, little brother. It sounded like James' Fowler rifle to me. I'll bet he just got us some meat."

Ten minutes later they heard James whistle. John responded with a shrill whistle of his own. Then James' smiling face came bobbing over a slight rise in the woods. He carried a rather large, plump turkey over his right shoulder and a huge grin on his face.

"Roast turkey!" William exclaimed.

"You haven't started that fire, yet?" James asked, incredulously, as he walked into camp.

"Twas just about to, right before you whistled. It won't take me long," retorted John.

John took his fire starting tin out of his leather bag and went to work. He grabbed a handful of pine needles and placed them beside his fire hole. He next unrolled his supply of char cloth, took out a small square of the blackened cotton fabric, and placed a healthy-sized wad of tow beside the cloth. It only took two strikes of his flint rock on a piece of steel to capture a spark on the char cloth. He picked it up in his hands and placed the tow on top, forming a perfect "bird's nest." Then he began to blow. The spark grew into a larger ember and rapidly heated the tow. It only took a few moments for the tow to burst into flame in his hands. He carefully placed the flaming wad in the hole and added a few pine needles and twigs. Soon he had a roaring little fire. The entire process took less than five minutes.

He looked at his older brother with a prideful look of self-satisfaction. James just smiled back and nodded.

It took a half-hour for James and William to pluck and clean the bird sufficiently for cooking, which gave John plenty of time to add some larger pieces of wood and build a substantial bed of piping hot coals in the fire hole. Once the bird was cleaned and washed in the creek, James rigged the meat on a makeshift spit. He cut the beautiful, pink breast meat off of the bone and removed the thigh and leg quarters from the carcass, mounting each piece separately along the spit for quicker cooking. He kept some of the fattier parts with skin attached and wrapped them around the breast meat to provided some extra grease.

"Them breasties will get all dried out of we don't grease 'em up a bit," he explained to his brothers.

For the next hour they took turns rotating the meat so that it would cook uniformly through. They snacked on some dried apples and pecans as they waited. When the meat was almost ready John fetched their water jugs and the basket that their mother had prepared for them. Though they had eaten most of her goodies at lunchtime, there was still a sack of fried cornbread cakes and about half a jar of their mama's elderberry jam.

James slid the succulent meat off of the spit onto a pewter plate from their mama's basket, John said grace, and then the Hamilton boys indulged in a delicious feast! They talked and laughed as they ate, and didn't stop eating until every morsel of the turkey was gone and every corn cake consumed. William lapped the final drops of jam out of the jar before returning it to the basket.

After dinner a raucous belching contest ensued, but James put a stop to it when it appeared that William might throw up his supper if they didn't quit. James took out his clay pipe to send the signal that it was time to calm down and relax. John retrieved his own pipe from the loop on the front of his tobacco sack that hung loosely from his neck. They each packed their pipes with aromatic tobacco and lit them with a coal from the campfire.

"Can I have a puff, Jamie?" begged William.

"Heck, no! You near 'bouts lost your supper from laughin'. If you get any of this baccy smoke in you I'm afraid you might turn green and die!"

John laughed. William pouted. James pondered.

"This shore is an adventure, ain't it, James?" mused John.

"I reckon," he replied. "But remember, we're ain't even goin' thirty miles from home. It ain't like we're a goin' down to Charlestown to spy on the Redcoats or nothing. Just going down to help out a poor widder lady for a spell."

"I know. But it's still excitin'! I mean, as long as I can remember I've never even been outta Mecklenburg County before this very day."

"Just don't go dreamin' up a bunch of nonsense," James cautioned. "There ain't no shootin' war down here in the Waxhaws. Just a few thievin' Tories that killed a good man. We're goin' down here to be good Christian neighbors and do us a good deed."

"I'm tryin'," John yawned, "But sometimes I can't help it."

"You boys better go ahead and get under that wagon and get some sleep. I thought maybe we'd better keep a lookout during the night, but I don't reckon we really need to. After you boys lay down a spell I'll cover this fire for the night. We should be just fine in the dark. I'll stay awake for a bit after I put the fire out just to be sure. But leave me some room. I'm plannin' to crawl under there with ya."

John got up and headed to the wagon with William. They got all three of their blankets out, leaving James' folded neatly in the center space under the wagon so that he could easily crawl into his make-shift bed in the dark. The two younger boys made their places on either side of James under the wheel axles and settled down into deep burrows of soft pine needles. They quickly drifted off into a deep, dreamless sleep.

3

NEW FRIENDS

John awakened just before dawn. He heard the rhythmic, deep breaths of sleep coming from James as he dozed deeply beside him. He knew, without doubt, that William was still asleep. He was always difficult to rouse, no matter the circumstance. There was a noticeable bite of chill in the air. John felt the cold in his bones and wished that he had prepared a thicker mattress of needles to help insulate him against the heat-sapping ground. He lay still in the pre-dawn silence for a few minutes, but was too chilled to doze. It had been an unusually cold night for late May. Or, perhaps, John just wasn't accustomed to sleeping outside on the ground. He slowly, quietly pried himself from his pine needle and wool blanket cocoon and crawled out from under the rear of the wagon.

Checking the fire pit he found a few small coals concealed under a thin blanket of ash. It took only two handfuls of the dry needles and some gentle blowing to revive the previous night's fire. A few branches and sticks added to the flames resulted in a vigorous campfire. Fetching his blanket from beneath the wagon, he draped it over his shoulders and warmed himself by the fire pit. The world around him was silent, except for the spooky call of an owl on a distant ridge. John enjoyed the solitude as the warmth crept back into his bones.

His solitude didn't last long. He soon heard James grunt his typical "wake-up snort," followed by a resounding and obnoxious fart.

James' exit from beneath the wagon was not nearly as stealthy as his own. He loudly extracted himself, dragging his blanket and half of the pine needle mattress with him, and joined John by the fire. They sat in silence for several minutes.

"Reckon we'll be at the McClelland place by mid-mornin'," stated James, breaking the quiet spell.

"Yep," responded John. He had nothing more to add to his brother's observation.

More silence ensued, this time broken by John.

"I sure hope Mrs. McClelland is a good cook. No offense, James, but it'll be nice to taste a woman's cookin' three times a day for a change."

James smiled in the darkness. He responded, "I just hope she has a handsome daughter or two. Might make all this workin' for free a bit more tolerable."

"I'm surprised you find your Christian duty so intolerable," teased John.

"What sounded good and holy in church don't seem quite so reasonable out here in the woods, little brother."

John grunted his acknowledgement, the firelight illuminating his toothy grin of agreement.

"I reckon we'd better get William up and get to movin'. Sun'll be up full in an hour. I'll rustle the boy if you'll put us together a little breakfast," James encouraged.

John pulled his body away from the fire and made his way to the wagon to fetch something from among the supplies that would suffice for a cold breakfast. He grinned as he listened to the combat of wills taking place beneath the wagon. William was none too excited to leave his sleeping nest. But he soon gave in and crawled from beneath the rig. James encouraged him to take his blanket and sit by the fire.

John grabbed a cloth sack from beneath the seat of the wagon. It contained a couple of pounds of salted, dried strips of beef. James had actually perfected a delicious black pepper cure recipe. He dried the strips on strings suspended in the smokehouse. James usually smoked them with hickory, but John preferred the milder flavor of apple wood. Either way, they were delicious. The boys ate the dried beef as a staple of their cold meals "on the go," or for snacks in the fields where they worked each day.

He grabbed a tin from the bed of the wagon, just behind the seat, that contained an assortment of dried apples, pears, and peaches, as well as a mixture of raw pecans and walnuts and salted, roasted hickory nuts. This would constitute their breakfast, such as it was. They sat down by the fire to eat. Slowly they gnawed at the tough beef and munched on the fruit and nuts. William was attacking the morsels of sweet, dried fruit with a little too much enthusiasm.

"Don't eat too much of them pears and peaches, Willie. You'll get the flucks. I ain't stopping every half-mile for you to drop your breeches on the side of the road," warned James.

"All right," replied William, pushing the tin toward John. "But don't worry about stopping for me. I'll just use Johnny's stinky hat."

John pushed him sideways, almost causing him to roll into the fire, bringing about a loud and boisterous protest.

"Stop it, you two," scolded James. "We're out here to do a man's job and you two need to be actin' like men. Keep your hands to yourself. None of that silly playin'."

They ate the remainder of their meager meal in silence and washed it down with spring water from one of the oak canteens. James poured the remainder of the water from the canteen onto the fire while John kicked in fresh dirt to cover the coals. Within minutes they had their gear stowed, the canvas cover re-stretched over the cargo, and were once again headed southward toward their destination. The rim of the sun was just breaking the horizon when William guided the wagon out of the glade and back onto the narrow, rutted road.

Once again William drove the wagon while James and John kept watch. The final leg of their trip was uneventful, but rather slow. The condition of the road deteriorated as they progressed southward. They had to stop at two homesteads to ask directions, and finally arrived at the Waxhaws Presbyterian Church around 10:00 in the morning. A familiar face met them in the doorway of the frame church. It was the Elder Thomas Crawford, the gentleman who had made the original appeal on Sunday before the Poplar Tent congregation. He called and waved to the Hamilton boys, smiling broadly and obviously happy to see them. As they pulled up in front of the church three young fellows emerged from behind the building. They looked to be a matching set, obviously brothers or close kin, and stair-stepped in age much like James, John, and William Hamilton.

"James Hamilton and brothers! We are so glad you have come! I trust that your journey was safe and free of travails," proclaimed Elder Crawford.

James was both surprised and humbled that the Elder remembered his name.

"Yes, sir, the trip was just fine. We moved a little slower than I had hoped, but we found us a good spot to camp last night, and we're rarin' to get to work," James responded.

"Excellent. Excellent. And what an amazing mass of cargo you have brought! Is this all for the McClelland family?"

"Yes sir. Every parcel and package. Folks were droppin' by with gifts for near on three days before we left," explained James.

"Oh, my! Such generous brothers and sisters in the Lord. The widow McClelland and her children will be most grateful, I assure you. Why don't we head out that way right now so that I can make the proper introductions and get you started in your ministry there?" prompted the elder. His speech was followed by the muted sound of a throat being cleared behind him.

"Oh, heavens!" he exclaimed. "How rude of me. We have some introductions to make right here, don't we. James, and ... I'm sorry boys ... I don't recall your names ..."

John spoke up quickly, "I'm John and this is our little brother, William."

"Yes, of course … James, John, and William … this is my son, Thomas, Jr., and the two younger boys are my nephews, Robert and Andy Jackson. They are my sister-in-law's boys. She was widowed over ten years ago, and their older brother died last year, so the boys spend quite a bit of time with me. They've been helping out a little at the McClelland farm these past couple of weeks, and will be working with you some while you are here. We believe that six strapping young fellows, like yourselves, will be able to accomplish much on that neglected farm in only a few days."

The boys all shook hands with mumbles of, "Howdy," and "Glad to meet you."

"Wonderful! So everyone is sufficiently acquainted? Then let us make haste to the McClelland farm so that the work can progress. James, if you boys would follow us."

The elder and his nephews retrieved their horses that were tethered to a bush beside the church building, mounted quickly, then led the Hamilton boys and their wagon westward. James drove the team with William beside him. John returned to his nest in the rear of the wagon. The McClelland farm was a mere quarter away and the trip required only a few minutes.

"Hello in the house!" exclaimed the Elder as they pulled off of the road into the small clearing in front of the cabin.

The widow McClelland emerged, wiping her hands on a stained towel, followed by a parade of curious children. First came three little boys, the oldest of which looked to be no more than seven or eight years of age. Two awkward, gangly looking preteen girls followed the boys, each covered with freckles, their brilliant red hair spilling down over the collars of their dresses.

The last person to come out of the little cabin caused James to give an almost audible gasp. He stared, eyes transfixed upon the most beautiful young woman that he had ever seen in his life. This eldest daughter of the widow McClelland radiated grace and beauty. Even John was captivated by her angelic appearance. Thomas Crawford and the Jackson boys all stared and smiled. William, oblivious to her feminine effects, focused his attention upon thumping the stinkbug that had landed on his knee.

The Elder began his introductions, "Mrs. McClelland, these are the brothers Hamilton from Mecklenburg County. The eldest is James, followed by John and William. Gentlemen, this is Mrs. Mary Kate McClelland and her eldest daughter, Margaret. The younger girls are Alice and Sharon, and the boys are David, James, and little Timothy."

James jumped down quickly from the wagon, "Good mornin', Mrs. McClelland, I'm pleased to finally meet you." He tipped his hat to the gorgeous young woman, "You, as well, ma'am."

She returned his gesture with a heart-stopping smile. For a moment he was lost in her perfect blue eyes and creamy face framed by shiny, cherry-blonde hair. Then she spoke, "Good morning, Mr. Hamilton, it is a pleasure to meet you."

Her voice was soft and smooth like velvet. It completed her beauty. James was overwhelmed, smitten. James and the young woman locked eyes with one another. An awkward silence ensued.

Mrs. McClelland ended the discomfort by extending her hand to James, which he shook gently and reverently.

She spoke to him in a thick Scottish brogue, "Mr. Hamilton, we are most grateful that you have come. It touched my heart when Elder Crawford told me of your plans to visit our humble home. I cannot express the depth of my gratitude for your sacrifice."

"It ain't a sacrifice at all, ma'am," James replied, "We were most eager to do our Christian duty and help a family in need."

John, sitting on the edge of the wagon directly behind James, remembering his brother's verbal regret regarding the trip spoken only hours before by the campfire, subtly dug his knee into James' back. James tried to ignore him.

"And we bring gifts to you and your family!" James continued. "Clothes, foodstuffs, supplies, and our folks even took up a modest monetary collection. We want you and your young 'uns to be blessed. We are so very sorry for the loss of your husband. And we hope your sons are safe and that they will soon be released by the British."

"You are most kind, Mr. Hamilton, and your church is, indeed, a blessing," she replied in a soft, broken voice. It appeared that she might begin to cry. "It has been difficult, indeed, since my dear husband departed from us. And my sons were the very backbone of this hardscrabble farm. Frankly, it's not much of a farm, at all, with them gone."

A cranky little voice piped from behind the Elder Crawford, "Your husband didn't depart you, Mrs. McClelland, them low down sons-a-bitches Tory dogs hunged him and took him from ya ... and your boys, too!"

"You watch your mouth, Andrew Jackson!" Elder Crawford scolded. "I'll not have you talking such profane speech around ladies. Apologize this instant!"

Andy glared for a moment at his uncle. "I'm sorry I said 'sons-a-bitches' Mrs. McClelland, and I'm extra sorry them Tory scum hung your husband."

The boy's uncle shot him another hateful glance. John could almost swear that he saw the widow McClelland's lip curl with the slightest of smiles through the tears welled up in her eyes.

"Thank you, Andy. Apology accepted. Now, boys, hop down off of that wagon and come sit down for a spell. Have you had anything decent to eat today?"

James responded, "We ate a little dried beef and fruit in camp this morning, ma'am."

"And we're powerful hungry!" William chimed in.

Everyone laughed, including Elder Crawford.

"But ..." James gazed at his brothers with a rock-hard stare, "we came here to work, not fill our bellies and socialize."

"Nonsense!" Mrs. McClelland corrected James. "You're here to encourage us with your company as much as your labor. It will take Margaret and meself about an hour to prepare a suitable dinner. Why don't you young men go ahead and unload the wagon? Just stack everything here in the shade under the stoop so that we can sort it all out this afternoon. Afterwards Robert and Andy will acquaint you with your sleeping quarters. They have been working here for the past couple of days and have prepared a place for you in the small loft in our barn. It's not much, but it will be a warm and comfortable place for you to rest."

"Of course, Mrs. McClelland," James replied. "We are most grateful."

He turned to his brothers, "You heard her, boys, let's unload this stuff."

With the help of the Thomas Crawford and the Jackson brothers they had the wagon unloaded and the supplies stacked in a matter of minutes. During the confusion of unloading, James pulled the Elder aside and entrusted to him the small doeskin coin bag containing the money collected by the Poplar Tent Church so that he might give it to the widow at a more appropriate and private time.

After the unloading was complete the Hamiltons grabbed their blankets and personal bags and followed Robert and Andy to the barn. Thomas lingered by the cabin and appeared to be stealing a glance at Margaret through the tiny window of the cabin.

The energetic Andy Jackson led them up the short ladder into the low loft. The lower level ceiling of the small stable-barn was no more than eight feet in height, with an extra six feet to the crown up in the loft. The Jacksons had already prepared a sleeping area at the front of the loft near the opening that faced the house. They had brought in fresh straw that they piled up to about one foot in depth. They limited the straw to the front of the loft. The rear of the loft room had an open, rough wooden floor. There was a single small table placed against the wall that contained two candle stands equipped with brand new beeswax candles. They leaned their weapons in the corner near the table.

James threw his belongings down on the straw and glanced at the Jackson boys, "This'll do just fine, fellers. Much obliged." Turning to his brothers, he declared, "I'm goin' back down to the house to see if there's anythin' I can do to help out."

"With the cookin'?" John questioned incredulously, "Not likely."

William covered his mouth and snickered.

"I'll see you at dinner," James shot back, ignoring to his brother's teasing.

"I'm goin', too! I saw a crick out behind the house. I'm gonna to do me some explorin'!" declared William. He shot down the ladder to go and explore his new surroundings, leaving John alone with Robert and Andy. All three plopped down in the thick hay to rest until dinner.

"Looks like your big brother's gone and got bit by Margie McClelland's love bug," observed Robert.

"I reckon so," responded John. "Can't say I didn't see it comin', though. He lit up like a sunrise when that girl came out the door. Cain't say I blame him none. She's one purty girl. Even I could 'bout get me some sore eyes starin' at her." John grinned when he saw the agreement on Robert's face.

"He'll have him some competition, though," observed Robert. "Thomas has been sweet on that gal for about a year now. He's been about to lose his mind lately now that he gets to see her most every day. He has marrying on his mind."

"Have you boys been stayin' here on the farm while you work it?" inquired John.

"No, we have to stay at our own place and keep an eye on our mama. We're all she's got, and she won't stay anywhere but home. The past couple of weeks we've been working our own farm and doing our chores in the mornings and then we come over here to help at Mrs. McClelland's with the basic chores for a while in the afternoon."

Andy jumped into the conversation, "There is no way we can leave our mama alone at night with King George's thugs on the loose. The bastards seem to be crawling up out of the ground now that the Lobsterbacks are in Charlestown. They're mighty courageous now that British patrols are roaming the countryside. It's been getting worse since the night they hung Mr. McClelland."

"Worse how?" responded John.

"Well, nothing military, for sure. Raiding houses mostly, and lots of them," explained Robert. "They have this little game of coming in the middle of the night to the homes of known Whigs and demanding payment of some kind of tax or other penalty that they conjure up for just such an occasion. They steal just about anything of value that they can, including food and livestock. And I've heard stories that they take what they want from the women, as well."

John's eyebrow shot up. He shook his head in disgust.

"Only good Tory is a cold, dead one," volunteered Andy.

Robert smiled in amusement. John ignored him and continued to question Robert.

"How old are you, Robert?"

"I'm sixteen, and the little bloodthirsty Tory-hunter over there just turned thirteen a couple of months ago." He threw a small pebble that ricocheted off of Andy's straw cocked hat.

"I'm sorry you lost your papa. Ours is gone, too. He passed back in '72, when I was just seven years old. Died one night after he fell off of a neighbor's barn that he was workin' on."

"At least you got to know him for a while," muttered Andy. "Our Papa died back in '67. They say he got crushed by a log while cutting timber. I wasn't even born yet. He died about a month before I came out of my mama. So they named me after him ... Andrew Jackson, Jr." Andy thumped his chest and smiled proudly.

"I was only two, so I don't remember him, either," offered Robert. "Hugh used to claim that he could remember him a bit, but he was only about four when he died. I tend to think that he's only remembering the stories that mama has told us about him."

"Who's Hugh?" asked William.

"He was our oldest brother. He died at the Battle at Stono Ferry, down near Charlestown last June. The worst part is that he wasn't even wounded or anything like that. He died of a heatstroke, they say."

"I'm sorry to hear that," offered John. "But I'm proud for you that he served the cause."

"Yeah, I miss him a lot. He was a good big brother."

Andy decided to change the subject, asking "Who's taking care of your mama while you're away?"

"Our mama got married just a little while after Papa died. She said her vows to a first-class arse named Ephraim Farr. We were all just little boys. He stuck us in an old cave on his place ... wouldn't let us live in the house with his own kids. As soon as James turned eighteen he bought back our Papa's old farm and we lit out. Been on our own for 'bout a year and a half now. So we're pretty much free to do what we want."

"Why aren't James or you in the army?" questioned Andy.

"Well, with all the bad news up north early in the war, James never saw fit to join the Continentals. Besides, he wanted to at least stay close to our mama. He's serving in the local militia in Mecklenburg County, though. He mustered with the call-up right after Charlestown fell. I reckon I'll report for the next muster since I'll be sixteen soon."

"I mustered some last year with Hugh and our Camden District militia. Andy's too young, but he always went to muster with us. He served as a messenger and runner for the officers. We practiced forming and shooting in lines and went on a few patrols, but have never fired a shot. But now with all the trouble being caused by these Tories, I suspect it's only a matter of time."

A sudden call emanated from the house, "Dinner! Come on, boys!"

John, Robert, and Andy all rose and peered through the window of the loft. They saw that two makeshift tables had been erected in front of the house with long benches down each side. James Hamilton and Margaret McClelland were sitting on one of the benches in a deep conversation. Thomas Crawford sat under a big oak tree about fifty feet away, obviously sulling.

"Yep, looks your cousin has him some serious competition," John observed.

"Sure enough. He will go crazy, for sure, knowing that you boys are sleeping right here in the McClelland barn every night. He won't be easy to be around." Robert smiled at John. "Let's go get some food and watch a few sparks fly. I have a feeling them boys are going to strike one another like flint and steel."

The boys hurried down the ladder and made their way to the enormous picnic. The McClelland women had prepared large platters of smoked ham, fried potatoes and onions, and boiled carrots. Four large loaves of fragrant bread were spaced evenly on the tables, along with three bowls full of fresh spring onions. There was fresh, cold water, apple cider, and hot tea to drink.

Mrs. McClelland invited her guests to sit at one of the tables then placed her children around the adjacent table. James quickly and strategically staked out the end seat adjacent to Margaret, a mere twelve inches away at the next table. The widow sat opposite her daughter while the Elder Crawford sat across from James. Thomas sat and fumed at the far end of the guest table, way on the other side of the younger boys, thoroughly displaced from the proximity to Margaret McClelland that he had so obviously enjoyed up until this particular morning.

The widow McClelland spoke, "We are most grateful for all you boys who have come forth to help our struggling family. We trust that the Good Lord will honor and reward your giving and your sacrifice. Now, Elder Crawford, will you do us the honor of blessing this meal?"

Andy Jackson released a semi-audible sigh. He had heard a few too many of his uncle's voluminous mealtime prayers.

The Elder unleashed a passionate diatribe that seemed to serve as both a sermon and a blessing. After calling down curses upon those who gave allegiance to the scoundrel King George, he prayed blessings upon the forces of freedom, as well as blessings for the boys who had come to assist the McClelland family. John opened one eye and stole a glance at the other young people at the tables. He met the stare of Andy Jackson, who rolled his eyes with a dramatic exaggeration. John suppressed a snicker. Finally, after what seemed like an eternity, the Elder asked God's blessing upon the food.

Everyone dug in with gusto. The delicious and ample meal was accompanied by boisterous laughter and conversation, with everyone except Thomas joining in the discussion and getting to know one another a bit better. About forty-five minutes later his irritated voice broke through the fellowship.

"Isn't about time, gentlemen, that we cease socializing and get to work? We only have about five hours of good daylight left today."

"My son is right, Mrs. McClelland," affirmed the Elder, "Let us be about our work. Thomas and I will get you gentlemen caught up on the tasks that need to be completed over these next couple of days."

The young men all rose out of respect for the widow as she stood to begin clearing the tables. James placed his brown wool cocked hat on his head and offered his elbow to Margaret, through which she extended her elegant hand, and James assisted her to her feet. He then bowed most politely and excused himself to join the other men.

Margaret batted her eyes, nodded her head gracefully, and responded, "I'll see you at suppertime, James. We can converse more this evening."

Thomas' ears turned red and a large vein pulsed on his forehead over his right eye. John and Robert observed all of the proceedings from a safe distance. James was entirely immune to the sight of the heartache that he was causing the other young man.

"Won't be long now," Robert whispered to John. "He's about to rupture." There was an obvious glee in his voice.

The survey of the impending work helped diffuse some of the tension as it took command of Thomas' attention. There was definitely plenty of work to accomplish. Several split-rail fences were in a state of disrepair. The north and west sides of the cabin needed to be re-chinked. The roofs of both the barn and the house had leaks and were in need of repair. There was one particularly large leak around a rotten spot where the roof met the stone fireplace. If the teenage work crew could accomplish those specialty tasks quickly, there was always firewood to be cut and stacked for winter and corn to hoe.

The boys divided their labor among the primary tasks. They decided to focus on the cabin first and make sure it was secured and weatherized for the family. Due to their experience in plugging leaks in the ceiling of their former cabin-cave, James and John volunteered to get to work on the fireplace and leaks. Thomas and Robert agreed to begin the chinking process. They would have to harvest fresh mud and clay from the creek bottom and haul it up in buckets as needed to the house. Andy agreed to take William and the three McClelland boys down to the corn patch and chop weeds. Once the labor was organized and divided, Elder Crawford announced that he had errands to run, and that he would check back in on them later. Andy rolled his eyes.

Robert whispered to John, "You won't see Uncle Tom until supper time ... I promise. He has a certain fear of hard work, I'm afraid."

The Elder Crawford gracefully mounted his horse, tipped his hat to the ladies, and proceeded down the road in the direction of the church.

The three work crews attacked their tasks with gusto. By mid-afternoon James and John had finished the roof patching on the cabin, repaired some dislodged, leaky stones on the chimney, and nailed fresh wood and shingles around the chimney leak. Since they needed some thick clay to seal the roof around the chimney, they helped collect and carry several buckets of mud and clay for Thomas and Robert, as well.

Once the cabin roof was completely repaired they proceeded to work on the roof of the barn. About an hour before sunset they replaced the last shake shingle on the barn roof. They were descending the ladder beside the barn when Mrs. McClelland announced that it was suppertime. Hugh and Robert were washing their hands in the creek, having finished sealing all of the open cracks in the cabin walls. Almost like magic, Elder Crawford appeared on horseback just in time for supper.

Once again the food at Mrs. McClelland's table was ample, hot, and delicious. The fellowship was warm and sweet. John and William were enjoying a splendid time with new friends. James was obviously enjoying the rather devoted attention of the lovely Margaret McClelland. The only unhappy soul in the crowd was Thomas Crawford, Jr.

Overwhelmed with disgust at Margaret's blatant romantic interest in James, young Thomas stood quickly from his bench and exhaled, "Robert, Andrew, say your good-nights. We need to go and you need to get home to check on your mama."

The Jackson boys shook hands with everyone, thanked Mrs. McClelland and Margaret for the delicious meal, and bid everyone good night and good rest. The Hamilton boys thanked the women for their supper. The ladies and girls began to carry platters and dishes back into the house. James cordially extended his hand to Thomas as he sat upon his horse, ready to leave. Thomas did not reciprocate. He merely peered at James with a cold stare of animosity and stated flatly, "I'll see you after dinner tomorrow, Hamilton." He tugged the reins of his horse and urged it onto the road at a quick trot.

"What in the world is his problem?" James asked obtusely.

Robert, Andy, and John snickered. William picked his nose, clueless. Elder Crawford grinned and shook his head.

"What?" inquired James.

The Jacksons and Elder Crawford turned their horses and followed Thomas, Jr., down the road.

Dumbfounded, James turned to John, "What is everyone actin' so strange about?"

Turning toward the barn, John replied, "Thomas has been sweet on Margaret for quite a spell, James, and you have invaded his territory. Can't you see it? That boy's been about to bust wide open ever since that girl first batted those blue eyes at you. I reckon when he does blow that you've got a thrashin' coming."

"Thunder!" James exclaimed. "I didn't notice."

"Because you've been blinded by her femaleness, big brother. You'd better wise up and work on puttin' this particular fire out tomorrow. I mean it. I didn't come down here to watch no cockfightin'."

"I reckon you're right, Johnny. I need to get my mind on our work, don't I?"

"I'd say so," John replied.

They took six or seven steps in silence.

"But she shore is a pretty thing, ain't she?" James observed.

John grinned and nodded as they climbed the ladder into the loft. Dusk was descending.

John lit the candles on the table so that they would have enough light to prepare their beds. James checked their rifles, making sure there was still powder in all three pans. William spread their blankets on the straw.

James insisted that William sleep by the window, as far from the ladder and hole to downstairs as possible, just in case he decided to get up and walk around during the night. Though he had not done so in a while, there was a time when the boy had been prone to walking in his sleep. Once everyone had removed their shoes and weskits and sufficiently prepared their nests for sleeping, John blew out the candles and crawled under his blanket beside James.

"Today sure was nice, wasn't it?" declared William.

"Yes, it was, William," affirmed John. "These are good people, and the Jacksons and Thomas Crawford are good boys, like us. If we do things right and throw a saddle on some of this romance, we might have us some lifelong friends down here in South Carolina."

"I hear ya, little brother," acknowledged James. "Tomorrow's a brand new day. I'm all about the work. My romancin' days are behind me, I promise."

"I'll believe that when I see it," responded John drowsily.

Quietly, rapidly they descended into a peaceful, deep sleep.

4

FRONTIER LOVE

A pair of the McClellands' roosters roused John in the pre-dawn darkness. The banging of buckets from one of the stalls downstairs added to the early morning din. He heard a muffled, shrill voice of reproof, presumably aimed at an uncooperative cow. Someone was milking downstairs in the rear of the barn. He kicked the wool blanket off of his body. He was hot, his shirt soaked with sweat. The loft had been much warmer than his previous night's bed in the woods. And his bladder was about to explode. He pulled on his shoes and headed down the ladder in search of a tree upon which he could relieve himself. He noticed the dull glow of a candle in the rear stall, no doubt the light carried by a young milkmaid.

It took only moments to find a tree to his liking that provided sufficient privacy for a young man's urination. Coming back around the front of the barn he noticed flickering candlelight emerging from the cabin. He surmised that the widow was already engaged in preparing breakfast for her youthful work crew.

John climbed back up the ladder, electing to crawl back into his makeshift bed and, perhaps, steal a few more minutes of sleep. He kicked off his buckle shoes and lay down on his back in his body-shaped depression in the hay. He dozed comfortably and effortlessly.

The sun was up full and bright when he was aroused by a kick in the leg. He opened his eyes to see William staring down at him.

"James wants to know if you are goin' to lay up in the loft all day or if you plan to come down and eat?"

Startled and disoriented, John jumped up and looked out the window. Sure enough, there were wood bowls and shiny pewter spoons on the tables in the clearing. There was a flurry of activity around the cabin as the McClelland children set the tables and brought out the food. And already James was sitting with the beautiful Margaret on a nearby bench.

"Well … so much for calming down the romance," John thought.

He donned his weskit and grabbed his hat and, for the second time that morning, descended the ladder to the world below. He smoothed the wrinkles on his weskit and breeches as he made his way to the breakfast table.

Several little voices called, "Good morning!" to him as he neared the breakfast tables.

The widow McClelland approached him, "Good morning, John. I trust you had a good sleep."

"Yes ma'am. I woke up before dark but somehow managed to fall back to sleep. I'm sorry if I've kept everyone waitin'."

"Not a'tall, not a'tall," she responded. "You're just in time. Besides, you needed your rest after that afternoon of labor you put in yesterday. There's fresh milk and cider on the table, so you can help yourself to a drink. Do you care for coffee, John? Your brother indicated that you have a taste for it."

His eyes lit up. "I love coffee, Mrs. McClelland! But I so rarely get to have any. It's so expensive and hard to come by and my brothers don't care for it. I have an occasional cup whenever my mama fixes some for me."

She beamed with pleasure. "Well, I discovered about a half-pound of coffee among the goods that you brought yesterday. It smelled a wee bit old, but it'll do, I suppose. I'm the only one in my household who drinks it, as well. I'm pleased to finally have someone who will enjoy a cup with me. After we say grace, I will go and brew us up some. It'll be ready in just a bit. Meanwhile, have a seat at the table and we can all get started with breakfast."

John sat down at the guest table just as the McClelland children were finding their seats. Mrs. McClelland stood at the end of the table, her hands resting on her ample hips, with a glowing smile on her face.

She commented, "Bless be, how it warms my soul to have a yard full of young 'uns. Just the sight of you all at my table is a pure joy. Now, who shall say grace for us on this fine mornin'?"

Margaret gently placed her hand on James' forearm, "James, you're the only man among us. I think it most appropriate if you pray over our meal."

James was somewhat startled at the invitation, but courageously rose to his feet to fulfill the damsel's request. He invited everyone to bow their heads, and then offered a simple farmer's prayer for their meal. Afterward Margaret smiled at him approvingly.

With the food sufficiently blessed, the young people dug in to a bowl of off-white porridge made from a mixture of oats, wheat, and hominy flavored with chunks of butter and sorghum molasses. John had taken only a few bites when Mrs. Mcclelland appeared with a pewter cup of steaming coffee.

"I put a wee bit o sugar in it for ya, Johnny. You might add a little squirt of that milk to dull the strength of it."

John did just that, and then sampled the creamy, tasty brew. It was absolutely delicious. He poured an additional squirt of the rich milk into his porridge.

The ravenous young people devoured their breakfasts in a matter of minutes. They sat for a few moments, enjoying the cool of the morning and the conversation.

"When do you plan to be returning home, James?" inquired the widow over the lip of her shiny coffee cup.

"Well, we aim to work all day today and get as much done as we can. Tomorrow we plan to spend the Lord's Day mornin' in worship with you folk, then start our journey back home some time in the afternoon. We hate to leave so soon, but we do have a farm to run," James responded.

"Nonsense! I'll not have you boys travelin' on the Lord's Day!" She sounded somewhat offended. "Such labor would not be appropriate on the Sabbath. No! You shall remain here to rest and visit with us tomorrow afternoon. Monday mornin' will be plenty soon enough for your voyage homeward. I simply won't accept any other arrangement. Besides, Mr. Crawford has plans to roast a whole hog in a pit this very night for the congregation to enjoy in a grand picnic after the meetin' tomorrow."

James was anxious to get back home to his land, but he savored the notion of an entire afternoon of leisure in the presence of Margaret. "Yes ma'am, of course, it will be as you say."

"Fine, then," she acknowledged. "Now, the girls and I will get things cleaned up here while you young men set about the work that was planned for and arranged yesterday."

"Yes ma'am." James wiped his mouth on his sleeve. He retrieved his fur felt round hat from the seat beside him as he stood and placed it confidently on his head. Turning to Margaret, he tipped his hat and said gently, "Miss Margaret, perhaps we can converse some more at dinner."

"Of course, James," she replied. "I will look forward to it."

As they walked toward the barn, John opened his mouth to speak but James cut him off. "I know, brother. Let it alone. I know what I'm doin'."

So there was no more talk between them about romance.

"We'll all be going to the corn patch this mornin', boys," James proclaimed. "William, you and your crew can continue choppin' weeds. I know it's a terrible borin' task, but it's necessary. You need to make sure these McClelland boys know how to do it right and proper. Understand?"

"Yes, James," William replied. His chest puffed up a little at the notion of actually being in charge of his own work crew.

James continued, "John and I will set about repairin' that busted fence."

The oldest McClelland boy, David, led them to the tool bin in the barn. They grabbed two hammers, a maul, a cross-cutting saw that had definitely seen its better days, a wood splitting wedge, and an axe. James inspected the hoes as William retrieved them from the bin and declared them unusable in their current condiiton. Before going to the field he and John took a few moments to put a better edge on them with a rough rasp and a sharpening stone. Soon they were all marching off to the corn patch, tools draped across their shoulders.

They discovered four places where the fence was damaged by fallen trees from a spring windstorm. Hogs had already gotten in and destroyed a pretty large patch of the ankle-high corn. He estimated the number of new split rails that they would need for the repair, and they set to work. The trees were not very large, so they made use of them as a convenient source for the fence rails. Once they had ideal-sized sections cut to length, James started expertly splitting rails. John brought their team of horses down to the field and used a chain to haul the remainder of the tree trunks and good-sized limbs down to the cabin to be used for firewood.

Rail splitting and hauling wood occupied the lion's share of their morning. William and the McClelland boys were thrilled to take a break from their monotonous hoeing and help haul smaller branches to the cabin for firewood and drag the tree-tops and limb remnants down into the woods. The actual placement of the rails didn't take very long. They had just completed the fencing job when the call for dinner emanated from the cabin.

The young ones dropped their hoes and took off running to the house. James and John were not far behind. They saw a rider approaching from the road as they neared the cabin. It was Andrew Jackson.

"Hello, Andy!" John called to him across the clearing, "Where are Robert and Thomas?"

Andy nimbly jumped off of his horse, rifle in hand, and responded. "They're not coming today."

"Really? Why not?" James inquired.

"Well, Uncle Tom has set about cooking a hog for a big picnic tomorrow. He made Thomas and Robert stay behind to help him with the pit and hog killing. They'll be busy till well after nightfall, and someone'll have to be up most of the night keeping an eye on that hog. So I reckon you won't see them again till church meeting tomorrow."

Hearing his report on the other boys, Mrs. McClelland inquired in her thick Scottish tongue, "Will you be a stayin' and eatin' dinner with us then, Andy?"

"Yes ma'am, if you don't mind. I'm not needed at the hog cooking operation, so I'm here to offer my services. I even brought a blanket with me. Mama said it would be fine if I stay here with the Hamilton boys in the loft tonight, if it suits you."

"Oh, that's grand," she replied. "You are most welcome. Find yourself a seat. Let's get you fed before you get to work."

Andy pulled John aside and whispered as they approached the table, "Ole Thomas, Jr., is none too happy, I'm here to tell you! I thought the top of his head was going to pop right off when Uncle Tom told him he couldn't come over here today. He got downright defiant ... I never saw him act that way. Your brother and Margaret's romance has really gotten under his skin, for sure."

"I hope things don't get nasty when they run into each other at the meetin' tomorrow," mused John.

"Well I hope they do!" countered Andy. "That sure would bring a little excitement to the meeting house. People will think that a bunch of Methodists or Baptists have shown up!"

John laughed out loud.

Dinner was a humble but hearty bowl of stew comprised of small cubes of venison, potatoes, carrots, and onions. As always, there was plenty of fresh-baked bread. There was plenty for a second or third bowlful for all who desired one.

"This is some fine, tasty venison Mrs. McClelland," complimented James. "It must have been a young doe."

"It was, indeed," she replied. "A gentleman from the church shot and dressed it and brought it by a few days ago. We have enjoyed it tremendously. But I'm afraid it's pretty much gone. I hope that some generous soul will supply us with another one very soon."

"You don't need to rely on charity for venison, Mrs. McClelland. Your boys can take a deer for you. These woods are swarmin' with 'em," observed John.

"Aye, that would be nice," she answered, "But we have no hunters left in this house. I'm afraid my little boys know even less about guns and hunting than I do. We have one Fowler rifle and an old trade musket in the house, but no one who can use them. You see, our oldest sons, Joshua and Caleb, supplied most of the game for our family. My dear, Edward … God rest his soul … he did a little hunting and shooting, on occasion, but the boys were so good at it that he truly didn't need to bother. So until they come back home we're in a bit of a spot, you see."

"Well, that's something we can definitely help with while we're here," responded James. "We can teach your boys how to load and shoot safely. They're plenty old enough to put some meat on the table."

"Land sakes, you're talkin' nonsense, Mr. Hamilton!" she protested. "David is only nine years of age and small for that. Little Jacob is only seven. And there's no way that I'm going to allow my baby Timothy to fire a gun!"

"I agree with you about Timothy," replied James. "But my brothers and I have been hunting and providing for ourselves since before we were Jacob's age. I assure you that they are both quite capable. Besides, there's a war on. You've experienced first-hand how people can treat one another during these treacherous times. Someone in this house needs to know how to handle a weapon."

Andy Jackson inserted himself into the conversation. "He's right, Mrs. McClelland. Those murdering Tories have inflicted violence upon this family once already. Who's to say they don't have plans to come back?"

Mrs. McClelland pondered what they had said, and seemed to be inclined toward James' proposal. "You're sure you can teach them to handle a gun properly?"

"Yes ma'am," James replied. "It's really not that difficult. And it will give you the opportunity for a little more self-sufficiency for your family."

Mrs. McClelland thought for a moment, and then nodded her assent. "Very well," she said. "It will be good for our family. There's plenty of room for shootin' in the meadow behind the cabin. Just don't be a shootin' toward me house."

"Of course, Mrs. McClelland," John replied. "We'll get started right now. After our shootin' lesson, we'll get to work on buildin' up your firewood supply. This green wood'll have plenty of time to cure before this winter."

Turning to David and Jacob he instructed, "Boys, get your guns and powder and meet us out back. We're gonna to have us a shootin' lesson!"

The young boys leapt with glee from the table and disappeared into the cabin.

"What about me, James?" inquired William. "Can I come along?"

"Sure enough, William. In fact, once we have them all schooled and ready, I want you to take them out huntin' for a deer whilst Andy, John, and me cut firewood."

William's face lit up with pride as he took off running for the barn. The hard leather soles of his shoes thumped loudly as he scaled the ladder into the loft. Minutes later he came running back out with his stubby sea service Brown Bess and powder horn. The McClelland boys soon emerged, as well. David, the older boy, carried an ancient .62 caliber musket. Jacob held a newer .54 caliber smooth bore Pennsylvania rifle. It was actually quite nice.

For the next hour and a half James, John, William, and Andy showed the boys how to measure the powder and load their guns.

They instructed them on measuring of the proper amount of powder for their guns, loading the ball with paper or a patch and using the ramrod to tamp it tightly against the breech plug. Finally, they showed them how to prime the pan, cock, and fire the gun. William took great joy in showing them how to aim down the sights.

For target practice they set up a small, lightly colored piece of lumber against the trunk of a huge oak tree about fifty yards down range. They guided the boys through five shots each with each weapon. Their first couple of shots were nowhere near the target. But by the fourth and fifth shots both boys were hitting the target piece of wood consistently. They proved proficient with both guns.

"That's fine, boys, Just fine," complimented James. "Just remember ... that gun is safe as long as the frizzen covers the pan and it remains half-cocked. Never put it on full cock unless you actually intend to fire. Do you understand?"

"Yes, sir," they replied in unison.

"Good. Now I want you both to load one more time. William, check your pan and make sure you have good powder. Then I want you boys to go get a drink of water and head out and get us a deer for supper," instructed James. "But make sure it's a small one. I want it to be something that you boys can dress and drag back to the house on your own. You shouldn't have to go far. There's been deer poppin' their heads out of these woods and lookin' at us all mornin' long. Then tonight, after supper, we'll all sit down and I'll teach you how to clean your gun proper. Sound good?"

"Yes, sir!" they both exclaimed.

James watched William supervise one last loading of the weapons then turned to John and Andy. He said, "Let's go cut some wood."

The three young men gave their attention to the rather large pile of unprocessed firewood. They cut short lengths of logs with the crosscut saw until their arms ached, took a short break, then they started splitting logs with the axe and maul. They had been hard at it for about an hour when John spoke up, "Why haven't we heard them shoot yet?"

"All of the shootin' we did at that target probably had them a bit spooked. It'll take a little while, but they'll ease back in here in just a bit," observed Andy.

Sure enough, about an hour later they heard the sharp crack of a rifle in the gulley to the north of the house.

"Sounded like the .54 caliber to me," mused John.

"I'd say you're right. Reckon little bitty David got him a critter?" chuckled Andy.

"He was carrying the rifle when they left the cabin. Reckon we'll see in a little while," affirmed James.

They continued their work, quickly hacking the logs down into manageable firewood. Their final task was to cut all of the smaller branches and limbs down to a size that would fit the fireplace. They were racking the last of the wood between two cedar trees when they saw three heads bobbing across the clearing. As the boys drew near their beet-red faces reflected the laborious task in which they were engaged ... dragging a deer carcass through the tall grass.

James called out to them, "Bring it on down here, boys! We'll butcher her up right now!"

It took another ten minutes, but at long last the boys got the small doe out of the tall grass and onto the open ground near the cabin. All three of them plopped down in the shade, panting from exhaustion, but with faces radiating joy in the midst of the sweat. They immediately began to chatter excitedly about the experience.

Mrs. McClelland, hearing the commotion outside, exited the cabin and walked around the corner of the house, followed closely by Margaret. "Saints alive! I can hardly believe me eyes. Did one of me own little boys shoot us a deer?"

The youngest boy, seven-year-old David, nodded and declared, "I got her, mama! Shot her clean through the bottom of the neck. She dropped right on the spot!"

"It was a good shot," affirmed William. "I showed Jacob and David how to cut a shooting stick to carry the weight of the barrel for them.

He laid it right in the 'y' of that stick and put her down! It was every bit of a seventy-yard shot."

"Oh, my!" their mother proclaimed. "Who would have thought that right here under me own roof I've raised a couple of genuine mountain men ... long hunters, at that?" She winked at James. "I'm so proud of you both. You boys will be blessing our table with tasty meat from now on!"

Examining the deer, John asked, "Who dressed it?"

"I did, of course," William replied. "These boys never dressed a deer before. It was goin' to be hard enough getting' it back to the house. I didn't see no need to drag it back guts and all."

"Good thinkin', and a pretty decent job, too," complimented James. "Let's string it up and skin it. We have just enough time to cut out the loins and get them on the spit for supper. You don't mind if we cook up the meat this evening, do you Mrs. McClelland?"

"Me mind? Heavens, no! It'll be a pleasure, indeed. Margaret and I will prepare all the fixins'. We shall have a feast tonight!"

"What shall we do with the rest of the carcass?" inquired James.

The widow replied, "We have a cold cave in a deep spot along the creek. It's a short walk upstream. The cave is nice and deep and plenty cool to keep meat for a week or more. If you would be so kind as to quarter and saw it up for me, Jacob and David will show you the way and how to hang it in the cave."

"Yes ma'am," he replied. Turning to William he commanded, "William, you and the boys go get us a cooking fire started out front in that rock pit. I think there is already an iron spit on it. Make sure all the iron is cleaned off. We'll have the backstraps and little tenderloins ready in just a few minutes. Get to it, and don't be a wastin' any time. We need a good bed of coals real quick."

Turning back to Mrs. McClelland, he requested, "Ma'am, do you have some bacon grease, salt, and black pepper that we can use on the meat. And about a quart of your apple cider?"

"Certainly," she replied. "I'll sit everything out on the front porch for you, along with some more cider and cold water for you boys to drink. I know you must all be suffrin' a terrible thirst." She turned and headed back to the cabin.

James and John hung the little doe head down from a nearby tree and expertly skinned it in a matter of minutes. They sliced the lean, tender backstraps and loins from the animal and placed them on a large wood platter that Margaret had brought out for them to use. Lastly he cut the shoulders free from the carcass and tied strings around the joints for ease of carry and hanging. He sawed the remainder of the carcass into small, manageable pieces for hanging, as well. He knew that Mrs. McClelland would make use of every edible morsel of the animal.

The boys returned from their fire making duties, reporting that they had a roaring blaze in the pit. James assigned John, William, and the McClelland boys the task of hauling the extra meat to the cold cave. "I'll get the meat cookin'," he promised.

The fire was, indeed, burning wonderfully. William had placed the three-foot-long iron spit on a bench, ready for use. James carefully impaled the sharp end into the doubled-over straps, forming a loose "U." He did the same with the smaller tenderloins, keeping them further from the heat so that they would not overcook. He rubbed the meat down with generous handfuls of the bacon grease, then sprinkled salt and black pepper over every exposed surface. He quickly spread the bed of coals and placed the meat over the oak and hickory wood fire. The boys soon returned from the cave, their meat storage task complete.

"All we can do now is wait, boys. I'd say about an hour and a half should do it. We want to cook it nice and slow and keep it on the edge of rare," James explained.

"What's the cider for?" queried Jacob.

"Well, Jacob, we're goin' to turn that meat every fifteen minutes or so. Right before we do it, we're goin' to wet it down with a little bit of the cider. It'll keep the meat nice and moist and add a little sweet to it."

Jacob licked his lips in response.

Dusk was less than an hour away, so it would be well after dark before they would be able to eat. Mrs. McClelland suggested that the boys relax and play games to amuse themselves. They were thrilled to accept such an invitation.

James noticed that Margaret was washing dishes in a large tub beside the front stoop of the cabin, so he elected to join her and assist. Mrs. McClelland brought out a well-used draught board for John and Andy. William and the younger boys amused themselves with a sack full of marbles.

Time passed quickly. Every few minutes James would tear himself away from the company of Margaret to check the meat, douse it with cider, and give it a one-quarter turn of the spit. Shortly after dark he declared that it was done. He placed the piping hot loins on two small wood platters and brought them to the table where he sliced them into inch-thick servings. The meat cut like butter, and the aroma was incredible.

Mrs. McClelland added her own platters of roasted potatoes and carrots, boiled greens, and hot bread. This time John said grace, and then they tore into the meal, dining by the light of candles spaced strategically on the tables. It was a delicious meal. The boys stuffed themselves with the tender, peppery loin until they were almost sick. They sat and talked for almost an hour. Sometime in the midst of the conversation James and Margaret had left the table and gone for a stroll. John was heartbroken when Mrs. McClelland declared that it was getting late and way past time for everyone to go to bed.

She ordered, "Just leave your dishes where they lay. I'm not about to try and clean up in the dark. We'll take the remainin' food inside and clean up in the light of mornin'."

She noticed James and Margaret in surprisingly close proximity to one another next to a big oak tree near the edge of the woods. James was whispering in her ear. Margaret covered her mouth and giggled. Her mother was more than a little disturbed.

"Maggie!" she barked. "Be a sayin' your 'good nights' now and get in the house. Dawn will be here before ya know it. Mr. Hamilton, I bid you good night. Boys, I'll be a seein' ya at breakfast." Margaret didn't move or acknowledge her. "Come along, now, Maggie. Don't make me call you again."

John saw Margaret squeeze James' hand and allow the touch to linger for just a moment. Just before she released him John saw her lips form a single word in the glow of the candlelight. It was, "Yes." James smiled. John was a bit puzzled, but not overly concerned.

James turned toward the barn. He was smiling ear to ear and, John thought, a bit overly-happy. "Let's hit the hay, boys."

"What about cleaning my rifle?" inquired Jacob.

"Just run a couple of dry patches through it tonight, Jacob," James instructed. "We'll clean it real good in the mornin'. Don't load it, though, or we'll have to shoot it again before we clean it."

"Yes, sir," he answered.

The boys all headed toward the barn. James reminded them, "Let's be sure to go around back and make water before we climb upstairs. We don't want to be makin' any middle-of-the night trips."

The entire group went behind the barn, formed what Andy called a 'Carolina firing line,' and gave the ground a thorough soaking. Then they climbed the ladder to the loft, shucked off weskits and shoes, and prepared for bed. Andy leaned his rifle in the corner, dug himself a fresh sleeping hole near John's, and tumbled in.

"I sure like having you fellows down here. It's been nice having someone else to talk to besides my brother and Thomas, Jr. I hate to see you all go so soon," bemoaned Andy.

"I ain't ready to go home," whined William. "I like being with David and Jacob, even if they are a bit younger that me. I think we've made pow'rful good friends."

John concurred, "It's been good bein' here. But we don't live so far away. We can probably make it back down for a visit someday."

James finally broke his strange silence from his spot near the wall. "I 'spect we'll be headin' back this way sooner than you think, little brothers. In fact, we might be a gettin' down this way right often."

"What are you talkin' about, James?" questioned John.

"Well … on this very night I asked the lovely Miss Margaret McClelland to marry me, and she said, 'yes.'" They could actually hear him smiling in the dark.

John and William were speechless, dumbfounded, overwhelmed.

Then the jocular voice of Andrew Jackson pierced the darkness, "Well, it's been nice knowing you, James Hamilton. When Thomas finds out about this we'll be having a funeral long before we have any wedding!"

The tension broken, they laughed hysterically. As the laughter died down they drifted into a deep sleep.

A thunderous 'Crack!' awakened John. Then he thought he heard a scream. He was disoriented, having forgotten momentarily where he was. He attempted to shake the fog of sleep from his brain. Then another loud, 'Crack!'

"That was a gunshot!" he thought, rising up on one elbow.

Fully awake now, he heard breaking glass and deep, harsh voices. Then he heard what sounded like children crying. Then another scream … this time a horrific, brief, blood-curdling scream that stopped suddenly, unnaturally. The piercing sound of it awakened James. His eyes met John's. John lifted his finger to his lips in a sign of silence. John woke up Andy and James woke up William, placing their hands over their mouths to keep them from making a noise. Both of them whispered, "Shhhh!"

The boys all crawled to the loft window and carefully peered over the rough sill. In the clearing beside the house stood three men in strange uniforms holding torches and pointing muskets at a sobbing huddle of terrified children. Through the tiny window of the cabin they saw flames dancing. There was more breaking glass. Then the screaming resumed, emanating from behind the house. It was unmistakably Margaret's voice. But this time the screaming didn't stop …

5

THIEVES IN THE NIGHT

"Them's British Legion dragoons!" hissed Andy. "Tarleton's men. Tories from up north. I can tell by the green coats. Them no good sumbitches. What are they doing this far from Charlestown?"

Another pain-filled scream emanated from the darkness, followed by the words, "Please, I beg you … no … "

"That's Margaret, for sure. It sounds like she's out back!" exclaimed James in an excited whisper. He was almost outside of his mind with fear and rage.

"I don't see Mrs. McClelland, either. And it looks one of the boys is missing, I can't tell which one," added John.

"I gotta go get Margaret!" James headed for the cluster of guns in the corner.

"James, you can't go a chargin' guns blazin' into a bunch of armed militia. They'll drop you as soon as you touch off your first shot," cautioned John. "We gotta think."

More screams filled the night. Frantic. Wailing. Piercing.

James rapidly assessed the situation and then voiced his plan. "I'm gonna work my way through the trees around back of the house. I've gotta help Margaret. I'm gonna shoot the first green coat that I see back there. I want you boys to get your guns and draw a bead on those three watchin' the kids. Make sure you know which one you're a shootin' at. Talk it all out. The second you hear my shot I want you to drop all of 'em. But be mindful you don't hit one of the kids. Got it?"

"All right, James, but what then?" asked John.

James wrapped his belt around his waist, sticking his sheathed knife inside the leather on his left hip, then replied, "Reload as quick as you can and be ready to drop any others that come out of the cabin or the woods. I don't think there's a lot of 'em, or we'd be able to see more from here," James replied. "If you don't see any more after a while, then come on down and check out the cabin, then work your way around back and find me."

Andy reached into his canvas shoulder bag and pulled out a tomahawk, handing it to James. "Take this hawk of mine, James. You might need it."

James tucked the tomahawk inside the belt on his other hip as he prepared to drop through the ladder hole to the barn floor below. "Good luck, boys. Don't get shot," he cautioned. Then he was gone.

John, Andy, and William retrieved their guns and shooting bags from the corner and made their way toward the window.

"Are you boys all loaded?" asked John.

"Yes," replied William.

"Always," answered Andy.

"Make sure your frizzen cover is off and that you have a good pile of powder in your pan. We want all of these shots to go off like they're supposed to," urged John.

John stepped up to the window to take another look at the Tory guards. They were still standing a rather loose watch over the kids, but seemed to be more entertained by the growing fire inside the cabin. All three had their backs to the barn.

"I'm gonna take the one on the left. William, you have the one in the middle. Andy, you take the one on the right. Let's go ahead and line up the shots. Nothing fancy. Aim dead center of the middle of the back. It won't take James too long to work his way around back of the house, so we need to be ready," stated John.

The boys stood well inside the room with their barrels resting on the high sill of the opening. It was a perfect height for Andy and William. John had to spread his legs a bit to stand comfortably and not hunch over. They each settled into a comfortable position.

"I don't like this," whined William. "Them's men down there. Not rabbits or deer. And we're shootin' 'em in the back. It don't seem right."

"Those men are Tory scum and they're aiming muskets at little kids … our friends, William," retorted Andy. "They deserve what they have coming."

"He's right, William. Nobody makes war on a house full of women and children. These Tories need to be shot down like the dogs that they are," affirmed John. "Now make ready, boys."

Two long rifles and one stubby musket issued a subtle "crack" as the boys pulled the hammers back to full cock.

"Sight in on your man," John ordered. "Now we wait."

James quietly made his way along the edge of the woods, just inside the rounded tree line that stood on the north side of the cabin. The further he went, the louder the voices became. He heard the voices of men. It sounded like two of them … laughing … an evil, teasing, celebrative laughter. The whimpers of a female voice were intermixed with their apparent celebration.

Suddenly a loud, angry voice roared, "I'll teach you a lesson, you traitorous wench!" Then James heard a loud slap followed by a muffled thud.

Another voice piped up, "Is she too much woman for you, Dan'l?"

"The ignorant hussy bit my lip!" the original voice exclaimed.

"Well, it looks like she's out cold now," the other voice proclaimed in disgust. "You didn't have to slam her head on the ground so hard. I prefer my women to be awake and wigglin' a little. Hurry it up and do your business. It's my turn next."

When he finally reached a point where he had a line of sight around the cabin, the vision that met his eyes almost caused him to vomit. Margaret was sprawled on the ground, illuminated by a torch stuck in the loose dirt nearby. She was not moving. The hem of her dress was pulled up over her waist and the upper part of the dress was ripped open from the neck down, exposing her breasts. Her legs were spread apart to an unnatural degree. One of the soldiers was on the ground between her legs, his pale, naked arse glowing in the light of the torch. He was riding her viciously … violating her. His musket lay on the ground beside him.

The other soldier stood about five feet from her head, his musket cradled loosely in his arm, holding another torch, smiling wickedly and watching the vulgar show before him. He cheered, "You're a getting' it now, Dan'l! Ride her on home, boy!"

James lost all sense of time and space. He didn't even think. He merely reacted instinctively. His rage and fear erupted from his heart and exploded in his members. He instantly threw up his rifle, taking aim at the standing soldier's head. He pulled the trigger. The deafening explosion cut through the evil darkness.

The ball entered the man's skull just behind and above his left ear and exited the other side of the soldier's head in a cloud of bone fragments, gray matter, and misty blood. The force of the lead slug carried his collapsing body sideways. He fell limp upon the torch that he was holding and knocked over the one sticking in the ground beside him, extinguishing both and plunging the yard into blackness.

The sudden crack of the gunshot startled all three of the boys, shaking them from their concentration upon their targets. The three soldiers jumped as well, instinctively lifting their weapons toward the sound of the report.

"Fire!" yelled John.

He and Andy fired their rifles simultaneously. William's shot was about a half-second behind theirs. All three bullets found their marks. Two of them sprawled forward onto their faces in the dirt. One pulled the trigger as he fell, his shot flying harmlessly into the wall of the cabin. Their torches exploded in sparks as they hit the ground. Both men kicked and clawed at the ground with their hands and feet in a feeble effort to crawl for cover, but their wounds were too severe.

The third soldier spun clockwise, propelled by the .69 caliber slug from William's musket that slammed into his left shoulder blade. His torch dropped as well. His wound was not mortal. He apparently saw the smoke of their shots emanating from the loft window and lifted his musket to fire. Unable to support the weapon with his left arm, he pulled the trigger prematurely and the shot sailed wide and low of his target. He tried for a moment to reload, fumbling for a cartridge from his case, but realized that his immobilized left arm would not allow him to complete the task. He dropped the musket and turned to run around the cabin, obviously hoping to take cover from his attackers. He sprinted in the direction of the outdoor eating tables, still covered with the dishes from the previous evening meal. The children scattered toward the woods.

As soon as they had fired, both John and Andy feverishly began reloading their rifles. John tore open one of his pre-wrapped cartridges, poured powder in his pan, and dropped his frizzen. He poured the rest of the powder down the barrel. Instead of attempting to tamp the paper and ball into the barrel, he tossed them aside and reached into his bag for a loose ball. He dropped it down into the smooth bore barrel, slammed the stock of the gun down hard on the floor to seat the ball, pulled back to full cock, and threw the gun to his shoulder. The entire maneuver took less than twenty seconds. He took careful aim at the fleeing militiaman.

A fiendish roaring scream erupted from behind the cabin, somewhere out of their field of view.

The rifle reported as he pulled the trigger. "Boom!"

The lead found its mark, striking the running man in his side just beneath and behind his left arm. The impact flung him sideways onto the table, landing him in a loud clatter of banging plates and utensils and cracking lumber. He shuddered momentarily and emitted a gurgling cough, spewing a cloud of blood into the air, the product of the gaping hole in his left lung. Both of his legs straightened in violent spasms as he died slowly, drowning in his own blood.

Andy, finished with his reloading, replaced his ramrod, cocked his rifle, and trained his sites on the cabin door. William fell down on his knees, spun around and sat against the wall, and burst into hysterical tears. He covered his face with his hands.

"I'm sorry, Johnny! I'm sorry, Johnny! I didn't mean to miss him. I swear, Johnny! I had my sites right on him! I don't know what happened."

John sought to console him as he reloaded, this time tamping his slug down tight, "You didn't miss him, William. You got him! He was hit in the shoulder, that's why he couldn't get that shot off right. You got him good!"

"I shoulda dropped him, Johnny! I shoulda!" William protested.

"It's all right, brother. It's that old musket of yours and that stubby barrel. It's nowhere near as accurate as these rifles. You done all right. We're all right. They're all dead or dyin'. Now quit bawlin' and reload. We gotta help James."

John rejoined Andy in the window with his rifle freshly loaded. "See anythin', Andy?"

"No. Nothing's moving as far as I can tell. Those kids are probably scattered to hell and back. I'll bet they're still running. Nice job on that quick reload. You need to teach me that trick sometime." He smiled in the darkness.

"I'm just glad it worked. We need to go check the bodies and the cabin and check on James. Little brother, are you loaded?"

"All loaded, Johnny."

"All right then, let's go. Both of you keep your eyes and ears open," cautioned John.

The startled rapist rose upright on his knees, staring in disbelief at his dead companion. He turned his petrified gaze in the direction of the shot. James was already on the move, running full speed as he bull-rushed his enemy. He spun his rifle around as he ran, taking hold of its barrel, preparing to use the stock as a club. He screamed in rage, his rattling voice reverberating with each impact of his feet on the hard earth. In fewer than ten steps he was upon his frozen prey. Swinging the rifle in a great arc to his right he unleashed a vicious blow to the man's head, striking him squarely in the center of the face. The impact drove broke his nasal bridge free from his skull, driving it deep into his brain and killing him almost instantly. His body dropped beside the motionless Margaret.

The sudden impact of the stock to the man's head vibrated violently up the barrel of the gun and broke the momentum of James' run. He tumbled head-first, rolling almost fifteen feet past the soldier. He quickly jumped to his feet, reached across his body, and drew his knife from the sheath inside his belt. He jumped astride his motionless enemy and drew the knife quickly and smoothly across his throat, plunging deep and feeling the blade brush across the front of his spinal column. Despite the obvious lifelessness of the man, James spun the knife around effortlessly in his hand, raised his right arm high in the air, and with a guttural roar of bound-up rage and pain, plunged the knife deep into the man's heart.

James jumped to his feet, grabbed the dead rapist's body by the leg, and pulled the violator away from his precious Margaret. He knelt on the ground beside her.

"Margaret!" he called to her. He reached for her dress and pulled it down to cover her nakedness. He attempted in vain to cover her breasts with the tattered pieces hanging loosely off of her chest.

"Margaret! Can you hear me? It's me, James! You're safe now. I have you. He can't hurt you anymore."

James lightly stroked her face. He shook her shoulder in an attempt to wake her, but she was unresponsive. The muscles in his thighs began to vibrate and ache as the adrenaline of the combat burned off. His head began to spin. He needed to sit down. He tumbled into a seated position beside Margaret's head and continued to speak softly to her, to try and reach her somewhere behind the wall of unconsciousness.

He lowered his left hand beneath her head, intending to lift it into his lap so that he might cradle her and comfort her. His hand touched something warm and wet. The back of her head was soaked in warm gelatinous goo. James lifted his hand, exposing it to the meager amount of light emanating from the fallen torch. It was covered with blood.

John and Andy exited the barn cautiously. They aimed their rifles left and right, prepared for possible enemy soldiers concealed in the woods. They saw no one. Even better, no one shot at them.

John barked an order to William, hiding in the cover of the barn, "William, you go around back and check on James. But be careful! Don't shoot at anything you can't see. Stay in the shadows. And whatever you do, don't shoot James!"

William trotted to their right, skirting the edge of the trees, and headed for the clearing behind the cabin.

"Let's check the bodies," Andy advised. John nodded.

The soldier that Andy shot first was dead. He lay in a huge puddle of black blood. He had bled out quickly. The target of John's first shot was breathing, but just barely. Blood oozed steadily from the wound in his back, soaking his green coat. His fingers extended and contracted slowly in an instinctive effort to crawl away. More blood oozed from his mouth and nose.

"This one's still alive!" exclaimed John.

"Leave him be," urged Andy. "He'll be dead soon enough. Let him bleed out."

The third soldier lay in a bloody heap on top of the shattered table. He was dead, as well.

They turned their attention to the cabin.

"I think they tried to set it on fire, but I don't see flames anymore. It must have burned itself out," observed Andy.

John picked up one of the still-burning torches and cautiously approached the door of the cabin, his rifle at the ready. Suddenly a strange cry, almost inhuman, emanated from beyond the cabin. John recognized the tone of the wailing voice. It was James.

Then the smaller, broken voice of William cried out, "Johnny! Come quick!"

John and Andrew let go of their caution and ran in the direction of William's voice. John's torch lighted the darkened carnage in the clearing. He was startled by the sight of a dead soldier, breeches around his knees and privates exposed, lying prone on the ground with a knife protruding from his chest. James sat only feet away from the body of the militiaman, cradling the motionless Margaret in his lap. His hands and shirt were covered in blood. He was weeping uncontrollably.

"James, are you hurt?" asked John.

James looked up, the torch illuminating the anguish on his face, and cried out, "She's dead, John! My Margaret is dead!"

"Are you sure?" asked John.

"She ain't breathin'. And her head's bleedin' so bad!" he wailed.

John knelt down beside his brother and placed his hand over her mouth. James was right, she was not breathing. He gently turned Margaret's head to the side and inspected the back of it. There was a small hole in her skull, about the size of a marble, from which the blood seeped. He shined the light of the torch on the ground where she had lay. He found a small pointed rock protruding from the hard ground, covered with blood.

"I'm so sorry, James. It looks like she hit her head on that rock so hard that it broke her skull." John shined the light upon the dead man beside them, illuminating his exposed, shrunken, bloody privates. He tried to console his brother, "At least she didn't feel anything else the bastard did to her."

James hugged Margaret to his breast, groaning, crying. He was in total disbelief, almost outside of his own mind. John didn't know what to say or do to bring him comfort or peace.

Andy placed his hand on James' shoulder and spoke, "Why don't we cover her up James? We'll go inside and get a blanket or quilt or something."

James merely nodded in response.

"C'mon John, let's finish checking the cabin. William, you stay with your brother."

William nodded in response, silent tears streaming down his face.

Andy picked up one of the extinguished torches and held it out to John to ignite off of his burning one. They proceeded back around to the front of the cabin to inspect the inside and retrieve a suitable covering for Margaret's body.

A pungent odor of burning flesh and hair slammed their nostrils as they neared the door. It reminded John of the smells of hog killing in the winter. John gagged when he saw what awaited them inside. The flames that they had seen earlier were not any form of arson. It was Mrs. McClelland's dress. She had been shot in the head and, apparently, had rolled partially into the fireplace. She lay flat on her back. Her cotton night dress had caught fire and burned completely up to her belly. Her wool stockings were singed and melted to her charred, black legs. The flesh was still smoldering. The stench was unbearable.

In the opposite corner they found the boy that had been missing from the cluster of children under guard outside. It was the nine-year-old Jacob, seated awkwardly on the foot of a bed, leaning against the wall. The old trade musket lay beside him on the floor. He had been bayoneted repeatedly in the chest and neck.

Andy picked up the musket and inspected it. "It's been fired," he informed John. "The little fellow fought back. Got off a shot."

"But he never had a chance," observed John.

"No, but he died like a man, I guess, protecting his family," returned Andy.

"But why shoot Mrs. McClelland?" wondered John.

"She must have tried to protect Margaret. Who's to say, really? One thing's for sure, though, this particular bunch of Tory bastards won't hurt anybody else."

John nodded his agreement.

"Let's cover these bodies. Then take a quilt out to your brother and try to help him any way you can. I'll go get some help."

"Just be careful," cautioned John. "There might be a whole company of 'em out there somewhere."

"Don't worry about me. I don' have far to go, and I know this country way better than any of these Tories."

They quickly and reverently placed bed sheets over Mrs. McClelland and little Jacob. John ripped a quilt from one of the other beds and headed out the door with Andy. He paused for a couple of minutes as his young friend fetched his horse from the barn, jumped on bareback, grabbed a handful of mane, and ride off into the darkness toward the direction of the church.

John took a deep breath and headed toward the clearing full of death behind the house to somehow comfort his despondent brother.

6

John heard a distant rumble of thunder mixing with the gallop of Andy's horse as he rode out of the clearing. A wind-driven downpour with booming thunder and lightning began about a half-hour after Andy disappeared into the darkness. After the initial storm soaked the Carolina countryside, the winds died down and the atmosphere settled into a steady, heavy rain. The temperature began to drop rapidly.

William had somehow managed to find the remaining scattered children before the storm began. They had hidden in fear in the nearby woods, but he managed to coax them out of hiding with his familiar, shrill voice. He would not let them near the cabin. Instead, he herded them up the ladder into the loft of the barn and placed them in the hay where he and his brothers and Andy had been sleeping. John soon joined him to help comfort the little ones. They tucked the children deep into the hay and covered them with their warm wool blankets. They were soon sleeping out of sheer physical exhaustion, despite their earlier emotional trauma. The steady patter of the rain on the roof deepened their sleep and masked the noises from below.

William and John quietly descended the ladder. Once downstairs they leaned their weapons against the wall and began to gather the resources to start a fire. The rain and dropping temperatures were going to make the night even more miserable than it already was.

While William stood watch at the door, John scraped a clear spot on the dirt floor about six feet inside the entrance to the barn, took out his fire-starting kit, and set about making a fire. He quickly had a small blaze going, fed with scraps of dry wood. A small woodpile against the western wall of the barn provided an ample supply to keep the blaze going.

John made two trips out into the rain to try and convince James to come inside the dry barn and get warm, but James ignored his pleas. He just sat and held Margaret's lifeless body, gently rocking back and forth as if he were comforting her.

John left him to his grief and returned to the barn.

"Riders comin'!" William announced only a few minutes later.

The first men to arrive were Andy's uncle, Thomas Crawford, and Thomas, Jr. Their faces registered visible shock at the carnage that marked this once-peaceful frontier home. They inspected the bodies both outside and inside the cabin, and discovered James, still in shock, holding Margaret's body across his lap. James was soaked to the bone and racked with shivering convulsions from both the emotional trauma and the cold rain.

Mr. Crawford squatted beside James, placing a firm hand on his shoulder. "Son, you'll catch your death of pneumonia out here. Let's get you in the barn and get you warmed up. Tom will help take care of Margaret."

James shook his head in the negative, pulling the body closer to his chest, and digging his arms underneath the soaked quilt.

"Look son, you don't want Margaret to be out here in this rain, do you? She deserves better than that. We need to get her inside where it's dry, and then we can take care of everything. Do you understand?"

James stared blankly into his face, and then subtly nodded his acknowledgement. Thomas, Jr., knelt down and slid his arms under the bend of Margaret's knees and her upper back and lifter her small body with ease. He turned and headed reverently toward the cabin.

"Come on, son," Crawford urged James, "Let's get you inside and make sure you're not hurt."

He led James around the cabin, and seeing the dull glow of the fire in the barn, led him toward the comfort of the light. William greeted his brother with a huge hug and urged him toward the fire. Mr. Crawford quickly inspected James in the firelight, discovering only a few scrapes and bruises.

He looked at William and John, "What about you boys? Are you hurt?"

"No, sir," answered John.

"Not a scratch," added William.

"And the children?"

"They're all up in the loft. William found them out in the woods pretty quick-like. We bedded them down together in the hay and they fell right to sleep. They were scared to death, but real tired. They're warm and dry," replied John.

"Good, good. Fine work, indeed, boys." He paused and gazed briefly into the fire, then looked at the boys with steely eyes. "Andy told us what you boys did here tonight. You're fine, courageous, brave men … all of you. And I'm grateful for your taking such good care of these little ones."

Thomas, Jr., emerged from the darkness, approaching the barn and carrying a large bundle under his arm. "I brought some of Mr. McClelland's old work clothes from the cabin, for anyone who might need something dry." He turned to James, "James, you're going to catch a bad chill if we don't get you into some of these dry clothes."

James smiled thinly and took the bundle from him. "Much obliged, Thomas. And thank you for taking Margaret inside. It means a lot to me."

"It was my honor, James. Just go get changed and we'll all get warm by this fire while we wait for the militia. Andy's sounding the alarm all over the countryside."

James retired to the darkness of a nearby stall and shed his wet clothes. The dry garments were an immediate relief and did much to brighten his spirits. He quickly returned to the fireside. William wrapped a dry coat around his shoulders.

It was only a matter of minutes before more men began to trickle in from the muddy road, all of them armed. Each of them followed basically the same routine when they arrived, inspecting the dead Loyalists and exploring the cabin in disbelief, then joining the growing group in the barn. Each and every man made the deliberate effort to shake the hands of each of the Hamilton boys, thank them for their intervention, and pronounce their judgment upon such men who could perpetrate this kind of an unthinkable act in their home district.

About an hour later a captain of the local Patriot militia arrived and took command of the scene. The gallant and proud Andrew Jackson rode at his side. Andy left the officer to his duties and joined the Hamilton boys by the fire. Like James, he was completely soaked by the torrential rains. His face was ashen white and his teeth chattered from the cold. John guided him to the rear of the barn and helped him get into some of the extra garments that Hugh had retrieved from the cabin.

Meanwhile the captain inspected the bodies of the dead, and then ordered that sentries be stationed along the road and at intervals around the house. He instructed that the bodies of the dead Tories should be moved to a nearby hillside away from the creek where they would be buried in the morning after the sunrise. He commanded soldiers to carefully and reverently place the bodies of the victims on the bed in the cabin and cover them with clean sheets.

Once the crowd inside the barn was sufficiently thinned the officer joined the four boys by the fire and introduced himself. "Gentlemen, I'm Captain John McKinney of the Camden District Militia. And who might you be?"

James, the eldest of the Hamiltons, spoke up, "Sir, I reckon you already know Andy Jackson. I'm James Hamilton and these are my brothers John and William. We're from up in Mecklenburg County, a few miles northeast of Charlotte."

"What brings you down this way?"

"Well, sir, we volunteered to come down this past week to bring a collection from our church to help the McClellands after the man of the house was hanged and killed here a couple weeks back. We brought down a load of clothing, food, and supplies mid-week and stayed on a couple days to help fix some things here on the farm ... leaky roofs, busted fences, and such."

"Well now, regular 'Good Samaritans' you are, then! But it seems you weren't so hospitable toward these green-coats strewn about the lawn," replied the Captain.

"No, sir, they all got what they deserved," growled James.

"No good sumbitches ..." added Andy, spitting into the fire.

The captain chuckled and nodded his agreement and then proceeded to interrogate the Hamiltons and Andy Jackson, attempting to glean every detail of the evening's engagement. After gathering all of the facts he formulated his analysis of the situation.

"Well, gentlemen, I cannot commend you enough for your resourcefulness and courage on this horrible night. When young Andy told me that the four of you had engaged and killed five soldiers of the British Legion I must admit that I did not lend much credence to his account. But the results of your combat this night are most astounding, indeed!"

"It is greatly disturbing to me that soldiers of the Legion are roaming this far outside Charlestown. This squad may have been a scout unit that saw an opportunity to take advantage of a defenseless family and in their depravity took that opportunity. Or they may be deserters and ruffians who have fled the British service. But from the well-kept look of their uniforms and equipment, I believe that they are, indeed, in the active service, and not simply outlaw ruffians. If that is the case, then we may have more than just a handful of the King's soldiers hereabouts."

"They didn't seem like runaways to me, Cap'n," replied James. "They looked pretty professional … in appearance, if not in their behavior."

The captain nodded his agreement. "We will have to be on the lookout, indeed. We could have an entire regiment of professional soldiers on the verge of invading our district. This could signal a major move by the British."

"Sergeant!" he barked at a tired-looking gentleman standing near the door of the barn.

"Sir!" the man replied, snapping to a not-so-professional attention.

"Send runners at once to the homes of all officers who have not yet reported to this location. Inform them that the district militia is called out, in its entirety, by my command. Tell them to gather their men and meet at the muster grounds in Lancaster by sundown tomorrow. Do you understand?"

"Yes, sir!" the sergeant replied. He hesitated, as if waiting for more instructions.

"Well … be gone, man! Ride hard and ride safely. I will see you at the muster ground tomorrow."

"Yes, sir," the man saluted rather loosely and ran for his horse.

The captain turned his attention back to the Hamilton boys and Andy.

"Are you men hungry? Do you need anything?"

"No, Sir. I think we're just wore plumb out," replied John. "I know I'm tired, but I'm not sure if I could even go to sleep."

"I know I can't sleep. How could I?" mused James. He almost wept, but choked back his tears, shuddering slightly.

The captain slapped James on his knee, "Son, I'm sure if we can find you a quiet, warm spot, you can get to sleep. You need to rest. We can handle anything else that comes our way tonight. Trust me."

He ordered several men to come into the barn and prepare a place for the Hamilton boys and Andy. The corncrib was the most logical spot. It was dry and in the rear of the barn. The militiamen brought in several armloads of hay and spread them over the previous season's stray corn shucks. They also managed to find three dry blankets for them to share. The boys reluctantly crawled through the low door and made their beds in the straw. William drew close to James. As they lay silently in the straw both of them sobbed.

John and Andy lay alone along the far wall, absorbed in their thoughts.

In minutes all of them lapsed into the unconsciousness of a deep, exhausted sleep.

John awakened to the sensation of a blinding light in his eyes. And there was an annoying noise. It was the buzz of what sounded like dozens of voices. James had already opened the door to the corncrib and was crawling out. The sun was up ... the obvious source of the bright light in John's face. He was completely disoriented for a moment, unable to remember where he was. Then the vivid memories of the events the night before flooded back into his mind. It was all too real. It was not a dream. And it was time to get up and face a very somber Sunday.

The other boys began to stir as well. They emerged from the warm comfort of their makeshift bedroom into a cold, wet world bustling with activity. Captain McKinney and most of the militia were gone. Indeed, the population of souls that occupied the small farm had changed completely, transformed from an assembly of armed militia into a gathering of smiling, kindly church folk.

The McClelland children sat crowded together on a single bench along one wall of the barn. They were being doted upon by kindly women who spoke soothing words, wrapped them in blankets, gave them tin cups of warm milk and coffee, and filled their hands with chunks of fresh bread with cheese. The two girls smiled and waved softly at the familiar Andy Jackson the moment they made eye contact.

Two large tents had been erected in the mud just outside the doors of the barn. Two sides of the tents were covered to shield from some of the rain. The other sides were open to the yard. The tables belonging to the McClelland family had been removed from the rain and placed under the tents. The table that was shattered by the fallen soldier had obviously been repaired. The rain had washed the raw blood away, but a dark, black stain covered almost half of its surface. The tables were covered with all kinds of hearty foods. Men and women alike stood about eating and talking. Suddenly John realized what he was looking upon. This was a funeral gathering. The people of the Waxhaws Church had gathered to minister to the children and bury the dead.

The boys quietly but swiftly made their way toward the food, suddenly aware of their ravenous hunger. The Elder Crawford spotted them from his perch, a chair sitting in the threshold of the cabin, safely protected from the rain.

"Boys!" he called out. He leapt from his chair and bounded through the thick mud and puddles toward the tent. "I was wondering how much longer you might sleep."

Undeterred from their mission of finding food, the boys all nodded and smiled as they reached for one of the pewter plates on the corner of the table.

James spoke first, "I reckon we was pretty dog tired, Elder. I can't hardly believe we slept plumb into the daylight. I don't recall ever doin' that, to be honest."

"Oh, it's quite understandable, James. You boys had quite a horrific experience last night."

James merely nodded in response. The boys piled their plates high with hot biscuits, slabs of salty ham, small sweet cakes, and cheese. Amazingly, there was also hot coffee and tea to drink, supplied steadily by women carrying pots from the cabin to the food tents and barn.

"What's goin' on now?" inquired young William, spraying bits of ham and biscuit as he spoke.

Mr. Crawford nodded toward the ridge to their right. "Well, a few of the militiamen are up top burying the enemy soldiers."

The boys all looked up the hill. A group of four militia soldiers were unceremoniously shoveling dirt into a hole on the hilltop. John could almost swear he saw one of the men spit in the hole.

"No Christian service for them, I assume," commented James mockingly.

"No, son. No service. Though one of our other elders did read the Scriptures over them a little while ago. We giving them a modest Christian burial together in a single grave."

"More than the bastards deserved," judged James. "What about the McClellands?"

"We will hold services for the three of them this afternoon. We're hoping that this rain will let up before long. It's slow going, but we have men digging their graves now at the church cemetery. They will, of course, be buried beside Mr. McClelland. We have cancelled our regular services this morning. We believe that our ministry to this family and to you boys takes precedence on this particular Lord's Day."

James stared at his plate. "Where is Margaret? I mean … where are the deceased now? I've seen people coming in and out of the cabin. They can't still be in there."

"No, son. They were moved at daybreak this morning. Taken by wagon to the church with the utmost care and respect, I assure you. Several women of the church are there now, bathing and dressing them, preparing them for the grave. I felt it best that we not have open caskets or viewing. You will understand, I hope."

"I agree. People need to remember them as they were, not as they are now," affirmed James.

"I thought you would. I could definitely see that there was an attraction between you and Margaret," stated Mr. Crawford.

"Oh, it was much more than that, sir," snapped James.

"Yeah, Elder, they was goin' to git married!" piped up William.

Crawford's face registered visible shock. He glanced at Andy Jackson, who raised both eyebrows and nodded gently in affirmation. Looking back at William, he queried, "What on earth are you talking about, boy?"

"It's true, Mr. Crawford. After dinner last night I asked Margaret to be my wife, and she consented. I loved her with every bit of my heart. We were goin' to speak to her mama after church this very mornin' and seek her blessin' and permission," confirmed James.

"Oh, my! Son ... I had no idea that your feelings and relationship had manifested themselves so quickly. Though it does make sense." Crawford paused. "I am so very sorry for your deep, personal loss, young man. Surely it makes the events of last night doubly offensive and tragic." He paused again, longer this time. "Did Thomas, Jr., know about this?"

"No, sir. We was goin' to tell him today, too. I could see how he liked Margaret. She knew it, too. She just didn't feel like that for him. But she didn't want to hurt him, neither," James explained.

Elder Crawford processed the information and the sentiments involved, then responded, "Well, it does not matter now ... who knew or who did not know, I mean. You know your own loss and grief all too well. Tom will bear some measure of hurt, as well, I'm sure. But life must go on."

"That's a whole lot easier to say than it is to live out, I'm a thinkin'," countered James.

"No doubt. But you are a young man. You have your whole life ahead of you, God willing. And I am quite confident that He will see you through this dark time. Besides, you have these fine young brothers standing by your side, don't you?" Crawford encouraged.

"I reckon. I just can't seem to see much past right here and right now. Past that graveyard this afternoon. Right now I almost can't imagine goin' home." James sounded distant, broken. He stared northeast over the ridge toward home, the grave-covering militiamen interrupting his line of sight.

Crawford turned his attention slightly to John and William, "Speaking of which, what are your plans, boys?"

"I don't rightly know," answered John. "We do need to head for home, though. We have our own place to take care of. What do you think, James. Are we headin' home today or tomorrow?"

"I don't see how we could leave today," responded James. "We have to pay our respects for this family. And if this rain keeps up, I don't look too forward to spendin' a night in the woods. I 'spect we will see things through here today and head for home in the mornin'. I don't reckon we'll be in any big hurry. We already know we'll likely have to camp on the way tomorrow night. We should be home mid-afternoon on Tuesday, I'd say."

"Excellent," responded the Elder. "I think that is a sound plan. Meanwhile, we want you to rest and eat and enjoy this Lord's Day as best you can. We will have the service and burial at the church at 3:00 this afternoon, rain or shine. We are already working on housing for the McClelland children. Several families have volunteered to take them in. You boys are welcome to stay here on the farm tonight, of course."

"Much obliged," stated James. "We'll make plans to stay in the barn one more night."

"Very well," Crawford gently patted William's bare head. "I'll leave you fellows to your breakfast. I pray God's blessings upon your day."

The boys stood in the shelter of the tent and finished their breakfast. John took the opportunity to drink an extra cup of coffee, syrupy sweet with sugar and pale with thick, fatty milk. He smacked his lips as he finished the last drop. The boys thanked the women who had prepared the food and headed back toward the barn.

"Boys, these guns all got wet and shot last night, so our first job this mornin' is to get 'em cleaned up real good. They'll rust up mighty fast if we don't," James proclaimed.

"We have most of the stuff we need," John stated, "but I reckon we could use some good rags and more gun oil. Alls I got is a tiny bottle of grease."

"I'll check the cabin," Andy volunteered. "There has to be some gun oil in there somewhere. I'll fetch some good cleaning rags, as well."

The Hamilton boys all grabbed their weapons from the corner of the barn and ascended the ladder back into their low-ceilinged loft retreat. James handed Andy's rifle up through the ladder hole to John. Ten minutes later Andy's smiling face popped up through the hole in the floor. He had, indeed, found an ample supply of cleaning cloths and oil. For the next hour the boys sat in the soft hay, chatting and diligently swiping and cleaning their barrels with small patches of white cloth. The distraction of the manual labor helped to clear their minds of the previous night's events. Their spirits began to lighten a bit.

When James finally declared each gun "clean," they each ran one more oiled patch down their barrels to keep them lubricated, and then thoroughly wiped down the exterior metal parts with an oil cloth. Finally, they primed their firelocks and loaded the weapons and stood them against the wall.

The remainder of the morning passed quietly. They remained in seclusion, talking … even joking and laughing. They told Andy tales about home, about their horrible step-father and loving mother, and many other adventures. They also shared about their struggles and victories involved in running their own farm. Andy told his stories as well. Indeed, he was quite a gifted storyteller and soon had the boys aching from laughter as he acted out some of the exploits of his brothers.

Shortly after noon the boys ventured down the ladder in search of more food. They were not disappointed. In true frontier form, the women of the area had piled tables high with delicious dishes, brought to encourage family members, guests, and soldiers still present on the farm. They boys ate their fill, returned to the loft, lay down in the soft hay, and drifted off into a deep, rainy-afternoon sleep.

Some time later John was awakened by a soft kick. Shaking the cobwebs from his brain, he looked up into the gently smiling face of the Elder Crawford. The others were sitting up and stretching, as well.

"It's time, boys. We need to head on down to the church-house. The graveside service will be in about a half-hour or so," he informed them. "The rain's let up a bit, thank Goodness."

The boys rolled out of their straw beds, retrieved their hats and guns, and followed the Elder down the ladder. Once at ground level they wrapped their firelocks with oiled cloths and headed for their wagon. They wrapped the guns in two rolls of canvas in the back of the wagon, and then climbed in for the ride to the church. They joined a small convoy of people on horses and in wagons. Elder Crawford rode on the seat beside James. John and William huddled in the back of the wagon. Andy rode his horse alongside them. There were a few people on foot in the beginning of the journey, but they easily found rides in one of the four wagons in the line.

The convoy rode in silence in a light, drizzling rain. After about twenty minutes the first horsemen in the line began to turn off the road to their right. Moments later James caught sight of the humble steeple atop the small, white church. A large circle of about two hundred people stood in a meadow about fifty yards beyond the building. A handful of headstones indicated that they were standing in the graveyard. As the Hamiltons and the large group from the McClelland farm approached the circle of mourners, their ranks opened, revealing three rain-soaked pine caskets ... two adult-sized and one small one.

"Which one is which?" James inquired of the Elder Crawford.

"Mrs. McClelland is on the right. Her husband already lies to her right. Margaret is beside her, in the middle. That is, of course, little Jacob on the left," he responded.

And James wept.

The service was amazingly simple and brief. There was little in the way of a eulogy. Several elders from the church shared from the Scriptures. Throughout the solemn event a few of the church ladies held the four remaining McClelland children close to them, offering hugs and comfort. The two girls were quite despondent. The little boys seemed a bit confused, but appeared to realize the gravity of the moment.

The men of the church were somber as they lowered the caskets with ropes into the hastily dug, water and mud-filled graves. Elder Crawford offered a very eloquent prayer, and with great suddenness it was over. The crowd dispersed quickly as the rain began to pick up again.

The Hamilton and Jackson boys hovered near the graves after the others left. Even as John, William, Robert, and Andy turned to leave, James and Thomas, Jr., remained in silence, watching the gravediggers shoveling mud into the holes.

Thomas finally interrupted the soft thumping of the rain, "Papa told me that you and Margaret were planning to marry. I have to confess that I was a might angry and jealous when he told me ..."

"Look, Tom ..." James interrupted.

"Wait, James. Hear me out. I came to realize how stupid it was to feel like that. Jealous, I mean. Margaret is gone. I know you're hurting. I miss her, as well. But she loved you and wanted you. And I am deeply sorry that you didn't get to make her your wife. I will keep you and your brothers in my prayers."

He extended his hand to James, smiling grimly.

James shook his hand with a single, strong stroke. "Thank you, Tom. It means a lot to me. I'd like to think that we Hamilton boys can count you and the Jackson brothers among our best friends."

"Friends. Compatriots. Always," affirmed Thomas.

Their solemn moment was broken by an authoritative voice from behind James, "Which of you is Mr. James Hamilton of Mecklenburg County?"

They turned to face a rather tall, distinguished looking fellow.

"That's me," responded James, "What can I do for you?"

"I am Sergeant David Faulkenberry, here under orders from Captain John McKinney. I believe you met him last night. He requests your presence at the muster grounds in Lancaster tomorrow morning," responded the messenger.

"Sergeant, me and my brothers were plannin' on headin' home in the mornin', if the weather will agree just a little."

"The captain understands that, Mr. Hamilton. He is well aware of the urgency of your return. He was hoping that you might postpone a short while and join him mid-morning. He desires to see you once more before you go, and he has something to give you. If you would be so kind as to arrive around 9:00, he is planning on a brief meeting and an early dinner so that you can be on your way. May I inform him of your intention to join him?"

James sighed. "Yes, Sergeant, that will be fine. A couple of hours shouldn't hurt us none."

"Excellent. Thank you, sir. I bid you a dry and restful night." The soldier turned and headed toward his horse.

"How about we get in out of this rain?" encouraged Thomas. "I need to get home and check on Mama. I didn't want her to get out in this weather and get soaked today. And you need to get back to the McClelland place. I bet these church mothers have a big supper all planned for you fellows."

"That's the best idea I've heard all day," responded James, grinning.

They paused for one last look toward the graves in the waning light, and then headed for the wagon. Andy and Robert Jackson sat on their horses beside the Hamilton wagon, talking to John and William. Andy held the reins to Thomas' horse.

"Andy, Robert … It's been an honor gettin' to know ya," stated John. "I hope we all meet again someday."

"I'm sure we will, Johnny," Andy responded.

The boys all shook hands in the misty rain, then headed their separate ways, certain that their paths would, indeed, cross again.

7

SPOILS OF WAR

The Hamiltons slept well. The rain came in torrents throughout the night, and the roar of its impact upon the barn roof drew them into a deep slumber. Shortly before Monday's sunrise the rain broke.

The boys awakened to peaceful silence. They were up and moving at dawn, excited about the prospect of going home. Even the hard-to-rouse William was bright-eyed and bushy-tailed on this particular morning. John started a fire in the previously-used spot just inside the barn door.

The church ladies had left ample food for their breakfast. There was a large bundle of biscuits, salted ham, a dozen hard-boiled eggs, and fried apple pies wrapped in cloth, along with a crock of strawberry jam sitting on the bench beside the barn door.

The boys enjoyed a leisurely breakfast beside the glowing fire as they watched the sun climb over the ridge to the east. Its warmth and radiance did much to brighten their spirits after thirty-six hours of darkness, death, and soul-soaking rains.

After breakfast they busied themselves with preparations for their journey. It would be easier travel home with their wagon emptied of all of its original cargo, but several inches of rain had fallen and would surely make a muddy quagmire of the rutted dirt roads.

Within an hour they were sufficiently loaded and packed. They climbed into the wagon, took one last look at the McClelland homestead, and then started on a southeasterly journey toward the village of Lancaster. James drove while John and William kept watch, weapons at the ready.

The journey was, indeed, monotonously slow. Once they passed the Waxhaws Church and left the firmer, well-drained western ridge road, they took the heavily-worn southward road to Lancaster. This road descended into several low-lying areas. Water had been across it in several places. More than once the boys had to dismount the wagon to clear small logs and debris from their path. In some places the mud was almost a foot deep. Their horses grunted and struggled against the sucking pull of the mud on their hooves. The wagon groaned from the ongoing struggle between the forward pull of the team and the downward tug of the thick mud.

Lancaster was easy enough to find. It was noisy and crawling with men and horses. The militia had come out in force. Tents of various shapes and sizes dotted the open meadows and fields. The air was thick with the acrid smoke of cooking fires. A sentry at the edge of town directed them toward the militia headquarters.

They soon spotted Captain McKinney sitting in a chair beside a rather large fire sipping from a cup and smoking a pipe. He waved a friendly hand at the boys and motioned for them to join him. The boys pulled their wagon into an open spot in the field and climbed down.

"Good morning, lads," he chirped as they approached. "How are our Mecklenburg County Patriots this fine morning?" His smile was wide and friendly.

"Mornin', Cap'n," responded James. "We're mighty fine, sir, and ready to be home, I reckon. No offense, but we've 'bout had our fill of South Carolina, I'd say."

The Captain laughed heartily, "I should think so! You boys saw more action in one night than most of these men have seen since the war began." His face clouded. "Nasty business, that. But I quite think that every man gathered on this green is proud that you did come to our fair district to visit, if only for a while. Your service, and your sacrifice, will not be forgotten, that much I will guarantee."

"I could have done without it all, myself," stated James, matter-of-factly.

"No doubt," affirmed the captain, "But, nonetheless, you're here and you are brave Patriots ... the whole lot of you. I'm grateful that you agreed to come and see me today before returning home."

"Any more sign of the British or Tories?" inquired James.

"None so far. We've had patrols out to the south and east, trying to observe all logical approaches from Charlestown. Though we haven't seen any sign of Redcoats, we plan to remain on station here for another two or three days, at least. With the entire Continental Army and many militias of the south captured at Charlestown, our northern fringe militias are the only forces blocking any potential move by the British into North Carolina. We've heard reports that the Virginians are sending some reinforcements, but it seems that they are all too little and too late. Things seem quite grim for our fledgling nation right now, boys."

"So why are we here, Cap'n?" interrupted John impatiently.

"Straight to the point, eh, Squire Hamilton? I like it," said the captain, nodding. "Quite frankly, I wanted to see you one last time and thank you for your service to our state. Maybe even convince you to remain here with us in the service."

"No, sir. Not interested," interrupted James. "We need to be on our way and tend to our property."

"I figured as much, but felt compelled to ask. Anyhow, I also have some things for you to take home with you."

"What do you mean?" inquired John, confused.

"Just the properties of the soldiers you killed. My men removed all of their valuables, personal effects, and weapons. Some of the boys tried to abscond with the items as spoils of war, but I informed them that the items were not theirs to take. They rightfully belong to you men who bested them in battle, not the ones who cleaned up afterward. I can have my men load it all in your wagon for you. Would you like to have a look first?"

"Yes, sir, I reckon so," responded James.

"Come, then." The captain tapped the ashes from his pipe and tucked it into the tie strings on the back of his cocked hat. "I have all of the items under guard and stored in a tent beside mine."

He led the boys to a medium-sized tent near the center of the field. Inside was a large wood table covered with weapons, leather goods, and smaller personal items from the pockets of the dead soldiers. A stack of bloody uniforms lay on the ground beside the table, along with five relatively new pair of leather riding boots. Five feathered leather dragoon helmets sat clustered on one end of the table. There were five short land pattern Brown Bess muskets with bayonets, two pistols, and a sword with a shoulder strap. There were also five British cartridge boxes, various belts and bags, three snapsacks with various items of clothing, money purses, and a small pile of gold and silver jewelry.

"There you go, gentlemen, all of the items recovered from the scene of the battle and the bodies of the dead. It's yours for the taking," proclaimed the captain. "Their horses are saddled out back, but I have taken the liberty of claiming those for the militia ... I hope you will understand. They are much needed for the war effort."

"You're not joking with us?" James asked in disbelief.

"No, sir. You were the victors, and to the victors go the spoils. It is only fair."

"How much money is there?" asked John.

"In real money, about thirty pounds in various coins, mostly silver with some gold, and fourteen Spanish milled dollars. There are a few British coppers included in that total. Plus several gold and silver rings, one quite exquisite silver comb, and a beautiful gold necklace."

James' eyes lit up. He was calculating the mathematics in his head. The currency and precious metals could perhaps total enough to pay off their mortgage on the farm! His mind raced, and his knees felt a bit wobbly. He made a deliberate effort not to appear to be too excited.

"Honestly, Cap'n, we don't have any use for the muskets, cartridge boxes, bayonets, or the uniforms. That's all army equipment. But if you're serious, we'll take all the rest of it," stated James. "We can easily sell what we don't need."

"And I want me one of them feathered devil-helmets, Cap'n," added John.

"Me, too!" chirped William.

James grinned. "I reckon we'll keep three of them dragoon helmets as keepsakes, Cap'n. Somethin' to look at and tell stories about when we get old someday."

"So you have no interest in the muskets and cartridges?" inquired the captain.

"No, sir. Not much use for them on the farm. And we want to do our part for the army down here. Just spread those around in your militia wherever you have a need. They'll be better used there. Tell the boys to blister a few Tories and Redcoats for us."

"I was hoping you would say that. Those muskets and the one hundred and fifty cartridges in those cases will be most valuable to our militia. I tell you what … in return for the weapons I will trade you two of the soldiers' mounts. You choose the animals. How does that sound?"

"More than fair," responded James.

"Excellent. Now, how about a meal with my officers before you're off?"

"We thank you, sir, but we've already eaten this mornin', and we have many a muddy mile to travel to get home. I reckon we'll just be on our way," responded James.

"All right, then. I understand. I'll draw up a receipt showing that you came by the horses legally and that they are, indeed, your property."

"I'm most grateful, sir," responded James.

He placed the silver and gold coins and jewelry in his shooting bag as the officer instructed a squad of privates as to which items were staying and which ones were to be loaded in the guests' wagon. James and John then selected the best two mounts from the five available.

It was about nine o'clock in the morning when the boys bid their farewells and headed for the wagon. The captain walked with them. As promised, the wagon was loaded and the two mounts tied to the back.

"James, it's been a pleasure. I hope that our paths may cross again some day. Here are your papers on the horses. I think I have sufficiently described how they came into your possession."

"Thank you, sir," James replied, accepting the folded document. "I 'spect that with this war coming our way, we might see each other again. But next time I'll probably just be Private Hamilton of the Mecklenburg County Militia. I reckon we'll be called out pretty soon. And it looks like most of the fightin' is gonna be down here in the southland," responded James.

"Until we meet again, then." The captain extended his hand to James, then to the two younger brothers. "And the same goes for you boys. We'll not soon forget what you little hornets did to that pack of Tory dogs. We are beholding to you all."

"So long, Cap'n, God be with ya," proclaimed James.

The boys clamored into the wagon and they struck out eastward along the turnpike that followed Gills Creek.

Once they were around the first bend, James looked at his brothers and stated matter-of-factly, "I hope you boys realize that we may have just got enough money to pay Farr off and get the deed on our farm."

"That's what I figured!" said John excitedly.

"We just have to protect our bounty all the way home. William, how's about you drive the team while Johnny and I keep watch. And I'm going to look for a spot in the wagon to stash this treasure."

William took the reigns from James, who climbed over the seat into the back of the wagon. James soon located a loose board behind the driver's seat that concealed a narrow, closed space, just large enough for a small money sack. He placed all of the coins and jewelry together, stashed them in the hole, and returned the board to its place.

They had about almost seven miles to travel before reaching the northward highway that would take them back into Mecklenburg County. William pushed the team hard, hoping to make it back into North Carolina before nightfall.

The road was muddy, but not impassable, and they made steady progress. The turnpike crossed the normally low creek about halfway to the crossroad. The ford was normally only four or five inches deep. But the water was over a foot deep on this day and flowing vigorously. William talked softly to the team and made the crossing carefully and slowly and without incident.

Time passed quickly and quietly. About an hour after noon they approached a small rise. As they neared the hilltop they heard the shouts, clanking metal sounds, creaking wagons, and the snorts of horses far off to their right. The sounds grew louder.

"We must be near the crossroad," observed John. "Sure sounds busy on the northern road, don't it?"

"A little too busy," mused James.

When they topped the hill they saw the source of all of the noise and activity. A large convoy of wagons and men was approaching steadily from the south. They were about a mile from the crossroad. There were several hundred men accompanying the wagons, some on horseback, but most on foot. Most wore blue and red Continental Army uniforms. There were several dozen men, obviously militia, in civilian clothing, as well.

"Them's Continentals!" exclaimed John. "But I thought they was all captured at Charlestown."

"Looks like they didn't catch 'em all," commented James. "They're movin' pretty fast and yellin' a lot. Must be in a hurry. I don't want to be in front of this bunch, for sure. They'll push us too hard. We'll just lay up here at this crossroad and let 'em pass, then we can follow at our own pace."

William eased the team to a stop about fifty yards short of the crossroad. John broke out a sack of snacks and passed them around for a makeshift meal. A cluster of five officers soon broke away from the head of the column and trotted across the field toward their wagon. It appeared that the column had paused as men were dismounting and sitting down along the side of the road to rest.

"We got company comin', boys," commented James.

They waited as the officers trotted up to the Hamilton wagon.

"Good day to you, gentlemen," one of the officers spoke, a kindly-looking middle-aged fellow.

"I'm Colonel Abraham Buford of the Third Virginia Regiment, in command of this detachment. I trust you boys are not of a loyalist persuasion."

"You would be right, sir. I'm James Hamilton, private in the Mecklenburg County militia of North Carolina. These are my brothers John and William."

"Outstanding! Are you in this area on official business for the military?" inquired the colonel.

"No, sir," responded James. "Personal business down here in the Waxhaws for a few days, but now we're headin' home. Thought that we would lay up here for a spell and let you gentlemen pass and then fall in behind you."

"I thought all the Continentals was surrendered at Charlestown," interjected John. "How did you get out of all that mess?"

The colonel smiled. "Well, son, we were not at Charlestown for the surrender, thank God! I was dispatched there to bring relief to the siege, but we arrived too late. We are returning to North Carolina to regroup with our forces there, but the British have been dogging us for days. General Lord Cornwallis is now out of Charlestown and seeking to subdue the countryside. We believe that he has elements seeking to run us to ground. Have you gentlemen seen any sign of the enemy?"

"We encountered a few of 'em night before last. Five men of the British Legion a few miles west of here," responded James.

"That is our nemesis, for sure! Loyalist cavalry and dragoons under the command of one Colonel Banastre Tarleton. They have pursued us for days. It must have been one of his forward patrols," observed the colonel.

"Well, whoever their commander might be, they attacked a helpless family that night near Lancaster. We happened to be staying on the farm, sleeping in the barn. We killed them all, but not before they killed two women and a child. They raped one of the women." James did not elaborate further.

"Absolutely horrible, but not surprising," commented the Colonel. "These beasts are unleashing many such horrors upon the people of South Carolina. They must be driven back into the sea." He nodded toward the horses that were following the wagon. "Those appear to be Legion markings on the saddles and leather of those mounts."

"Yes, sir. I reckon they are," responded James, staring into the eyes of the Colonel. There was an uncomfortable moment of silence.

"Good for you boys," the Colonel winked at them.

"Sir, a rider under white flag!" exclaimed one of the other officers.

A lone rider, dressed in the unmistakable bright green and red of the British Legion, rode rapidly along the road beside the column. He paused briefly, then following the directions of several finger-pointing men, galloped across the short grass toward the officers gathered around the Hamilton wagon. He yanked the reins and pulled to a rapid halt twenty feet from the wagon. He pridefully sized up the gathering of officers before him, stealing a glance at the wagon and the two horses tethered to it.

"Whom, may I ask, is the officer commanding this column?" he inquired with a thick, educated British accent.

"That would be me, Lieutenant. Colonel Abraham Buford, Third Virginia Regiment, representing the Continental Congress of the United States of America, in command of this column and detachment. State your business, son."

"Colonel, I am Lieutenant Andrew Mayfair of the British Legion, at your service. I bear a message from Lieutenant Colonel Banastre

Tarleton, commandant of the Legion, currently following in your pursuit." He reached into his pocket, retrieved a folded paper, and thrust it toward Colonel Buford.

"Just read it to me, son. I have neither the time nor the inclination to decipher a message from the King's servant today."

"As you wish." He cleared his throat, lifted his chin, and delivered the message.

"Sir. Resistance being in vain, to prevent the effusion of human blood, I make offers which can never be repeated: You are now almost encompassed by a corps of seven hundred light troops on horseback; half of that number are infantry with cannon, the rest cavalry: earl Cornwallis is likewise within a short march with nine British battalions.

"I warn you of the temerity of farther inimical proceedings, and I hold out the following conditions, which are nearly the same as were accepted by Charles town: But if any persons attempt to fly after this flag is received, rest assured, that their rank shall not protect them, if taken, from rigorous treatment.

"Article 1: All officers to be prisoners of war, but admitted to parole, and allowed to return to their habitations till exchanged.

"Article 2: All Continental soldiers to go to Lamprie's Point, or any neighboring post, to remain there till exchanged, and to receive the same provisions as British soldiers.

"Article 3: All militia soldiers to be prisoners upon parole at their respective habitations.

"Article 4: All arms, artillery, ammunition, stores, provisions, wagons, horses, etc. to be faithfully delivered.

"Article 5: All officers to be allowed their private baggage and horses, and to have their side arms returned.

"I expect an answer to these presuppositions as soon as possible; if they are accepted, you will order every person under your command to pile high his arms in one hour after you

receive the flag; If you are rash enough to reject them, the blood be upon your hand.

"I have the honour to be, Banastre Tarleton, Lieutenant Colonel, Commandant of the British Legion."

The lieutenant swiftly folded the paper and returned it to his weskit pocket.

The eyes of the Continental officers were wide with shock. A couple displayed obvious worry on their faces. The others just stared.

One of the worried-looking officers spoke up, "Perhaps we should entertain the terms, Colonel. It sounds as if there is a formidable force arrayed against us."

The colonel ignored him, peering at the messenger. Fishing for more information, he countered, "Seven hundred men, you say? And Cornwallis with nine battalions nearby? Not likely! How close is 'nearby?'"

"I can offer no other comment, sir. I am only authorized to deliver the commandant's terms ... nothing more. And I am to await your response," countered the British messenger.

The officers stared expectantly at the face of their colonel. At long last he spoke, "You may deliver the following message to your commandant, Lieutenant.

"Sir, I reject your proposals, and shall defend myself to the last extremity.

"I have the honor to be, Abraham Buford, Colonel."

"As you wish," the officer countered snidely. He lifted his reins, preparing to turn and make his exit, but then subtly eased his horse toward the driver's seat of the wagon. "Young man, those horses are familiar to me, with the clear markings of the British Legion, no less. Were you aware of that fact? How did they come into your possession?"

James glared hatefully into the face of the pompous officer. "I didn't figger that dead men needed horses, so I brung 'em along with me to take home."

"Is that a fact?" the officer growled.

"Tis a fact," proclaimed James. "I kind of like that horse you're riding, too. Maybe I'll tie him up to my wagon here in just a bit."

"We'll just have to see about that!" the officer snapped, spinning his horse on its heels and galloping southward, white flag dancing in the soft breeze.

The colonel smiled at James. "I don't think he cares for you, son."

"Feelin's mutual, sir. I promise you," James responded.

"Gentlemen!" the colonel addressed his officers. "Fifteen more minutes of rest, then we proceed northward. I do not believe a single word of that pompous brat, but we still need to move and quickly so. Send a small detail as rear guard; one sergeant and a squad of four men. We don't want to risk losing any more of our men than that. Tell them to signal the main force if they see the enemy approaching."

"Yes, sir," a major responded. "Gentlemen ..." The officers tipped their hats at the boys. "Good luck."

"Well, Colonel, looks like we're in for a fight. We'll go ahead and fall in with your boys."

The officer shook his head. "No, son. This is not your fight. I want you to move on. Three more rifles won't make a difference if Tarleton has the numbers of men that he claims to have. Besides, you will better serve the cause by getting ahead to Charlotte and warning them about the British move out of Charlestown."

The colonel pointed to a tree-covered ridge about a half-mile to the northwest, on the left side of the north-bound road. "You boys need to get moving now and get under cover of those trees. If there is action, it will be in this open land here near this crossroad. You should be safe there. Once there is no danger of pursuit, proceed northward."

"Are you sure, Colonel? We don't want to run from a fight ..."

"Private!" the colonel barked. "Do not question my orders. Get your brothers under cover and then deliver the news of this British incursion to Charlotte and areas northward. Do I make myself clear?"

"Yes, sir."

The colonel extended his hand to James. "Good luck, Mr. Hamilton. And God speed." He turned his horse and trotted back toward the column.

"You heard him, boys, let's hit the tree line," muttered James.

William clucked at his team and popped the reins, slowly leading the wagon onto the highway north. The road was horribly thick with mud, but they managed to cover the half-mile in about thirty minutes. William guided the horses off of the road and sought refuge in the trees. He hid the wagon and team behind a small knoll, next to a depression with ample water for the horses, and then the boys dismounted, stretched their muscles, and took a drink of water themselves. William grabbed a sack of corn to feed the horses a meal. James and John sat down against an oak tree, watching the Continentals in the clearing to their south.

"James, do you reckon reckon there's a big fight comin'?" asked William.

"I assume so. Sounds like that Colonel Tarleton is achin' for one."

"Will we be safe up here?" William countered, sounding worried.

"Oh, sure. We'll be fine up here. We've even got a first class seat to watch the whole show." James smiled at his little brother. "Don't you worry, tadpole, I won't let them green coats get hold of you. "

"James, the column is back on the move, looks like," interrupted John. "And I see riders way off on that far ridge! Look! There's smoke way down the road!"

Seconds later the muffled crack of musket fire reached their ears. There were six or seven shots, followed by hollow silence.

8

WAXHAWS MASSACRE

"What happened, James?" John asked. "Was that it? Was that the battle?"

"No ... that was likely just the rear guard. That was a ways down the road from the sound of it. They were probably shooting to warn Colonel Buford. Or they could be dead, or captured. There wasn't many of 'em. There's no way to tell."

The boys watched the action unfolding below. The wagons moved northward along the road while the infantry fanned out into a single line on both sides of the muddy trail. Riders in dark green uniforms came over the far ridge and began forming up, as well. There were three separate groups of them, one lined up the left flank of the Patriots, one on their right flank, and the other spread out across the center. They looked to be about three hundred yards out from the Continentals.

"That doesn't look like seven hundred men to me," observed John.

"No, I'd say they number two hundred, maybe two fifty at most," affirmed James. "But they're pretty much all on horseback. I see a few infantry, but not a whole lot. Buford has about a hundred more men, but almost all of them are on foot. And look at how he has 'em all strung out along a thin line. I swear, it don't make any sense. They should be lined up tighter, and two men deep, at least. And why didn't they use the wagons for cover? Brothers, I've got me a bad feelin' about this ..."

Moments later the cavalrymen on the right flank began their charge toward the Continentals, led by a flashy officer on the right who was vigorously waving his sword in the air.

"That's gotta be Colonel Tarleton," commented James. "That feisty fellow over on the right flank. Do you see him?"

"I see him," responded John. "He didn't waste any time at all, did he?"

"I told you he was achin' for a fight," affirmed James.

The other groups of green-clad horsemen followed the Colonel's enthusiastic charge. They all converged upon the line of foot soldiers. It took a couple of seconds before the thunder or their hooves traveled across the expanse of the field and reached the boys' ears. The horses increased in speed as they continued down the hill. They were almost upon the infantrymen.

"Why ain't they firin'? They're right on top of 'em!" wailed William.

The smoke of the first shots erupted as William's final word still hung in the air, followed by the echo of their explosions. There was one modest volley of musket fire from the Continentals, but that was all. Colonel Tarleton and several of his men on the right went down hard, their horses apparently shot beneath them. They couldn't tell if the Colonel had been hit because of the volume of smoke hovering over the field.

Amazingly, the left flank of the Continentals did not appear to even fire a single shot. Within seconds the thundering cavalry cascaded over the hapless infantry. Only sporadic shots rang out along the line after that. The poor Virginians didn't even have the time to reload. The primary sound coming from the smoky crossroads was that of ringing steel and screaming men.

Suddenly John saw movement to the left as a handful of riders emerged from the smoke. They were leaning low over their mounts and galloping hard toward the woods to the east of the boys' position.

"Is that Colonel Buford?" asked John, incredulously.

"Yep. That's Buford. And most of his staff, it looks like. Cowards!" James spat on the ground. "I reckon the boys of the Third Virginia are on their own."

Screams continued to emanate from the battlefield. Men on horseback rode to and fro, swinging their swords in high, powerful arcs. The battle was over in minutes. Actually, it was over before it even began. The British Legion had routed the Continentals.

The boys watched in disbelief as the horsemen pranced about the battlefield and then descended upon the wagons. On the far right flank of the carnage they saw one Legionnaire pick up a white flag and wave it in the air as the men around him laughed and jeered. Moments later the men snapped to attention and demonstrated discipline when an officer with the appearance of Colonel Tarleton rode up on a horse and pointed his sword at them. He was obviously alive and well and had found another horse to replace his fallen mount. He did not appear to be pleased with the behavior of his men. They crisply saluted their commandant and then returned to the business of surveying the battlefield.

The Hamiltons watched in horror as some of the men on the far right appeared to be plunging their swords and bayonets into the ground at their very feet.

"What are those men doing, James?" questioned William.

"I think they're killing the wounded. At least that's what it looks like, little brother."

"Are they s'posed to do that?" he inquired innocently.

"No, buddy. They're not supposed to do that. In fact, it's just about the most horrible, cowardly thing that any man could do on a battlefield. It's a crime, and it violates the rules of civilized war."

"When are we headin' out?" asked John, obviously worried.

"I don't think we need to move yet. We don't want to risk bein' spotted. We'll lay low here until about an hour before sundown, then we'll ease out on the road and head toward home ... get as far as we can before dark. If any of 'em start headin' this way, we'll either take to the deep woods or hit the road, dependin' on what direction they're goin'. Right now let's get our guns and settle in on this spot, wait, and watch."

The boys grabbed their weapons and sat down behind a small outcropping of rock to observe the activities on the battlefield. Other riders and wagons approached from the south. They appeared to be carrying wounded to the wagons, both Continentals and Legionnaires, but mostly blue coats. About a half-hour later the boys heard a stick crack in the woods to their right.

"What was that?" hissed John.

"Somethin' big … most likely a deer. Could be a man, though," replied James. "Stay alert."

The boys all lowered themselves against the rocks for better concealment and kept their eyes peeled in the direction of the sound.

Moments later one of the Virginians emerged, hatless and bloody, from the thick undergrowth about fifty yards to their right. He stumbled over a tree root and slammed into a small sapling, emitting a faint, muffled cry. He collapsed to his knees.

"C'mon!" urged James, running toward the man.

Hearing their approaching footsteps, the wounded man rolled onto his back and immediately began to cry out, "Don't! Please! I surrender! Good God, I surrender! Please don't cut me again! I surrender!"

"Hush, soldier!" James slapped his hand over the man's mouth. "Half of the countryside can hear all that wailin'! We ain't from the Legion. We're Patriots out of North Carolina. You're safe. Now lay still and let me look you over."

Relief washed across the man's bloody, mangled face. Clotted blood covered his eye sockets and cheeks from a deep gash across his forehead at the hairline. His ears were also full of blood. James carefully lifted the man's scalp to inspect the wound, revealing his exposed skull underneath. Poor William gasped when he heard the sucking sound of the blood. He quickly turned his head and vomited profusely.

"Can I please have some water?" the man begged.

"I'll get it," volunteered William, wiping his mouth with a look of shame.

James nodded at him with a soft gaze of affirmation, "It's all right, little brother. Nothin' to be ashamed of. Go fetch a couple of canteens. We need some extra water to wash him up a bit. And grab anything you can find that will work for some bandages. We gotta dress this wound."

"What's your name, soldier?" asked James.

"Alexander Macon, Third Virginia. Just call me Alex." He extended his right hand to James and John.

"I'm James Hamilton, Mecklenburg County Militia. This here's my brother John, and our younger brother William is the one fetching water. We're gonna check you over real good and get you taken care of. Just rest easy, now."

The man was covered so completely with blood that it was impossible for a superficial inspection to identify any other wounds.

"I can't see nothin' but blood," proclaimed John, exasperated. "Alex, are you hurt anywhere else besides this head wound?"

"My right knee is numb and my boot feels like it's full of blood. And I have a horrible burning across my lower back." His breathing was labored and short.

They looked at the leg first. John found a small vertical cut in his breeches. He stuck his fingers into the hole in the linen and ripped it open. There was a deep horizontal puncture wound in the front of his thigh, just above his right knee. It was bleeding profusely.

"Get that boot off of him, John. And try to get some pressure on that wound."

John tugged at the boot, which slid easily off of his blood-soaked leg. The coagulating crimson liquid poured out into a large puddle on the ground. He removed the leather sock garter and slid the man's bloody sock off of his leg, wound it up into a tight ball, squeezed out the excess blood, and pressed it over the oozing hole. He grabbed the leather garter and wrapped it around the leg and improvised bandage, barely managing to get it to buckle closed in the last available hole.

"Good job. Now help me lift him up so's I can check his back, Johnny."

They gently tilted the man onto his left side, causing him to let out a long hiss. "Something burns like hell back there," he explained.

James pulled open a wide cut in the man's coat and shirt and inspected the wound on his back. "You're sliced pretty good back there, right across the kidneys, but it's not that deep and not bleedin' a whole lot. The wool of your coat took most of the blow of the blade, I think. It'll have to be sewed up later, but it's not bleedin' much and it's for sure not fatal. Same for that scalp wound. It's bloody as hell and down to the bone, but it'll heal. It's that leg wound I'm most worried about. It's still bleedin'."

William returned with two and a half gourds of water and two linen food sacks. The dehydrated man quickly downed the half-filled gourd. James took one of the other gourds and slowly poured the water over his face, gently rubbing away the clots and rinsing the blood from his eyes, nose, and ears. The cleansing water revealed the tender face of a young man, probably not much older than James.

James folded over one of the food sacks and lay the makeshift bandage across the scalp wound, then took his patch knife and sliced the other sack into long strips, making a tie to secure the bandage on the front of his skull.

"This sock is soaked again, James," reported John. "I don't know what else to do."

"Take the strap off," James instructed.

Once the bandage was removed, James rinsed the wound, which quickly filled again with thick blood. He shook his head grimly.

"Alex, this cut is deep. I think it's cut a blood vessel of some kind. The good news is that it's dark blood, not bright red. But we still have to get it stopped or you're gonna bleed out eventually. I'm gonna try somethin'. I saw it done once on a feller with a real bad axe wound on his thigh. I reckon you gotta trust me," urged James.

"I trust you. Do whatever you have to do. I don't want to lay here and bleed to death."

"It's gonna hurt like hell," James advised.

"I've already been to Hell today. Let's get it done."

James nodded grimly. He reached down at his side and took hold of his powder horn. He nodded to John, "Johnny, get out your flint and steel."

"What for? We can't make a fire, them British'll see the smoke!"

"We're not makin' a fire, little brother. But we need a spark to get his wound closed."

"How?" asked John, confused.

"Just get ready to strike when I tell you," James commanded.

He turned his attention to the wounded Virginian. "Alex, here's what's got to happen. We gotta burn that wound to make the bleedin' stop. I'm gonna to sprinkle a little gunpowder right into the hole and Johnny is going to set if off with his flint and steel. It's gonna burn something horrible for just a little while, but it should sear the flesh and close the hole. And you must not yell, or the enemy will hear you. Do you understand?"

"I understand. Grab me something to bite down on and let's get it over with," muttered Alex.

John whipped off his shooting bag, doubled over the strap, and wedged it onto the soldier's open mouth. He chomped down hard on the thick leather.

"You ready, Johnny?"

John clicked his flint and steel three times on the ground to make sure he had a sharp edge and a good spark.

"Ready, James."

James stuck a piece of clean cloth into the hole in an attempt to absorb as much of the oozing blood as possible. Alex winced in pain at the invasion.

James looked at John, "Johnny, as soon as I pull this rag out of the wound I'm going to pour in a dash of powder from my horn. You've got to make a spark fast because the blood will wet the powder if you take too long."

John clicked two more showers of sparks onto the ground, and then nodded at James. James nodded back in response, then rapidly whipped the cloth from the hole and poured in a small pile of powder.

"Now, Johnny!"

John hit the steel across the edge of the flint three times, throwing a shower of sparks. In the moment between the second and third strike the powder ignited with a hollow fizzle and a quick pop. Frothy blood erupted from the wound along with a small cloud of white smoke and steam. The smell of seared flesh mixed rapidly with the acrid burn of the gunpowder. The wound glowed orange and red, almost resembling a tiny volcano.

Alex howled through his teeth as he clamped them down on the leather. James reached over quickly and placed his hand over his mouth to help muffle the sound. Alex's muffled screams continued for about ten seconds, and then subsided to a dull groan. The burned flesh and cooked blood closed the hole and the flow of blood was stopped.

"It worked, Alex. You ain't bleedin' any more," said James, excitedly. "John, get a fresh piece of cloth to put over that burn."

After covering the charred hole in his leg, the boys began their work on the back wound. They rolled the soldier onto his belly. James cut roughly twelve inches from around the bottom hem of the wounded man's white cotton shirt. He rolled the long piece of clean cloth three times, making it four layers thick and roughly four inches wide. He carefully placed the cloth over the long sword wound across the small of his lower back, and then gently rolled him back over onto his back and tied the loose ends tightly across his belly.

"Alex, the bandage on your back wound ain't much, but it should keep good pressure on the cut until we can get some more help," James informed him.

"Thanks again, gents. I don't know how I'll ever be able to repay you."

"T'aint necessary, Alex. It's our honor and our duty. You just rest easy and drink some more water. Are you hungry?" asked James.

"Now that you mention it, I'm starved. I don't see how I could think about food at a time like this. But I think I could eat. We've been on the move so long, I haven't had a bite since last night."

"I'll fetch some ham and biscuits," volunteered William.

"And fellows, I'm so, so cold. Down to my bones. I feel a rigor coming on."

"It's all that blood you lost, I'll bet. William, grab a couple of blankets, also, will you?"

William nodded and trotted to the wagon to grab the food and blankets.

"Johnny, can you go back up to the rock we were watchin' from earlier and keep an eye on things? Make sure nobody is nosin' up our way?"

"All right, James. I'll check and be back in a bit."

He retrieved his shooting bag, freshly decorated with a new set of Alex's teeth marks, grabbed his rifle, and trotted back up the rise toward the vantage point.

"Alex, if you're comfortable enough, we're gonna set right here and lay low for just a little while longer, and then head north along the road toward nightfall … try to put as much distance as we can between us and the Legion before we make a cold camp," James explained.

"Suits me. It feels good just to lie still a bit. And it's real good to be able to see without all that blood in my eyes," he smiled at James, his spirits lifting.

"How'd you get away from down there, Alex?" inquired James, "We didn't see any more foot soldiers gettin' off that battlefield. Just a bunch of officers riding low and fast toward the north right after the shootin' started."

"Is that a fact?" inquired Alex, eyes wide.

"Yes, sir. Colonel Buford was right in the front of all of 'em, gallopin' like there was a sack full of gold at the end of the ride."

Alex looked sullen, disappointed. "I can't say as I blame them. If I'd had a horse I probably would have been running off, too. We never had a chance on that field today. The boys all knew it as soon as we saw all those dragoons lining up on us."

"So how did you get loose?" James inquired again.

"I was way out on our right flank, about ten men from the end of the line. We were under orders not to fire until they were ten yards out … which I thought was insane … but we followed our orders. We cut loose on them with a single volley at ten yards. It dropped quite a few of their horses, actually, but they kept coming and rolled right over us. I never even had a chance to reload. We truly thought Colonel Buford was going to surrender. After that first shot lots of the men were dropping their muskets and surrendering. I threw mine down, too, and had my hands in the air. I even caught a glimpse of a white flag over on the left, but the man carrying it went down. I assume he was hit."

"You actually saw a white flag?" asked James in disbelief.

"Yes. Definitely. But the horse soldiers still didn't stop. They rode right into us, dozens of us with hands up to surrender. The first rider that came by me was swinging his sword. If I hadn't ducked he would have taken my head off. Instead he caught me right across the line of my cap. It felt like a brick had hit me. I felt the jab in my leg a few seconds later. I never saw who did that to me. I think I passed out for just a bit."

He continued, "As I was going down I heard some of their men yelling, 'The colonel is down! The colonel is down! They've slain Tarleton! No quarter for the rebels!' I had a lot of blood in my eyes, but I could see their soldiers on foot slashing at men on the ground. Their infantry came up and were bayoneting our wounded as they lay." His voice was breaking with emotion. He paused for a moment to compose himself.

"I rolled over on my belly and started crawling toward some high grass to the right of our line. I had only made it about twenty feet when I heard voices nearby, so I stopped moving and lay still. I figured my best bet was to just play dead. No time later something sliced me across the back. It felt like my back had caught fire. I assume it was a sword. I didn't move or make a sound, even though it hurt so badly! I lay still and played dead until I heard no more movement or voices, then started crawling again."

"So they cut you, on the ground, whilst you was laying there still and lookin' dead?" confirmed James.

"Yes. I was not moving. I was barely breathing. But even after all of that I still managed to make it to the tall grass and kept going. A couple of minutes later I rolled into a small creek. I washed my eyes out, made sure I wasn't being followed, and then lit out up the creek. My leg felt heavier and more numb as I went along. I was pretty much dragging it for dead weight when I finally hit the woods and eventually stumbled into you fellows."

William returned, carrying a sack of food and dragging two blankets. He helped James cover the shivering soldier.

"William, can you just pinch off some small pieces for Alex and feed it to him? Let's let him get warmed up a bit," suggested James.

William nodded and sat down near the soldier's head, and then started feeding him small morsels of the moist biscuit, with an occasional piece of salty ham.

"You're lucky you got outta there. They've been haulin' the wounded out by the wagon load, mostly Continentals," commented James. "And that Colonel Tarleton ain't dead, either. We saw him again a little later on with a fresh mount. He looked to be chewin' out some of the men for what they was doin', didn't seem none too pleased with 'em."

"Well, no matter," replied Alex. "They were still Tarleton's men. He was in command. The blood of those Patriots is on his hands. He is already well known for his ruthlessness. Now we have an actual record of what Tarleton's quarter looks like. I just pray that the blood of the men massacred on this field will not be forgotten … that my friends and compatriots will not be forgotten. I have served with some of those boys for two years, and now I'll never see any of them again," his voice trailed off, forlorn. A single, bloody tear trickled into his ear.

"We'll make sure that people know what happened here today, Alex," James promised.

William, curiously quiet since the embarrassing loss of his lunch, spoke up, "You said you've served two years. Exactly how old are you, Mr. Alex?"

"I'm twenty years old, William … that's your name, isn't it?"

William nodded and smiled. He was clearly proud that the soldier had remembered his name.

"But I feel much older than that today, William."

"You're just a year older than James!" William replied.

"I imagined that we were about the same age when I first saw your brother. So tell me, how old are you, William?"

"Oh, I'm just thirteen … way too young to be in the army."

"But not too young to fight the legion," James interrupted. He went on to describe the events of Saturday night and how they had killed the squad of British Legionnaires with the help of their friend Andy Jackson.

"Well, that's quite a feat, indeed! So you have seen action then, young William. I have a brother back home who is almost your age, I think. I've been gone far too long. Shadrack … we all call him Shad … is twelve by now I think. I hope and pray that he will never have to fight in this war or fire his weapon at another man."

"What about you, Alex? Been in any big fights before today?" inquired William.

"Well, I was in one real battle in the summer of '78. The entire regiment fought at Monmouth in New Jersey soon after I enlisted. I will forever remember that day as the hottest in my life! I bet I fired fifty times, and never got a single scratch, even though men fell all around me. God was watching over me, I guess. We fought the Redcoats to a draw and held our ground that day," he proclaimed, grimly but proudly.

"Since then I've been in several minor skirmishes and raids. But mostly it's been marching, maneuvering, drilling, foraging for supplies, and making camp. Much of my regiment was captured at the surrender of Charlestown. I was on furlough when the regiment moved south, and was recalled to join this detail under Buford to relieve the city. But we didn't make it in time."

"Well, I reckon your soldierin' days are most likely over now, Alex. You'll need six months, maybe more to recover from these wounds. That leg might not ever get back all the way right," advised James.

"Perhaps you are right. We shall see," Alex responded, and then changed the subject. "So what happens now? Where are we going when we leave these woods?"

"We're only a few hours ride from Charlotte. We live a few miles northeast of town. We'll get you loaded into our wagon and head that way. We'll have to camp tonight. We've had way too much rain and the roads are mighty bad, as you well know. But if we pull out at first light we should have you there a little after noon-time if the mud cooperates a little. We need to warn the people there about the British bein' so close. Our Colonel will most likely call out the militia pretty quick. There's a good doctor in town, so we'll leave you with him and then head on toward home. We'll have to get things in order on the farm before I answer a muster," explained James.

John returned from his hilltop perch.

"Nobody's comin' up here, James. They're all busy picking over the bodies and lootin' the wagons. Looks like all of the wounded are gone already. There ain't two dozen men left down there now. It'll be pitch dark in an hour and a half, reckon we ought to head on out?" asked John.

"Yep, let's go. Let's get Alex to the wagon." He looked at Alex, "Now listen, friend, you need to let us do all the work. I want you to keep that leg straight and try not to bear any weight on it. I'll get under your right arm, and Johnny will help you on your left. We're gonna head up this hill nice and slow. William will go on up and make you a pallet in the back of the wagon."

Alex nodded in response. It took several minutes to wrestle the exhausted soldier up the hill, but they finally made it. William had prepared a first-rate bed for Alex to rest upon. William took the reins and John joined him on the seat. James took the rear watch, keeping his eye on the direction of the British and Tory forces. William skillfully led the team through a shallow gully and back onto the road below the crest of the ridge, well out of sight of the battlefield to the south.

They headed northward toward Charlotte ... back toward home.

PART II

James' War

9

WHEELING AND DEALING

The roads did not cooperate as they had hoped. The boys struggled to make even two miles for each hour of travel. The twilight appearance of the Hamilton boys in downtown Charlotte on Tuesday afternoon with two British Army horses in tow was a curiosity to the town folk. Their discovery that they carried with them a wounded, bloody Continental soldier in their wagon caused a general disturbance. The news that a major battle had just occurred forty miles to the south threw the town into an absolute uproar.

The boys left their wounded friend in the local doctor's good care and continued on toward home in the dark, leaving the townsfolk to their hysteria. They arrived at their cabin late in the evening. Emotionally and physically drained from their ordeal and journey, they kicked off their leggings and shoes and tumbled into their beds.

Sunrise brought a parade of visitors and curiosity-seekers, anxious for news and information about the British. Their mother and little brother, Hugh, were among the first visitors on Wednesday morning. She embraced her boys and wept, relieved that they had returned home safely. She brought with her two chickens and all of the fixings for a feast and insisted upon cleaning up the cabin and cooking the boys a huge "welcome home" dinner. It was exactly the homecoming that they all needed.

Folks continued to drop by for several days. The boys shared about the political situation down south, the movements of the British, and Monday's battle, but they elected to keep the story of their own violent introduction to the war all to themselves. Somehow, though, word got out about the violent events at the McClelland cabin. There was much talk about it in the community, but no one dared approach the Hamilton boys regarding their experience. By week's end life had settled back into its familiar routine of chores, farming, livestock care, and hunting.

On Friday evening after supper the boys built a small campfire on the ground near the cabin and sat down to watch the sunset. James and John puffed on their clay pipes while William played with his marbles in the smooth dirt. John soon joined in a friendly game with his little brother. It was a pleasant, peaceful, restful evening.

"Boys, I've been doing some cipherin' on the money and valuables we got from that militia colonel in Lancaster," stated James, breaking the silence. "As best I can tell, we have what amounts to about forty-five dollars in Spanish and English silver and gold coin. We have several more dollars in the silver and gold jewelry and the silver comb. I'm not quite sure how much value we have in all of the leather goods we got, not to mention those two fine cavalry horses."

"We don't really need those mounts, do we?" asked John.

"No, we each have our own horses that are servin' us just fine. And if we can get them two British army horses within sight of some Continental officers, I bet they could fetch quite a sum," answered James.

"There's a Continental post and all manner of militia up at Salisbury, ain't it?" observed William.

"You're thinkin' like I'm thinkin', little brother. So here's what I have in mind. I'm plannin' to head on up there early tomorrow. I can sell the jewelry at a store in town and then see what I can get for the leather goods and horses out at the army camp. I don't plan on takin' anythin' but gold and silver, and I don't plan on bringin' any of the stuff back home."

"It'll be better not to sell it all in Charlotte, anyway," commented John. "Too many nosy people that we know askin' too many questions."

"Exactly," affirmed James. "Then, maybe, by this time tomorrow we might have close to enough to pay off this farm full and clear. That would give me plenty of peace of mind, seein's how I'm probably goin' off to this war pretty soon. It'll be good to know that you boys have this place for your own if somethin' happens to me."

"Well, if you go with the militia, I'm goin', too," declared John.

"Oh no you're not!" scolded James. "You're gonna stay right here and take care of this farm, and our stock, and our little brother. We've got too much sweat and blood invested in this ground. You'll do as I say."

"Johnny, you can't go off and leave me!" exclaimed William. "I ain't staying here by myself and ole Farr ain't exactly gonna give me a bed to sleep in."

"T'aint fair, James. I wanna fight for my home, too," muttered John bitterly.

"I know you do. Heck, you already have! And you might have to again, right here on our own land someday. That's why it's important that you stay. I'm already committed. I'm part of the Mecklenburg Regiment. I have to go to the war when they call me. But you gotta stay," urged James. "Heck, this war might just come to you one of these days. We already know that it's just down the road!"

"I reckon," replied John. "But I ain't gotta like it."

"It'll grow on ya, Johnny. You're a good man. And you're the only man I trust to take care of this place ... with William's help, of course!" James winked at William.

"Can I go to Salisbury with you tomorrow, James?" begged William.

"No, little brother, I'm gonna go alone on this one. I'll be moving fast and doin' some wheelin' and dealin'. Don't worry, though; I'll be home by dark. You won't even miss me. Besides, I need you two to chop out that south cornfield tomorrow. It's gettin' to where I can't hardly tell the weeds from the corn after all this rain we had last week."

"Oh, boy! Excitin' stuff!" mocked William, rolling his eyes.

"I know it ain't quite as full of excitement as you've gotten used to lately, but it's important. Especially if you plan on eatin' this winter," corrected James.

"All right, all right. Choppin' corn tomorrow. Got it. Can't wait," William grunted.

"Let's go ahead and call it a night, brothers. We've all got a long day ahead of us tomorrow," suggested James.

John and James tapped the smoldering remnants of tobacco out of their pipes. William tossed his marbles into his doeskin bag and ran for the cabin door while the older brothers kicked dirt into the coals of the fire. They followed William inside where they all stripped down to their shirts and settled into the comfort of their corn shuck beds.

James awakened an hour before dawn, dressed quietly, and stepped out into the darkness. He double-checked his leather pouch to make sure he had the gold and silver jewelry, and then headed to the barn. He swiftly saddled his horse and the two cavalry horses, looping the various leather belts and bags from the dead Legionnaires across the saddles of the prized animals. He mounted his horse and pointed his little convoy northeast toward the Rowan County village of Salisbury. He estimated a generous five hours of riding time, more than enough to cover the seventeen miles to his destination.

He made pretty good time on the journey, stopping once to rest and water the horses at a small creek and eat a cold breakfast. He arrived in the village of Salisbury about an hour before noon, proceeding at once to the biggest general store to inquire about possible buyers for precious metals. The shopkeeper referred him to a jeweler who lived above a doctor's office on the same block.

The jeweler welcomed him in, weighed his merchandise, and calculated the gold and silver content. The amount of pure gold turned out to be surprisingly high, almost three quarters of an ounce thanks to one unusually large ring. Since James insisted in being paid in Spanish silver, the jeweler made an offer of twenty-three and three-fourths Spanish milled dollars for the entire lot. James happily accepted the offer, pocketed the silver coins, and made his way toward the military camp outside of town.

John and William arose in the dull glow of dawn. After milking and feeding the cows, feeding the chickens and collecting eggs, and checking the goats' water and feed, John fixed them a hot breakfast. He scrambled six of the morning's fresh eggs and toasted some bread in the stone fireplace oven. William was quite subdued and not his usual chatty self, obviously dreading a hot day of work in the field.

After breakfast they put together a sack full of food for dinner and a couple of canteens full of water, grabbed their hoes and files from the barn, and then headed off to the assigned field to chop weeds. The relative cool of the morning would, at least, make the monotonous task a little more bearable. They worked steadily until noon and then took a break for dinner and a short nap in the cool of the trees. Both boys lounged in tall, cool clover with their straw cocked hats covering their faces. Sleep came quickly, easily, and deeply. Suddenly the sound of a voice pulled John from his blissful slumber.

He heard the crooning voice off in the distance, coming from the direction of the cabin. It didn't sound familiar, at all. And he suddenly realized that they had both left their weapons in the cabin and gone to the fields unarmed.

"Idiot!" John scolded himself.

He left William asleep in the shade and scampered along the edge of the field toward the house.

The voice called out again, discernable this time, "James! Where are you, boy?" But John still did not recognize the voice.

He quickly made it to the corner of the clearing beside the cabin and stole a glance at the visitor. The man was facing partially away from him, so he couldn't catch a full-on look at his face. He looked somewhat familiar to John, but he still could remember neither the man's name nor the context in which he had encountered him before. The man wasn't brandishing any weapons and appeared familiar and harmless enough, so John stealthily stepped out into the open.

"James ain't here, mister. What can I do for ya?"

The man spun around in his saddle, startled by the unexpected voice to his rear.

"Where's he at, boy?" the man inquired.

"Gone to Salisbury on business before daybreak this mornin'. I expect him back by nightfall."

"I see. Are you his kin?"

"Yes, sir. I'm his brother, John. My other brother, William, is hidin' in the trees with his sights on you right now, mister," John lied, aiming to bluff his way through any possible trouble.

"Is he, now?" the man asked, his mouth bending into something of an amused grin. "Well, there's no need for that, James and I are well acquainted."

"So says *you*." John paused, with a heavy emphasis upon the last word spoken. "But I ask again, what can I do for you?"

"Well, since ole Jamie isn't here, can I trust you to give him a message for me, son?"

"Yes, sir. Of course. What's it pertainin' to?" inquired John, nosily.

"It's official business pertaining to the Regiment of the Mecklenburg County Militia, to which your brother, James, has sworn his service," the man stated. "I am Lieutenant Thomas Givins of the company commanded by my brother, Captain Samuel Givins. I bring a message regarding the call up of the regiment."

"Oh, I see," stated John, perking up and walking toward the man. He extended his hand. "I'm pleased to meet you, sir. Sorry about the way I was actin', you just can't be too careful these days with the Tories so close by."

"I understand ... John, is it?"

"Yes, sir. John Hamilton."

"I see ... were you one of the boys involved in that shoot-out with the British Legion patrol down in the Waxhaws?"

"Yes, sir," John responded proudly, his chest expanding. "We took care of five of 'em that was raidin' a house where we was stayin'."

"Indeed. Well, Mr. Hamilton, I would be most appreciative if you could deliver this very important message to your brother. Do you need to write it down?"

"No, sir. I'm not so good at writin', but I'll be faithful to deliver your message just like you give it to me," John promised.

"Very well, then. Please inform Private James Hamilton that the Regiment is now officially on alert. Command has caught wind of a Tory uprising in the neighborhood of Lincolnton. If, indeed, the regiment is called up, riders will be dispatched with a report date. Our headquarters will be Phifer's Mill. Can you handle that message?"

"Yes, sir! Regiment on alert, Tories in Lincolnton, riders will instruct, muster at Phifer's Mill. Got it."

"Excellent! I bid you good day, then, John Hamilton. Perhaps I will see you at a muster one of these days soon?"

"Could be," John responded, head drooping. "But for now James says I have to stay home and take care of the farm."

"Well, I'm sure your brother knows best. Take care, Mr. Hamilton. It was a pleasure speaking with you."

"You, too, sir."

The lieutenant clucked at his horse, spun her around, and trotted back down the road toward Charlotte. William appeared out of the field just as he was leaving.

"Who was that?" he asked.

"Just the lieutenant from James' militia regiment. They're getting ready for a call-up. He says there's Tories actin' up near Lincolnton. They must be gettin' pretty bold, knowin' that the Redcoats are so close by."

"Does that mean James is leavin' us?" his little brother whined.

"I reckon so. It's only a matter of time till he goes off to the real shootin' war."

❧

James saw the Patriot camp from a half-mile away. Several hundred troops, mostly militia, dotted the open field. There were ample two-man tents in the center of the camp and larger tents around the periphery. James rode up to a sentry post on the road leading into the camp manned by blue-uniformed Continental soldiers.

A sergeant greeted him professionally and sternly, "State your business, sir."

"Sergeant, I am James Hamilton, from down near Charlotte. I am a private in the Mecklenburg Second Regiment. I'm here today on my own accord lookin' to sell these two mounts I have with me along with some other soldierin' goods. I was hopin' you might point me in the right direction."

The sergeant took a quick glance the horses and accouterments.

"British cavalry mounts, eh? Where in the hell did you get those?"

"It's a long story, Sergeant," James replied, exhaling. "But their original owners are now under the dirt and I'm a lookin' to unload 'em for the right price. Who do I need to talk to?"

"Well, if you were just looking to sell some ordinary horses, I'd send you to the quartermaster. But you wouldn't want to sell them to him, anyway, because he's just going to give you some worthless script or a receipt in return. I doubt you're interested in going back home with nothing but musket wadding."

The soldier winked and smiled.

"Well, you're absolutely right about that, Sergeant. Any other suggestions?"

"If I were you I would talk directly to some of these officers around here. There's bound to be someone looking for a good horse. There's actually a group of Marylanders camped just the other side of these trees that have at least a couple of colonels and a few majors and a boatload of captains. One of them has to be on the lookout for a horse."

"Sounds good, just point me in their direction."

"Well … I'm under orders not to let just anyone through into camp right now. There's talk of Tories getting stirred up hereabouts. I tell you what, though, why don't you go have a rest under that shade tree over there and I'll send someone over to fetch some of the Maryland regiment's higher-ups. If they're not interested, I'll see what I can do to get you a pass into camp. Sound reasonable?"

"That sounds fine to me. I just don't have a lot of time, though. I need to be home before dark and I've got a solid four or five hours ride back."

"I'll send one of my boys right now."

The sergeant called to a nearby private and gave him orders to fetch some officers from the Maryland regiment to come and look at some fine horses for sale. The lad took off through the thick trees. James settled down with his back against an oak tree and waited. Fifteen minutes later, four gentlemen wearing continental black hats, unusual gray regimental coats with green facings and cuffs, and matching gray breeches emerged from a pathway in the thicket. Their uniforms, though not threadbare, were well worn and showed the stains of many months of service. The eyes of the officer in the front of the line grew wide when he saw the horses tied to James' mare. The four officers approached him suspiciously.

The lead officer spoke. "Good day, sir. I'm Colonel Otho Williams of the Maryland Brigade. This is Major Thomas Hewlett and Captains Burrell Henry and Edwin Stapleton. And you are?"

"James Hamilton of Mecklenburg County, just a few hours southwest of here, sir. I rode up today hopin' to sell these two mounts to someone who could really use them."

The colonel responded, "Well, son, we were told that you had some horses for sale, but I must admit that I did not expect such fine animals as these."

"Indeed, with saddles and markings of the British army, no less," added the major. "Exactly how did you come to be in possession of these animals and materials, sir?" His tone was incredulous.

Again James exhaled. "Well, Major, like I keep telling everybody else, it's a bit of a long story and I don't care to go into all the details. But the short version is that my brothers and I fought a patrol of the British Legion down near Lancaster in the Waxhaws when they fell upon the home of my fiancé and her family. Tories already hanged the man of the house a few weeks before. And one week ago this very day the dragoon patrol raped and killed my fiancé. They also killed her mama and one of her little brothers. So we killed all five of them where they stood and took possession of their belongings."

James paused, allowing a moment for his story to sink in, and then he resumed. "The local militia captain confiscated their horses, but traded me back two of 'em for the Legionnaires' muskets, cartridges, and cartridge pouches. So now I'm here to sell 'em to anybody that's got silver and gold coin to pay for 'em."

The officers were speechless and stared at one another with eyebrows raised.

"We've heard stories of such atrocities down Charlestown way," commented the colonel. Then a look of realization came over his face. "Are you the same lads who were at the engagement in the Waxhaws and rescued that Virginian?"

"Yes, sir. My brothers and I came upon a detail from the Third Virginia right before the battle. Colonel Buford ordered us to take cover on a ridge to the north and stay out of sight. We saw the whole thing, including the colonel and his staff riding full speed to the north while his men were being carved up on that battlefield."

The officers looked at one another knowingly. The major nodded at the colonel as if affirming James' account of the events.

"Go on ..." urged the colonel.

"Well that boy from Virginia stumbled into us in the woods a while later. We doctored him there and then brought him back to Charlotte."

The colonel extended his hand, as did the other officers. "Good show, indeed, young man! We've heard stories about you, as well!"

"Really?" queried James, puzzled by the thought.

"Absolutely! Word came up from Charlotte a couple of days ago about a private of the Third Virginia Regiment hauled out of the woods by some young fellows out of North Carolina. There was some preposterous nonsense about having a gunpowder charge burned off in one of his wounds ... or something to that effect," replied the officer, shaking his head incredulously.

James just smiled in response.

"Be that as it may ... the major and I are much in need of new horses. I'm afraid that ours are in poor shape after our rugged travel down from Yorktown. We've heard rumors that we will soon be heading southward to engage the British in South Carolina. I would very much like to have a new beast to ride when that time comes." He paused. "Can I assume that you have sufficient papers of ownership for these animals?"

James reached into his bag and produced the authorization given to him by Captain McKinney in Lancaster. The colonel read it quickly, nodded, and handed it back to James.

"That will do nicely, Mr. Hamilton. I'm prepared to offer you four guineas each for these animals and their saddles."

James' mind reeled. That was roughly the equivalent of forty Spanish dollars, more than he ever expected to get for them. Still, he decided to try a little bargaining.

"Well, Colonel, the saddles do come with the animals, but not the other leather goods. And I was hopin' for a wee bit more for this fine British horseflesh. I'm plannin' to see if your quartermaster might buy them belts and bags off of me, unless you're willin' to sweeten the deal a bit and take 'em off my hands."

The junior officers smiled at the colonel, entertained by James' obvious amateur status as a negotiator.

The colonel countered, "I tell you what, son, I'll give you ten guineas for the whole lot and save you the trouble of fooling with the quartermaster of this post. He is an absolute thief and scoundrel. I'm sure there are some men in my regiment who could use some of that equipment. I'll pay you right here on the spot with British gold."

"Done!" James proclaimed, extending his hand.

The colonel shook his hand, reached into his haversack, and pulled out a black leather purse. He counted out ten of the shiny gold coins and placed them in James' hand. James turned each of them over and inspected them closely.

Looking at the bust of King George III, James stated, "I gotta admit, Colonel, I'm not all too fond of the fella in the picture on them guineas."

"I quite agree with you, son, but gold is still gold, isn't it?"

"That's a fact, sir. Well, I appreciate you doin' business with me, colonel. And I wish all of you the best of luck." James carefully dropped the gold coins into his leather bag alongside the silver coins from his previous sale that morning.

"I wish the same for you, young man. God speed on your journey home. And thank you for blessing me with these fine animals."

James tipped his hat to the men, effortlessly mounted his mare, and headed back down the rutted road toward home. Once he was out of view of the camp he pulled off into some thick woods and removed the stack of gold and silver coins. He then peeled back a thick flap of leather just behind his saddle horn, revealing a flat hidden compartment. He carefully stuffed the coins beneath the flap and then returned the leather to it place. Once the money was sufficiently hidden he resumed his journey.

His heart leapt as he mentally calculated the total from his sales. With the other silver and gold hidden at home, he figured that he had almost one hundred and thirty dollars in hand … more than enough to pay off the mortgage that they owed Ephraim Farr!

He urged his mare to pick up the pace, anxious to get home with the news.

James arrived back home shortly before dark. His brothers peppered him with questions about his experience, the army and Salisbury, and the financial deals he had made. He beamed with pride as he counted out the veritable treasure of silver and gold coins. The jaws of both boys dropped. Neither of them had seen that many gold coins before.

John informed James about the visit from Lieutenant Givins and the impending call-up of the regiment. He was not surprised, as the local information seemed to verify the rumors that he heard in Salisbury.

After a supper of venison stew and cornbread the Hamilton brothers crowded around a small table by the fireplace to count their total haul. It was an assortment of coinage: gold British guineas, silver sovereigns and shillings, copper pennies, and quite a large stack of Spanish silver dollars … the famous "pieces of eight" coins welcomed as currency throughout the colonies.

William's eyes were huge. He asked, "How much is it, James?"

"Well, the exchange between these British coins and Spanish coins can be a matter of dispute sometimes, but near as I figure we have right at one hundred and thirty dollars worth, more or less, in Spanish silver."

"What do we owe on the land?" inquired John.

"We've paid on it for just over a year now, so we've paid out right at seven dollars on our one hundred dollar mortgage. But most of that is probably interest. We most likely owe about ninety-seven dollars or so."

"So we have more than enough money!" exclaimed John.

"For sure. I'm thinkin' that we approach mama's husband after meetin' tomorrow with a deal. We will offer him ninety-five dollars as payment in full and see if he will go ahead and take it and give us the papers. That'll leave us another thirty-five dollars for operatin' money for the farm. That's enough to last us for a few years."

John looked doubtful. "You think that greedy cuss will actually take that deal, with us owing him another two dollars?"

"Cash in your pocket is better than a note at the courthouse, I reckon," responded James. "I'd like to see someone take him for a little money on a deal for a change! We'll find out tomorrow, won't we?"

The next morning, immediately after church services were over, James approached his mother and stepfather. He smiled and nodded at his mama.

"Mr. Farr, can I speak to you for a moment?"

"What's on your mind, James?" Farr responded, coldly.

"I was wonderin' if my brothers and I might come by this afternoon and speak to you about somethin'."

"Pertaining' to what, reckon?" Farr inquired, now curious.

"Well ... we would like to talk to you and mama about our land and the money we owe you."

Farr interrupted him, "Now, boy, there's no need to drag your mama into your business and money problems. We have made us a square deal on that land. You signed the papers and you need to make your payments. You know what happens if you don't. And I ain't renegotiatin', if that's what you have in mind."

"I don't reckon we've missed a payment so far, have we?" retorted James, his anger rising. "We're fine with the arrangement we made. Anyhow, I don't want to hash it out here on church grounds. It would be more fittin' to talk at your place, or you could come by and see us if you would prefer."

"Of course you're welcome to come by the house," James' mother interjected. "You boys come on over for supper and you can talk your business then." She glanced sternly at her husband.

Farr exhaled, "Sounds all right to me." Although he did not sound like it sounded all right to him. "Reckon we'll see you boys this evenin'."

James kissed his mother on the cheek.

"We'll see you in a bit, Mama."

The boys arrived by wagon at the Farr homestead around mid-afternoon. Their stepfather was waiting for them on the porch, smoking a pipe and drinking cool cider. He intercepted them before they could see their mother.

"What's so all-fired important that you boys need to talk business on a Sunday afternoon?" he demanded.

"We want to speak to you about payin' off the farm full and clear," James stated matter-of-factly.

Ephraim Farr stared at him for a moment, then broke out into semi-hysterical laughter and slapped his knee. "That's a good one! Real good one, James! You had me skeerd! I thought you were serious about somethin'! Pay off your land … ha! That'll be the day!"

James never broke his stare as he reached into his leather bag and pulled out his linen sack of coins. He poured out ninety-five dollars in gold and silver on the rough table next to Ephraim's cider glass. The man stopped laughing at the sight of a pile of silver and gold.

"Where in the bloody blazes did you boys get that?" he exclaimed. He looked around to make sure his wife hadn't heard him swear.

"We come by it honest, don't you worry about that," James responded. "We're hopin' that you'll settle up with us on our land today."

Farr looked at all three of the boys. James was stone-faced. John and William smiled broadly.

"How much is there?" Farr asked.

"With a simple five Spanish dollars to a guinea, I calculate there is ninety-five dollars, give or take. Pretty close to what we still owe you for the farm," James explained.

"You owe just a bit more than that," countered Farr. He seemed to be doing calculations in his head.

"I understand that full well, but there can't be more'n two or three dollars difference. There might even be more on the table than we owe you dependin' on the exchange you might get. Anyhow, we're hopin' that you'll settle up with us with this sum today and go ahead and give us the deed. Hard money might come in handy for you with the war on. No tellin' how things might get in the days ahead with the British roamin' around."

Their stepfather remained silent for a moment, thinking and calculating, clearly intrigued.

"You boys didn't steal this money, did you?"

"No sir, we came by it fair and square, for somethin' we done down in the Waxhaws," James shared.

"Was it somethin' to do with that soldier boy ya'll brought into Charlotte and that British Legion?" he inquired further.

"Yes sir, it was for service we rendered while we was down there." He would elaborate no further.

"So ... this pile of silver and gold for the deed, free and clear?" Farr clarified.

"Yes, sir. That's what we're proposin'," agreed James.

Farr thought for a moment, took one last glance at the pile of money, and then finally extended his right hand to James.

"You have a deal, son."

"Good," James stated, relieved.

"But I'm all tied up in my salt operation this week. There's no way I can make it to the courthouse before Monday next. We won't be able to make it official until then."

"I ain't sure how much longer I'm gonna be here, with the regiment about to be called up. If somethin' happens this week you're gonna have to change your plans and get this done. I ain't leaving my brothers in the lurch," explained James.

"All right, then. If you get the call, we'll make a special trip to town. Otherwise we'll plan on a week from tomorrow. Agreed?" asked Farr.

"Agreed. Meantime ..." James started placing the money back into his bag, "I'm gonna hold on to our coin until we make it official. We can count it out and have the clerk be our witness."

Farr nodded his response, looking a bit disappointed. Then he slapped James on the back, smiled, and said, "Now! Let's go see what your mother is fixin' for supper!"

As he rose and headed for the door of the house, John whispered to James, "Are you sure that's Ephraim Farr? He sounded downright cordial!"

The boys giggled silently, and followed their stepfather into his cabin.

10

REPORTING FOR DUTY

The following week passed without incident. Though rumors abounded regarding the war and marauding British forces, the anxiously awaited muster of the regiment did not occur. Finally, the day arrived for the closure of the deal and the deed transfer from Ephraim Farr.

The Hamilton boys took their wagon into town right after breakfast on Monday. They arrived at the courthouse just as it was opening for the day. Ephraim Farr wasn't far behind. They asked the county clerk to close and lock the doors for just a little while so that they could conduct a money transaction. Since it was so early in the morning he gladly obliged.

The clerk drew up all of the necessary paperwork while James and Ephraim counted out the coins. John and William looked on with great interest. They exchanged the money and then signed the deed transfer. The clerk attested to the transaction and registered the deed, and as soon as James paid the modest transfer fee, the deal was done. They shook hands, Ephraim pocketed his cash, and James carefully folded his precious document.

Ephraim excused himself while the Hamiltons remained in the courthouse. James wanted to complete one last document naming both of his brothers as co-owners of the land, so that there would be no question regarding ownership should he be lost in the war.

It took another half-hour to draw up that paper to his satisfaction. Again, with fee paid, the record was registered and official. The boys walked out of the courthouse as the proud co-owners of one hundred and ninety acres of land ... free and clear of any lien. It was an amazing accomplishment for a trio of brothers not even twenty years of age.

They were clamoring into the wagon when a voice called out from across the dusty street, "James Hamilton! Hold on there, son!"

A distinguished-looking gentleman approached from the direction of the tavern. He was dressed in a fine blue wool weskit and wore an exquisite black cocked hat.

"It's a mite early for the rum, ain't it, Cap'n?" quipped James.

"I'll be the judge of that, Private. Though I haven't had a single drop today, thank you very much. I merely stopped by the tavern to spread the word regarding the regiment. I'm pleased I ran into you today. Saves me a trip out to your place. And who might these two young men be?" the gentleman inquired.

"Captain Givins, these are my brothers John and William. Boys, this is the captain of my company, Mr. Samuel Givins."

"Please to make your acquaintance, gentlemen. Your reputations precede you. I've heard all about your escapades in the Waxhaws. I salute your bravery and your patriotism." The captain bowed and tipped his hat to the boys.

The younger boys merely grinned in response to the awkward gesture.

"What news of the regiment, sir?" asked John curiously. "Your brother came by our place about a week ago and left me a message for James."

"Indeed," the captain replied. Turning to James he said, "Well, the time for action is upon us, I'm afraid. We will muster at Colonel Phifer's place on Friday and prepare to march. We are being assigned to a Continental command, I think. I am not sure what direction we will be heading, but my instinct tells me it will be into South Carolina to join the effort to stop the advance of Cornwallis into North Carolina. So … you have four days to get your affairs in order and provide for these brothers of yours."

"Yes, sir. We're workin' on that right now, in fact. What's the enlistment time?"

"Three months," the captain responded.

"All right. Well, I reckon we had better get on our way then, seein' as we only have four days to prepare," James responded.

The captain extended his hand. "Excellent. I will see you bright and early on Friday then. Turn out with enough personal supplies for at least five days in the field, with all of the food that you can carry. The Continentals may provide lead and powder at some point, but there's no guarantee. Boys …" Again, the captain tipped his hat to John and William, then turned and walked toward another building down the street.

"Well, brothers, you heard him," James stated flatly. "We've got four days to get you boys set up on the farm. At least I'll be back around harvest time in September."

Friday approached quickly. Throughout the week they took time after their regular chores and farm labor to plan out the next three months. James compiled a thorough list of priorities and tasks that John and William needed to perform during that time period. Though the boys knew all too well what was expected of them, it gave James some peace of mind to write everything down.

The boys also helped James prepare for his three months of duty. James organized his own clothing, electing to wear his prized pair of lace-up black leather half-boots with buckskin breeches and leggings. He planned to wear his favorite green, checkered homespun shirt, covered by his heavy off-white linen hunting frock and a thick three-inch-wide leather belt.

The brothers packed both of James' shooting bags with as much lead as they would hold. They filled his personal haversack with bundles of dried beef strips, dried beans, and dried fruit. William spent the entire day on Thursday baking sheets of hardtack. Once the rock-hard crackers cooled he carefully broke them and filled a second haversack for James. They packed a snapsack full with extra socks, a thick wool blanket, and two extra shirts. Two full horns of powder finished out his supply load.

All of the work and preparation helped keep their minds off of the fact that James was leaving for a long time. The brothers had been basically on their own and inseparable for almost seven years. Though James was excited about going off and doing his duty, he still felt a pang of guilt for his brothers. And they dreaded his going.

None of them slept very well on Thursday night. James was too excited. John and William were too conflicted. They dozed fitfully during the wee hours of the morning, and then finally gave up about an hour before dawn. John cooked a hot breakfast while James gathered his things. William hovered close to James, doting over his every action.

After breakfast and a trip to the outhouse, James began to strap on his supplies. John volunteered to saddle his horse.

"Saddle yours, too, little brother," James instructed. "I'll need you to go along with me. I can't take my horse on the march, so I'll need you to bring her back home from Phifer's Mill."

It didn't take John long to saddle the horses. He brought them from the barn just as James was emerging from beneath the stoop of the cabin. He had his rifle in hand and was tucking his tomahawk into his leather belt. He turned to face William.

"Now I know you're almost a grown man, little brother. But you need to know that John is in charge while I'm gone. I need you two to work together and take care of our home."

"I know what's expected of me, James. Don't you worry about Johnny and me. We'll be just fine. And Mama's just across the ridge. You just worry about stayin' alive, and getting' back home in September."

James wrapped both arms around his little brother and smothered him with a huge hug. He turned and laboriously mounted his horse. William actually gave him a little push in the rump to help him lift all of the extra weight of his food and gear. John climbed up on his horse as well. They turned and headed west in the direction of the muster ground to the northwest of Charlotte.

John called over his shoulder, "I'll be back before dinner, William!"

William waved to them both. Once they disappeared around the bend William sighed and walked back into the empty cabin.

The eight-mile ride to Phifer's Mill passed quickly. The location was bustling with activity when they arrived. It appeared that several dozen men had camped in the field the night before. Thin trails of smoke from campfires rose high into the air. Men were pulling up tent pegs and folding canvas. The camp was definitely preparing to move. Near the edge of the field a few small groups of men were practicing formation and marching drills. Other men were trickling onto the green on foot and horseback in response to the muster call.

James recognized one of his best friends since early childhood, Joel Moffat, leaning on his rifle near one of the campfires on the western side of the field. He and John guided their horses to where he stood.

"Hello, James!" Joel called out. "Is little Johnny goin' with us, too?"

"Naw, he's just here to take my mare back home. The cap'n said we was probably marchin' out today. I wasn't taking no chances."

"That's what they say. Everybody's tearin' down camp and gettin' ready to move, for sure. I bet we're headin' down through the Waxhaws. Folks says they's covered up with Redcoats down yonder way and tain't no Continentals to stop 'em," stated Joel.

"That's what I've been hearin', too," affirmed James. "Can't say as I'm lookin' forward to it."

"Well, I am!" exclaimed Joel. "I'm achin' for some action! Ready to whup me some Redcoats ..."

James chuckled. "We'll see how achin' for action you are when the smoke and lead is flyin'."

There was a sudden flurry of excitement on the north end of the camp as a fast rider galloped in on a sweat-lathered horse. He reported directly to the two colonels in the camp, George Alexander and Edward Phifer. They reacted briskly to his report.

Shouts of "Fall in! Fall in! Formation, men!" echoed across the field.

The militiamen stopped what they were doing and ran to the location of their commanders, forming up in loose lines. It took only a few moments for the men of the regiment to gather.

"Gentlemen!" boomed the voice of Colonel Alexander. "We have received an alarming report from the vicinity of Lincolnton. The Tory scoundrel, Colonel John Moore, has apparently gathered an impressive force of Tory militia at a place called Ramseur's Mill. General Rutherford is on the verge of engaging this force and we have been ordered to that location in support of his attack."

"How many are we talking about, sir?" inquired one of the captains.

"The rider says at least one thousand, probably more."

A murmur of worry and excitement washed through the cluster of men.

The colonel encouraged the soldiers, "Not to worry, men. General Rutherford has amassed an impressive force to deal with this insurgency to the Patriot cause. We will be in good company. Captains, see to your troops! We march overland to Lincolnton within the hour. Be prepared for action upon our arrival. Dismissed!"

The formation broke as men scattered to the various corners of the camp and completed their preparations. James, being already prepared to march, had no such preparations to make. But he did need to say his goodbyes to his brother. He walked back to where John stood holding the tethers to their horses.

"Johnny, we're about to head out. Tories are on the rampage up at Lincolnton."

"Yeah, I heard," John replied. "I reckon I'll head on home and leave you to your soldierin'."

"I'm gonna miss you, brother. Hold everythin' together whilst I'm gone. And don't you hesitate to go to Mama or old man Farr if you hit up on any trouble. Mama'll see that you get help if you need it."

"I will. Don't worry 'bout us, James. We'll be all right. You just keep your head low and come back home."

John reached out his right hand to his brother. James took him by the hand, pulling him close and wrapping his other arm around John's head. He hugged him tight, knocking John's hat sideways.

"I love you, Johnny."

"I love you too, James. You come home when you're s'posed to. Don't make me come after ya."

James punched him in the shoulder, cradled his rifle across his chest, and then turned and walked toward the cluster of men gathering near the officers. John somberly climbed up on his horse and headed home.

The march to Lincolnton was excruciating. It was a distance well over twenty miles, perhaps closer to twenty-five. James was beginning to doubt the wisdom of bringing so much food and gear. The regiment marched hard all morning and straight through dinner. They had to eat what they could while they marched. Many of the men complained incessantly about their feet. Blisters and loose shoes were beginning to take their toll. Then dehydration set in. One man actually fell out unconscious along the roadside. His captain assigned a man to remain with him and render aid.

Around mid-afternoon the men heard the distant sounds of shots being carried on the wind. They were not steady or loud. Instead, the sounds were faint and intermittent. But someone was definitely shooting up ahead of them.

"Let's pick up the pace, men!" shouted the colonel.

"That's easy for him to say from the back of his fine horse," muttered Joel Moffat.

Several other men grunted their agreement. James merely lowered his shoulders and plowed ahead. His feet were feeling fine, thanks to a fine pair of shoes and some plush wool socks. His right knee was starting to bother him a little bit, though. It was not debilitating, just a bit worrisome.

The sound of gunfire grew louder. They heard shots for well over an hour, then the shooting ceased. The woods along the roadway became eerily quiet.

"Stay alert, boys," Captain Givins urged. "We don't know how the fight's been going up there. There might be Tories in these woods."

James and the other men kept their feet moving and their eyes peeled on the trees and undergrowth, looking for any possible sign of the enemy. A short time later they emerged from the narrow road into an open field beside a meandering river. A gristmill sat alongside the river's edge.

It was clearly the site of the battle. Bodies lay strewn about in the short grass and along the edge of the woods. Fibers of musket wadding lay on the ground everywhere. The grass had burned in some places. Many of the men on the ground were wounded and attempting to crawl toward some vision of imaginary relief. There were two or three hundred of them altogether. There was no way to tell which of the bodies were Tory or Whig since they were all local men dressed in their everyday clothing. Indeed, they were mostly neighbors from the same region. All over the field men wandered and stared. Groups of soldiers huddled talking near the edges of the woods. Some sat on the ground, dazed.

Colonel Alexander called a halt at the edge of the field. Several men collapsed where they stood. The remainder sat down gingerly, favoring their sore feet. Many immediately shucked off their shoes and socks.

"Captain Givins, take a squad and find out what's going on!" barked the colonel.

"Yes, sir! Hamilton, Moffat, Bainbridge, Beverly, you're with me ..."

James and the other privates exhaled in disgust as they rose once again to their feet. The group of five men moved forward onto the field, inspecting as they walked.

They had covered roughly a quarter of a mile when they encountered a giddy, snaggle-toothed, middle-aged man perched on a stump in the middle of the field. He jumped up and ran toward them, waving excitedly.

"Whar you fellers frum?" he drawled.

"Mecklenburg Regiment, here under orders of General Rutherford," responded the captain. "Who's in charge here?"

"Cain't rightly tell you that, friend. Everybody's kinda busted up and headed off in ever die-reckshun. But you boys is too late now, anyhows. We uns has already whupped them thar Tories and sent 'em packin'. I got two of 'em my own self! Tain't been a shot farred in a whal now."

Captain Givins looked over the field once more. He inquired, "Is there a hospital or station for medical aid nearby? Why isn't anyone tending to these wounded men?"

"I heered they's settin' up for the wounded in that thar mill," the hillbilly responded, scratching his nasty head. "We uns has been too busy fightin' to do any doctorin'."

"You didn't look particularly busy when you had your lazy arse parked on that tree stump," retorted the captain.

"Well, you don't know squat, do ya now, friend?" the man retorted. "Least I wuz here for tha fightin', mister fancy-hat."

"That's 'Captain fancy-hat' to you, mister. Now go find out who's in charge here and ask them to send a representative to link up here with me! Do you understand, you Cretin?"

"Uh … most of it, I reckon. But I ain't no creeton. I'm from Burke County."

"Just get going!" the captain snapped.

He looked at James. "Private Hamilton, inform the colonel that the battle is done and that the wounded are unattended and desperately in need of care. I will set up a rally point here. Bring the regiment to this central spot on the field. We will set up an aid station and process the dead and wounded, transporting the latter to the hospital that we hope is located the mill."

"Right away, sir." James trotted back toward the regiment with his captain's message.

The regiment spent the next six hours locating and tending the wounded and gathering the dead. They worked well into the dark of night. The Colonel finally called a halt to their relief and "mopping up" duties late in the evening. The men didn't bother with tents or campfires. They simply lay down where they stood and drifted into the unconsciousness of sheer exhaustion.

Snores abounded in the field all around James. The smell of death and gunpowder still hung in the air. As he drifted off into his own deep sleep he thought, "This 'real' shooting war ain't quite what I expected it would be."

11

AN UNEXPECTED GUEST

Life on the Hamilton farm settled back into a steady routine. James had been gone for almost a month. Managing the crops was difficult with James away, but John and William were holding their own. The oppressive heat of July had blanketed the countryside, but so far there had been abundant rains. The corn crop was well watered, high, and healthy, as was their vegetable garden. Their hoeing days were well behind them. The shadows of the thick corn stalks now kept the weeds at bay. The boys had plenty to eat and plenty of tasks around the farm to keep them occupied.

There had been no word from John since his quick departure for Lincolnton. John learned through the rumor mill that the Mecklenburg boys had arrived too late for the battle, but it had been a great victory for the Patriot forces. There had been little news after that. Until today ...

William had taken to the woods in search of a turkey for supper. John was picking tomatoes in the garden in the early afternoon when a wagon pulled up in front of the cabin. It was Angus McHenry, an older gentleman who lived about a half-mile down the road toward Charlotte. The Scotsman's oldest son, Colin, served in the same regiment as James.

"Hallo, Johnny!" he called out in his jolly, thick Scottish tongue. "I was a hopin' that I would catch ye here at the hoose whilst I was on me way home."

"Howdy, Mr. McHenry. I haven't seen you in a while. Is everythin' all right?"

"Aye, aye. All is grand, laddie! I'm just on me way home from Salisbury. I went up yesterday in search of me boy, Colin. I had no trouble a findin' him. None a'tall."

"So the regiment is camped there now?"

"Aye, Johnny. They've been sleepin' in that field ever since their first march up to Lincolnton. As soon as that battle was over the army marched 'em to Salisbury and put them into that camp. They've been a practicin' their soldierin' ever since. All manner of marchin' and drillin' and shootin' and such."

"So they're all well, then. Everyone is all right?"

"How I wish they were, laddie! There's horrible want up there. Terrible sickness and hunger! The boys have almost nothin' to eat. No provision a'tall from the Congress and, apparently, the state has nay funds, either. Our boys are scavengin' what they can from the woods and countryside, but it's a poor, pitiful sight."

John was disheartened but not surprised. Stories abounded about the lack of supplies available for the Patriot militias and the Continentals.

"What should we do?" inquired John.

"Well, son, we can do our part to help 'em all we can. I took some food to me boy yesterday and stayed the night with him in the camp. Now that I'm back home I'm a doin' all I can to spread the word regardin' their want and need. So consider yourself informed, Johnny. I know that Jamie would be most grateful for some supplies and provisions. And a visit from his brothers would be most welcome, I have nay doubt."

"Thank you, Mr. McHenry. I'll think on it and see what we can do."

"You are most welcome, Johnny. Farewell, then."

The enthusiastic Scotsman clucked at his mules and headed off in the direction of his home.

William returned from his hunting a couple of hours later with two fine turkeys tied together at the feet and hanging over his left shoulder. John greeted him near the barn.

"We had a visit earlier."

"Who was it?"

"Mr. McHenry. He just got back from Salisbury. The regiment is camped there. He says they're mighty bad off. No supplies and very little food. The army isn't providin' 'em with nothin', so they pretty much have to fend for themselves. He's spreadin' the word so that folks might try to help."

"That sounds like a good idea. But what happens when people from down here start showin' up with provisions for the Mecklenburg boys but everyone else is goin' hungry? That could get messy," observed William.

"Maybe so, but I don't reckon we can worry about that. We just need to help James as best we can. I know I won't be able to sleep at night knowin' that we have all this plenty here and James is goin' without."

"I agree. So when we you goin'?" asked William.

"I say let's load the wagon tonight and then take off in the mornin'."

"What do you plan to take?"

"Well, we need to take as much food as we can. We have four or five hundred pounds of corn meal in the shed that's still good. We can haul almost all of that. We'll be harvestin' corn soon enough, anyhow. James can share it with the other boys. Plus there's plenty of dried beef and venison. We can take a couple of bushels of fresh vegetables from the garden. And we can be on the lookout for deer on the way up. If we could shoot a couple of the critters along the road we could just dress 'em and throw 'em on the wagon. They should keep a couple of hours, at least. I doubt the meat would last very long once it hit camp. It'll get cooked up quick, for sure."

"Sounds like a good plan to me. Let's get to it." William paused thoughtfully. "But to be honest, Johnny, I don't like the idea of leavin' the farm empty. I think it'll be best if one of us goes up to deliver the food and one stays here. I want to see James real bad, but it's probably best that you go and I stay put."

John nodded his agreement and smiled. "I reckon you're right. You're gettin' mighty wise in your old age, little brother."

"I'm just a tad bit more comfortable stayin' put on my own place."

"All right, William. You go ahead and get them turkeys cleaned. I'll pull the wagon around and load the corn meal and dried meat. That's all we really need to do tonight. We can pick all the vegetables fresh right before I leave in the mornin'. I can also take a couple of jugs of fresh milk for James and his buddies."

"Boy, they'll love that for sure! As long as it don't turn before you get there," William chuckled. "I'll have these turkeys cleaned up and over the fire in no time. You can take one of them for Jamie tomorrow, too!"

For the next couple of hours the boys busied themselves in their work. William loaded eight fifty-pound sacks of corn meal into the wagon. He placed them in the front of the cargo space, right behind the seat. He wanted to leave the rest of the wagon clear just in case he might be able to get a deer or two along the road. He also dug a bushel of new potatoes out of the garden and placed them in the wagon. He would wait to pick the fresh tomatoes, cucumbers, and melons in the morning. Meanwhile, William prepared the birds for supper.

They ate themselves sick on the delicious, smoky meat that night and barely ate half of one bird. Afterwards they cut up the remainder of the meat and wrapped it in clean cloth to take to James. John cleaned his rifle, packed a full shooting bag, and topped off his powder horn and then they went to bed early.

John was up before dawn to prepare for his journey. He went out to the barn to milk the cows. He filled two one-gallon jugs with the delicious, fatty treat. William awakened soon after sunup. After a quick breakfast they went to the garden and picked a bushel of to-matoes, a bushel of cucumbers, two bushels of squash, and six large watermelons. William stashed the leftover roast turkey and jugs of milk under the seat beneath John's feet.

Once all of the food was loaded and covered with canvas, John hopped into the driver's seat, anxious to get on the road and main-tain the freshness of the milk and vegetables.

"Keep your eyes open, Johnny," warned William. "Don't worry about me none. I'll keep a good eye on things here."

"I should be back by dinner tomorrow. It'll be best if I stay to-night instead of trying to get up there and back before dark. I don't want to wear out the team."

William reached his hand up to John. "Be safe, Johnny."

"You too, William."

John snapped the reins and headed toward the northern road.

The journey was considerably longer than James' earlier trip on horseback. It took just over seven hours for John to arrive at the camp. Of course, a good chunk of that time was spent harvesting deer. Amazingly, John spotted and killed three does near the road as he traveled. He managed to shoot two of them up ahead of the wagon almost along the shoulder of the road. All he had to do was drive up to the spot of the kill, field dress the animals, and then wrestle them into the back of the wagon. He had to drag the third one about a hundred feet, but it was not too tough a task. He shot all three animals within two hours of reaching Salisbury.

Finding the camp was easy. An older gentleman in town point-ed him down the eastern road and less than a quarter mile later he encountered the sentries posted at a makeshift gate. He eased the wagon to a stop.

A burly militia soldier walked up to the wagon. "What's your busi-ness, boy?"

John hadn't even considered the notion of having trouble getting into the camp. To make things go as smoothly as possible, he cooked up a quick lie.

"Sir, I'm John Hamilton, wagoner with the Mecklenburg County Regiment. I'm here from Charlotte with their supplies."

"Hauling what, exactly, son?" challenged the guard.

"Food, sir. We received a message that there is a shortage of food in the camp, so we are startin' a supply chain to provide for our boys."

"Well, that might cause some problems amongst some of the other outfits. Lots of hungry men in this camp and not much forage left around here."

"I'm sure that the folks down in our county will be helpin' out all they can. But we gotta start somewhere. It's only right that we try and help out our own first," responded John matter-of-factly.

"I reckon," the soldier replied. He rubbed his chin and stared curiously at the canvas cover.

John, thinking quickly, hopped down from the seat and reached under the canvas on the left side of the wagon. He pulled out a beautiful watermelon.

"Here's a little somethin' for you, mister. Might help cool you down a little on this hot afternoon."

The soldier's eyes lit up. "Tarnation! I ain't seen a melon in two years! Much obliged, boy." He took the watermelon into his arms and held it like it was a newborn baby. He pointed with his head over his left shoulder. "The Mecklenburg boys are over on the far left side of the field next to the woods. You'll find 'em easily enough. If you got any meat on that wagon, I aim to find 'em myself in a bit." The soldier smiled broadly at John.

"Well, soldier, there's a couple of fresh doe critters on the back of this rig. I imagine they'll be smokin' over some fires here pretty quick."

The soldier licked his lips hungrily. "Well then, maybe I'll see you at supper, my young friend. What's your name again?"

"John Hamilton. My brother, James, is here in camp. What's your name, sir?"

"Thomas Jefferson, corporal, from Virginia."

John grinned, doubt covering his face.

"I ain't kiddin', John. Honest to God, my name is Thomas Jefferson. But I'm from Washington County ... no connection to the governor or that Declaration of Independence. But I do get picked on quite a bit because of my name. My friends just call me Tom."

"Well, Tom, swing on by and find me at suppertime."

"You can count on that! I'll for sure see you then."

John mounted the wagon and headed out in search of his brother. Ten minutes later he spotted some of the Mecklenburg officers and angled the wagon toward their campsite.

James' friend Joel Moffat was the first to spot John as he guided the wagon across the bumpy field. He was sitting in the shade of the trees, as were most of the men. Several were actually laid out on the ground, hats over their faces, napping.

Joel kicked the leg of the man lying beside him. "Well, I'll be hanged! Jamie! Lookie there! If it ain't you're little brother on that there wagon!"

James snatched his hat off of his face and sat up in disbelief. He jumped to his feet and ran to the wagon. John was shocked. James looked gaunt, maybe ten pounds lighter than when he left home. He caught John just as he jumped down from the wagon and grabbed him up in a huge bear hug.

"Johnny, what are you doing here? Is everything all right at home?"

"Everything's fine," John reassured him. "William stayed home to keep an eye on the place. Crops are all good. The garden is comin' in strong. Huntin' is good. We're blessed for sure. We got word yesterday that you boys are hurtin' for provisions, so I came to help."

"Old man McHenry?" James asked.

"Yep. He came by yesterday and told me how things were here in camp. So I brought up a load for the regiment."

By this time a small crowd was gathering around the wagon.

"Whatcha got, Johnny?" asked Joel. "Not to be nosy, but we 'uns is hungry."

"Oh, not much. About four hundred pounds of corn meal, and a few bushels of taters, maters, cukes, and squash. There's a few fresh watermelons in there, too. Oh … and I shot three deer critters on the way up here. I got 'em dressed and in the rear of the wagon." He smiled broadly.

The men gathered around the wagon stared in disbelief.

"Well, don't just stand there boys, let's get it unloaded. This venison ain't gonna keep for too long in this heat. Just leave the stuff under the front of my seat. That's personal property."

The excited group of militiamen erupted in a small cheer then attacked the task of unloading with gusto. All of the activity aroused the attention of the officers gathered near the regimental tent. Several of them began to walk toward the commotion.

"What's going on here?" a voice boomed. It was Captain Givins, James' company commander.

James spoke up, "It's my brother, John, Cap'n. You met him in Charlotte a couple of months ago. He's done brought up a load of rations for the men. Even dropped three does on the way in and dressed 'em for us."

"Well, well, you do not fail to disappoint do you, John Hamilton?" He extended his hand to John. "Son, we are mighty grateful for your generosity. The men in this camp are hungry. We haven't seen a deer near this place in two weeks. They've been cleaned out, I suspect."

"Well, Captain, I sure couldn't let my own brother go hungry. And I figured that corn meal would go a long way if you fellers stretch it out. I imagine there will be some more folk comin' with goods in the comin' days. Old man McHenry is spreadin' the word all over the county."

"That is, indeed, good news … though I don't know how much longer we will be here in this camp. There are rumors that we will be moving south soon. But in the meantime, we welcome these supplies. Are you going back home today?" inquired the captain.

"No, sir. I figured on stayin' tonight and visitin' with James and then gettin' an early start tomorrow."

"Good. That is good. I will draw up a voucher for you detailing the goods that you have provided. I am hopeful that you will be reimbursed for your supplies at a later date. You will need to hold on to this voucher until such time as funds become available. Do you understand?"

"Yes, sir," John responded. "It ain't necessary. We're happy to share. But I'll do as you say."

"My document will reflect your service as a wagoner for this regiment, as well. It takes some skill to handle a team and deliver such a load of cargo. I want that reflected in our records."

"Thank you, sir. It's been my honor," replied John.

"Very well, then. I suppose I will see you at dinner then, won't I? You're dismissed to perform your duty, Wagoner John Hamilton. See to your cargo."

John responded crisply, "Yes, sir!"

While John was talking to the Captain, the men were busy sorting and processing the food. Several militiamen were hoisting the three does up onto limbs at the edge of the woods, preparing to skin them and butcher the meat. The corn meal was stacked and already under guard. The vegetables were sitting in the shade, covered with the canvas.

John found his brother in the group. "James, I have a little special somethin' for you. He led his brother to the wagon and retrieved the first cloth sack from underneath the seat. "This is some of your smoked beef and venison. Hide this in your pack for when you're back on the march."

"Thanks, Johnny. That'll come in mighty handy."

"And here's a little special somethin' for you to enjoy right now, and maybe share with a couple of your pals." He handed a large cloth sack to James.

"That's roast turkey! I can smell it through the sack!"

"And you'll need somethin' to wash it down with." John carefully untied and pulled down the cloth sack from around the two one-gallon, cork-sealed brown jugs.

"What is that? Rum?"

"Naw! You ain't never tasted a sip of rum in your life. Somethin' even better ..." He popped the cork of one jug and handed it to James. "You might want to slosh it around and shake it up a bit. I kept it in the shade and as cold as I could."

James lifted the jug to his nose and took a deep whiff, then smiled as he lifted it to his lips. He closed his eyes in ecstasy as the cool, creamy milk poured down his throat. A fatty, yellow stream trickled from the corner of his mouth and ran down his neck, disappearing behind his collar.

"Slow down there, brother, that'll make you sick for sure if you ain't had much to eat in a while. Take your time," John cautioned.

James finally stopped gulping, took a breath, and wiped his frothy lips.

"Good Lord, that's like Heaven, Johnny." He called to his friends, "Joel! Henry! Come here real quick!"

His two closest friends meandered over and joined James and John on the far side of the wagon.

"Take a swig of this, boys," James encouraged.

Joel grabbed the jug out of James' hands, threw back his head, and took a quick drink. His eyes registered confusion for a moment, and then closed in contentment. He eventually stopped to take a breath.

"Jamie, I have to confess, I thought that was a jug of rum or corn likker ... so I was a might bewildered at first. But I also have to confess to ya that this jug of cow's milk is better'n any rum I ever tasted."

Henry Pippin's eyes lit up. "Milk?" he exclaimed, and grabbed for the other jug. It didn't take long for the three men to drain both gallons. They returned the empty jugs to John with resounding belches.

"You all deserve a belly ache after that," commented John, smiling.

"Believe me, it'll be worth it, Johhny ... the best case of the trots I'll ever have!" retorted Joel Moffat.

"We'll share the turkey with the boys. C'mon, John, sit with me and tell me all about home," encouraged James.

For the next hour John caught James and his friends up on the limited news from home. In return, they told him all about camp life and the utter boredom of being soldiers. They also filled him in on the lowly state of militia in the southern army.

"It's a barrel full of piss, is what it is, Johnny," commented Joel. "The Continentals get what little supplies there is. They tell us that it's up to the states to take care of their own militia. But the great state of North Carolina don't even know we're camped in this field! And even if they did, they ain't got no money, anyhow. So here we sit, sucking hind teat as always."

James added, "Word has it, though, that General Gates is formin' a big army to go into South Carolina and run off the British. We reckon we'll be joinin' that grand army soon enough. In the meantime we just lay around here and hurt for food."

"Don't you practice and drill?" asked John.

"Oh, yeah, we do some of that. Not near as much as we did when we first got here, mind you. We mostly lay up under the shade and go out a foragin' for supplies whenever we can. But this countryside is pretty much picked over and the locals ain't lettin' go of no more goods in exchange for vouchers."

"I'm ready to just get on with it," added Joel. "Let's get to fightin' or get home."

Several of the other fellows murmured their affirmation.

A voice interrupted their conversation, "Plotting treason over here, are we?"

The men looked up into the face of Colonel George Alexander, regimental commander. The men began clamoring to their feet.

"As you were, men, as you were! Remain seated. I just stopped by to thank young Mr. Hamilton for his service to the regiment."

John stood and shook hands with the colonel. "It was my pleasure, sir. I'm glad we could help the men out."

"It won't just be our men you are helping. I hope you don't mind, but I'm ordering that this meat be shared with the men from Caswell and Guilford Counties. They are hurting for provisions," stated the colonel.

"Of course, sir. That meat will turn bad pretty quick, anyhow. I was hopin' that it would feed a bunch of men at least one good meal."

"Indeed. We'll send one carcass to each of those other regiments to dispose of as they see fit. Meanwhile, I've rounded up two large iron cook pots. We're going to take that bushel of potatoes, along with the tomatoes and squash, and cook up two huge pots of venison stew for all the men to enjoy. Truly, we will feast tonight!"

"Give this to the fellers who are cookin', sir," James requested. He reached into one of his bags and pulled out a small sack. "It's some of our salt from home. Should be more'n enough to flavor up that stew."

The colonel smiled and took the salt. "Most excellent! Again, we thank you for your service and for blessing these men with a fine supper and rations of corn meal that will last us for many days."

"You're mighty welcome, Colonel," John replied.

The colonel turned and headed toward the area where a group of soldiers were stoking two large cook fires.

"You're just gettin' in good with all the important folk, ain't you, you little turd?" mocked Joel Moffat.

The men chuckled, several of them slapping John approvingly on the back.

Another voice piped up from somewhere behind the group, "Did I hear something about some venison stew?"

John saw the familiar face, "Tom! Come on over here! Boys, I want you all to meet a friend of mine ... none other than Thomas Jefferson of Virginia."

Silence ensued. Incredulous, dumbfounded looks abounded.

"No ... really, boys. This here is Thomas Jefferson, down visitin' from Virginia," John stated again.

"Washington County, Virginia, gents," Tom clarified. "I'm a corporal in the militia, and I haven't signed any Declaration of Independence, either. I am thinking about running for governor, though!"

Laughter ensued.

"How do you know my brother?" inquired James, confused.

"Well, the lad bribed his way past me at the check point this morning with an exceptionally large watermelon and gave me an invitation to supper, as well. So here I am!"

"Well, welcome, then!" crooned Joel Moffat. "If you're responsible for lettin' this carriage full of goodies through, then we'll feed you a double portion! Have a seat and let's smoke till supper's cooked."

The men enjoyed over an hour of camaraderie, laughter, and fellowship while the stew boiled over the nearby fires. Finally, at long last, came the call to, "Come and get it!" Men grabbed their spoons and all manner of plates, bowls, cups, and mugs and ran toward the bubbling stew. Almost two hundred men ate their fill of the thick, tasty substance. They also enjoyed fresh cucumbers with a pinch of salt. Each man received a small slice of the watermelon for dessert. It was truly a joyous time.

The fellowship went on well into the evening, made even livelier when the officers produced a few bottles of rum. The men drank, smoked their pipes, and sang songs. Their bellies and hearts were full. The weary men slowly melted into their tents and shelters throughout the evening until, finally, there was silence in the Mecklenburg Regiment's camp. Everyone was bedded down for the night.

John slept soundly beside his brother. Morning came quickly. Most of the men were up and moving around at dawn, scrounging for breakfast. John began to make preparations for his trip home. Since there was no cargo to carry back, his only task was to gather and organize his personal belongings. James walked him to the wagon. He had just climbed up into the driver's seat when he saw Captain Givins approaching from the "officer's counrty" portion of the camp.

The captain called out, "John Hamilton, wait just a moment!" The officer covered the ground between them quickly. "I wanted to thank you again for your service to the regiment, and to advise you to be prepared for future assignments of hauling goods and supplies in your family's wagon. We may need you in the days ahead."

John responded, "Of course, Cap'n. I'm plannin' to make another trip up with more supplies and meat in another three or four days"

"Don't bother, son. We won't be here. Colonel Alexander just received the news this morning ... we will be breaking camp and heading south within the hour. Colonel William Lee Davidson of the Continental Army has been assigned as an Acting Colonel in the militia and will be taking over temporary command of our regiment. We are headed toward Anson County to deal with yet another Tory uprising. But should the need arise for your services as a wagoner, we will send appropriate messengers. We also ask, since you have now been added to our regimental rolls for duty on wagons, that you might return home and seek out other wagon owners and recruit them to the service for future supply assignments."

"Of course, Cap'n. It'll be an honor."

"Very well, then. I will report your acceptance of this mission to Colonel Alexander. He asked me to give you this official voucher for your goods." He handed John a worn, folded piece of paper. "John, it was good to see you again. I bid you good day and good luck." The Captain tipped his hat to John, turned on his heels, and headed back to headquarters.

James' stare met John's. "Well, little brother, I guess this is it for a while. No tellin' where we'll be a goin' from here on out. But I'm glad I got to see ya for a little while, at least. Don't go gettin' too caught up in the wagoneerin' thing. If there's a big fight brewin', I don't want you anywhere near it. You hear me?"

"I hear ya, James. I'll do what I gotta do, but only what I gotta do, I promise."

John extended his hand down to his brother. "You just take care of yourself, Jamie. Don't go doin' anything brave or stupid. Just do your duty and come back home."

"That's all I got on my mind, John ... gettin' home. But the Lobsterbacks and Tories have to answer for what they've done. And I aim to make a few of 'em do just that."

"Just be careful. I love you, Jamie."

"I love you, too, John. Give William a big hug for me."

John nodded, snapped the reins and whistled to the team, turned them to his right, and meandered toward the trail leading from camp. James turned toward his gear and, once again, began to pack and make ready for war.

12

A CERTAIN KIND OF VICTORY

There was a new colonel in the Mecklenburg Regiment. And this one was a battle-tested soldier and commander.

Colonel William Lee Davidson was an impressive-looking character. He stood out brilliantly among the rag-tag militia soldiers who surrounded him. He was impressively tall and distinguished in his beautiful Continental Army uniform. He was powerful and confident in his demeanor and seemed to be a worthy commander. How he came to be commanding a detachment of Mecklenburg County Militia was something of a mystery.

He was an experienced warrior, to be sure, having served the cause since his commission as a captain in the Rowan County militia in 1775. In 1776 he received a commission from Congress as a major in the North Carolina Continental Line and then served in several North Carolina regiments. He had been in the thick of the fighting in the northeast, and had wintered with General Washington at Valley Forge. He rose to the position of commander of the First North Carolina Regiment as a lieutenant colonel in 1779. Then he was quite suddenly and without explanation replaced by Colonel Thomas Clark and left without a Continental command.

The rumor among the troops was that he had refused outright to resign his commission in the North Carolina Continental Line. And now here he was, promoted to full colonel, and added in amongst the cadre of colonels already in command of the Mecklenburg County Regiment. Because of the sheer fact of his years of experience and his current Continental Line commission, the other colonels naturally deferred to his leadership. On this particular day, so did General Rutherford.

John Hamilton had barely disappeared down the road toward Salisbury when the men were called into formation. The officers seemed focused and attentive. Clearly, the regiment was headed into action.

The various captains issued a loud call for the men to gather around. The elegant Colonel Davidson stepped up on a stump to address the men.

"Boys, I have not yet had the pleasure or meeting all of you. I am Colonel William Lee Davidson of the North Carolina Line, now acting commander of this regiment and our forthcoming mission. I suspect we will get to know one another well in the coming days as we take action against our common enemy."

He continued, "For the past few weeks, since our victory at Ramseur's Mill, General Rutherford has been in pursuit of several hundred Tory militiamen under the command of a traitorous South Carolinian by the name of Samuel Bryan. He has pursued Bryan on the east side of the Yadkin River in an effort to prevent his forces from linking up with the British in the south. Unfortunately, he has been unable to flank Bryan's army.

"Elements of militia from our district have been ordered to proceed southeast along the western side of the Yadkin and Pee Dee Rivers and prevent Bryan from crossing and adding his numbers to the army of General Cornwallis. I will command this detachment, which will include militia companies from several other counties. You are a critical part of this force. Gentlemen, we will depart forthwith for our rendezvous. You have one half-hour to gather your gear and properties before we commence the march. Pack lightly, but equip yourselves well. That is all."

The men broke camp quickly. A short time later they were on the march. And they marched hard, following a relatively straight line to the southwest with the Yadkin River as their reference. The officers encouraged the men and prodded them forward. They walked well into the darkness of night. Exhaustion among the men forced the officers to call a halt and make a late camp. The men slept where they fell. They had covered over forty miles through difficult terrain in roughly fourteen hours.

At dawn they were on the move again. There was no stopping for fires or cooking. The men were on rations of corn meal. They soaked the coarse powder in water during brief breaks, allowing it to swell as it absorbed the water, and then ate it with spoons and washed it down with water. Some of the men had molasses to add to the gruel. That was the only food available to most of the men. James was blessed, having a sack full of dried venison and beef. He shared it liberally with his closest friends. They gnawed on the tough, tasty fibers as they marched.

They covered several more miles by mid-morning when they finally broke for some much-needed food and rest. Many of the men chose to sleep rather than eat. A few men built small fires to facilitate the cooking of their corn meal mush. Many others were unable to sleep and merely sat to relieve their feet and re-hydrate. Not long after they stopped a fast rider approached from the rear of the column, setting the entire detachment on edge. It was a messenger sent by General Rutherford. He by-passed the men, rode directly up to Colonel Davidson, and dismounted.

"Begging the colonel's pardon, sir … I bring a message and instructions from General Rutherford."

"How did you get across the river?" inquired the colonel.

"Sir, I am native of this county. I rode to a passable ford that is approximately five miles upstream and crossed there, saw the evidence of your recent passing through that location, and consequently headed south in your pursuit."

"Good work, son. What is the message?"

"Sir, General Rutherford wishes to inform you that he was unable to cut off the Tory force during their southward approach along the Yadkin River. The Tory Colonel Bryant has, apparently, rendezvoused with the forces under the command of a Major McArthur. This combined force now greatly outnumbers our forces on the east side of the Yadkin, therefore the General has elected not to enter into an engagement."

"Hmm ... that is most unfortunate," commented the colonel.

Colonel Alexander spoke up. "Sir, it appears that our pincer movement has failed. There is nothing now that can stop the Tories from linking up with Cornwallis in the south. He could potentially add another 3,000 loyalists to the Redcoat armies!"

Colonel Davidson responded, "Indeed, that would be debilitating for our floundering southern army." He turned his attention back to the patient messenger. "What are our orders, son? Are we to turn back?"

"By no means, sir. General Rutherford has received intelligence that another force of Tories is located near the confluence of the Pee Dee and Rocky Rivers. This force has not yet crossed the river to join the larger Tory army attempting to link up with the British. The General's order is that you take your force to that location, engage the enemy now encamped along the Rocky River at Colson's Mill, and hamper their efforts to rendezvous with Bryant and McArthur."

"You say you're from this area, son?" confirmed the Colonel.

"Yes, sir. My home is in this county. I am very familiar with the terrain."

"Then how far away are we from this Colson's Mill?"

The messenger rose up in his stirrups and surveyed southward, examining the contour of the nearby river. "Sir, I believe that we are no more than four or five miles from that location."

"What is located there, besides the gristmill?" inquired the commander.

"Well, sir, it's a pretty central location, within a mile of where the Pee Dee and Rocky Rivers meet. There is a highly frequented tavern that serves as a stop for the stagecoach. But more importantly, there is a ferry near the mill that crosses the Rocky River to the south."

The colonel exploded, "Good God, man! They could be making their escape now! How large is the ferry?"

"Not very large, sir. It is a modest flat boat, hand-drawn on a rope spanning the narrow river. No more than ten or twelve men can cross at any one time. Sir, I know that time is of the essence. I would be honored to guide you to the spot so that you can engage the enemy quickly."

"Most excellent!" He turned to the other officers. "We move out in fifteen minutes. Inform the men."

Colonel Alexander spoke up, "Sir, most of these men have yet to face the enemy in an actual engagement. Unlike the battlefields inhabited by uniformed opponents, these men and the men that they face are all Carolinians and all militia. They will all be dressed alike and appear, in every conceivable way, to be the same. How can we prevent our men from turning their guns upon one another?"

"An excellent point," confirmed Colonel Davidson. "We must differentiate our forces or risk absolute confusion on the field." He pondered for a moment, and then his eyes lit up as an idea occurred to him. He turned to one of the regiment's captains standing nearby.

"Captain, I have inside the satchel on my horse a significant supply of unused writing paper. I want you to distribute this white paper to the men by companies. Have each man secure a strip of the paper inside the ties or bands of his hat. Have each man use two pieces. One must be visible from the back and the other must be visible from the front. Do you understand?"

"Absolutely, sir. And a fine idea it is, sir," the captain responded.

"Off you go then. See that it's done as quickly as possible. By God, I don't plan to let this pack of Tory traitors slip through my fingers and across that river today!"

The numerous captains spread out throughout their regiments, distributing paper and giving instructions.

Captain Givins approached the men of his company, "Boys, the Colonel doesn't want us shooting each other. Place these strips of paper in the front and rear of your hats to identify yourselves. We move out in fifteen minutes, so make it quick."

The men stared at him, confused.

"C'mon now, boys. I know it's not fine Continental wool, but it's all the uniform that you'll be needing today. We just have to make sure we shoot the Tories and not each other. Understand?"

The men nodded and mumbled their affirmation. James wasn't quite sure how much he liked the whole idea. He appreciated the help in preventing getting shot from behind. But he wasn't a great fan of the notion of displaying a huge, bright white flap on the front of his head as an aiming point for the enemy. Still, he obeyed his officers and tucked the paper inside the cotton ribbons that tied the flaps on his brown fur felt cocked hat. Moments later the men were on the move.

The detachment of roughly two hundred and fifty men moved quickly. They covered four miles in less than an hour and a half. The colonel called a halt when the guide informed him that they were less than one-quarter mile from Colson's Mill. The men were ordered to take cover in the woods and remain silent. Colonel Davidson called a meeting of the officers.

"Gentlemen, we need to send spies ahead to determine the enemy's position and strength. I would like men from our Mecklenburg Regiment to take this mission. Volunteers?"

Captain Givins spoke up immediately, "Sir, I'll take a squad from my company and scout forward. I actually have one man who has seen action against the Tories in South Carolina. His experience may be of great help."

"Good. Take your men, Captain, and scout forward. Take the local scout with you, as well. Do not ... I repeat ... do not reveal yourself or engage the enemy. Merely ascertain their strength and position and report back to me forthwith. Go now."

"Yes, sir!" Captain Givins responded.

He nodded to General Rutherford's scout. Both men hurried back to the spot where Captain Givens had left his company under the concealment of the woods.

He called out quietly as he approached, "Hamilton, Moffat, Williams, Hennessey, Pippin, come with us. Leave everything but your rifle and shooting bag. We have a scouting mission."

The five men jumped up, dumped their haversacks, snapsacks, and baskets, grabbed their rifles, and followed Captain Givins through the woods. After they had traveled a couple hundred yards, the captain paused and squatted between two huge oak trees.

He began to brief his men. "Gentlemen we have been tasked with spying out the enemy at a place called Colson's Mill. This scout will lead us. What's your name, son?"

"Andrew Halstead, from Anson County, sir."

"Mr. Halstead will guide us to the site of the mill and we will reconnoiter."

Private Williams spoke up, "I've been there before, Captain. It was a long time ago, but as I recall there's a ferry there. It's not far from where the Rocky River comes off of the Pee Dee."

"That's the place," affirmed the Captain. "This is not the main body of Tories that the general has been pursuing. That group has already crossed into South Carolina and has likely joined with the British. It is, however, a significant number of enemy soldiers. We simply cannot allow this bunch to make it across and join the army of Cornwallis. We are instructed to make reconnaissance and report back to the Colonel as rapidly as possible."

"Sounds easy enough," commented James.

The captain continued, "We must remain silent and undetected, and under no circumstances engage the enemy. Is that clear?"

"Yes, sir," the men responded, quietly.

"Good. Check your gear and make sure there's nothing that will make any unnecessary noise. Mr. Halstead, lead the way."

The scout led the men down a well-worn deer trail. He moved deliberately and cautiously. The group had gone about five or six hundred yards when they spotted what appeared the outer edge of the tree line to their south. Halstead stopped rapidly and dropped to one knee, raising a silencing finger to his lips. The other six men followed suit. James had an uneasy feeling that they may have brought a few too many spies along for their mission.

Halstead turned to the Mecklenburg County men. "Colson's Mill is just ahead of us, about a hundred yards on the other side of the trees. We should have excellent cover as long as we stay in the trees. But we have to watch for sentries and patrols. Captain, my recommendation is that you and your men stay here while I go up ahead and check. If the way is clear, I will come back and signal. Then we can disperse along this tree line at intervals of twenty or thirty yards. With seven sets of eyes we should be able to get a good picture of things to report back to the colonel."

"That sounds good, Andrew. But make it quick," the captain ordered. "I don't want us to be dangling out here alone any longer than we have to."

"Yes sir. I'll be back shortly."

The scout scurried silently toward the boundary of the forest. In a matter of moments he disappeared completely from view.

"Boys, get under cover and let's watch all directions. Keep your eyes peeled. There may be patrols in these woods," warned the captain.

The men scattered out in a small circle and took cover behind fallen logs and tree trunks. The forest was eerily silent. Halstead was gone for what seemed like an eternity. He reappeared quite suddenly from behind a large rock directly in front of Joel Moffat. Joel jumped as if he had been shot and fell over flat on his back in a mass of undergrowth and flailing limbs. He was generating entirely too much noise. James chuckled silently and went to his rescue, extending a hand and helping extract him from briars and vines.

"Tarnation, boy!" Joel hissed. "You 'bout made me mess my breeches. I dang near blew a hole in ya!"

"Moffat, you were flat on your skinny arse! The only way you would have hit him was if he was swingin' through the tree tops ... and then, maybe," mocked Henry Pippin.

The other men choked down a silent snicker, drawing a look of reproof from the captain.

Halstead appeared apologetic, "Sorry, friend. I didn't want to risk any signal or noise. There are lots of men in that open field, not even two hundred yards away from where we are right now. I didn't want to risk giving away your position."

"Did you see any patrols?" asked the captain.

"No, sir. It doesn't appear that they are too concerned about things in our direction. They look to be more focused on what's going on east and south of them. I don't think they suspect anything from our side of the river."

"Excellent. We will proceed forward then. Halstead, you lead the way. Hamilton, I want you to extend out along the far left flank. Pippin, I want you on the right flank. The rest of us will disperse at intervals. Keep low and keep silent, men. Try to get a good count of their troops, wagons, and supplies. Be especially on the lookout for artillery. See if you can determine the location of their headquarters. We will meet back here in a quarter hour."

The men followed the Halstead toward the outer edge of the trees. About fifteen yards from the periphery he dropped down low and turned, directing the scouts laterally along a narrow game trail. James went first, taking the left flank to the east. He stayed low and moved carefully, stopping every twenty feet to observe and listen. He soon reached the far left side of the Tory camp. Dropping down on his belly, he low-crawled almost to the edge of the trees.

It only took a few moments to locate the perfect vantage point. It was the convergence of two large fallen logs at the very edge of the trees. The two logs met like a hinge with an outward v-shape toward the enemy's position. There was an opening that was half the width of a man's head at the convergence of the two-foot-thick logs, covered with dense foliage behind. James was able to crawl from the rear of the logs, under heavy cover, and observe freely through the small opening between them. There was a horrid, foul stench of dung and death, but it was an ideal observation post.

James pinched his nostrils to relieve his offended nose. "Good, Lord! They must have thrown a carcass or scraps into these woods," thought James.

The mill was directly in front of him. He could see men entering and exiting the building. There were lookouts in the upper windows of the mill, watching mostly toward the east. The Rocky River flowed behind their camp. The tavern stood roughly forty yards east of the mill. Men were milling about along the riverbank and throughout the open meadow. There was one cluster of militiamen a mere thirty yards from James' position in the trees.

There were several small fires, obviously for cooking, spaced among dozens of two-man tents. Though a handful of men were on the ferryboat headed south across the river, they did not appear to be in a particular hurry. It did not seem like this was a regiment that was on the move. James made a mental note of the layout of the encampment. He did not see any pieces of artillery. He estimated the number of men to be somewhere around three hundred and fifty.

He was just about to start backing out of his hide when he noticed movement to his left. One of the militiamen standing watch near the eastern border of the camp was walking directly toward him. His eyes were focused intently on James' position.

James thought, "Good God, I've been spotted!"

The man approached him, brandishing a rather old long land Brown Bess musket. James sized up his enemy. The man was stoutly built, almost a little overweight. He likely outweighed James by a good thirty or forty pounds. James determined that he would have to take the man with his blade. He silently set his rifle aside, drew his hunting knife, and waited.

One of the fellows' compatriots called from their observation post, "What's the matter, Otis? You feelin' the movement of the Lord amongst your nasty bowels again?"

The approaching man yelled over his shoulder, "I told you that rabbit stew didn't smell right! Just be glad I ain't dropping my load beside your tree, Billy!"

The man picked up his pace, almost trotting directly at James, who suddenly realized the source of the stench. He was hiding in the midst of a makeshift latrine. James watched in horror as the man first dropped his musket and then his breeches, spun quickly, and then planted his naked arse right over the opening between the two logs. James nimbly rolled to his right, silently concealing himself.

As soon as the skin or the man's arse touched the bark of the log, the man's bowels exploded with a thunderous belch, blowing a cloud of mucoid feces downward and backward through the opening in the logs. The foul mass sprayed across the ground and leaves less than two feet from James' face.

"Thank you, Lord!" exclaimed the foul-boweled Tory. "Whoo-eee!"

James held both his nose and his breath and thought, "Yes, Lord. Thank you for letting me get out of the way of *that*!"

Someone called from across the clearing, "Good God, Otis! I can smell that all the way over here. Somethin' done crawled up in you in your sleep and died!"

Jeers and laughter emanated from among the other men along the river.

The Tory named Otis remained perched over the gap in the logs for several minutes, spewing an unspeakable volume of foul, watery death from his bowels. James jumped when he heard the leaves shaking directly over his head. The man broke off a fair-sized branch and began ripping off the leaves to wipe his hind parts. It took quite a while to clean himself up after such a mess. James had to take several silent, labored breaths throughout the process. Each time he barely resisted the urge to vomit. Finally, after what seemed like an eternity, the man stood, pulled up his breeches, and walked away from the latrine.

Once James could no longer hear the man's footsteps he carefully retrieved his rifle and crawled back to the game trail. He paused and checked his surroundings and then headed nimbly back toward the rendezvous point for the scouts. The other men were waiting, wide-eyed.

Joel Moffat hissed, "Where in Hades have you been, Jamie? We was scared plumb to death. We heard some shoutin' down that way and thought you'd been caught, for sure!"

Captain Givins followed, "What happened down there, James? Were you spotted?"

"No, sir. Let's just say that I know how David felt when King Saul was a squattin' in the cave."

"Huh?" asked Joel. "King who? Was there a cave down yonder?"

"No, you backwoods idiot. When King Saul was chasing David, from First Samuel."

"David who? Which Samuel?" replied Joel. "Boy, you is speakin' jibberish."

The other men snickered silently. Captain Givins covered his smile with his hand.

"Joel, one of the soldiers dropped his breeches right beside me. I was hidin' right at the spot they done picked for a shat hole. He blew his brown thunder out right beside my head."

"Good God, Almighty!" Joel exclaimed under his breath.

"That's what I said." James smiled.

"Enough of the chatter, fellows. Let's get on back," ordered Captain Givins. "James, we've already compared our observations. You can add to the report any differences you observed when we see the colonel."

James nodded in reply.

The men skillfully and silently made their way back to the assault force's holding position. Colonel Davidson anxiously awaited their return. Surrounded by a bevy of officers, he wasted no time on pleasantries.

"Report, Captain Givins. What is the status of the enemy?"

"Sir, it appears that the enemy is camped at the mill and shows little intention of moving. We saw no artillery. By our best estimate, there are maybe three hundred fifty to four hundred men total. Many were inside the buildings, so our numbers are not exact."

"And the enemy's headquarters?"

"Sir, we couldn't discern the exact location of any headquarters."

James spoke up, "Colonel, it appeared to me that the main activity was all centered 'round the mill itself. If I had to guess, I'd say their higher-ups are in the lower floor of the mill. There were lookouts posted in the top windows watching toward the east."

"Interesting. What about the ferry? Was it in use?"

"We couldn't see the ferry from our direction." Captain Givins looked to James, "Did you have the angle on it, Private Hamilton?"

"Yes, sir. The ferry-boat was crossin' to the south, but I only counted five or six men on it. There wasn't any considerable activity south of the river crossin'. They ain't on the move, far as I could tell."

"Did you encounter any patrols in our direction?" asked the colonel.

Captain Givins responded, "No, sir. All their attention seemed to be focused to the east. I think they have Rutherford's force on their minds, sir."

"Excellent! Most Excellent! Good work, Captain," proclaimed the Colonel. He turned his attention to his other officers. "Gentlemen, we have caught them by surprise. We will attack from the north and the west. I will lead the Rowan, Montgomery, and Mecklenburg regiments in a direct assault from the woods. Major Armstrong, you will lead all of the other companies in a wheel right maneuver. You will swing around to the west and slam the door shut on these Tories. We will have them entrapped by the rivers to their east and south and our regiments to the north and west. They will have no option but to surrender. Questions?"

The men were silent.

"All right, then. Major, gather the men for the flanking force. We will attack immediately. Colonel Alexander, you will join me in the forward attack group. We must crush these Tories!"

Minutes later the force was on the move. Captain Givens and his scouts led Colonel Davidson's force single-file down the game trail. They were one hundred and fifty men strong. Major Armstrong had a force of roughly one hundred men on the right flank. Once they arrived at the periphery of the woods the Colonel stationed his men over a two hundred yard front that extended from the eastern edge of the camp on their left. James joined his company in the area near the eastern flank. He was close to his original outpost behind the logs, but intentionally avoided the latrine. He checked the powder in his pan, stayed low, and waited.

Back up the line Colonel Alexander of the Mecklenburg Regiment and Colonel Francis Locke of the Rowan County Regiment joined Colonel Davidson at the center of the line, directly opposite the tavern.

The mission commander addressed his fellow officers, "Gentlemen, we will remain in position to give Major Armstrong and his men a few more minutes to get into position. Pass the word along to your men. Instruct them to remain in position and fire only on my command."

He had no sooner spoken those words than a shot rang out to his right, followed by a loud and resounding, "Damnation!"

"It must have been an accidental discharge, sir," observed Colonel Alexander.

Whether accidental or intentional, it didn't matter. The alarm rang out in the Tory camp. Men scrambled for cover and for their guns. The fight was on.

Colonel Davidson stood to his feet and exclaimed, "Prepare to charge men! Form ranks!"

The colonel stepped out of the cover of the trees into the open field. He pulled his sword and began walking up and down the tree line, yelling at his men, "Out of the trees boys! Form ranks now! Dress it right! We are going to charge this field!"

The Colonel made quite a spectacle alone and out in the open. He was the only man wearing the brilliant red, white, and blue of a Continental uniform, and in so doing stood out like a sore thumb.

Lead whizzed by overhead, slamming into the tree trunks and leaves. The larger musket balls made a haunting howling sound as they sailed past. What started out as a trickle of fire soon escalated into a flood. Almost four hundred men were pouring lead into their position.

Joel Moffat was right beside James. He muttered, "What in the world is he talkin' about, 'form ranks?' We need to be poppin' these boys off from right here amongst these trees. That numbskull's gonna get his arse shot off out there in the open. He's been in the regular army way too long!"

The colonel cried out again, "Men, I have ordered you to form ranks! Get your cowardly arses out of those woods and form up on me now!"

Slowly, reluctantly, the men of the North Carolina regiments obeyed and followed the colonel's lead, stepping out onto the edge of the field. Amazingly, no one was getting hit. The inaccurate muskets of the Tories were having no effect at all. The courage of the Patriots began to rise.

"C'mon, Joel. We can't hide here all day. Let's get in the fight!" encouraged James.

He grabbed Moffat by the flap of his hunting frock and pulled him to his feet. The two men darted just outside the cover of the trees and joined the line forming there. It was an impressive sight … almost two hundred men lining the side of the field spaced out a mere one yard apart.

"Fix bayonets, if you have them, boys!" yelled the colonel. "Hold your fire until I give the command. We're going to run these Tory dogs off of this field!"

The colonel turned and faced the enemy. Then, holding his sword high in the air, screamed, "Prepare to charge!"

Just as Colonel Davidson was waving his sword forward the sharp crack of a long rifle came from the direction of the mill. The Colonel's body buckled at the center, his back pushed rearward in a grotesque arch. His sword flew from his hand and his lovely cocked hat tumbled forward off of his head. The impact of the round striking his flesh seemed to lift him off of the ground. He fell backwards and landed flat on his back.

From twenty yards away James could see the colonel clutching at his belly as a large, expanding crimson stain soaked his white linen weskit. The man screamed in pain and horror. The colonel was down. His wound looked mortal.

James looked quickly for the origin of the deadly shot. He spotted a marksman standing in an open window of the second floor of the mill. He was actually leaning out of the window and cradling a long rifle, a cloud of smoke slowly drifting upward toward the roof.

"To blazes with bloody orders!" thought James.

He threw his beautiful Pennsylvania smooth bore rifle to his shoulder, sighted in on the shooter's chest, exhaled slightly, and then pulled the trigger.

The ball sailed a little high, but not much. It slapped into the man's throat just below his Adam's apple and exited through his spine. The Tory recoiled and then fell backwards out of view.

"Good shot, Jamie!" yelled Joel over the din of gunfire and screams.

The other men near James were just raising their weapons to fire when another voice from down the line yelled out, "Charge men! Let 'em have it!"

James glanced to his right and saw Colonel Francis Locke of Rowan County leading the charge. Colonel Alexander was kneeling beside the thrashing body of Colonel Davidson.

The men in the line all unleashed blood-curdling screams as they charged across the open field. Many fired as they ran. On the right flank Major Armstrong's group attacked, as well. It appeared that the Patriots had sprung Colonel Davidson's trap.

James reloaded his rifle on the run. He was prepared to fire by the time he reached the center of the field, but he didn't see any good targets. He fixed his eyes upon the mill as the finish line of his run. He knew he could make it if he could only reach the cover of the stone foundation wall. He willed his heavy legs to move and heard his heart pumping in his ears. The trip across that field was taking forever! All around him little geysers of dirt and grass flew up into the air. James heard the dull thud of lead impacting the ground all around him. He prayed as he ran, thanking God for the inaccuracy of muskets.

At long last he reached the wall. He pivoted his body and slammed his back into the stone, landing in a partial squat beside the open downstairs door. He paused to gather his wits and catch his breath, shocked that he was so exhausted from the relatively short run. His legs were wobbling and achy. James looked to his right and saw that about a dozen men had joined him in taking cover behind the thick stones. Joel Moffat and Henry Pippin were to his immediate right.

James rallied the men, "Let's clear the building out, boys. Follow me!"

He looked quickly and carefully over his left shoulder into the open door. He could see no one in the downstairs of the mill. He shifted his rifle to his left hand and then pulled his tomahawk from his belt and gripped it in his right hand. Jumping to his feet, he turned and ran through the door, not stopping until he reached the far wall. Moffat and Pippin, along with two other men, followed his lead.

"See anything?" hissed Pippin.

"Nary a soul," answered Moffat. "Which is just fine with me!"

James whispered, "Check the whole bottom level, then we go up." He pointed to a stairway at the far end of the large room. He nodded to the other two men. "Which regiment are you boys with?"

"Rowan County," they answered, simultaneously.

One of the men extended his hand. "I'm John Hunt. This here's William Bone."

John shook his hand. "I'm James Hamilton. These two rough-necks are Joel Moffat and Henry Pippin."

They men nodded at one another.

"All right, then. Is everyone acquainted?" James grinned. "John, you and Mr. Bone stay right here and watch this door. Just don't shoot anybody with a white paper in their hat."

"Sounds good," John Hunt replied. "We'll watch your backs."

It took about a minute to clear the bottom level, then the trio headed for the stairs. Henry Pippin led the way. The door at the top of the stairway was closed. Henry waited until James and Joel were ready. He counted to three and then burst through the door leveling his rifle in the direction of the far wall.

There was a body lying in the floor several feet from the open window facing the battlefield. Two other men sat huddled together behind an overturned table in the southeast corner of the room. All that James and his compatriots could see were the feathers of their hats and four empty hands sticking up from behind the table.

"Don't shoot, fellers!" one of the men screamed. "We ain't armed no more. We surrender! We surrender!"

Two muskets lay on the floor in front of the table.

"Stand up so's I can see you!" Joel commanded.

The two men rose to their feet. They were boys, actually. No older than fifteen or sixteen years of age. Their faces were ashen. They were obviously in a state of shock and horror.

Henry chimed in, "Keep them hands where I can see 'em, boys. Now move over against that other wall and turn around."

The boys obeyed his commands. Henry checked the muskets. Neither one of them had been fired.

"Good. Now put your hands up on the wall. You got any pistols on 'ya?" asked Moffat.

"N-n-n-no s-s-s-sir …"

"That's too bad," sneered Moffat. "I've been a wantin' me a good pistol. What are you two pups doin' here, anyways?"

The older of the two boys responded, "Our uncle made us come with him two days ago. We ain't Tories, really. We've been for you fellers and George Washington all along, I swear!"

"Funny how them sentiments come out when a man is on the wrong end of a smoke stick, ain't it?" quipped Joel.

"I ain't lying, mister. I swear we's Patriots through and through. Just put us in front of a officer and we'll swear our oaths right here and now."

"All right, all right. Just stop your jabberin.'"

Joel and Henry checked the boys for weapons but found none, not even a pocketknife.

"You're safe enough, I reckon," Joel commented. "Now turn around and sit back down on the floor and keep your mouths shut."

"Yes, sir," the youngest boy replied. "But why are you fellers wearing paper stuck all in your hats?"

"None of your dang business! Now shut up!" barked Joel.

With the boys checked and declared disarmed, James moved to check the dead body. It was the man that he had shot from the far side of the field. The neck wound was almost instantly fatal. The man was most likely dead before his head hit the pine floor.

"That's the boy you shot, ain't it?" asked Joel.

"Yep."

"Twas a helluva shot, Jamie. Every bit of a hundred yards, and you popped him right through the gullet. I bet he tasted lead in his mouth right before the lights went out. Serves him right for shootin' the colonel." Joel spat on the floor.

"That there's our uncle!" the younger boy exclaimed.

"I done told you little fartcatchers twice to shut up!" snapped Joel, winking at James.

"Yes, sir," the chastised boy mumbled.

James checked the man's pockets and bags. He had a little money, but not much to speak of. He had a well-worn pistol inserted inside his belt. James checked the pan and then tucked the pistol into his own belt. The rifle that the man had used to shoot the Colonel lay beside the window. It was an exquisite .50 caliber rifle from Virginia. James checked the barrel, which proved to be rifled. It was much more accurate than his own smoothbore.

He looked at the lads sitting quietly against the wall. "Boys, I'm leavin' this man's money and other belongin's for you. He's you're kin. But I'm claimin' his pistol and rifle, powder and lead. You got any problem with that?"

Both boys silently shook their heads.

"Good. I didn't think so."

The volume of shooting had died down considerably outside, but there were still shots some distance off to the east.

"Reckon we need to get out there and get back in the fight?" asked Henry.

"Forget that, son! We done secured this mill and took prisoners. We 'uns has got responsibilities right here in this room. Let them other boys finish up outside," commented Joel.

James spoke up, "For once I agree with Joel. It sounds like the fight's almost over, anyhow. Let's just check this buildin' for papers and such."

Henry guarded the prisoners while James and Joel searched the building for any useful intelligence. They found none. About a half-hour later the shooting stopped entirely, so the men thought it safe enough to venture back outside. They exited cautiously with their prisoners. All around them the Patriot militiamen were gleefully searching the tents and wagons and celebrating their victory. It had the look of an organized form of chaos.

James and his chums soon found Captain Givins.

"Ah, there you are, Hamilton. I lost sight of you boys after the charge. I was afraid that something might have happened to you. Where have you fellows been?"

James spoke for the group, "Sir, we made it to the wall of the mill once we crossed the field. Privates Moffat and Pippin and two boys from the Rowan County Regiment went in with me and made sure the building was clear. We found one dead man and took these two boys prisoner."

"One dead, you say? It wouldn't perhaps be the sharpshooter that took out Colonel Davidson, would it?"

James hesitated, not wanting to respond.

"It's all right James. I saw that shot you took. And an impressive shot it was, too. Worth a salute." The captain smiled as he tipped his cocked hat to James.

"Just doin' my duty sir," James responded. He changed the subject. "How is Colonel Davidson?"

"He's gut-shot pretty bad. We've got him in a wagon headed northwest already. There's supposedly a doctor in a town not too far from here. He might pull through ... he's a tough old cuss."

James looked around the battlefield and then asked, "What about the Tories?"

"Most of them made their escape, I'm afraid. The biggest part of the group escaped to the east. I quite imagine that most of them are from this area and know it very well. A few slipped by the flank to the west. Some swam the river. Counting your sharpshooter we've confirmed three killed and another four or five wounded. I think we took a mere ten to twelve prisoners. A disappointing outcome, to say the least."

"What about our losses?"

"Surprisingly low. None dead. The Colonel received the only serious wound. There was one other fellow wounded slightly, but it's hardly worth mentioning. It seems that we attacked a gaggle of Tories that know their way around the woods but can't bloody shoot!"

"Well, I reckon we won, didn't we Cap'n?" chimed in Joel.

"Yes, Moffat. We won. The enemy is dispersed."

"I don't reckon I know what 'dispersed" is. I'm just happy that we 'uns is all still above the dirt," Joel added.

"Amen. Amen to that," declared Captain Givins.

13

HOME SWEET HOME

The gravely wounded Colonel Davidson was evacuated back to Salisbury on the day of the battle. There was a rumor that he might possibly survive the wound, but most of the men doubted it. Still they hoped and prayed for his recovery. He was a brave officer and even though he had only been with the regiment for a few days, he had endeared himself with the men through his courage under fire.

Five days later the North Carolina militia received orders to return from Colson's Mill to their encampment at Salisbury. While camped at the mill they had enjoyed the ample provisions abandoned by the fleeing Tory army, all of it supplied by the British in Charlestown. The North Carolinians drank the British rum and ate ample British rations. The two-man tents that dotted the nearby pasture were special prizes, indeed. Emblazoned with the 'GB' and crown emblem, these wonderful shelters had been provided courtesy of General Lord Cornwallis and His Majesty, King George III.

It took two entire days to ferry over all of the abandoned British equipment on the far side of the Rocky River. After all of the goods were across, Colonel Locke, who had assumed command, ordered that the ferry crossing be destroyed. James Hamilton had become something of a backwoods celebrity in camp once the news of his long-distance shooting of the Tory sniper made the rounds. So when the order came down to disable the ferry crossing, after much teasing and cajoling, James agreed to attempt to shoot and cut the ferry rope on the far side of the river.

The rope was of a large diameter ... almost an inch and a half. It was wound tight and tied off on sturdy tree trunks on each side of the quick-flowing river. There was a high volume of wagering going on. Men placed bets on how many shots it would take. Some bet on whether or not he could even hit the rope, at all, at such a range. The entire event turned into quite a spectacle.

James made himself a tall shooting stick and took his position on the northern bank. Every soul on the detail was present to watch the event ... almost four hundred men. Some men laughed, teased, and yelled in an attempt to distract James. Others shouted for them to be quiet. A couple of rum-induced bouts of fisticuffs broke out before the first shot was even fired. Despite the racket, James sighted in his beautiful Virginia rifle that he had taken off of the dead Tory. He nicked the rope right at the tree trunk with the first shot. Dozens of men erupted in cheers. Others groaned in disbelief.

James carefully measured his powder and poured it down his barrel. He popped a lead ball into his mouth and moistened it liberally and then pressed it down over the top of a piece of ticking patch soaked in middlin' grease. He pressed the ball down into the end of the barrel and then trimmed the extra cloth off of the patch with scientific precision. He tamped the load tight with his ramrod and prepared to fire. He took a deep breath, released it halfway, and then gently squeezed the trigger. The shot struck the rope at the exact point where it met the tree, shredding it. The far end of the rope fell limply from the tree and drifted downstream with the current.

A huge cheer erupted from the camp. Men exchanged coin as bets were won and lost. Even the officers were shaking hands and exchanging money. Men by the droves tracked down James to slap him on the back or shake his hand. It was a rare moment of fun and celebration in the midst of war.

One of the men standing near the tree where the other end of the rope was tied whipped out his hunting knife and sliced it free, letting it tumble into the river and disappear downstream. Soon other men came from the tavern carrying bowls and tubs of oil and grease. They doused the ferry raft with the oil and then set it ablaze with some gunpowder sparked with flint and steel. They released the burning boat into the current and watched it disappear around a bend in the river.

The men spent their final day at Colson's Mill packing the spoils of the battle into a dozen wagons abandoned by the Tories. Though tempted to torch the mill and tavern, Colonel Locke elected to leave the structures intact. Both were important to the culture and commerce of the region. It was a clear sign of goodwill to leave them unharmed and available for future use.

The journey back to Salisbury was much more leisurely than the hard march that took the regiments to Colson's Mill. The men paced themselves with the wagons. The journey took two full days of marching, but the men entered camp well fed, relatively well rested, and none the worse for wear. They settled into a dull routine. Though the officers led them in the occasional marching or shooting drill, for the most part they lay around camp and waited.

James hated the dullness of camp. He volunteered for every possible task and mission that he could find. He went out into the countryside to forage supplies. He even volunteered for night patrols, gate duty, and being stationed at observation posts. Anything to break the monotony and boredom and get away from the antics at camp.

Three weeks later James was napping soundly in his comfortable British army tent when the flap flew open and a shrill, obnoxious voice ripped him from his slumber.

"Good news, good news, good news! I can't hardly believe it. I got some good news, son!" It was the one-of-a-kind Joel Moffat.

"What, Joel? What kind of news can you possibly have that's worth wakin' me up from a good nap in the shade?"

"We 'uns is goin' home! Goin' home! Goin' home! Yessiree ... a furlough's come down. I heerd we's gettin' a whole week to go home and rest!"

"You're drunk! Leave me alone."

"I ain't had a drop, I swear, Jamie! I heerd Colonel Alexander tell the captains over at the headquarters tent just a little while ago. They was all jabberin' about how they's worried most of us won't come back once we get us a taste of home cookin'.'"

"They're probably right," commented James. "Truth be told, they're probably just sendin' us home because we've done ate all the food from Colson's and there ain't no more provisions to be had around here."

"True, to be sure. But who gives a bloody blame? Just so long as I get to go home for a spell. Ain't you achin' to go home?"

"Sure, I am. I'll just believe it when I hear it out of an officer's mouth. No offense, Joel."

"Suit yourself, you grumpy fartleberry. I'm goin' to pack my gear. My arse is road bound just as soon as Captain Givins hollers, "Git!'"

Joel disappeared behind the tent flap. James drifted back to sleep.

It turned out that, for once in his misguided life, Joel Moffat had stumbled upon some actual trustworthy information. Colonel Alexander called a formation of all companies about an hour later. He stood to address the men on one of the two Tory wagons that the Mecklenburg regiment had claimed after the battle at Colson's Mill.

"Gentlemen! Today we have received orders from General Rutherford that as of daybreak tomorrow morning the men of the Mecklenburg Regiment will be placed on a one-week furlough. Tomorrow is August 10. That means you must report back to camp before sundown on Wednesday, August 16. You are responsible for your own transport home and your own transport back to this camp. If you do not report back before sundown I will declare you a deserter and you will be punished to the fullest extent of North Carolina law. So make sure you're back on time."

"Run out of food again, have we Colonel?" someone shouted from the back.

The men erupted in laughter, almost disbelieving that a soldier would actually voice such a question.

The colonel chuckled, "Something like that, son. Just be glad you're only twenty-five miles from home. Some of these poor creatures in these other regiments have nowhere else to go."

The colonel's observation seemed to kill the excited mood.

A voice yelled from the crowd, "Can we go on and leave right now, Colonel?"

"No, son. By no means is anyone to leave before daylight tomorrow. You are still on duty at this post until then. Early departures will be regarded as desertion. Now ... to change the subject. Upon our return to camp I anticipate that we will be assigned to the great Southern Army that General Gates is assembling to drive the Redcoats out of South Carolina!"

A resounding chorus of, "Huzzah!" broke out among the men. Hats flew into the air. The men cheered and danced.

The colonel attempted to quiet his men. He shouted, "One more thing ..."

The levity and celebration continued.

The colonel's patience finally reached its limit. He almost screamed, "Gentlemen, shut your mouths and listen!"

Silence swept across the formation.

"Thank you. One more very important matter must be addressed. Should we be called back to duty for some unforeseen reason, company commanders will be notified and that notification will proceed through the chain of command. You will be instructed where to report. Captains, make sure you know where you can find all of your men. Understood?"

"Yes, sir!" shouted the chorus of captains from the formation.

"Very well, men. Enjoy your visits home. These two wagons will be detailed to make the trip at first light. They will carry anyone too sick or injured to travel by foot. That is all."

James didn't stick around for the post-formation celebration. He had gear to pack, a weapon to clean, and preparations to make. He was going home!

Thursday morning was clear and uncharacteristically cool for August in the North Carolina piedmont. Men began streaming out of the camp as soon as the dull glow of dawn invaded the night sky. James Hamilton was one of the first, accompanied by the ever-outspoken Joel Moffat and their other close pal, Henry Pippin. The boys hadn't eaten anything since the previous morning, and hunger gnawed angrily at their insides. James knew that their journey home would be most difficult on an empty stomach.

Unlike most of the other men from Mecklenburg County, James was blessed to have a little real money in his pocket. He had stashed all of the copper coins and a few pieces of cut Spanish silver taken off the Tories in South Carolina in the bottom of his fire-starting tin. It was John's idea, really. He thought that it might come in handy during James' time away from home. Besides, with the sale of the horses, John and William still had plenty of money on hand back home in case of emergencies.

James was thankful for his little brother's wisdom. On the way through Salisbury he tugged at Joel's frock and whispered, "Grab Henry and follow me."

"Where the blazes are you goin', James? Home is yonder way!" he exclaimed, pointing to the southwest.

"Just shut up and come with me and be glad I asked ya!" James scolded.

Joel signaled to Henry and both of them followed James as he exited the human convoy headed toward Charlotte. They walked down a narrow alley between the general store and a small tavern.

"What's this all about, James?" asked Henry.

James smiled, "I'm about to get us some breakfast."

"How you figger on doin' that, Jamie? These tight-arsed folk stopped givin' hand-outs to us soldier-boys weeks ago," observed Joel.

"I ain't lookin' for no hand-out," James declared.

"You plannin' on robbin' somebody, then?" asked Joel, confused as usual.

"No, you dumb arse, I ain't gonna rob nobody. Just bite your tongue and hold out your hands."

He handed Henry his rifles, reached deep into his haversack, and pulled out his fire starting tin. He cracked open the lid and removed the flint and steel, placing them in Joel's palm. He lifted the wad of tow and extracted four copper pennies and two one-bit wedges of Spanish silver.

Joel's eyes lit up. "You been holdin' out on us, Jamie-boy! Where'd you stumble on such a treasure?"

"I've been sittin' on it since before we got called up. Just been lettin' it rest for such a time as this. Now stay here and I'll be right back."

James disappeared around the corner of the tavern. A few minutes later he returned with a cloth bundle and a huge grin. Inside the package were three loaves of steaming hot bread, three huge slabs of salt pork, and three abnormally large fried apple pies.

"God, Almighty, Jamie. You keep cookin' like this and I might just have to marry up with you!" exclaimed Joel.

"I'm mighty grateful to you, James," Henry added meekly.

"You're welcome, Henry. You, too Joel. And thanks for the proposal, but I think I'll just have to hold out for somethin' a little less stinkier and a whole lot prettier than you."

The men ravenously inhaled the three apple pies. Henry checked around the corner to make sure that the crowd of walking soldiers had moved on and then they fell in well behind them. They didn't want any questions and they weren't in the mood to share their food. The men talked merrily, munched on the crispy bread, and savored the succulent, salty meat. They wisely saved half of the meat and bread for snacks later in the day since they had several hours of walking ahead of them. They settled into a steady pace with their minds and hearts fixed on home.

It wasn't every day that John got to go into Charlotte. This was one of those special days. Caleb Madison, a neighbor about a half-mile east of the Hamilton place, had offered John one Spanish dollar to take his wagon and pick up a load of lumber for him. These little wagon jobs were becoming more numerous. It was his third request in the last two weeks. Word was definitely getting out. It was easy money, and John had the time, so he jumped at each opportunity.

He parked his rig at the mill, unhitched his team, and tied them off in some nearby shade with plenty of grass to graze. He had about an hour to kill, so he headed to Patrick Jack's tavern for a cup of his beloved coffee.

A familiar voice called out to him from a store across the way.

"Johnny Hamilton! Wait!"

John stopped reluctantly.

"Oh, Lord," he thought. "Not Mary Skillington!"

Mary was a nice enough girl, and it was abundantly clear that she had romantic designs on John. But he had never shared a similar interest. And he definitely wasn't in the mood to fend off her feminine assault on this fine day.

John heard the crunch of footsteps. She was walking toward him. There was no getting away from it now. John took a deep, exasperated breath and turned slowly to face her. But he wasn't prepared for the vision that awaited him.

Mary was wearing a stunning blue dress. He auburn hair was tucked under a simple white bonnet, with just a whisper peeking out on the right side of her forehead. The blue dress drew out the deep blue-gray color of her eyes. Her lips were parted thinly in a mischievous smile. She held her chin low, shielding her eyes from the sun. Her face was radiant. It was obvious that she was very happy to see John Hamilton.

John reeled at the vision of her. In fact, he was dumbfounded. He and his brothers, much to their mother's disappointment, had gotten out of the habit of attending church meetings, so it had been close to three months since he had last seen Mary. And it looked as if she had undergone some sort of metamorphosis. His memory was filled with the youngster he had grown up around ... a lanky, freckle-faced farm girl. But the young woman who stood before him was, in her own simple and humble way, breathtakingly beautiful. John progressed from being dumbfounded to being captivated. What manner of chrysalis had transformed this creature?

John finally forced a greeting through his female-induced fog, "Hello, Mary. It's been a long time."

"It certainly has, Johnny. Too long. Your mama's not a bit pleased with your church-going as of late."

"I know ... we need to do better, but we just don't like leavin' the farm unattended with James away in the war. William has to stay home alone every time I have to go someplace."

"I know. Lots of folks are doing the same thing these days."

She paused, waiting for John to speak. It was an incredibly awkward moment. Finally John said something.

"You look different."

Mary blushed and looked down, pressing some of the wrinkles in her dress.

"Papa bought me this new dress last week. I absolutely love it."

"It's not just the dress. It's somethin' else. You hair's different. And you look older, maybe."

"Is that bad?" she teased, the right side of her lip curling into an embarrassed smile.

"No. No. Not bad, at all. It's good, in fact. I think it suits you."

This time John blushed, and then turned and looked up the street.

"What are you doing in town today?" he asked, changing the subject.

"Oh, Papa had some business to attend to with Mr. Avery. He invited me to come along for the ride. I was just browsing in the store while I was waiting for him."

"How are your folks?"

"Oh, they're just fine. Same as usual, I suppose."

John looked across the street at the tavern.

"I was just about to go over to Mr. Jack's tavern and get me a cup of hot coffee. Would you like something to drink?" He couldn't believe the words that were coming out of his own mouth.

"Oh, no! Papa would blister me if I went inside a tavern!"

"You don't have to go inside. I'll bring you something. We can sit over yonder in the shade beside doc's office and wait for Mr. John to finish his business. You don't need to be standing around town all alone, anyways."

"How noble and kind of you, Mr. Hamilton."

She batted her eyes at him. And for the first time ever, he actually liked it. His heart fluttered a bit.

"What would you like then, Mary?"

Suddenly, for the first time ever, he actually liked hearing that name ...

"I would love a cup of spiced tea with sugar."

"That's grand. I'll fetch it. Just go have a seat under that apple tree and I'll be back in a bit."

John turned and trotted off to the tavern. A few minutes later he emerged with two steaming-hot pewter mugs. He was pleased to see Mary waiting for him beneath the tree.

"Here you go, spiced tea, extra sweet. And a little something else."

After he handed her the hot mug he reached up and took off his straw cocked hat, revealing a cloth napkin bundle perched on the crown of his head.

Mary giggled, "What on earth is that?"

"A little rum cake to go with your tea." He winked and grinned, "And we don't have to tell your Papa about the rum part."

Mary giggled again.

"They only had this one slice, so we'll have to share."

"That suits me just fine," Mary responded.

And for the next half-hour Johnny Hamilton and Mary Skillington sat together under Doc Holcomb's apple tree. They told stories and talked about memories. They shared about their families. It was a delightful time. John couldn't believe how much he enjoyed it. He decided, as they talked, that he desired more times like this. The conversation eventually became deeper, personal, and more serious.

"I heard about what happened to you and your brothers down in the Waxhaws. How you fought and killed those Tories. John, I can't even imagine. You were so brave."

"It wasn't about bein' brave, Mary. We were just tryin' to help those people."

Mary allowed some silence to linger, and then spoke, "They say that James was sweet on the girl that … that got hurt and died."

John smiled and nodded. "That was somethin' else, I tell you. James fell for that gal the minute he saw her. And her for him, too."

"Do you really think a man and woman can love one another like that? In an instant, I mean … " queried Mary.

"I'm startin' to, Mary Skillington."

He looked into her eyes. No smile, this time.

"Anyhow … in less than two days they were already talkin' marriage. James asked for her hand and she consented." His face clouded. "But she died that night before they could tell her mama or anybody else."

"Oh, how horrible! I heard talk about James being engaged, but I didn't quite believe it."

"It was true, sure enough."

"Was he absolutely heartbroken?"

"Yes, Mary, he was. We liked to never got him to let go of her body. He sat and held her forever in a blindin' rainstorm. It was pitiful. And the burial was awful. I was hurtin' for him. But then we headed home the next day, and then got caught up in Buford's battle, and then we was home. Next thing you know James was called up and gone. So we ain't been able to talk about it much."

A shout echoed from the mill yard, "Hamilton! Your load's ready! Get this rig out of the way!"

John's heart fell.

"Mary, I reckon I gotta go."

"I know. Papa should be ready any time now. I'm surprised it's taken him this long. Mr. Avery is probably talking more politics than law."

"Let me take these cups back inside. Then will you walk with me, Mary?"

"Of course, John."

John trotted to the tavern and unceremoniously dropped the pewter mugs on the first empty table nearest the door and then ran back to where Mary was still sitting under the tree.

John reached his hands down and, taking Mary by both hands, helped her to her feet. Her fingers lingered on his palms for just a moment. His heart raced. John extended his right arm and then Mary slipped her left hand inside his elbow. Together they strolled up the street toward the mill.

"I've enjoyed our conversation, John."

"So have I, Mary. Maybe we can do this again sometime."

"Soon, I hope. It would be a shame to let another three months pass by."

John laughed out loud. "Well, maybe we won't wait so long this next time."

Mary answered, "I hope not."

They reached the fence beside the mill. Mary waited there while John retrieved his team and hitched the animals to his rig. She came nearer as he prepared to climb up into the seat.

"Take care of yourself on the way home, Johnny Hamilton. Keep an eye out for Tories."

"Oh, I don't 'spect there's any Tories 'round these parts right now. But I'll be a watchin', of that you can be sure."

They stared into one another's eyes. John was smitten. And delighted. And confused.

"I swear, Mary, somethin's different. You've changed."

"I think maybe we've both changed, John."

"I think maybe I want to kiss you, Mary."

Mary blushed brightly and shot glances in both directions. Then she stared at her feet, too embarrassed to look John in the eye. She tapped her toe in the dirt.

"Not here in the middle of the street, John!" she hissed. Then she looked him directly in the eyes and whispered, "Soon."

She turned and ran down the street toward the law office, moving much like the little girl that John had always known. John smiled, shook his head, and then jumped up onto the seat of his wagon. He whistled a jolly tune as he headed north toward home.

James feasted his eyes upon his cabin like it was a gourmet meal. He had only been away for a few weeks, but he missed home and his brothers so badly!

As he walked up the well-worn dirt path that approached the front of the cabin he shouted, "Hello in the house! Can you spare a bite for a wayward soldier?"

The door cracked open and the barrel of a musket poked out of the crack.

"What's the matter with you fellers, don't you recognize your big brother's voice when you hear it?"

The door flung open as William ran out, dropping his musket in the grass.

"Jamie!"

He ran to his brother with all the speed his legs could provide, tackling him to the ground and smothering him with a huge hug. James howled with joy as he clung to his little brother in the cool grass. After a few moments James extricated himself from William's grasp.

"Are you home for good?"

"No, just for one week. We all got a furlough. Where's Johnny?"

"He went into town to pick up a load of lumber for Mr. Madison. Lately folks have been payin' him to haul cargo in the wagon. I keep an eye on things whilst he makes a little extra money. He should be back any time now. I got supper warmin' on the hearth."

"That sounds good to me! I'm danged near starved to death. Whatcha got?"

"I made a stew with chicken, onions, and taters. And a pone of cornbread is cookin' now."

"Little brother, that sounds dee-licious! John had better get on home, or I might not leave a single bite for him."

"You've got plenty of time to wash up before supper. And I don't mean to be getting' in your business, or nothin' … but you're a might rank. How's about letting a little soap and water in under them arms or yours?"

James smacked him in the head. "I gotcha. Don't worry, I'll smell like a field of daisies when I'm done."

"I'll believe it when I smell it," William responded.

William trotted back into the house. He grabbed James a basin, a small cloth, and chunk of lye soap and then went back inside to check on his cornbread. James poured a half-bucket of water in the basin and stripped off his shirt. He was busy taking a basin bath when John pulled the wagon off the road and approached the house. John was a bit confused at first by the sight of a man covered in mud and lather, but soon recognized his older brother. He brought his wagon to a halt and jumped down.

"I would hug ya, but you're too much a mix of nasty and slippery right now." He beamed. "Welcome home, James."

"It's good to be home, brother."

"How long ya got?"

"I gotta be back at Salisbury in seven days. The whole regiment got sent home for a week."

"Well, that's good. It'll give us a chance to fatten you up a bit."

"That's what I'm a hopin' for. Supper's almost ready, according to William."

"Good, I'll take care of the horses and wash up," replied John.

By the time John finished turning watering and housing the horses, James had rinsed off and put on a crisp white shirt.

"You almost look human again," commented John as he walked up to the cabin.

"I almost feel human again. Maybe some hot food will finish the job. Let's eat!"

The boys went inside and, for the first time in over a month, had a meal together. They ate the entire pot of stew and every crumb of William's cornbread. James guzzled mug after mug full of fresh milk. After dinner they took their chairs outside to watch the sunset and smoke their pipes. They talked and laughed until late into the night. James was almost too excited to go to bed, but he forced himself, anyway.

The boys were up early the next morning and set about working on the farm. James loved being back on his own place again. He loved the smell of the dirt. He loved everything about it. He determined that he was going to savor every moment.

They worked all day Friday and Saturday. On Sunday they stepped out in faith and all of them went to meeting, leaving their cabin unattended. They sang and worshiped. Their mother wept. They went to the Farr home for dinner and were invited to stay until supper. They played games with Hugh and their half-brothers and half-sisters. It was one gloriously fine and memorable day.

Mundane work on the farm continued on Monday morning. The time for the corn harvest was growing near. James would have to miss that, unfortunately. But there were still plenty of other tasks to take care of. They worked on fences until dinner, and then lay down for an afternoon nap.

James lay awake for quite some time. He was thinking too much. He was already dreading leaving. Thursday was approaching too quickly. Soon it would be time to march back to camp ... back to the hunger, want, and violence of the war. Despite his racing mind he eventually drifted off into a fitful sleep.

Something was shaking his leg. The sensation grew stronger, more irritating. Someone was trying to rouse him.

"Leave me alone!" he exclaimed.

"Someone's comin'," John hissed. "I hear a horse."

James shook the cobwebs of sleep from his brain. Sure enough, he heard the high-pitched thud of a horse's hooves striking hard dirt and rock.

"Fast rider," stated James.

"Sounds like it," confirmed John.

The sound of the horse grew louder as it approached. James jumped from his bed. John was already holding his rifle. He tossed it to James and then they both bolted for the door. They both cocked their flintlocks. John lifted the latch and flung the rough wooden door open as James lunged out, rifle at the ready.

"Don't shoot, gentlemen!"

It was Ensign John McFalls, from James' company. James and John lowered their rifles, exhaling in relief.

"Private Hamilton, the regiment is recalled at once. The British are out of Charlestown in force and headed north. We have been ordered to join Gates' army in South Carolina. Muster is at the Charlotte Courthouse at sunset. Bring all of the powder, lead, and food that you can carry. We will be hard marching, probably into the night and again all day until tomorrow. We have many miles to travel. I'll see you there. I need you to inform Privates Moffat and Pippin. Understood?"

James replied, "Yes, sir. I'll be there. And I'll tell the boys."

The Ensign shouted, "Huzzah!" and then spun his horse and galloped to the east, headed to the next homestead.

James looked at his brother and shrugged. "Well, Johnny, I guess that's it. Cornwallis calls."

John didn't respond. He was already heading back inside the cabin to help organize and pack his brother's gear.

14

HUMILIATION AT CAMDEN

Once again John prepared to take James to the place of muster for the regiment, this time in the wagon. James sent William on horseback to pass the word to Joel and Henry. While James was making his preparations for the deployment John packed some extra foodstuffs to take to the other soldiers. He loaded three bushels of freshly dug potatoes, two bushels of sweet corn, and two bushels of tomatoes. Since the corn crop would be in within a couple of weeks, John tossed in their last hundred pounds of corn meal.

William killed a deer about every three days, so the boys had a huge supply of dried, smoked venison. John loaded four large grain sacks full of the dried meat into the wagon as well. He figured that the men would be able to take what they wanted of the vegetables and meat to fill their haversacks.

William soon returned from his mission as messenger. Once again older brothers left him at home and headed for the muster. They arrived in front of the courthouse a half-hour before sundown. Men were trickling into the village from every direction. John hopped down and tied up his team to a post. Joel Moffat was already sitting on the courthouse steps. He rose and walked toward them, a frown frozen on is usually jolly face.

"So much for restin' and gettin' fed, huh Jamie?"

"I reckon. The British don't care about our sleepin' and eatin' habits," responded James. "Where are we goin', exactly?"

"Well, I just happened be in a spot where I heerd some officers talkin' about a place called Rugeley's Mills down in the south of Carolina. Not quite to Camden. They say Gates ran out the Tories and set up camp there."

"I reckon it's good a place as any to pick a fight," responded James.

"Sure enough. Though I'da liked for 'em to have waited another couple of days. I see you brung your little cub with ya."

"John's just here to drop me off. And he packed a load of food to share with the boys." He nodded at John and smiled. "My little brother's a Patriot through and through."

John spoke up, "Joel, them sacks is full of dried venison. Help yourself and fill up your sack before everybody else lights into it."

"Why, thankee kindy, Johnny. I believe I will, at that!"

Joel got busy loading his haversack with meat and began stuffing potatoes into any opening in his baggage that he could find. A stern voice from across the street interrupted his stockpiling.

"Private Moffat, I trust you are not raiding the regiment's stores."

It was Captain Givins, striding toward the wagon.

"Naw, sir. Johnny brung this stuff and told me to help myself."

"You will cease immediately, Private. These are now part of the provisions for the regiment."

"Private Hamilton, I'm pleased you made it. And it's good to see you again, as well, John. The regiment is grateful for your contribution. Once again, I will provide a receipt voucher for the provisions furnished. But I need you to compact these supplies as efficiently as you can to make room for more cargo. We have several more items coming from the mill and the store."

"Sir, I'm just leavin' this stuff for the soldiers and headin' back home. I figured they could use a little extra food for the road. I ain't here for the muster."

"Nonsense. Your country needs you, lad. We only have three other wagons and all of them are filled to capacity and beyond. Consider yourself called up for wagoner service in support of the regiment as of this moment. You will be added to the roster and reimbursed accordingly someday, I trust."

James intervened, "Sir, I don't want John goin' with us and I sure don't want him goin' near no battlefield. I'm gonna have to put my foot down on this one. This boy has to go home."

"Private Hamilton, you are forgetting your place. I am afraid that this affair is not up to you." He looked at John. "Son, how old are you?"

"I turned sixteen back in June."

"Well, there you have it, gentlemen. North Carolina law requires that all males age sixteen and over swear their oaths to the state of North Carolina and enlist in their county's militia. John, have you taken your oath?"

John swallowed hard and looked at his brother. "No, sir. I ain't."

"Very well, as I am an elected magistrate in this county, I will administer it now and enter the event in our regimental record. Please raise your right hand."

John's head was swimming. He only meant to give his brother a ride to muster, not take a ride himself into the middle of the war. Nevertheless, he raised his right hand.

"John Hamilton, do you solemnly swear that you renounce all allegiance to King George III and the nation of Great Britain, that you will faithfully serve the free and independent State of North Carolina and the United States of America, and that you call upon yourself the judgment of Almighty God should you fail in this oath and dishonor your home and country, so help you God?"

"I ... I do."

"Excellent! Welcome to the Mecklenburg Regiment. As wagoner you are responsible for your cargo, your vehicle, and your team. You may be called upon to carry and care for wounded in addition to the movement of food and supplies of war. Prepare your rig for the journey. We move out within the hour."

The Captain spun on his heels and ambled off to his next area of responsibility. John looked at James wide-eyed. James bit his lower lip grimly and shook his head.

"I shoulda never brought you down here, Johnny. I had no idea somethin' like this might happen."

"Heck fire, Jamie, whatcha whinin' about? He gets to ride all the way to where we is goin'. Shoot … I might sign up to be his assistant!" quipped Joel.

"This ain't no time for playin' around, Joel," James scolded.

"I know it. I'm just tryin' to cheer you up. Stop worryin'. Johnny-boy is gonna be just fine. He won't be near the shootin'. We'll just make sure he knows how to skedattle iffin it comes to it."

James nodded. He soon spotted a familiar face among the spectators gathering across the street. It was old Ned Carlisle, another neighbor. James ran over to him and asked him to get word to William that John had been unexpectedly drafted into the militia and would not be returning home for a while. Ned promised that he would give William the message on his way back home. James trotted back across the street.

"Well, you heard the Cap'n," he said to John. "Let's get the rig ready. They're bringin' more stuff."

James and Joel stowed their rifles and began helping John rearrange his cargo. Henry Pippin showed up a few minutes later and pitched in to help. They were able to place another twelve bags of corn meal on the wagon, along with two small barrels of rum.

"Now I know for sure I'm puttin' in as your assistant!" joked Joel Moffat. He licked his lips and patted one of the rum barrels.

Shortly after sundown the march was on. John joined the tiny formation of wagons in the rear of the column. The Mecklenburg boys were headed for war.

The regiment marched hard and fast. Their destination was, indeed, the home of a Tory colonel by the name of Henry Rugeley, some sixty miles to the south. General Gates was encamped there and awaiting the arrival of militia regiments to increase the size of his army. The Mecklenburg Regiment marched until well after midnight, covering about twenty-five miles. They pitched a cold camp and tried to get a little sleep.

Colonel Alexander and the officers roused the men at daylight and the march was on again. The regiment did not tarry. They force marched throughout the entire day, stopping briefly only twice to allow the men to relieve themselves and eat a little. The bedraggled regiment stumbled into the encampment at Rugeley's Mills shortly after dark. As soon as they received their assigned area the men collapsed and slept out of total exhaustion. John took his wagon to the supply depot and helped unload cargo for about an hour.

Just as he was about to climb back up into the seat of his wagon and go look for the regimental area Captain Givins stepped out of the darkness. John jumped, startled at his sudden appearance. The captain chuckled.

"John, I'm sorry I frightened you. I just wanted you to know that I think you've done fine work today. You moved that wagon and load as good as any grown man. And I'm honored to have you serving with us."

"It's my pleasure, Cap'n. I want to do my part."

"I know you do. And I have yet another mission for you, one that I believe your brother will appreciate and approve."

John was curious. "Sir?"

"There are six men in need of medical care that cannot be provided here in this camp, especially on the eve of battle. Four are suffering from various maladies ... fever, flux, and the like. Two of the men were wounded in recent skirmishes and require a surgeon's care. The General wants them evacuated from the camp at the first possible opportunity. I have volunteered you for this mission."

"Sir, I'm mighty tired, and I know that my team can't handle any more walkin' tonight."

"No, son … not tonight. First light is fine. The company is located about two hundred yards that way," the captain pointed northward. "Go find your brother and get some rest. There is plenty of grass and a small pond where you can tie off your team. Just be prepared to depart at dawn."

"Yes, sir. And thank you, sir."

"My pleasure, Mr. Hamilton. You be careful on the return trip. I hope to be joining you back home in Charlotte in a month or two."

"Yes, sir. Good night, sir."

"Sleep well, John Hamilton."

The captain disappeared into the darkness in the direction of the army's headquarters tent. John headed toward the company area and quickly found the pond. He tied the team loosely to a nearby bush, grabbed his rifle and blanket, and went in search of the boys from Mecklenburg. Ten minutes later he was bedded down in the company area and sleeping soundly.

John felt like he had just lain down. Suddenly yelling men, clanking gear, and the dull glow of fires and torches awakened him. He sat up and rubbed his eyes. His vision was blurred by fatigue and smoke. He finally caught sight of his brother. James was slinging his bags over his shoulder and checking his rifle. John clamored to his feet and ran to him

"What's goin' on, James?"

"We're movin' out, Johnny. Our spies found out that the British are right down the road from us in Camden. They're tryin' to get us in place by mornin' light, I reckon."

"How far is Camden?"

"I ain't sure. Ten or twelve miles, maybe. I don't know how far they're plannin' to march us. But don't worry, you'll be at the tail end of the column."

"I ain't goin', James."

"Why? What are you talkin' about?"

"Cap'n Givins came to see me a while ago. He said they have a wagonload of men they want taken back to Charlotte. Sick and wounded. He volunteered me for the job. I'm s'posed to pull out of here at first light."

"That's mighty good of the Cap'n," commented James, relieved.

"I thought so, too. But I hate to leave you, Jamie."

"I'll be fine. Don't worry about me. You just get goin' before the shootin' starts and watch yourself. The Tory snakes will be crawlin' up out of the ground with the Lobsterbacks this close by."

"I will. I promise." John was on the edge of tears. "Jamie, please come back home."

James embraced his brother. "It ain't up to me, but I'll do my best."

A loud voice called out behind James, "Form up, men! Let's go!" It was Captain Givins. The regiment was already on the move.

James gripped John by the shoulders and held him at arm's length. "I love you, little brother. Now go and bed down under your wagon and try to get some rest. You've got a long day tomorrow."

He hugged John again, then released him and fell in with the southward column. Within minutes the field was empty except for a little candlelight and movement around the hospital tent. John walked over to that tent and confirmed with the doctor that he was the driver for the men being evacuated, and then he took his blanket and crawled under his wagon. Sleep came with surprising ease.

The army marched for hours into the throat of darkness. There were almost four thousand of them. There were the First and Second Maryland Brigades of the Line, a regiment out of Delaware, almost two thousand Virginia and North Carolina Militia, and various cavalry and artillery units.

It was James' first time to see cannon. He couldn't believe the size of them. He tried to imagine how powerful and loud they must surely be. Silently he prayed that the enemy did not have any of those huge, fire-belching beasts.

The shrill voice of Joel Moffat emanated from the darkness to his left, "Reckon we's in Georgia by now, boys? I declare I think we might've walked right past Cornwallis in the dark!"

Laughter echoed through the ranks.

"I do declare! I hope I see that wig-headed General over the top of my barrel today. I'll blast his fancy arse right back to Charlestown," Joel bragged.

"Maybe we won't even have to fire a shot, Joel. You could just talk him to death," remarked a soldier in the darkness.

Hearty laughter ensued, followed by a harsh rebuke from their ensign.

The men marched on in silence, the sounds of footsteps and labored breathing filling the night. Suddenly a shout broke the darkness far off in the distance ahead of them, followed almost instantly by the crack of a musket. More shots followed. Then came more shouting, the thunder of horses' hooves, and dozens of shots.

"You men take cover! Everyone off the road!" It was the voice of Colonel Alexander.

"What's going on, Colonel?" echoed a soldier's frightened voice.

"I'm not sure son, but I'm going to find out." The colonel clucked at his horse in the darkness and then galloped off down the road.

The shooting soon tapered off to just occasional shots, and within a few minutes stopped completely. About a half-hour later the men heard the familiar sound of the colonel's voice calling out to them in the darkness, "Mecklenburg Regiment, where are you boys?" He was about fifty yards down the road.

Several men called out, "Here, Colonel!"

The colonel trotted his horse to their position and dismounted.

"Gather 'round, men! Someone light a torch. Officers to the front."

A torch was ignited, piercing the darkness. One hundred and fifty men of the regiment crowded in close around their colonel.

"Here's the situation, gentlemen. The shooting was Colonel Van's advanced guard. They encountered the forward patrols of the British and exchanged fire. There was a brief attack by British cavalry and some infantry, but they quickly withdrew. The colonel's men took one prisoner in the exchange. The prisoner was interrogated and has confirmed that Cornwallis, himself, is in Camden. He has an army of three thousand or so men and had planned to attack us to-morrow at Rugeley's, but we have foiled his plan. No doubt there will be an engagement up ahead of us at first light."

"What is our position in the order of battle, sir?" inquired one of the Captains.

"We will proceed forward approximately one-half mile, at which point we will fan out left immediately alongside the road. The North Carolina militia is under the command of General Caswell. We will occupy the left center of the immediate front. The Virginia Militia will be on our left and Porterfield's light infantry will occupy the far left flank. The Second Maryland and Delaware Brigades will be to our right on the other side of the road. Artillery will be in the center. Smallwood's First Maryland will hold reserve across the road to our rear."

The Colonel paused. The men stood in silence, staring at the ground.

"This is it, boys. This is what we have been waiting for. We have the opportunity to deal the British a crushing blow and liberate South Carolina from these invaders. Captains, see to your men. We move out immediately."

The colonel turned and strutted toward his horse.

As soon as he was out of earshot, Joel Moffat muttered, "It might be what he's been waitin' for ... alls I'm waitin' for is to get my skinny arse back home where I belong!"

Several of the men murmured and grumbled their affirmation in the darkness.

"Let's go, gentlemen," urged Captain Givins.

The men were on the march again. They passed by cornfields and dark houses. About a half-hour later they were directed off of the road to their left. They lined up two men deep along the back of a slight rise. The enemy was somewhere in the darkness to their front.

Soon Captain Givins came down the line. "Boys, lay down where you stand. Cuddle up with your rifles and try to get some sleep. Daylight will be on us soon. Drink plenty of water and get a little something to eat. No more marching tonight. The next marching that we do will be at the British."

There were no quips, comments, or jokes, not even from Joel Moffat. This was no joking matter. Combat against a real army ... the best army in the world ... was only hours away. Each man along the line withdrew into his own thoughts and preparations. Some wept. Many prayed. Others slept.

James finally made himself moderately comfortable in the tall grass. He felt amazingly at ease. Instead of thinking about the British he thought of home. He thought of his mother and brothers. He thought of Margaret and the intense love he felt for her, despite the brevity and tragedy of that love. Then he slept. He dreamed about Margaret and marriage and babies.

John awakened about an hour before dawn. He made sure his team was well watered, hitched them to the rig, and then drove across the empty field to the hospital tent. A doctor sitting on a stool in front of the tent greeted him.

"You're up early, son."

"Yes, sir. I didn't sleep much, anyways. I figured we might as well get a move on."

"That is probably for the best. We need to clear these men on out of here. No doubt I will be needing the room for new patients before this day is done."

"How many men will I be taking, sir?"

"Only five. Sadly, we lost one of the fellows with fever in the evening. The other gentlemen are not that bad off, but they are certainly too debilitated to march or fight."

"Well, then, I reckon we might as well go, if that's all right with you."

"Certainly. Let me get some assistants to help load the men. We will also pack some rations and water for them for the trip."

The doctor walked to a nearby tent and roused two sleepy, cranky attendants. While John loaded jugs of water and a crate of food the attendants loaded the five sick men. John felt sorry for the poor creatures. The boys with the flux were pale and gaunt. He wondered if they might ever recover from their loss of health and weight. Each man received a blanket and a small, lumpy pillow. They settled into the crowded wagon as best they could. Two of them sat with their backs to John's seat. The other three lay down in the bottom of the wagon.

The doctor approached John as he climbed up into his seat. "Son, you be careful on the road back. You need to put as many miles as possible behind you this morning. There's no telling how things might turn out here today."

"Yes, sir. That's my plan."

The doctor extended his hand, "Good luck, and God speed, son."

"Good luck to you, as well, Doc."

John carefully guided his wagon onto a well-worn trail across the field, making every attempt to reduce the jostling of his sickly passengers. He soon found the edge of the field and pulled the wagon out onto the road headed north to Charlotte. The sun was on the verge of breaking through the horizon. He had traveled only a half-mile when he heard the dull, rumbling thunder of cannon fire.

An explosion rocked James from his sleep and the bliss of his dreams. He was completely disoriented. For a moment he thought that he was in the midst of a thunderstorm.

But it was not thunder. It was the cannons beside him in the road, barking their death southward in the direction of the British. James and the other North Carolinians clamored to their feet. The dull glow of dawn washed across the field. He saw huge clusters of men forming to his right and left. The cannons were barely a hundred feet away, strung across and along the shoulder of the hard-packed road. Again they belched fire and thunder. Then James heard drums across the field.

He turned and got his first glimpse of the British. The sight of their beautiful and immense army took his breath. Directly in front of him were amassed three uniformly dressed regiments, sporting their read and white coats and black cocked hats. Their regimental colors danced upon tall poles in the morning wind. Other regiments extended to the right, some dressed differently. It appeared that some loyalist militia regiments were massed on the far right flank. And behind them all James saw men on horseback. They wore the familiar green coats and helmets that he remembered all too well from that horrid night in the Waxhaws. It was the British Legion. Over one hundred and fifty of them.

Then the explosions began. Two cannon rounds impacted into the field fifty yards in front of his position, hurling chunks of dirt and burning grass into the sky, raining the crumbling debris upon the North Carolinians.

"Aww, hell naw!" drawled Joel Moffat. James' eyes met Joel's. His face was awash with terror.

"What did you expect?" asked Henry Pippin.

"I don't rightly know, but not that! That's a real army! Look at them boys marchin'. They got their bayonets on and drums a bangin'. Cannon balls flyin'. Them's professionals, boys. We gotta git!"

"Too late for that now," commented James. "The fight is on us. We're on the front of the line. There ain't nowhere to go but forward."

"That's for sure," snapped Joel. "Have you looked to either side of us? Tain't nuthin' but swamps in both directions. Them Redcoats have us bottled in here betwixt two swamps to our sides and two gulleys wrappin' round us to the rear. The only way in and out of this spot is right along this here road. We 'uns is cooked, for sure boys. This here is a great big trap, and we 'uns is the bait. Mark my words."

More explosions rocked up and down the line, a little closer this time. The British were adjusting their aim. Surely the next rounds would land among the soldiers of the American army.

The Continental and militia officers wound their way back and forth in front of their men, waving their swords and barking orders. The captains of the Mecklenburg Regiment and their lieutenants worked feverishly to get the men into ranks. James checked his pan along with his powder and lead supply. He brought his old straight bore rifle for this fight. He wanted something he could load easily and quickly in an open field battle. He followed the orders of the Captain and lined up alongside his friends. He stood in the forward of two rows of soldiers. Everything was happening so fast. Too fast.

Suddenly confusion reigned among the Virginians and North Carolinians. Someone claimed that General Gates had ordered the militiamen to shift their positions toward the center. Then two cannon balls exploded among the massing soldiers. One decimated a group of Marylanders on the right side of the road. The other landed among the North Carolina militia to the left. It seemed that the officers didn't even know where the men were supposed to be. Confusion reigned.

Then the British came. Row after row of crimson soldiers marched orderly and deliberately toward the American line. Drums thumped harder, faster, and louder. The canon fire increased. The smoke from the cannons and the fires that they started began to hang low over the ground in the haze. Visibility was rapidly reduced.

"I thought it would all take longer than this!" yelled James. "But they're rushin' right into us!"

"They ain't comin' to dance, that's for sure!" exclaimed Joel. "I told you we shoulda lit out already. This is gonna get bad. And quick!"

"They're coming, boys! Prepare to engage!" yelled Captain Givins. He stood in front of the line with his hands on his hips, facing the enemy defiantly. Then he walked back toward the men, cutting through the line to stand beside them.

He called out, "We're going to fire by twos, men. Front row kneel! The second row will fire over your head. We will fire the first shot together. After that you will fire at will. Understood?"

"Yes, sir!" the men sang.

Another captain from a Lincoln County regiment called out from down the line, "Captain Givins, we have not received the order to fire!"

He responded, "Captain, I don't need an order to shoot at an army of Redcoats about to run their bayonets through my gullet. All I need is common sense! You just mind your own regiment's business!"

The British were about seventy-five yards away, muskets still held smartly against their shoulders, marching in unison. The sight of this huge red military machine was unnerving. The panic in the line was palpable. At long last some of the Marylanders on the right opened fire.

Captain Givins called out, "Boys, make ready!"

Dozens of hollow clicks echoed down the line as the men brought their weapons to full cock.

"Take aim!"

The two rows of dirt farmers lowered their rifles into the firing position. The British were getting closer and closer. They stopped at sixty yards, standing at perfect attention. They provided stationary targets for the men of the militia.

James thought, "This is insane!" He picked his target ... an officer standing almost directly in front of him.

"Fire!"

The Mecklenburg Regiment unleashed a hail of lead into the British line. Several soldiers fell. James saw his target fall as his slug slammed into the man's heart. Other British appeared wounded. The smoke of the Patriots' volley hung in position right in front of the line, mixing with the haze to form a dull battlefield fog. The men rapidly began to reload their weapons. Then they heard the dreaded commands from across the field ...

"Make ready! Level! Fire!"

Musket balls hummed and screamed overhead and slammed into the ground in front of the line. Some found their mark. All around James was the sound of lead striking metal, wood, leather, and meat, especially on the second row of standing shooters.

Something heavy slammed into his back and threw him forward onto the ground, weighing him down. It was the dead weight of a body. James finally managed to extricate himself from the pile of immobile flesh. It was David McKenzie, a boy he had known since early childhood. There was a huge hole in the center of his chest from which black blood flowed. David was dead before he even landed on James. There were at least another dozen men from the regiment lying prone in grotesque, unnatural poses on the ground along the firing line.

All around men were feverishly reloading. James shot a glance at Henry and Joel. Joel seemed fine. He was cussing a blue mile, but unhurt. Henry had blood running down his right cheek and was missing a large chunk of his ear on that side. It must've hurt badly, but a fellow could live without an ear.

James was just finishing his reload when an inhuman chorus of screams erupted from the smoke in front of him. Through the haze he could see that the lines of British soldiers were no longer marching. They were running, muskets extended in front of them with bayonets fixed. James and several of the men near him fired again, but there were precious few shots coming from their side of the line. He could hear hundreds of rounds being fired on the right side and flank across the roadway, but almost nothing from the North Carolinians and Virginians. Many were frozen in fear. Well over half of them never even fired a single shot.

Screams of stark terror erupted from the militiamen as they turned and ran. The entire line melted away as men by the droves threw down their weapons and fled for their lives. The Continentals across the road were standing tough and fighting. But the militia were done and headed north, fleeing the battlefield.

"We're done for, let's git!" exclaimed Joel Moffat.

The Redcoats were already pouring through the line to both their right and left. British infantry were already sweeping around behind the Continentals clear over on the right flank. The artillery was captured.

Finally, Captain Givins shouted, "That's it, boys! Retreat! Fall back to Rugeley's Mills!"

The Mecklenburg Regiment joined the torrent of citizen-soldiers running to the north. They could not escape into the creeks and swamps on the flanks, so the entire force headed straight up the road. The militiamen simply ran over and through the secondary line of Maryland Continentals that spanned the road. Those men were also swept away in the terror.

It was over in a matter of minutes. It was a complete rout of General Horatio Gates' "grand army of the south." And as his men perished from lead and steel, General Gates galloped north as fast as his horse could carry him. He was already a full mile to the north-east, leaving his subordinates to carry on the dwindling fight, and leaving the men under his command to die.

15

PRISONER OF WAR

J ames ran with the horde of fleeing soldiers northward along the narrow road, caught up in the compelling common desire to stay alive. Those who were not swift of foot perished, mostly by the bayonet and blade. It was the most horrible and humiliating thing that James had ever experienced. All around him men fell as musket balls tore into their backs. The road was littered with the dead.

James, Joel, and Henry ran fast. They leapt over the bodies of the dead. They soon outran both their pursuers and most of their fellow soldiers.

Joel Moffat shouted, "The wagons, boys!"

James was reading his mind. The cluster of wagons in the rear offered the only cover for at least a quarter mile. The men ran with a singular goal ... to get behind the wooden shield of those wagons. They finally reached the first one in the line, diving behind its cover. All three of them doubled over, their bodies screaming for oxygen, the muscles of their chests aching from the effort to draw more air into their lungs.

"I told ya what was goin' to happen, didn't I?" barked Joel. "I told ya it was a bushwack!" He gasped for air.

James and Henry both nodded. They couldn't argue. Everything happened just as the backwoods farmer said it would.

James looked over the corner of the wagon. More men were coming, hundreds of them. Some of them had already passed by and were taking cover among the other wagons. Unlike James, Joel, and Henry, precious few of them were carrying weapons.

"We gotta get back to Rugeley's," James determined. "The army will surely regroup there. But we gotta get past them two ravines first so's we can can get around back of these swamps and hit the open woods. It's gonna be a bottleneck right there. Sooner or later the Redcoats are going to hit that ravine and cut off this retreat."

Henry stole a glance over the wagon, as well, and spied the combat still taking place on the right flank. "Look at them Maryland boys, still in the thick of it! Those are some real fightin' men! Not a one of them ran!"

Joel countered, "T'aint no shame in runnin' today, Henry. Everybody else lit out. Only a fool would stay put and play target practice for a thousand Redcoats, no matter how bad they shoot."

"Do you see anyone else from our regiment?" asked James.

"Not a soul," responded Henry. "Not since we ran through the Marylanders. That's when everythin' got mixed up."

"Well, we gotta move right now. They'll keep comin' after us. You boys good to get goin'?" asked James.

Henry and Joel nodded grimly in response.

James stole one last glance around the wagon. What he saw curdled his blood. It was the horsemen of the British Legion. They were riding among the fleeing Patriots, slashing wildly with swords. Some fired pistols at point blank range into the backs and heads of the terrified men.

James hissed, "Boys, look!"

Joel and Henry peeked over the gate of the wagon.

"Aww ... hell, naw!" moaned Joel.

James exclaimed, "British Legion dragoons! Shoot the murderin' bastards!"

He threw up his rifle over the corner of the wagon and drew a bead on the nearest horse soldier. He touched off his trigger and the man recoiled backward and tumbled off of his horse. As James reloaded Henry and Joel swung their rifles over the rear of the wagon and dropped two more of the dragoons.

"There's too many of them, Jamie!" exclaimed Henry.

Joel pointed to their left, "Look! Them dragoons are in the tree line and headed to the rear. They aim to cut us off."

It was true. At least twenty of the green-clad horsemen were galloping full speed around the periphery of the field. James looked to the right flank. Another similarly sized group was making their way along the creek bank on that side.

"Let's git now, boys! If they hit them gullies we're done for!" Joel screamed.

He was already running up the road. James and Henry fell in behind them. They could see that some men were already clear of the choke point at the ravines and scattering into the woods and fields. They found themselves in the middle of a mass of about fifty militiamen and Continentals running full speed along the road. The occasional man fell from the rear of group as shots rang out from behind them and the lead found a target within the cluster of fleeing bodies.

They were almost to their goal. If they could only clear the narrow bridge over the small ravine they could find refuge in the woods and escape this hellish killing field.

But there would be no escape for these Mecklenburg County boys, for in front of them the green-coated dragoons of the British Legion popped up out of the ravine on both sides of the road, pistols drawn. The cluster of running men stopped. The enemy completely blocked the road. James and his friends were cut off. They were captured.

One of the officers of the dragoons spoke loudly in a snobby, obnoxious British voice, "Gentlemen, it would be in your best interests to lay down your weapons if you are still holding any and raise your hands high in the air. You are now prisoners of His Majesty's army. I assure you that you will be afforded all of the courtesies that are due a soldier captured on the battlefield."

The few men carrying weapons, including James, Joel, and Henry, all dropped them to the ground and raised their hands high.

"Didn't I tell ya?" mouthed Joel.

"We will tolerate no talking among the prisoners!" snapped the officer. "Now, gentlemen, line up along the edge of the road and face toward me."

The men slowly and angrily obeyed.

One of the other Legionnaires spoke to the officer, "Captain Mayfair, the rebels realize they are cut off and have begun to scatter into the swamps."

"No matter," remarked the Captain arrogantly. "They will return to this road soon enough when they see that their efforts are futile. Meanwhile, disperse the legion along both sides and make every effort to cut off all means of egress. General Lord Cornwallis has tasked us with the capture of as many of the enemy as humanly possible. I intend to have this entire army incarcerated by noontime."

In addition to being frustrated, James was also a bit puzzled. Standing in the line, his hands high in the air, he thought, "Where have I heard that name … Mayfair?"

The captain turned his attention back to the prisoners before him. He slowly walked his horse around the back of the men, all the way down the line, inspecting their belts for weapons. Most of the men carried knives and tomahawks.

The officer commented angrily, "Gentlemen, when I ordered you to drop your weapons, my expectation included those barbaric axes and blades strapped to your sides. You will immediately remove all of your belts, bags, and equipment and drop them on the ground, as well. And keep your hands well away from your bladed weaponry."

He spoke to his soldiers, "Men, keep these rebels under the barrel of your weapons until we are sure that they are completely disarmed. Remain vigilant. Sergeant Williams, take your men and disarm and apprehend the next group of rebels approaching on the road."

"Yes, sir!" responded the sergeant as he took a small group of the Legionnaires and led them back down the road.

He turned his attention back to his captives, "Prisoners! I order you to turn and face toward your right and place your hands on the shoulders of the man in front of you. Do it now!"

The men complied. There was no use in resisting. Their situation was hopeless. Hundreds of Patriot captives were being disarmed all over the field. The noise of battle was winding down significantly. The British cannon had not fired since the opening minutes of the battle. Musket and rifle fire were sporadic, at most, with most shots echoing from the swamps and surrounding woods.

The Patriot soldiers stood silently as ordered. The captain and two of his men continued to inspect the group of prisoners to which James, Joel, and Henry belonged. He slowly made his way down the front of the line of dejected, humiliated men. As he drew nearer to where James and his friends were standing, James realized who the pompous captain was. It was the officer who delivered the terms of surrender to Colonel Buford in the Waxhaws! James had actually made a veiled threat on that day that he would kill the man. And now he was his captor!

James stared at the ground in front of him, attempting to allow his hat to shield his face from view. He definitely didn't want to be recognized. He prayed fervently that the officer would pass him by. But it was not to be …

The officer barked, "You, boy! You seem familiar to me. Have we met before?"

James lowered his head even more, pretending not to hear … trying to convince himself that the man was talking to someone else. The officer kicked him in the shoulder with his boot.

"I'm talking to you, rebel scum. Where have we met before? I know you from somewhere."

"I don't know what you're talkin' about," James lied.

"Yes. Even your voice is familiar to me. We have most definitely encountered one another before."

"I'm just a dirt farmer from the woods of North Carolina. I ain't got no call to be knowin' any uppity-arse British officers."

Joel, standing behind James, snickered and choked down a laugh.

James thought to himself, "Hamilton, you're an idiot …"

"Uppity, indeed. Bold words for a boy headed to a British prison. Perhaps we can work some of that sass out of you while you are our guest aboard ship in Charlestown. I know a couple of officers who specialize in such endeavors. They should have some measure of amusement with you."

The Captain turned his horse to move away when suddenly he stopped. He wheeled his horse back around and removed his sword. He leaned across his saddle and placed the sword under James' chin, slowly turning his face into full view. James looked away at first, but finally shifted his eyes to look directly into the eyes of the officer. Bitter hatred spewed from James' gaze.

"Oh, yes!" the Captain hissed victoriously. "I do know you! You were the lad in that wagon with the coward Buford in the Waxhaws. What was it you said, 'Maybe I'll take your horse from you?' Or something to that effect … Well, now, isn't this an interesting turn of events? And as I recall, you were in possession of the mounts of some of my fellow servicemen. Yes … I have special plans for you."

The captain flicked James' hat off of his head with a quick swipe of his sword.

"Sergeant! Take these rebel prisoners to the collection point. All but this one. Take him to our headquarters for interrogation."

"Yes, sir," answered the Sergeant.

Joel's hands squeezed James' shoulders tightly. Two musket-wielding Legionnaires plucked James from the line of prisoners, ripping him from Joel's grip.

"You hang in there, James," encouraged Joel.

"Shut up!" barked one of the soldiers, slamming the butt of his musket into the side of Joel's skull.

"I'll be fine, Joel. Don't you worry 'bout me."

The other soldier slammed James in the back. "You'll speak only with permission, boy!"

The guards pushed James in the direction of the body-littered battlefield.

John wondered about the course of the battle. He didn't hear the cannons for very long, which was a curiosity. He expected to hear many, many more of their thunderous booms. But there was silence in the direction of Camden. Whether that was good or bad he did not know.

He took his time as he headed north toward Charlotte. The load was heavy and he didn't want to stress the horses. He covered roughly ten miles before he guided the team off of the road for a rest. The poor animals had covered many miles in the past two days and had precious little rest the night before. They were fine, costly animals and he did not want to run them to ground. He pulled up to a small stream that ran alongside the road. There was ample shade.

The men who could move about climbed down from the wagon and lay down in the cool shade. Two of the fellows were too sickly to move. John made sure that each of them had ample water and what-ever food they desired. They rested for about an hour. John actually fell asleep for a short while. He awakened from his brief nap and in-structed the men to get back in the wagon and prepare to move out. He helped one of the wounded soldiers who was having difficulty climbing back into the wagon. And then they were off.

John's makeshift ambulance was only a mile further north when a rider approached from the south.

"There's a rider coming, I see his dust kicking up," stated one of the wounded men. "It looks like he's moving pretty fast."

John pulled on the reins and guided the horses to the shoulder of the road. He turned and watched the rider approaching, wondering who he was and why he was in such a rush. He soon came into full view. It was a Continental officer. John wasn't sure of the rank. He rode up to the wagon. He was sweating and winded. His horse was soaking wet and lathered.

"I'm Lieutenant David Pressman, First Maryland Regiment of the Line. How on earth did you men get so far north so quickly?" he demanded.

John responded, "I'm John Hamilton, wagoner with the Mecklenburg Regiment out of Charlotte. These men are sick and wounded. I was ordered to evacuate 'em to Charlotte before the battle. We pulled out of Rugeley's Mills at sunup this mornin'."

"Ahh, that makes sense then. I didn't think there was any possible way you could have been in the engagement at Camden."

"No, but my brother and the rest of the regiment is. How are they doin'? What's happenin'? We could hear the cannons for a bit, then they stopped all of a sudden."

The Lieutenant stared coldly at John. "The battle is lost, son. It was a rout. General Gates fled the field. The militia regiments threw down their weapons and ran. It was an absolute disgrace. I am on my way to Charlotte and points north and east to deliver the news."

John reeled at the news. His heart sank in his chest. "Where is the militia now? What happened to them?"

"They're dead, son. Dead or captured."

"How many?" John's voice trembled.

"All of them."

James lost count of the days. He was in a cell in the basement of the courthouse at Camden. He was given a bucket of water and some stale bread on the second day. He was kept in isolation. He had no idea where his friends were. At least it was summer. The cool basement room was actually pleasant ... or at least it would have been if he had a civilized method to relieve himself. As things were he had to perform his bodily functions in a shallow depression in one corner of the stone floor. The room was completely dark except for what little light filtered through the floorboards over his head. Those boards rained down dust and debris on him constantly as men walked across the floor above.

He was beginning to wonder if he had been forgotten, since he hadn't seen or heard a soul in the basement since the delivery of the water and bread. At long last he heard footsteps in the hallway outside. Moments later the door flung open, banging against the wall.

"Good God, the stench!" exclaimed the unidentified visitor in a thick Irish voice.

"I don't know what you fools expect, lockin' me up in here without a slop jar," retorted James. "You should try livin' in it for a week … or however long you Redcoats have kept me locked up down here."

"Shut your stinkin' mouth, you louse! You got what you had a comin' to ya, ungrateful rebel! Anyways, you're getting out of here, now. Get on your nasty feet!"

James obeyed grudgingly.

"Where are you takin' me?" he demanded.

"You're bein' taken to the colonel for interrogation."

"What does that mean?"

"It means he's goin' to ask you a lot of questions and you'd better have the right answers or you'll be swingin' from the king's rope!"

"I don't know nuthin' 'bout nuthin'! I'm just in the militia!"

"That remains to be seen. Word in the Legion is that you murdered some our own. If that be so I'll be happy to stretch your sorry neck meself."

James said nothing in response. He followed the instructions of his captor who took him up a narrow stairway and out the back of the courthouse. Once his eyes adjusted to the light James saw that the Irishman wore the green colors of the British Legion.

He thought, "That's just great!"

The soldier prodded him across the street to a large brick house. Two Legion soldiers stood guard beside the front door. One of them turned and opened the door, allowing the soldier to take James inside. They stepped into a beautiful foyer. It was unlike any house that James had ever seen.

The soldier pointed at a spot on the floor. "Stand right here. Don't move an inch or I'll put a bullet in your stupid head."

The man walked to a set of sliding pocket doors and opened them just enough to walk inside. A calm, dignified British voice drifted through the opening.

"Sergeant O'Neill, there you are. I trust that you have our special guest with you?"

"Yes, sir. The boy's waiting in the outer room."

"Bring him in, then. Let's get to the bottom of this."

The Sergeant's face appeared in the open door.

"In here, boy. Now! Mind your tongue and speak only when addressed."

James warily stepped through the door. The sergeant grabbed him by the arm and pulled him to a spot beside an elegant, cloth-covered chair in front of two seated Legion officers. One was Captain Mayfair. The other was an older officer unknown to James. He was examining a piece of paper and thoroughly ignoring him. James stood in awkward silence. Captain Mayfair stared at him in disgust. Finally, the other officer broke the silence.

"Have a seat, son. I am Lieutenant Colonel Banastre Tarleton, commandant of the British Legion. I have some questions for you."

James nodded his acknowledgement.

"What is your name, young man?"

"I'm James Hamilton, sir."

"And where is your home?"

"Mecklenburg County, North Carolina ... a little northeast of Charlotte."

"I see. A militiaman of North Carolina." He paused thoughtfully, and then reached for a teacup sitting on the end table beside him. He took a sip, and then continued, "Captain Mayfair has shared some alarming information about you that I find somewhat hard to conceive. I believe you are familiar with the captain, are you not?"

James glanced at the other officer. "Yes, sir. We met once."

"On the day of our glorious victory in the Waxhaws?"

"Yes, sir. We happened to be at the crossroads when Buford's column came up. We were just waitin' for them to pass. He and some officers came over to talk to us when the captain showed up with your surrender demands."

"Who, then is the 'we' that you mention?"

"My two younger brothers and me. We had been visitin' a church in the area to help a family in need."

"I see. So you were on a humanitarian mission, then?"

"A humana-what?" queried James.

"A humanitarian mission … a quest to do a good deed."

"Yes, sir. We went there to help a widder woman whose husband had died." He didn't elaborate any further.

"How very noble of you," the Colonel stated mockingly. His voice became very deliberate and slowly shifted upward in intensity. "So then, can you explain to me how you and your brothers, gentlemen traveling into the wilds of South Carolina to do a good deed, came into the possession of two horses and saddles of the British Legion?" He was almost shouting by the end of the question.

James thought carefully and quickly.

"Sir, I traded for them."

"You what?"

"I traded for them with a militia Captain in Lancaster. We had some guns and goods that he wanted, so he traded us for them. He had five horses like them, actually. But we only traded for two of them."

It was a brilliant answer, really. Every single word of it was absolutely true. James was just careful and clever enough to include the full number of horses, but leave out what actually happened to the five Legionnaires.

"So you have no idea what happened to the five soldiers who were originally in possession of those animals?"

"Well, sir, as I understand it they was all killed in a raid a couple of nights before that battle you just mentioned. That's how the militia Captain got hold of their mounts. We got the horses from him that morning when we stopped in their camp in Lancaster to do some tradin'."

"I see ... so you had no part in the killing of those men?"

James manufactured his best possible look of incredulity. "Colonel, how is it you think that me and my little brothers would ever tangle with five of your dragoons? That would be plumb stupid, and suicide!"

The Colonel looked at the Captain, raising his left eyebrow. James thought he even saw a smile.

"Son, that is exactly what I told the captain moments before you entered this room."

The colonel looked down at the paper in his hand.

"One more question, Mr. Hamilton," said the Colonel.

"Yes, sir?"

"Were you involved in the combat at the Waxhaws?"

James bit hard and squared his jaw, looking directly at the eyes of the Colonel.

"No, sir. I was not. My brothers and I offered to serve, but Colonel Buford ordered us to take to the road and go home."

The two officers of the Legion stared into his eyes. James paused. He weighed his words. It seemed that things were going well for him. The Colonel was inclined to believe him, it seemed. He was well on his way toward being dismissed, perhaps even released. But then his mouth got in front of his thinking. The words poured out of him before he could try to stop them. And once they began, he let them flow.

"But we did observe your battle, Colonel, such as it was. We was on the ridge just to the north. We saw your Legion overrun the Continentals. We saw a white flag. We saw your men slashin' and shootin' surrenderin' men. We even saw your infantry come in and bayonet the wounded right there on the ground. I had a hard time explainin' that part of it to my baby brother. We saw it all."

"So *you* say," hissed the Colonel. "But then, what do you know, really? Just a lad ... a rabble farmer from the frontier?"

"I know this is a real fine bunch of soldiers you command here, Colonel," James growled, sarcastically. "Nothin' but a well-dressed pack of thieves, rapists, and murderers. I reckon them five you lost over in the Waxhaws probably got what was comin' to 'em."

The Colonel glared at James with contempt.

"Young man, I *was* of a mind to offer you clemency. It was my full intention to give you the opportunity to renounce your rebel ways and go home. All I was planning to require was that you give your oath to King George and the British Empire."

"Colonel, all I want to give your King George is my foot up his royal arse."

The Colonel exhaled. "Indeed. Well. You have made my job much easier and considerably more enjoyable. Captain!"

"Yes, sir!"

"Assign a detail to add the eloquent Mr. Hamilton to our next group of prisoners to be marched to Charlestown. We will introduce him to some of our maritime endeavors in the harbor there. Perhaps a little salt water and moist ocean air will quench the fires of his rebellion."

"Right away, sir."

The captain rose from his chair.

"Let's go, lad."

He grabbed James by the arm and hauled him out of the house. Within the hour he was marching toward Charlestown with a mass of over two hundred other Patriot soldiers. Five days and one hundred twenty-five miles later he was thrown into the crowded hold of the British prison schooner *Pack Horse*.

James' war was over.

PART III

Johnny's War

16

THE HOME FRONT

J ohn rolled into Charlotte with his makeshift ambulance around nightfall on the day of Gates' defeat. The messenger he encountered along the road had already been through and shared the distressing news. The entire village was in an uproar. John deposited his wounded and sick at a makeshift aid station on the northern outskirts of town and then headed home. In so doing he managed to avoid much of the hysteria and confusion that racked Charlotte town for the next several days.

The day after the battle this tiny hamlet of twenty houses and small businesses was transformed into a military processing center. Charlotte, simply because of its geographic location along the road north out of Camden, became the collecting area for the wounded soldiers and displaced refugees from the battle. The few officers who had evaded capture on the battlefield worked feverishly to organize the troops into an actual army and prepare them to march back to the camp at Salisbury.

A couple of days later their haphazard column moved out of town headed northeast. The wounded were piled into wagons and pulled on horse-drawn litters. Those who were able to sit upright traveled on horseback. Hundreds of refugees, many of them women and children, joined the column. But the most pitiful sight came behind the military formation. Over three hundred displaced, scantily clad

Catawba Indians joined the mass of humanity headed north, fleeing the British occupation of their native lands.

A handful of officers and militia from Mecklenburg County remained at home to attempt to organize some semblance of a defense in case the British continued their move to the north. But their pitiful remnant stood little chance of slowing the British juggernaut.

A full month passed after James' disappearance at Camden. For John and William it was the not knowing that was so hard. Not knowing if James was dead or alive. And if by some miracle he was alive, not knowing where he was being held, or if he was wounded, sick, or had enough food to eat. Not knowing was what kept the boys awake at night.

So to combat their disillusionment and despair the Hamilton brothers stayed busy on the farm. Work was one of the few mechanisms at their disposal to help alleviate the absence of James. Yet at the same time his absence was such a huge burden on their work. For years James had been the true leader and workhorse on their small farm. He was the foreman and his brothers were the laborers. It had always been that way and it had always worked well.

Somehow John and William managed. The corn crop came in around the first of September. It was a bumper crop. They managed to bring in the harvest with a little help from Ephraim Farr and his hired workmen. Ephraim required a small percentage of the profit, of course, but in the end it was worth it. John traded the bulk of the corn to the mill in exchange for ground corn meal and flour for winter storage. The boys fully stocked their own corncrib and even built a second crib to store ear corn for the livestock throughout the winter.

The vegetable garden was still producing into early September. William worked the garden like a master. The boy had a real talent for it. He put in the cold-weather crops at the end of August. They would have ample turnips to add to the potatoes, onions, carrots, and beets in the root cellar. There would also be plenty of tasty cabbage for the fall.

Their social lives evolved a bit as well in James' absence. For many years the three brothers had lived within their small, closed family support system. During that time they had little else to do with other folk in the community outside of the normal flow of life and commerce and church, but with James absent from home, John and William discovered that their social needs changed. They enjoyed being together, but something was definitely missing. So they sought fellowship outside their own cabin more than ever before.

William spent quite a bit more time at their mother's place. He was still young enough and close enough in age to the other half-siblings that his presence didn't aggravate Ephraim too much. He ate often at his mother's table. He played with the other kids. He even spent some nights at the Farr home, something that he would have never done if James were at home.

John, on the other hand, had other priorities. He had courting on his mind. He began to spend lots of time at the John Skillington homestead. Each week he spent Friday and Saturday evenings and Sunday afternoons with Mary. They went for long walks and enjoyed long talks. Even though they had grown up together, the discovery experienced during their evolving courtship made it seem like they had never even met before. It had only been a month since John first saw Mary with "new eyes" in the street in Charlotte, yet in that month's time he had fallen helplessly, hopelessly in love with her. The emotion was nothing new for Mary … she had loved Johnny Hamilton for as long as she could remember. With each visit John hoped that he might be able to steal that elusive first kiss. Theirs was a blossoming, precious, innocent love.

Amazingly, despite the proximity of recent battles and the loss of over two hundred men from the local area at the Battle of Camden, the war had still not encroached upon the actual borders of the county of Mecklenburg. There were still skirmishes and engagements ongoing down in South Carolina, and the Tories to the north and east seemed emboldened by the British victories. Cornwallis, however, had stopped his army in the Waxhaws in South Carolina after his huge victory at Camden. The reason for his pause was unknown, but it was most welcome. And so the people of Charlotte and its environs had enjoyed an entire month of peaceful respite.

But all of that changed in late September of 1780.

John was enjoying a leisurely Sunday afternoon at the Skillington home. He had already enjoyed church services and a wonderful late dinner with Mary's family. It was about an hour before sundown. He and Mary were swinging together in a large, two-person swing suspended from a huge oak tree beside the Skillington house when his step-father rode in on horseback. John was absolutely flabbergasted at his unexpected and unwelcome appearance.

He whispered to Mary, "Mary, go inside now."

"What for? I know Mr. Farr."

"I know you do, but somethin's not right. Just go inside and I'll come get you in a bit."

"All right, Johnny. But I'll be watching from the house."

Mary scampered toward her home. John rose and approached Ephraim Farr. Then fear struck deep in his chest as he realized that something must be horribly, terribly wrong for him to make such a trip. There was no other explanation.

"What's wrong, sir? Did somethin' happen to William?"

"No, John. I'm just here to deliver a message. Patriot spies have gotten word through that the British are preparing to move north. The report is that they will pull out of the Waxhaws and head north in the next few days. General Davidson has called up all the area militiamen who can and will serve and is asking every able-bodied man to report for duty at the courthouse at dawn day after tomorrow. I promised to bring the message out this way."

"All right. Thank you, sir. I will be there. Is there anythin' else?"

"No, son. I'll see you Tuesday at dawn. And I'll make sure William just stays at our house with your mother until this all blows over."

"Thank you, sir. That really does help set my mind at ease."

"I knew it would." He smiled at John ... a sincere, caring smile. It seemed strange to John, but not unpleasant. "Bring lots of food and lead. I'll have a horn of powder for you."

Farr turned his horse and rode back toward his home. Mary came quickly from the house, her parents right behind her.

"What is it, Johnny? What's wrong? Is somebody hurt?"

She reached her hand toward John and he took it in his own, smiling reassuringly.

"No, Mary. No one is hurt. It was about the militia. Ephraim was just delivering a message."

"What message?" inquired John Skillington, walking up to the young couple.

"It's about the British, sir. General Davidson has gotten word that the Redcoats are pullin' out of the Waxhaws and headin' north. They expect them to be here some time Tuesday or after. The militia's been called up. All able-bodied men who will serve are expected at the courthouse at dawn day after tomorrow."

"So you're going?" inquired Mrs. Skillington.

"Yes, ma'am. I'm a sworn member of the regiment."

"I guess I'll see you Tuesday morning, then," remarked John Skillington.

His wife rebuked him, "No, John! You will not! You are not going off to get killed in some cursed war!"

He reached out and touched his wife's face. "My love, it's not 'some war.' It's our war. These people have invaded our land and now they're invading our own county. They may even come here and confiscate our property or take our livestock or occupy our own home. I can't let other men fight for me, anymore. I have to go."

His wife's eyes began to swell and turn red. Huge tears formed and instantly began to drain down her cheeks. Trembling from her emotions, she turned her back to her husband and walked away.

"John ... Mary, I'll give you two a moment, but not long. Mary, you need to get inside directly. It'll be dark soon, and John needs to be home before sundown. John, I'll swing by your place and meet up with you before dawn on Tuesday. We can ride in together."

John extended his hand. "Yes, sir. And thank you, sir. I'll see you then."

Mr. Skillington turned and went off in pursuit of his unhappy wife, leaving John and Mary standing alone beside the pathway to the road.

Mary fell into John's arms and began to weep.

"Oh, Johnny, I don't know what I'll do if something happens to you. I can't stand the thought of it."

She clung tightly to him. John cradled her face against his chest and stroked her hair with his hand.

"It'll be all right, Mary. Your papa will be with me. Mr. Farr, too. And all of the other fellers. There'll be hundreds of us, most likely. You gotta have faith, Mary. You gotta know that I'll come back to you."

"You promise?"

"I promise."

He held her silently, gently rocking back and forth. Her tears began to soak the front of his shirt. They didn't talk. They just held one another.

Mary pulled her head away from John's chest and looked him directly in the eyes.

"Johnny, do you even love me?"

He cradled her cheek with his hand.

"Mary, I know I never paid much attention to you before, but I fell in love with you the minute I turned around and saw you on the street in Charlotte town. And I've grown to love you more and more every day since then. I live for the times when I can come here and just be with you. Times just like this."

Mary smiled broadly as tears of joy intermingled with her tears of sorrow and worry.

"And I aim to make you my wife someday, if you'll have me," John concluded.

"Nothing would make me happier than to be your wife, Johnny Hamilton," Mary responded. Then she rose up on her tiptoes and melted her mouth with his. John and Mary lost themselves in that magical, long-awaited first kiss.

Tuesday, September 26, came quickly. John Hamilton and John Skillington rode their horses silently along the road headed southwest toward Charlotte just as the dull light of dawn filtered into the eastern sky. They encountered several more riders along the road, including Ephraim Farr. They arrived at the Mecklenburg County courthouse just after sunrise. There were roughly fifty men milling about and waiting in the streets. The newcomers tied off their horses and joined the group.

John scanned the crowd but didn't recognize many of the men. It seemed pretty clear that most of them were from other counties and regiments. No doubt the makeup of the assembled militia force was impacted greatly by the number of men lost and captured at Camden.

John soon spotted a very familiar face. It was Daniel Pippin, Henry's younger brother. He was the same age as John and they had known one another since the Hamilton family first arrived in North Carolina in 1770. Daniel was sitting cross-legged on the brick wall that surrounded the foundation of the courthouse. He waved at John and motioned for him to come over to where he was sitting.

"I was a wonderin' if I might see you this mornin'," crooned Daniel in his singsong voice.

"Don't see as I had much choice," John responded. "I've been on the regimental books for a couple of months now."

"Not that there's even a regiment or a book anymore," corrected Daniel.

"True. But I'm not one to run from doin' my duty. Have you heard what's goin' on yet?" John asked.

"Nothin' yet. Just a lot of rumors. There's some South Carolina lads in this bunch that say they've been shadowin' the Redcoats for days with a Colonel Davie, runnin' patrols and bushwhacks and such. Cornwallis pulled out of Camden a couple of weeks ago but got held up in the Waxhaws when most of his army took sick."

"Poor fellers," drawled John sarcastically.

Daniel cackled, "Ha! That's for sure! Maybe they left some of their will to fight in the outhouses of Lancaster."

John smiled. "That might be a little much to hope for."

"True, true. But an Irishman can hope, can't he?"

John looked at the loitering militiamen. "Well, what are we supposed to do now?"

"Wait here, I reckon. Until somebody with some rank tells us what to do."

And so they waited. They waited all morning long. Most of the men were growing restless and perturbed. Several of the locals felt they had done their duty by showing up at the courthouse at dawn. After a few hours of waiting they gave up in disgust and went home. About an hour before noon John and Daniel walked over to Patrick Jack's tavern and John treated Daniel to a hot dinner. They were just finishing their meal when they heard yelling and excitement out in the street. A large contingent of horsemen rode into the center of town and joined the local militiamen. A crowd was gathering at the courthouse steps. John paid the bill and the boys headed out to see what was going on.

A voice called out from the platform at the top of the courthouse stairs, "Gentlemen, if you please! Can I have your attention?"

All conversation stopped.

"For those of you who do not know me, I am Colonel William Davie, commander of the North Carolina State Cavalry of the Western District. This is my adjutant, Captain Joseph Graham. Our men have been engaged against the British invaders in and around Camden over the past month. Ours has been the only intact corps since Camden standing between the British in South Carolina and the Continental forces in North Carolina. We have attempted to harass the enemy at every possible opportunity and have remained in contact with the enemy for the past several days. We have skirmished with them, harassed their patrols, and intercepted their communications.

"I must inform you that the enemy is only a few miles down this road to the south, and they are headed this way. I expect that their lead cavalry elements will attempt to enter this village in about one or two hours. Our mission is simple. General William Lee Davidson has ordered us to fight a holding action and delay Cornwallis for as long as we possibly can. This will give our forces in Salisbury and points north and east the opportunity to withdraw and regroup for a future campaign.

"I harbor no illusions, men. We cannot defeat this army. They are over two thousand strong with a corps of dragoons at their disposal. If they want this crossroads they will have it. The only question is, how long will it take them to take it from us and how many of Cornwallis' men will die in the process? We will hold until it becomes clear that the town is lost. At that time I will order a covered retreat to the northeast. Questions?"

There was silence for a moment, and then John spoke up, "Colonel, I reckon I have a question."

"And who might you be, young fellow?"

"My name is John Hamilton, sir. I'm in the Mecklenburg Regiment ... what's left of it, anyways. What about us fellers who live right here in and around Charlotte town? We ain't got no place to retreat to. What happens to us when your horse soldiers mount up and ride?"

"Son, all I can tell you is that you local men need to figure out your own method of retreat, whether back to your homes or to other safe hideouts in the woods. You can then lay low until the British are gone."

"And what if they don't go?" another voice questioned from the crowd.

"Well, I can't tell you what to do then. I won't be here and I won't be in command. But I don't think I would take too kindly to the Redcoats occupying my home and my lands. I believe that I would find every way that I could to fight them until they did leave, and I would encourage you to do the same."

The local men nodded and grunted their affirmation. They didn't know this Colonel Davie, but they were beginning to like him.

The Colonel continued, "For those who intend to make a stand with us, my officers will place you in defensive positions immediately. I want this south road covered from both sides from this point to at least one hundred yards to the south. There will be a small troop of cavalry in reserve. We will not be lining up and blazing away at lines of Redcoats like a regular army. This is a good old-fashioned ambush, boys. Find you some good cover. I want men behind these stone walls, behind the brick walls under this courthouse, behind trees, foundation stones, buildings … anything that will stop lead. I want you to pick your targets carefully and I want you to kill the enemy. Inflict as much death upon them as you possibly can. Do you understand?"

"Yes, sir!" the men responded in unison.

"Very well, then. Officers, take charge of your men. I want everyone positioned and prepared in fifteen minutes. Lieutenant Drake will command the forward group to the south. Boys, when you hear his men shooting, you be ready to fire. Now get to it!"

John and Daniel intentionally sought out other local men. They quickly located Ephraim Farr and John Skillington.

"Boys, I want you to stick close to me," Skillington ordered.

"Yes, sir. Glad to," responded John.

A handful of other local men joined them. They all grabbed the reins of their horses and waited for someone to tell them what to do. Within minutes a cavalry officer took charge of the small group and positioned them along the right side of the road. There was a short stacked-stone wall that led up to one of the cabins right at the edge of town. After they tied their horses in cover about twenty yards deep in the woods, the officer positioned them roughly five feet apart in a defensive line along the wall. It was the perfect height for concealing a shooter. Each man checked his rifle and powder and began to prepare for action.

Once they were in place, the officer got their attention. "Boys, I'm Ensign Michael Davis. I'll be right here with you through the whole fight. I want you to hold your fire until I give you the order. Shoot anything in a uniform. These should all be regulars coming at us, no militia. If you can tell the difference between officers and enlisted, aim for the officers and sergeants first. All right?"

The men nodded their understanding, and then turned toward the road. John's mind was spinning. Not even a half-hour ago he and Daniel were eating beans and cornbread at the tavern. Now here they were, about to go toe to toe with Cornwallis and the Redcoats!

John looked to his left. Daniel Pippin was busy laying out cartridges for his smooth bore rifle along the top of the wall. His hands were shaking violently. The boy was terrified. John looked to his right. John Skillington, his future father-in-law, was beside him. He was actually sitting down and leaning back against the wall with his eyes closed. John was amused, thinking that he was trying to catch a nap. How could he be so relaxed? But then John saw his lips moving. The man was praying. On the other side of Mr. Skillington was Ephraim Farr. He leaned comfortably on his elbows on top of the wall, calmly puffing a clay pipe and squinting as he peered southward down the road.

They waited. And they waited some more. For over an hour they waited. Soon the adrenaline of fear gave way to the wandering minds of boredom. John could see that most of the men were no longer watching the road. Many sat and relaxed. Some slept. Others drank water and munched on food from their haversacks. John was actually beginning to wonder if someone had made a mistake.

He thought, "Maybe the Redcoats aren't coming after all!"

His notion of a grand military miscalculation still occupied his mind when Ensign David hissed, "Here they come, boys!"

John heard the thunder of horses on the road. It sounded like dozens of them. Maybe even hundreds. They were incredibly loud. Like the other men lining the road and the area around the courthouse, John took cover and made as low a profile as he possibly could. The thunder of cavalry grew louder and louder.

Suddenly the boom of rifles and muskets unleashed down the road. There were dozens of shots. The forward group had engaged, but the thunderous horde drove right through their hail of lead. John's heart leapt into his throat when he saw the riders approaching his hiding spot. They sported emerald green and red coats. On their heads were black helmets with plumes of feathers. The brass of their hardware and gear glistened in the sun.

"That's the British Legion!" John exclaimed.

"The who?" hissed Daniel Pippin.

"The British Legion! The ones me and my brothers fought down in the Waxhaws! Tories from up north!"

Ensign Davis commanded sternly, "Boys, make ready!"

The clicks of hammers cocking echoed up and down the wall.

"Get a good aim, now! Remember, they're moving at you and to the left. Aim to your left, just ahead of them."

John stared down the barrel of his father's Fowler rifle and took aim at one of the Legionnaires. He was captivated by the strange motion of the feathers bouncing on the man's leather helmet. He could see his face clearly. He could see that the man had red hair.

The attackers were less than fifty yards out when the officers lining the crossroads cried out, almost in unison, "Fire!"

John touched off the trigger on his rifle. Almost a hundred other shots unleashed at the same time, throwing a deadly cloud of lead into the dragoons. Men and horses fell, tumbling and writhing on the road. Even through the cloud of smoke John could see that his shot had found its mark. The red-haired man tumbled backwards off his horse.

John quickly dropped down behind the cover of the wall and began to reload his weapon. He poured the powder of a cartridge down the barrel, stuffed the paper tube and ball into the end of the barrel, and quickly tamped them down with his ramrod. Random, isolated shots rang out throughout the village as defenders accomplished their reloading. John replaced his ramrod as he rose and then aimed over the wall, prepared to fire again. But there was no one to shoot at. The dragoons had retreated. They left about a dozen dead or wounded men lying in the dusty road and almost as many horses.

The ensign barked at his men behind the wall, "Is everyone all right?"

"I don't think they even got off a shot!" exclaimed Daniel Pippin.

"No, I don't think so either. But they'll be back. We surprised them this time, but it'll be different on the next charge. Mark my words. They'll come in shooting and they may have infantry in support. You men need to do a quicker job of reloading. You'll have many more targets when they come in again."

John felt a sudden thirst. The salty beans and mid-afternoon heat had left him parched. He grabbed his gourd canteen, popped the large cork, and took a huge drink. He could taste the sweetness of the beeswax lining of the gourd. It tasted good. The cool water relieved his dry throat. He poured some of the water over his head to cool off.

Daniel asked, "Can I have a little swig, Johnny?"

John grinned, popped the cork back in, and tossed the gourd to his pal. Daniel took a big drink as well.

"Man, that's good, Johnny. Tastes like spring water with a little squirt of honey."

The voice of the ensign interrupted their water break, "They're coming back, boys! Make ready!"

Again they heard the thunder of charging horses. It sounded like even more riders this time.

Rifle barrels bristled over every wall, around every corner, and from behind every tree that John could see. It was a grand horseshoe-shaped barricade of deadly iron, all aiming at the same point to the south.

The ensign encouraged the men, "This time we're going to shoot a little sooner, gentlemen. I want to give you some extra time to reload. So aim tight and make that first shot count. You should have plenty of time to reload before they're on us."

The attacking force was roughly one hundred yards from the courthouse. Again the forward elements opened fire.

"Take aim, boys! Make every shot count!" barked the ensign. Seconds later he screamed, "Fire!"

Again a hail of lead unleashed on the dragoons. But this time they kept coming. Men reloaded feverishly. John didn't bother to duck down this time. He quickly ripped open the powder end of a cartridge and poured the powder into the muzzle of his gun. He tore the projectile from the paper wrapping and dropped it directly into the barrel. Then just like he did on that deadly night in the Waxhaws, he slammed the stock of the rifle onto the ground to seat the ball on the charge and threw his rifle to his shoulder. He fired again. This time he couldn't tell if either of his shots found a target.

The dragoons made it further into the heart of town on their second charge, but once again the attack was broken and they turned and fled in retreat. This time a tremendous cheer erupted from the mouths of the Patriots. Men stood, waved their hats, and screamed, "Huzzah! Huzzah! Huzzah!"

Colonel Davie's voice shattered the celebration. He literally screamed from his vantage point at the courthouse, "Get back in your positions, men! Reload! That's just their cavalry advance. They will be back again, and in force. Prepare to fire and make ready your retreat!"

His words seemed almost prophetic as once again the thunder of a third cavalry charge echoed up the road. Men tore into cartridges, spitting the foul powder and paper from their mouths, and pouring the explosive loads into their barrels. Ramrods pounded up and down.

The ensign yelled at his men along the wall, "This is it, boys. There will, without doubt, be infantry supporting these dragoons. I expect each of you to fire two shots and then retreat. You Mecklenburg boys hit the woods, get to your horses, and ride fast. You know this area well, so you should know where to go. You'll be just fine. The British will stop and secure their gains as soon as they take the town, so you should have some time to get clear. It's been an honor serving with all of you. You have fought well. Now let's give it to them one more time."

The riders came into view. There seemed to be twice as many of them as there were on the first and second attacks.

"Good God! How many more of them can there be?" John wondered.

"Make ready, boys!" shouted the ensign.

The cavalry drove forward. The men leaned low over the necks of their horses. Some waved swords. Others held pistols. It was clear that they had no intention of stopping this time. They were one hundred yards down the road.

"Take aim! Make it count!" Ensign Davis paused momentarily. "Fire!"

A billowing white cloud of smoke exhaled from their rifles. John could hear lead striking meat downrange. He heard the screams of men and horses, yet still they came. He reloaded his weapon as fast as he could, but they were coming so fast!

The dragoons were almost upon them. Three of the riders turned in the direction of the Mecklenburg detachment, obviously intending to jump the stone wall. John couldn't see anything but the chest of one of the horses. It filled his entire field of view … that's how close the horse was. He squeezed the trigger without even taking aim.

The rifle ball struck the beautiful animal at the base of its neck. John watched, mesmerized, as the animal folded and fell, almost like a bird that was shot from the sky. Its legs simply stopped moving, yet the powerful forward momentum of its speed and mass carried the wounded animal forward. The horse slammed chest-first into the stone wall right in front of John. He had almost no time to move. The top row of rocks on the wall shifted subtly toward him. He attempted to duck to his left, but he couldn't drop fast enough. The horse's head whiplashed over the top of the wall. John felt the horse's teeth slam into the left side of his head, just behind his eye. He dropped to his knees behind the wall. Blood ran down his face, quickly filling the eye. He could hear the horse still thrashing against the stones.

John barely glimpsed the Legionnaire as he flew over him, propelled over the wall at roughly the same speed he was traveling when the horse impacted with the stones. The man landed shoulder first with a tremendous grunt fifteen feet beyond the wall and then rolled nimbly to his feet. John held his hand to the left side of his face, trying to stem the flow of the blood. He couldn't see his rifle ... not that it mattered. It was no longer loaded. He looked at the Legionnaire in horror as the man pulled his pistol and aimed it directly at him.

John prayed, "God help me!"

Suddenly an object flew into view from John's left. A huge tomahawk tumbled end over end, hurled in the direction of the enemy soldier. The tomahawk struck with a gigantic thud, slicing into the man's neck just above his collarbone. It severed his jugular artery, throwing a fountain of bright red blood high into the air and soaking the ground in front of him.

Reflex caused the man to squeeze the trigger on his pistol. John heard the bullet scream over his head. It struck the skull of the wounded horse with a thud, exploding its head like a melon. The animal lurched forward one last time against the stone wall.

John could barely see out of his bloody eye, but he heard the sound of grinding stones. Something heavy and hard struck him in the back of the head. And then there was darkness.

17

OCCUPATION

John had the strangest dreams. He dreamt of lying across the back of a horse. He dreamt of a crackling fire and blood and screaming men. And he dreamt of Mary. He saw her smiling face and heard her soothing voice. He dreamt of anger and pain and darkness. Then somehow he fought his way through a fog of unconsciousness and emerged into the waking world.

He was lying on his left side on a soft bed in a dark room. A fire burned brightly in a fireplace. He heard a woman singing somewhere nearby and the soft clinking of silverware.

Then a voice exclaimed, "Papa, he's awake!"

Instantly Mary was hovering over him, her face just inches above his. Her eyes filled with joyous tears.

She whispered excitedly, "There you are! There's my Johnny!"

John tried to move his head to look around the room. He desperately wanted to discern where he was. His neck locked in sharp pain, refusing to move left or right. His head throbbed with a horrific, pounding ache. He reached back with his right hand and felt a bulbous bandage across the back of his head.

"What … what happened?" he stammered.

John Skillington's smiling face came into view.

He explained, "You took quite a lick in the back of the head, John. That horse you shot knocked off a big chunk of the rock wall and it landed right on you. You're lucky you've got a thick Hamilton skull."

"I didn't get shot, then?"

"No, son."

"But I saw that soldier fire his pistol and … no … wait! I saw a tomahawk split his neck wide open! Was that you?"

John Skillington nodded modestly.

"That was one fine throw, Mr. Skillington."

"Well, it was enough to make his shot go high. But the bullet blew that horses' head wide open. It kicked a big death lurch and pressed against the wall. That's what knocked the big rocks off on your head."

"Then how did I get here?"

"Ephraim and I pulled you out of there. We dragged you to your horse and threw you across the saddle and then hit the woods. We headed due west for a mile or so then cut north and east and made our way back here. We ran a big, wide circle around Charlotte town. You're at our cabin. No one followed us. You're safe here."

Mary interrupted, "Oh, Johnny, we were so worried! You bled so much! You had the strangest wound beside your eye. It looked like someone bit you!"

John chuckled, "It was that horse's teeth. His blamed head whipped over that wall and his teeth sliced me open."

"Must've been one bucktoothed horse," quipped Mr. Skillington.

Mary ignored him and continued, "Johnny, you have a huge gash right at the top of your neck from the rock that hit you. You lost so much blood, and then the knot on your head got so big. And you've been asleep for so long!"

"How long?"

"Two days," stated Mary's father, matter-of-factly.

"Two days?" John exclaimed, almost shouting. A sharp pain shot through his neck, causing him to wince.

"You came out of it a couple of times, but not for long. Mary's been trickling water into your mouth with a spoon. You swallowed them on your own just fine, so we weren't too worried. Your body just needed the rest, so it could heal itself. But you haven't had any fever or anything like that. You'll be all right with a little more quiet and rest," encouraged Mr. Skillington.

John reached for Mary's hand. She smiled tenderly.

"So Mary's been takin' care of me, huh?"

"She's been hovering over you like an old mother hen. It's a wonder you could sleep at all, the way she's been checking you for fever and fluffing pillows, covering you and uncovering you. She's checked you every five minutes just to make sure you're still breathing! You'd think she's partial to you, or something." Mr. Skillington winked at John.

John smiled and squeezed Mary's soft hand.

"What about Daniel Pippin? Is he all right?"

"Daniel's fine," reassured Mary's father. "He lit out at the same time we did. He stopped by yesterday to check on you."

"Have ya'll heard anythin' from my brother or my mama?"

"William's fine, and so is your mother. She's been here to check on you at least once, usually twice every day. Ephraim made it back home after the skirmish with no trouble. I've talked to him twice. I've checked on your place, too. The farm's fine. William and Hugh are milking the cows and taking care of the chores in the morning and afternoon."

"What about the Redcoats? Are they gone?"

John Skillington shook his head. "No, John. It looks like they're planning to stay for a while. Cornwallis has set up his headquarters in Colonel Polk's house in town. His officers have pretty much taken over every other house and building for their quarters. His army is camped just south of town along the road. Cornwallis has started issuing proclamations and acting all governmental, lording over the local folk."

"Proclamations? What do you mean?"

"Well, the day after he took the town he issued a decree to all of the folk of Charlotte and Mecklenburg that they were to give up all of their firearms and stay peacefully in their homes." Skillington sneered, "He said that we are all 'now under the protection of the King's army.'"

John laughed out loud, sending another wave of pain down the back of his neck and head.

"He must not understand where he's set up house," commented John. "Good luck gettin' these roughnecks to lay down their arms. How did that proclamation thing work out for him?"

"Well, they say he was spitting fire when only two men showed up to give up their guns."

John chuckled again.

Skillington continued, "So now he's after goods and provisions. They're out peoples goods and supplies in and around Charlotte town. They have over two thousand soldiers to feed. They've taken almost 30,000 pounds of flour and grain from Col. Polk's mill in these first two days. Word has it they're slaughtering a hundred head of cattle a day. Cornwallis is promising British money for all the goods, but outside of town nobody's giving up anything. Most of the local farmers have taken to hiding their food and supplies ... even their cattle and sheep ... deep in the woods. I even heard of one fellow who burned his full barn to keep the British from getting his grain!"

"Lord, Almighty!" exclaimed John. His face darkened. "The Colonel had all of our corn for grindin'. We was expectin' meal and flour from him for winter."

"Well, it's gone now, son. I'm sorry."

John's face reddened with anger. "What about the militia? Is there any resistance to all of this?"

"Oh, there's plenty of that, to be sure!" exclaimed Skillington. "Farmers and militiamen are bushwhacking the Redcoats at every turn. Dozens of them have been killed, and lots more wounded. The local boys hide in the trees and along the roads, shoot up the wagons and troops, and then disappear into the woods. I may have been out on a few trips myself." He smiled at John. "Cornwallis is mighty frustrated, indeed."

"Well, that's what I need to be doin', then. I gotta get into this fight."

"You'll do no such thing, Johnny Hamilton," scolded Mary. "You've been asleep for two whole days. Your neck is still oozing blood. You're white as a ghost. It's obvious that your head hurts mighty bad. There's sickness in your eyes. You're in no shape to go anywhere. You have to rest and take care of yourself. Cornwallis and the war will still be here when you're well enough to get about."

Mr. Skillington chimed in, "She's right, son. You're in no condition to leave this bed, much less ride, shoot, or fight. You just rest easy and let us take care of you for a couple of days, and *then* we'll talk about fighting the British."

"I reckon you're right. My head and neck do hurt somethin' fierce. But I just can't stand to think about layin' up whilst other men are doin' the fightin' for me."

"You'll know when it's the right time to fight, John … and when you're able to do it. Right now you need to get some food in you and get your strength back."

"I am powerful hungry, now that you mention it."

"Can you sit up?"

"I think so."

"Good. Mrs. Skillington has some stew that's still warm from dinner, and plenty of cornbread. Let's get you cleaned up a bit and fed. I'll send one of my boys over to your mama's and let her know you're awake."

"Thank you, sir."

He looked at his daughter. "Mary, I want you to go outside for a bit while your mama and I help clean John up and change his clothes. Then you can come back in and get him fed."

"Yes, Papa." She looked at John. "I'll have you up and running after Redcoats in no time." She winked, turned, and headed for the cabin door.

It was very early morning. It was still pitch black, but the sun would be up soon. These last minutes right before dawn were always the worst. Men wailed and cried in the bleak darkness. Some were no longer wailing because death had finally claimed them during the night. The stench of urine, feces, rotting flesh, and death filled their chamber. It seemed like the sun might never rise ... that he might never be free of the dark, damp, putrid hold of this prison ship.

James Hamilton lived for the daylight. It meant that he could leave the death chamber below decks. He could take his threadbare blanket and hammock upstairs and rest in the sunshine. And there would be water. He was so thirsty! The men of the ship suffered incessantly from a never-ending, burning thirst, aggravated by the brackish water that the Redcoats pumped into the tubs on the open deck.

James prayed silently in the darkness that the daylight might bring some food as well. How he longed for just one boiled potato or a strip of his smoked beef from home. Anything cooked properly and free of insects and vermin would satisfy. There hadn't been anything significant for the prisoners to eat for the past three days. Their last semblance of a meal was a small bowl of maggot-infested, half-cooked rice mixed with rancid pork and covered with a slice of mold-covered bread.

James gave his entire ration to Henry Pippin that day. Joel Moffat did, as well. The poor lad was so very sick. Henry didn't want to eat the disgusting food, but James and Joel made him swallow it down. Henry was deteriorating quickly. He was so dehydrated that his eyes had sunk deep into their sockets. He had lost well over one third of his body weight. He couldn't climb the ladder topside by himself anymore. His friends had to lift him up the ladder and through the hatch in order to lay him in the rejuvenating sunshine up top. They had to get him out of the hold if there was any hope of keeping him alive. The British would not allow James and Joel to take water below decks to him.

Poor Henry suffered terribly from the bloody flucks ... dysentery. Well over half of the men on the prison ship suffered from the debilitating illness. Though they did not understand the disease or its source, it was actually caused by the fecal contamination of their water supply. And nasty, bloody, pus-filled human feces was the one thing that was in ample supply on this ship. It covered the decks and walls, despite the daily rinsing required by the British. The seawater merely served to rearrange the putrid filth.

The wretched men who suffered from the bloody diarrhea had absolutely no control over their bowels. Most of them had their friends cut the backsides out of their breeches to save them the trouble of attempting to pull them down. Those who were able dangled their buttocks over the side rail of the ship and held on to a friend for support as they emptied their bloody bowels into the water below. But most men lost the strength and will to do that after two or three days. Each sufferer finally succumbed to lying helplessly in his own excrement. Few men recovered from the flucks. Death was the only deliverance from the grip of the disease, and many longed for its coming.

As usual, James couldn't sleep at night. He savored sleeping in the pleasant air on the outside decks during the daytime. He could barely breathe through the stench of death that inhabited their chamber beneath the decks of the ship. All night long he made a game of taking partial breaths and trying to figure out ways to filter out the stinking smell from his nostrils and expel the taste that never left his tongue.

Some nights he thought that he might go mad. But it was the thoughts of home that kept him going. He tried to imagine what John and William were doing. The corn crop was in by now. William planted turnips and cabbage some weeks ago. Nights were starting to become crisp and cool in the Piedmont. It was prime season for hunting rabbits and squirrels.

Ahh ... roasted rabbit! James' mouth began to water. He could taste the blackened meat, the salt, and the zesty black pepper. He thought of carrots and onions, apple cider and hot tea, hot oats and sorghum. His stomach knotted up into a tiny ball and sent a shudder of pain through his abdomen.

"Stop it, Hamilton!" he thought. "Stop torturing yourself!"

James rolled over onto his empty belly and removed his writing utensil from a crack between the planks. It was a small nail. With it he scratched another mark on the rough wall of his floating prison, just above the floor. Since his arrival on the *HMS Pack Horse* he had kept a careful count of his days in captivity. He wasn't sure if knowing the days and keeping a calendar made his plight better or worse. But still, he didn't want to lose track of time altogether. Somehow he had to keep a connection to what was going on in the outside world.

Joel Moffat's voice whispered in the dark, "I hear you a scratchin' over there. I thought you might be a mouse. Was figgerin' on eatin' ya." He chuckled lightly.

"You could try, but I doubt that I would taste very good. You might want to fatten me up on some corn and taters first," quipped James. "Besides, no mouse in his right mind would be on this ship."

Joel giggled in response. It was amazing, really, that they could find levity in their situation. But their humor was sometimes the only thing that kept them from going crazy.

"You're still keepin' your calendar over there, I reckon."

"Yep. Another scratch on the wall. Just over five weeks now for me."

"Six for me, you lucky turd," joked Joel.

"I still can't believe I wound up on the same ship as you boys," mused James.

"Just the Good Lord lookin' out for a fine little Presbyterian boy, I reckon. Or maybe He knew that we would be a needin' you, Jamie boy."

"I s'pect He was lookin' out for all of us," James pondered deeply.

"No disrespect, Jamie, but it kinda feels like the Almighty has done gone and forgot us boys."

James didn't respond. He was afraid to comment, because he was beginning to feel the same way that Joel was. Where was God in all of this? And how could He allow good men to suffer so needlessly in this hellish place? He just lay on his aching belly on the hard floor and tried to make his mind go somewhere else.

Joel's voice interrupted the darkness again, "Reckon what day it is now, Jamie?"

"I'm pretty sure it's September 30. Saturday, if I have my marks right and haven't lost count somewhere along the way."

"Folks back home is prob'ly livin' high on the hog right now. Corn's in. Good huntin' and fishin'. I s'pect there's a picnic or two planned for today," Joel mused.

"I'd venture there's probably more drinkin' and fightin' bein' planned in Mecklenburg County today than anythin' else," corrected James.

"Yep ... that, too." He paused. "Sounds fun, don't it?"

"Kinda does, though my mama would whup my arse if I even tasted a drop of rum."

"No need to worry. She ain't got much to whup on, anyways. You look like you traded legs with a jaybird and got cheated out of your arse."

They both howled with laughter and were instantly greeted with a growling chorus of, "Shut up!" and "Quiet!"

"Aw, get stuffed!" retorted James.

"Yeah ... and which one of you farted?" yelled Joel.

Men all over their bay burst out in laughter. It took James and Joel a few moments to compose themselves. They struggled between outright laughter and a controlled giggle for the longest time. Laughing felt good, despite the pain in their bellies and the darkness in their hearts. Finally, they were able to calm and quiet themselves.

"Joel, have you checked on Henry, lately? I haven't heard anything from the other side of you for a while now. He sure is restin' easy tonight. He cried and carried on so much the past couple of nights. I'm glad he could finally get some sleep."

There was a moment of silence, followed by a deep breath and a long exhale from Joel.

"Jamie, Henry's resting, sure enough. He stopped breathin' about an hour after we laid down. You was actually sleepin' right then so I didn't want to bother ya'. Wouldn't have mattered, anyways. But our dear friend Henry Pippin has gone to meet his Maker."

Just in that moment the screeching metal of the rusty gate sounded above their heads as the guards above threw open the cover to the ship's hold.

A thick Irish voice called down into the hole, "All right you dirty, thievin' rebel scum! It's mornin' time. Another day in me very own paradise. Time to turn out your dead!"

John recuperated nicely over the next couple few days under the watchful eyes and capable hands of Mary Skillington. His wounds were clean and healing nicely. The swelling on the back of his head went down dramatically after he began to sit up and move around. His headache subsided to a dull throb, mostly when he exerted himself. And he could almost swear that he had gained at least five pounds. Mary was force-feeding him most enthusiastically.

The third day after his "awakening" was October 1. It was Sunday, and John was determined to go to church and see his family and friends. Mr. Skillington agreed that it was time for him to get out of the house, and church was certainly the safest place to go.

The turnout for services was huge. The Poplar Tent Church was filled to overflowing. There were people that John had never seen at the meeting before, many who weren't even Presbyterians. The people of Mecklenburg, it seemed, were looking to faith and to God for answers in this time of great crisis and oppression.

John enjoyed the morning immensely and was rejuvenated by the gathering and the worship. His mother invited the Skillingtons to the Farr home after church for dinner and fellowship. Both families enjoyed a beautiful afternoon and a hearty meal.

After dinner the men sat together in the shade of the trees beside the cabin, smoking their pipes and talking about life, the war, and Cornwallis' occupation.

"They say that Cornwallis is about to lose his mind and his temper over this resistance," commented Ephraim Farr. "I think he expected a warmer welcome from the local folk."

"Somebody gave him some bad information, I reckon," stated John Hamilton.

Ephraim chuckled, "Did you boys hear about little Susannah Barnett?"

"No," both Johns answered.

"Well, the Redcoats went to the Barnett house and commenced to taking whatever they pleased. One of them put a bridle on one of John's best horses and was about to take it when little Susannah walked right up and snatched it off the horse's head! And then one of them brought up a crock of milk from the cellar, intending to load it up and take it with him, and she up and knocked it over and poured out all the milk!" Ephraim howled with laughter, and the other men joined him.

"They told that little girl they was going to kill her and cut her to pieces, and she told 'em, 'Go ahead, if you dare. But you'll be shot at from every bush in the county!' Can you imagine that? That skinny little girl! Anyhow, them boys hopped in their wagons and took their foraging someplace else!"

More laughter ensued.

As the laughter waned John Skillington added, "That is funny, to be sure. But I know for a fact that Cornwallis has turned vengeful on men of a Patriot persuasion." His face and voice darkened. "He's taken to torching homes and businesses. He burned Avery's law office to the ground yesterday."

"Really?" asked John in disbelief.

"Yep. He's rooting out what he considers the worst of the lot when it comes to the rebellion against King George. He's looking for signers of the Mecklenburg Resolves, state assembly members, public officials, families with soldiers off in the Continental Army, and the like. The Redcoats will use any excuse to torch a building."

Ephraim added, "He's paying a high price, though. Captain Thompson told me that the Mecklenburg boys have killed over forty Redcoats and Tories since Cornwallis took Charlotte town, and that doesn't even count the ones who died in the original attack. And the more men our resistance kills, the more guns are showing up in the woods and along the roads. They're not even organized attacks, anymore. Boys are just going out and shooting British every day like it's as ordinary as milking cows or feeding chickens! It's getting to where the Redcoats won't even leave town unless they're moving in force."

"I gotta get up off my hind parts and get in this fight!" exclaimed John.

"Like I've told you before, you'll be at it soon enough. You just need to rest easy and take advantage of my hospitality," encouraged Mr. Skillington.

"Well I've noticed that little Mary Skillington sure seems hospitable to our Johnny Hamilton, doesn't she?" Ephraim teased.

John grinned sheepishly and was saved having to comment further when Mrs. Skillington came walking from the Farr cabin.

"John, dear, it's time to be heading home, don't you think? Cows will need milking soon."

"Yes, my love, it is about that time." He extended his hand to his host, "Ephraim, we are grateful for your hospitality. We have truly enjoyed this afternoon of rest. Maybe we can treat you folks next Sunday."

"That sounds good to me, John. We'll plan on it."

John Hamilton spoke up, "Mr. Skillington, I would sure like to take a look at my place before headin' back to your cabin. William and Hugh will be goin' over to milk our cows here in a bit. Would you be all right with the notion of Mary ridin' with me and payin' the place a visit? We won't be long, I promise."

John Skillington pondered for a moment. "I reckon it'll be all right, John. Just make sure you boys are all armed, and don't take any chances. Cut cross-country and stay off the road."

"Yes, sir. I was thinkin' exactly the same thing."

"And make sure you're both back well before dark. If I have to come looking for you you're liable to get another knot on your skull."

"Yes, sir." John smiled.

A few minutes later three horses were headed east through the thick woods to make the quarter-mile journey to the Hamilton farm. William and Hugh Hamilton had an odd assortment of empty jars and jugs tied across the necks of their horses for carrying Sylvia and Barthenia's rich milk back to the Farr cabin. Mary rode behind John, her arms locked tightly around his waist. It was a perfect afternoon for a ride. The air was cool and pleasant. And John was so excited to be able to visit his home.

William, who was leading the small column, brought his horse to a rather sudden stop.

"Do you smell that?" he asked.

John took a deep breath. He smelled smoke.

"Smells like a campfire," John remarked.

Hugh commented, "Odd place for a campfire. Smells mighty strong to me. I hope the woods ain't on fire."

John rose up in his stirrups and looked around. He didn't see anything suspicious.

"Let's keep our guns handy, just in case," he cautioned.

The boys all took out their rifles and laid them across their laps, and then they were quickly back on their way. The smell of smoke grew progressively stronger the further they journeyed into the woods.

"Somethin' ain't right, Johnny," William stated urgently. "I think I see black smoke up ahead."

A sudden fear gripped John. The smell of fire grew more intense the closer they got to their home.

"The cabin!" John exclaimed. He screamed at his horse, "Hyah!" He dug his feet into her sides and galloped off toward the cabin as quickly as the mare would run.

John's heart almost ripped in two at the sight that awaited him when he emerged from the trees. Their beloved cabin and barn, built by their father's own hands, were engulfed in flames. He ripped himself from Mary's grasp and tumbled off of his horse before it even stopped moving. He ran to the barn and tried to see if there were any livestock inside. The milk cows were gone. The horses were gone. All of their goats and chickens were gone. Even William's beautiful garden was emptied of its vegetables and the plants were torn from the ground.

John fell to his knees and wept. Mary approached him cautiously from behind and placed her hand lightly on his shoulder. He reached up and took hold of it. William and Hugh walked up beside him, as well.

John looked up at William, his eyes sunken and forlorn. "Oh, William! They took everything! All the livestock, the horses, the wagon, everything!"

"No, they didn't take everythin', Johnny. I hid most of our stock way out in the woods two days ago. The wagon, too. The Redcoats have been takin' every wagon they see. I was skeered somethin' like this might happen. The stock's a couple hundred yards north of here in that little clearin' along Coddle Creek. I did leave Sylvia and Barthenia here in the barn, cause that's where they've always been used to stayin'. And I left all the chickens here in the pen, too. I reckon the British got 'em all."

John stood and grabbed his brother in a huge embrace.

"I'm proud of you, little brother. You took care of everythin' whilst I was down, didn't you?"

WIlliam just smiled and nodded. Then he looked at the house. "It's ain't nothin' but logs, Johnny. We can build us a new house and barn as soon as James gets back home."

John smiled back. "We surely will. I promise you that."

Hugh's shrill voice interrupted their tender brotherly moment, "What's that?" He was pointing at three fence posts on the far side of the barn. There was something strange sitting on top of each post. The objects were round and had black feathers. They walked closer to try and see what they were.

Then John realized what he was looking at. There were three British Legion helmets stretched open and perched on the fence posts. It was the three helmets that they had kept as trophies from the Waxhaws ... the leather helmets of the men they killed at the McClelland house. They also saw a piece of paper nailed to the center post beneath the middle helmet. John ran over and snatched the paper from the post. Mary appeared over his shoulder to read what it said. She gasped, covering her mouth with her hand.

William exclaimed, "What does it say, John?"

John trembled as he read it out loud, *"REWARD. Ten Guineas Gold for the Capture or Bodies of the Traitors and Outlaws James Hamilton & William Hamilton & John Hamilton. Wanted for the Murder of His Majesty's Brave and Faithful Soldiers. By Order of His Excellency General Lord Cornwallis."*

18

INSURRECTION

"How did they find out what we done?" wailed William. John replied, "Word was already out not too long after we got home, brother. I'm not sure how, but people found out about what happened at the McClelland place. There's a couple of Tories lurkin' hereabouts. I reckon one of them passed the word along to the Redcoats. Then when they came here and searched the cabin and found these Legion helmets, they had all the convincin' they needed."

"What does it mean?" asked Mary.

"Nothin' really, I don't think. They went and put a price on our heads ... a lot of good that'll do 'em. I don't know of anybody around here who's likely to turn us in. We'll just lay low and fight the Redcoats when we can. We can always take to the woods if needs be."

"We need to tell Papa about this," stated Mary.

"Ephraim, too," replied John, nodding. "Especially since he's harboring a stone cold killer fugitive under his roof."

John smiled at his brother. William looked like he was about to cry.

John tried to reassure him, "I'm tellin' ya, William, this ain't nothin' to be frettin' over. Nobody's comin' after you, I promise."

William didn't appear to believe him.

"Let's just go," said John. "We've been standin' around here too long, already. We're lucky the Redcoats didn't leave a spy behind to keep watch."

The little group mounted their horses quickly and headed back into the trees. They were about halfway back to the Farr home when William finally spoke.

"I reckon since the British took Sylvia and Barthenia, that means I don't have to milk cows no more, right?"

"That's right," confirmed John. "Not our cows, anyway. The poor girls are probably headed for the slaughter right now. Stupid Redcoats are gonna waste two fine milk cows by roastin' 'em on a spit."

"Yeah. But the no more milkin' part is good … I hate milkin' stupid cows," remarked William.

The British declared war on the clan Hamilton, so John elected to declare war right back on them. The day after the British burned his home he made contact with Captain James Thompson of the Mecklenburg militia. He made his intentions clear and stated his desire to join the growing guerilla force that was so ably thwarting the efforts of Cornwallis. The captain welcomed him and added John to the contact list for future action. John Skillington requested that he be added to the list, as well. Now all they had to do was wait for a call-up. Captain Thompson informed them that they were free to harass the British as they saw fit, but they did so at their own risk.

The first contact did not take long. The following morning John was doing some light work in the Skillington garden with Mary and her mother when a young barefoot boy in a straw hat rode in on a mule. The boy, no more than eight or nine years of age, rode his animal right up to them, stopping at the garden fence.

"Mister, are you John Skillington or John Hamilton? I'm lookin' for both of 'em."

"I'm John Hamilton. Mr. Skillington is out in the fields right now. What can I do for you?"

"Captain Thomas sent me out to spread the word to the militia ... the British are out of Charlotte town. It's a powerful lot of them."

"How many and where?"

"Between four and five hundred men and some forty or fifty wagons. They pulled out of Beattie's Ford Road about an hour ago headed north. It looks like they're movin' on the McIntyre place. The Captain already has a bunch of men headin' out to bushwhack 'em at the farm. He wants militia to set up along the road back to Charlotte so's they can light 'em up as they're a headin' back."

John made his way to the garden gate. "How long have we got?"

"Don't rightly know, Mr. Hamilton. But you likely need to get on out there as quick as you can. The captain wants lots of guns on that road."

"All right, boy. Thanks for the message. I'll tell Mr. Skillington. You head on out to the next farm."

"Yes, sir. Good huntin'!" The boy waved and trotted away on his mule.

John turned to Mary. "Can you run out to the west field and tell your Papa what's goin' on? I'm headin' out right now. Tell him to meet me on this side of the north road where it crosses Torrence Creek. We'll try to slow 'em down on that big hill. He'll know the spot."

"I'll tell him. Be safe out there, Johnny." She moved swiftly toward him, rose up on her toes and kissed him on the cheek, and then took off running toward the field.

It took less than five minutes for John to fetch his rifle, bags, and powder horn and then mount his horse. It would take almost an hour for him to make the trip cross-country to the ambush spot. He moved swiftly.

A little less than an hour later he hit the creek bank and then followed it northwest toward the road that led north out of Charlotte. As he approached the road he crossed the shallow creek. He quickly found the spot that he wanted. It was just south of the place where the slow-running creek crossed the road. The land rose rapidly, climbing almost one hundred feet in elevation over a one-quarter mile stretch. James had traveled this road many times. Lately, because of his wagon business, he had negotiated the hill with a full load. Wagon teams always had a hard time getting up that hill, especially when carrying a load or cargo. It was the perfect place for an ambush.

He tied his mare about a hundred yards deep in the woods and then made his way on foot to the roadbed. He found the ideal vantage point. It was halfway up the steep hill, and it gave him a commanding view of the road to the north. He would be able to see the approaching enemy more than a quarter-mile away. He settled into a perfect spot behind a fallen log and waited.

Not long after he sat down on the cool ground he heard shooting off in the distance. It sounded like a large concentration of several shots, and then it was followed by isolated single shots afterward.

John thought, "Captain Thompson has sprung his trap!" Now all John had to do was wait.

He heard movement behind him and spun around to take a look. It was John Skillington with Daniel Pippin in tow.

"You sure found me easy enough," remarked John.

"Wasn't hard. It looked like a buffalo has been running through the woods. You were easy enough to track."

"Well, I was tryin' to travel fast. Didn't have any reason to hide my tracks. Besides, I wanted you to find me."

"It's good to see you again, John. Last time I saw you, you didn't see me. You was laid up with a knot on your noggin," said Daniel.

"It's good to be back among the land of the livin', my friend." He shook hands with Daniel.

"It sounds like the fighting's already started up at McIntyre's. What's your plan here, John?" asked Mr. Skillington.

"I aim to let go on the Redcoats when they get about halfway up this hill. It's hard for wagons and horses, and even harder for men on foot. They should be huffin' and puffin' when they get to where we are on this hillside. Should be easy targets."

"Sounds good to me," agreed Skillington. "I just wish we had a few more men."

"Maybe a few more will be along. Let's all settle in on a good spot. We should be able to touch off a couple of shots before we have to light out," stated John.

Sure enough, it wasn't long before more men began to materialize out of the woods. A group of four approached the road cautiously downhill and to their right. Daniel let out a shrill whistle and waved. The four men waved back and then spread out at a comfortable distance from the road. Sporadic shooting continued to the north and continued for the next several minutes.

"Rider comin'!" hissed Daniel. "Definitely not a Redcoat."

The man was riding full speed and headed straight toward them.

"That's George Graham!" exclaimed Mr. Skillington. He jumped to his feet and yelled out, "Hey, George!"

The man yanked back on his reins and brought his horse to a sliding stop.

"George Graham! It's John Skillington! Over here!"

The man trotted his horse off of the road in their direction.

"Daniel, get his horse," Skillington commanded. "Go tie it up with ours."

"Yes, sir."

Graham jumped off of his horse and handed the reins to Daniel. He ran over to where both Johns were hiding.

"Dang, John! I'm glad to see you boys. Cap'n Thompson sent me ahead to try and round up more guns and get 'em on this road. The Redcoats will be through here soon. They done lit out southbound back to Charlotte! How many of you are up here on this hill?"

"Just three of us here, but four more are about fifty yards down the slope."

"That's good, that's good! That'll add some more lead to their step. I think there's about another twenty or so a half-mile north. I'm wore plum out from fightin' and ridin'. Reckon I'll stay here with you fellers. Either you boys got any water? I'm parched."

"I do," answered John Hamilton.

"What's your name, boy? You look familiar to me."

"I'm John Hamilton, sir. James' younger brother."

"Ahh! A member of that fee-rocious Hamilton gang, huh?" He grinned at John. "Well, any young feller with a price of gold on his head from Cornwallis is a friend of mine!" He shook John's hand.

"What happened at the McIntyre's place, George?" inquired Skillington.

"You won't believe it, I swear. I was there and saw it all with my own two eyes. I still don't think I believe it, myself! We was staked out in the trees beside McIntyre's barn, waitin' for the right time to let loose on 'em. They was raidin' the livestock and loadin' grain in their wagons ... a dang train full of wagons. Must've been fifty of 'em or more! Anyways, in the midst of all their thievin' and pillagin' one of the Redcoat boys knocked over one of McIntyre's beehives.

"Boy, did them bees unleash! Them Tories and Redcoats was screamin', swattin', and runnin' all over the place. Dogs, chickens, men ... they was a runnin' every which way. It was the funniest thing I ever did see! There was a British officer standin' on the porch of the house laughing his arse off. Well, since they was all caught up in the battle of the bees, Cap'n Thompson decided it was time to start shootin'. We each picked a target and then we lit 'em up. Cap'n Thompson dropped that Tory officer right there on the porch. He was dead when his head hit wood."

"What did the Redcoats do?" asked John.

"Well, they mounted up all military-like and formed 'em a nice straight line. The whole time they was a gittin' organized we 'uns all re-loaded. We cut loose on 'em a second time before any of them numb-skulls fired a single shot. They set loose some dogs on us so we lit out. Them dogs nearly 'bout got Edward Shipley, but he turned around and dropped the first one with a pistol shot. The rest of 'em commenced to howlin' and screamin' and then they all turned tail and run off.

"I worked my way back around to the road and watched 'em ride out. And, boy, they was haulin' arse, let me tell you! I reckon they thought there was a whole battalion after 'em or somethin'. I cut cross-country and got ahead of 'em on the road to try and find some reinforcements. A few minutes later I heard you hollerin', and now here I'm settin' behind this log."

"How far out do you think they are now?" inquired Skillngton.

"Not sure, but they can't be long. We'll have an idea when we hear that bunch up the road start to shootin'. They'll be movin' pretty fast. Wagons are runnin' in the front, infantry runnin' as fast as they can behind 'em. But that farm is eight miles out. That's a long way for men to be a runnin' on foot. They should be 'bout done for when they get here."

Moments later shots rang out up the road.

"That's the boys I was tellin' you about. Won't be long now," stated George excitedly. "Better get 'em cocked and ready."

It wasn't long before the first wagons appeared. They were moving at breakneck speed, the horses running all out and the wagons swimming side to side all over the road. They were at a hundred yards out when the men down the hill began to shoot. Their rounds struck the sides of the wagons with little effect. They were clearly shooting at the drivers.

"We ain't even gonna be able to slow 'em down, boys! They's movin' too fast," lamented George Graham.

"Oh yes we can!" exclaimed John Hamilton.

He laid his rifle across the log and sighted in carefully on the first wagon. He led his target and gently squeezed the trigger. His rifle barked smoke and fire, and his ball found its mark. The left horse on the lead wagon dropped like a rock. The animal's sudden fall jerked the head of the right side horse downward and dragged it face first into the ground. The tongue of the wagon snapped with a thunderous crack as the forward momentum of the loaded wagon carried it right over both of the doomed animals. The wagon tumbled sideways, spreading a dusty cloud of wheat all over the roadbed. The wreck completely blocked the road, and the next two wagons plowed full speed into the mass of wood, grain, and horseflesh. The other men beside John sat and stared, mesmerized by the spectacle before them.

"What are you waitin' for? Shoot!" screamed John.

His voice snatched Daniel, John Skillington, and George Mason from their collective stupor. They all opened fire with their rifles, as did the other men down the hill. The wagons were stacked up in a massive pile-up on the colonial turnpike. Wagon drivers dropped like flies as the snipers picked them off one by one. A few minutes later the infantry arrived and established a perimeter line down both sides of the road. The Patriots took cover as the Redcoats unleashed their first volley into the trees.

As soon as the line of soldiers began to reload, the Meckenburg boys took off running for their horses. Right before the second shot they heard a British officer shout, "Make ready!" They instantly took cover behind trees and listened to the second volley sail harmlessly by. They were all mounted on their horses and riding fast toward the east before the third shot was fired. They rode in silence.

Finally, when it seemed clear that they were safe from any pursuit, they pulled up in a thicket to allow both horses and men to catch their breaths.

Daniel Pippin leaned over the pommel of his saddle and looked John in the eye.

"So, Johnny, tell me ... 'xactly what kind of grudge are you holdin' against horses, anyways? What did them poor critters ever do to you? It seems like every time I see you another horse is gettin' a lead ball in the brainpan."

George looked puzzled, John grinned sheepishly, and Mr. Skillington howled with laughter.

The frustrated, decimated convoy of British wagons finally cleared their barricade and completed the trek back to Charlotte. The drivers ran the wagon teams so hard that several of the horses fell dead in the streets of the town. They were still tied to the tongues of their wagons. Dead Redcoats littered the road all over the eight-mile stretch to the McIntyre farm. Dozens more were wounded. It was a humiliating defeat, indeed.

Cornwallis' frustrations reached their breaking point. It was inexcusable that four hundred and fifty of his best soldiers had been humiliated by a gaggle of farmers and a hive full of bees. The General stood on the deck at the top of the courthouse steps and surveyed the mess in the streets before him.

He turned and declared to his officers, "This damnable place is an agreeable enough village, but it is a veritable hornet's nest of rebellion. The people of this county are more hostile to England than any other place in America."

Because of the continued harassment by guerilla forces, General Cornwallis decided to change his tactics and take the fight to the enemy. He learned that a party of rebel troops commanded by General Jethro Sumner was encamped at Alexander's Mill on a branch of the Rocky River to the northeast of Charlotte. He decided to send a corps to attack that outpost. He placed Lieutenant Colonel James Webster in command of the operation and ordered that the men of the expedition draw two days rations for the march.

Because of the intense resistance around Mecklenburg County, the general decided that it would be prudent to protect his flanks. He sent out armies to the east and the west to insure against any surprise maneuvers by the American forces. The western force was comprised of 1,100 loyalist and provincial troops under the capable command of Major Patrick Ferguson. His force deployed about thirty miles west of Charlotte in the low mountains of South Carolina. Major Ferguson established an encampment at a remote place that the locals called King's Mountain.

The Patriots of Mecklenburg County kept constant pressure on the occupying British. The terrain was very much in their favor. The roads of the county were narrow and surrounded by thick woods. The local sharpshooters continued regular attacks on the British along the roadways. Though they did not inflict serious losses upon the enemy, their constant, stinging attacks did much to hamper the foraging efforts. The British radius of influence shrunk smaller and smaller, and their area of pacification began to dwindle. The hornets of Mecklenburg County were most definitely "out of the nest." Cornwallis' army was beginning to run low on supplies. His men were getting hungry, and he was not happy.

The British occupiers established a fortified outpost at Colonel Thomas Polk's gristmill just southwest of town. It was their central supply depot and the center of operations for all of the foraging parties. The stone blockhouse of the mill provided ample storage space for the goods that the British collected and also served as an easily defendable position.

For the Mecklenburg men and the other Patriot forces operating in the area the time had come to move beyond harassment and ambushes. It was time to hit the enemy where it would hurt the most. They would attack the British supply dump.

John Hamilton learned of the plan at church on Sunday, October 8, as he walked with the Skillington family out of the tent after services. Most people greatly enjoyed the time immediately following church. It was the perfect opportunity to visit with friends and, though they would never own up to it, share in the latest community gossip. John noticed a group of eight men gathered near the wagons, huddled together tightly, engaged in some type of covert discussion. He excused himself from Mary and her family and quickly moved to investigate the conversation.

He noticed that his ambushing buddy, George Graham, was part of the huddle. Despite his questionable communicative skills, George actually looked like he was leading the conversation. John made eye contact with him, so George motioned for John to come and join the group.

"What's going on here, gents? Plotting a little treason, are we?" John teased.

"What else would you be expectin' from this bunch of rough-necks?" retorted George. He smiled and then spoke to the other men in the group, "Boys, I think you all know the infamous cutthroat outlaw Johnny Hamilton. Lord Cornwallis has a special length of rope all saved up for him."

The other men nodded and grinned at John.

George continued, "Johnny, I was just lettin' our Patriot friends here know about an upcomin' chance to cause a little trouble for our out-of-town visitors."

"You've got my attention," responded John.

"I'm sure that most of you fellers heerd that the Redcoats have commenced to operatin' out of Colonel Polk's mill. They's usin' the blockhouse to store all the goods they go 'bout confiscatin' from the goodly folk of Mecklenburg. Well, Colonel Taylor of the brand new Mounted Volunteers has a plan to attack that mill and do some damage."

"When?" asked John.

"Morra' night. He's got about a hunnert men in his outfit, but he's lookin' for a few more. But they gots to be mounted. It's gonna be a horseback fight. The colonel wants to hit the mill and hit it hard, and maybe even put an end to the Redcoats' thievin' ways."

"Where do we meet up?" asked one of the other men.

"Cap'n Thompson asked me to pass on the word that militia needs to be at the Randolph cabin on Paw Creek right at sundown. He says you need to stay off the roads, and iff'n you see any Redcoats, at all, you 'uns need to turn tail and go back home. T'aint worth givin' away all the rest of us."

"Do you need our word right now?" asked another listener.

"Naw. No need for that. If you can make it, just show up. But keep your mouths shut! Not a word to nobody! We don't need no loose lips flappin' and settin' us up to get bushwhacked our own selves. Got it?"

The men solemnly nodded their affirmation.

"Good," George responded. "I heerd that Cornwallis has called our fair county a hornet's nest. How's about we give that fat lump of butter a sting that he ain't gonna soon forget!"

The following evening John arrived at the appointed location at sunset. Roughly twenty men answered the call to join Captain James Thompson for the nighttime cavalry raid on the British supply depot. They headed out toward the south for their rendezvous with Colonel Philip Taylor and his Mounted Volunteers. The two groups met at an old Indian camp just west of Charlotte. John recognized some of the men of Taylor's detachment. They were the same fellows he fought alongside in the battle in Charlotte less than two weeks ago. The Colonel called the men together for a briefing.

He nodded to the boys from Mecklenburg County, "Gentlemen, I'm glad you've joined us. Before we discuss our plan of action for tonight's attack, I have some wonderful news to share. Two days ago, an army of over one thousand men from the high country in North Carolina and Virginia surrounded, attacked, and wiped out Ferguson's army at King's Mountain in South Carolina not thirty miles west of here."

He paused for a moment to allow the news to sink in. The men stared at him in disbelief.

"Are you sure? Why ain't we already heard about it?" inquired one of the Mecklenburg boys.

"The information has been confirmed. There were almost five hundred loyalists killed or wounded, and almost another eight hundred captured. It was an absolute, decisive victory."

"What does that mean to us, Colonel?" asked another man.

"It means, boys, that for the first time in a long time we have the Redcoats on their heels. Cornwallis is open to attack from the west. He's had intentions in the past couple of days of moving further deeper into North Carolina. We hope that this loss will help change his plans."

"So are we still going ahead with the attack tonight?" asked John.

"Absolutely! We are going to do our best to kick the enemy while he's down. Here's the situation … most of you know that the Redcoats have been using Colonel Polk's mill for all of their supply operations. They're sending out all of their foraging parties from that location and are housing all their goods in the mill house. I believe that the mill is ripe for attack. It is lightly defended. My lookouts have spotted a small detachment of about twenty Royal Welsh Fusiliers and about the same number of Tory Militia. We should be able to overwhelm the outpost with sheer force of numbers. Our objective is simple. We will attack, repatriate or destroy all possible supplies, kill the enemy, and take prisoners and horses. Questions?"

The men remained silent in the darkness.

"All right, then. We will attack in two lines from the north and west. I don't want to surround the place and get caught in our own crossfire. We will drive the enemy out of the mill and back toward Charlotte. You Mecklenburg boys will ride with my team from the west. Captain Tuttle will lead the second team from the north. Once we are in position I will signal the attack. Now, let's move. I want to take this mill within the half-hour!"

John mounted his horse and followed the other men into the darkness. He couldn't see anything in the pitch black of the woods. He just hoped that the men leading the force knew where they were going. Soon the group came to a stop in the woods. A message made its way through the ranks of the cavalry, "Spread right and left. We attack in five minutes."

"Attack what?" John thought. He couldn't see anything. No light, no fires. Not even a candle. He was beginning to wonder if he had made a mistake by volunteering for this mission.

A familiar voice emanated from the darkness behind him, "I can't see a blamed thing. What 'bout you, Johnny?" It was George Graham.

"Nope. I have no idea where we are or what's goin' on."

A volley of shots rang out from about a hundred yards in front of them and lead whizzed through the trees just over their heads.

"Well all righty, then. I reckon we's in the right spot, after all," commented George.

The voice of the cavalry colonel echoed through the trees, "Charge the blockhouse men!"

Instead of forming up as a solid force, the assault turned into more of a slow trickle as the riders struggled to make their way through the dense trees. One by one they emerged into the open meadow surrounding the mill. And as they did a hail of gunfire greeted them. One man near John was hit and tumbled off of his horse. He soon heard another scream in agony from a wound. John's heart skipped a beat when a musket round knocked his straw hat off of his head.

It seemed clear to John that there was no way for this haphazard, disoriented mounted force to dislodge the enemy from the mill house. He let off one shot from his rifle toward the door of the mill and then turned around and rode fast toward the woods behind him. Most of the other attackers did the same. In a matter of minutes he heard the colonel call for a general retreat. After that the men fled with enthusiasm.

The nighttime assault on Polk's Mill was an abysmal failure. The only redeeming outcome of the night was that part of the attacking force managed to steal fifty British horses from the nearby Polk plantation.

John broke away from the raiding party, skirted around Charlotte, and made his way back home in the darkness. He rubbed his bare head and imagined what might have happened if that stray ball had ventured three inches lower. He decided that his days as a cavalryman, especially one who operated at night, were officially over.

Though the raid on Polk's mill was ultimately a failure, the fact that the Patriot forces exhibited such boldness to even attempt such an attack served to test the already frail hold that the British enjoyed upon Mecklenburg County. Cornwallis was livid. His men were hungry and depressed. His couriers were being ambushed at every turn, making it impossible for Cornwallis and his officers to procure any useful military intelligence. Even the experienced and tested soldiers under his command were ready to return to the relative safety and peace of South Carolina.

The final blow to the British morale came in the form of a message early in the morning on October 10. Somehow one of the British couriers managed to make his way through to Charlotte. The man informed General Cornwallis of the news that Colonel Taylor had shared with his men the evening prior. The command of Major Patrick Ferguson, the protector of Cornwallis' western flank, had been wiped out by a ragtag army of North Carolina and Virginia mountain men three days prior at a place called King's Mountain. The messenger also bore the news that Major Ferguson, himself, was dead.

Cornwallis refused to believe the report. He immediately dispatched Tarleton's British Legion with instructions to reinforce and render aid to Ferguson as needed. By nightfall he received the confirmation from Tarleton that he dreaded. Ferguson was, indeed, routed. Cornwallis' left flank was exposed.

On the afternoon of Thursday, October 12, 1780, the British Army began its evacuation of Charlotte. A pouring rain and persistent harsh wind began just as the entourage of over two thousand soldiers, another two thousand Tories and civilian camp followers, and one hundred wagons made their way southward toward Camden. In their haste the force abandoned twenty wagons full of equipment that included tents, uniforms, and muskets. They also left behind dozens of dead soldiers, all buried in shallow graves in the yard of their makeshift hospital at Liberty Hall School.

In just fifteen days Cornwallis' first invasion of North Carolina ended in dismal failure. The occupation was over. Mecklenburg County was, once again, free.

19

GOOD AND BETTER NEWS

J ames thought that the raging storm would never end. For three days an enormous tempest churned somewhere in the Atlantic Ocean. It began with modest waves and torrential rain. On the second night of the storm gale winds howled and huge waves slammed against the prison ships anchored in Charleston Harbor. Their anchor chains stretched to the maximum limit. Some of them broke, releasing the ships to be tossed about in the harbor. These loose ships slammed into the other ones that managed to hold fast by their anchors in the sandy bottom of the harbor floor.

The third day brought some respite. The winds subsided and the waves calmed somewhat. The torrential rains continued. The men below decks didn't mind the rain. They gathered under every barred hatch and crack overhead that allowed the fresh rainwater to spill through. It was the cleanest water they had tasted since their arrival aboard ship. They captured the sweet, pure substance in their mouths and drank until they thought their bellies might explode.

The prisoners were basically abandoned to the mercy of the storm. No one had bothered to check on them during those three days. Perhaps the British were hoping that the storm might do them a favor and sink a few of the ships and put the rebels out of their misery. They hadn't seen a morsel of food since the day before the rains began. In the end, that was probably for the best, as well. There was universal seasickness on board all of the ships, causing almost every man to heave out the rainwater that they drank. Surely if they had consumed any food the infernal sickness would have caused every man to vomit it right back up.

No one missed the sadistic prison keepers who had been watching over the ships, anyway. It was almost a vacation for the men who managed to survive for those three days. But the storm did break, at long last. Unbeknownst to the people in America, the storm that barely brushed the coast would one day be known as the Great Hurricane of 1780. It was the costliest hurricane, in human lives, in all of recorded history. It claimed over 22,000 souls, including an entire fleet of French troops bound for America for service in the Revolution.

The last night of the storm was a strange one, indeed. It was strangely quiet on board the *War Horse*. Men actually slept. Perhaps it was the ample fresh water that they enjoyed for the past three days, or maybe the gentle rocking of the ship in the diminishing harbor waves. Most likely it was the fact that all of the men who were critically ill had finally died. But whatever the reason, it was a quiet, peaceful night.

On the morning after the storm broke the men were roused from their slumber by the grinding rust of the iron bars that covered the hatch. Sergeant Micheline Flanagan, the hated Irishman who served as the sergeant of the guards, stuck his head down in the hole.

He screamed with his horrendously thick Irish brogue, "Rise and shine you bloody rebel bastards … time to turn out your dead, if any of ya's still kickin'! Oh, Holy Father, shine your favor upon me and let these filthy creatures all be dead and drowned!"

Angry voices cursed him from below, informing him that he was more than welcome to jump overboard and drown himself.

He cackled his wicked laugh. "Ahh, there's me sweet li'ul boys. Did ya miss me, lads? Well let's get on with it then! Get those stinkin' rotten bodies up here. And bring up all your worldly possessions, if ya have any. You're all goin' for a wee li'ul ride."

Joel kicked James in the leg, "What in tarnation is he talkin' 'bout?"

"Danged if I know, Joel. Maybe they're movin' us."

"Why would they do that? Where ya reckon they'll take us?"

"I don't know, brother, but it can't be worse'n this God-forsaken ship!"

When they made it topside after helping remove the bodies from below deck, they discovered that their luxury shipboard accommodations had suffered quite a bit of damage in the storm. Repairs were needed, so the prisoners were to be transferred to the Charleston barracks.

James, Joel, and what was left of their Mecklenburg pals were headed back to dry land.

"It just doesn't look right."

That's what Mr. Skillington said to John regarding his continuing stay at the Skillington house. It was almost two months since John's injury during the battle in Charlotte. He recovered fully and was no longer in need of any special care or nursing. And it just didn't look right, socially speaking, for John to remain under the same roof with Mary. After all, they were not married and they were not kin. Sooner or later people would begin to talk. John Skillington felt bad about John's homeless predicament after the Redcoats burned his house down, but some other type of arrangement had to be made.

John understood his sentiments and concerns. In reality, he agreed. He definitely didn't want to impugn the character or damage the reputation of his beloved Mary. She hated to see John go because she enjoyed being around him every waking moment. But she understood the social and moral dilemma, as well.

So John packed his knapsack and moved out. He kissed Mary goodbye, loaded his gear on his horse, and went "hat in hand" to Ephraim Farr to see if he might be able to live in his old cave house until James came back home or until he was able to make other arrangements. Upon hearing John's plan, William elected to join his brother in their old home, as well.

Incredibly, Ephraim wasn't only agreeable to the notion, he actually helped John and William clean the place out and make it livable again. He relocated all of the food in storage back deep into the cave and made plenty of space for the boys in the front add-on. He made sure that their flue was serviceable and drawing well. He helped construct two small beds and some other simple furnishings. He even encouraged the boys' mother to provide them with all the linens they needed and a few garments of new clothing. Ephraim shared liberally of their foodstuffs and made sure the boys knew that they were welcome to take their meals at the table with the family. And he spoke differently to the boys ... with kindness, courtesy, and respect.

Perhaps it was their service in combat together, or maybe the fortitude that the boys had shown since their brother was lost at Camden. But whatever the reason, something had changed in the heart of Ephraim Farr. He acted less and less like an angry and jealous stepfather and more like a real father to William and John. The boys reciprocated in response to his kindness and in the coming weeks began to develop a deeper respect and even a form of reserved and careful love for the man who was their mother's husband.

So peace returned once again to the lives of the Hamilton brothers and to Mecklenburg County. Shortly after Cornwallis pulled out of Charlotte and crossed back into South Carolina General Gates marched his army from Hillsborough and occupied the town. He tried to act like something of a conquering hero but no one was impressed. The locals knew full well that it was the local guerilla forces and the defeat at King's Mountain that dislodged Cornwallis, not the impotent Horatio Gates. The story of his cowardly flight from the battlefield at Camden was common knowledge, as well as the fact that many Patriots in the south were calling for his removal from command.

Still, his army was a welcome sight, indeed. They still required supplies to survive, but at least his soldiers were asking for voluntary contributions and issuing vouchers in return. So the people of Charlotte and Mecklenburg County did what they could to help feed the Patriot soldiers.

With the threat of confiscation and outright theft gone, the boys elected to relocate all of their livestock to the Farr farm for safety and ease of care. They wholeheartedly joined in the work of the farm. They had no other choice, really. Their home was destroyed and the British army had already stolen and consumed their year's crop of grain. They were dependent upon the good graces of Ephraim Farr, but they were also determined to earn their keep. When not performing the everyday chores involved in running the farm, John and William joined Ephraim in his salt-mining operation. His product was still much in demand with the Continental Army.

Farm work began to dwindle dramatically as the autumn ceded its daylight and warmer air to the shorter, colder days of winter. The boys turned to hunting and tanning hides to occupy their extra time in the cooler weather. With the help of their mother they built a small, but profitable, cottage industry that produced deerskin leggings for sale and trade to the soldiers encamped near Charlotte.

In late November William shot an enormous bull elk. He and John had to cut down a couple of small saplings so that their team of horses could pull the massive animal out of the forest. The meat was delicious and abundant and a tremendous blessing to the Hamiltons and the Farrs. The hide was so expansive that it made an incredible seventeen sets of leggings.

Early December brought a radical change to military life in and around Charlotte, North Carolina. George Washington, under order of the Continental Congress, had appointed a replacement for Horatio Gates to command the Southern Army. Gates just didn't know it yet. On December 5, a stern-looking, stocky Major General by the name of Nathanael Greene, the "fighting Quaker," rode into town and relieved the shocked Horatio Gates of his command of the entire Southern Army.

Two other officers rode in with General Greene. Both were Virginians. One was the huge, hulking Brigadier General Daniel Morgan and his company of gifted marksmen known as, "Morgan's Riflemen." Morgan hated the British with a passion and had been fighting them for the past five years all the way from Canada to South Carolina.

The other officer was Lieutenant Colonel Henry Lee, better known as "Light Horse Harry." His American Legion of cavalrymen wore white leather breeches, beautiful green wool coats, and plumed leather helmets much like the enemy's British Legion. They were, without doubt, the finest dressed soldiers in the Patriot army.

Yes, things were changing around Charlotte. The attitude of the army was changing. And the direction of the war was changing. The people could sense it.

James warmed his fingers by the small fireplace in his hut. December had brought an unusually bitter chill to Charlestown. He thanked God every day that he was no longer on board the prison ship. He could only imagine how cold the men must be on board all of the other ships that dotted the harbor.

The British prison barracks, such as they were, were not really barracks at all. They were log huts constructed by the prisoners into the sides of the hills of the prison yard. The men first dug out partial holes into the faces of the hills and then lined them with the pitiful, rotten logs supplied by their captors. They built as much pitch into the rooftops as they could. There was no rock or brick or mortar to speak of, so the men formed crude bricks out of the mud. They constructed their fireplaces out of sticks and coated them with layer upon layer of mud to produce a fireproof coating. The little fireplaces worked quite well. Their roofs were comprised of mud and sod.

James and Joel shared their log hut with eight other men. Six of them were other militiamen from North and South Carolina. Two of them were Continental soldiers from Maryland. All had been captured at Camden. Though they did not know one another before becoming roommates, they quickly forged bonds of friendship and mutual survival.

This particular group of men was quite blessed, actually, in that they had very little work to do on their shelter when they arrived in the camp. Other prisoners who, for reasons unknown, were no longer present in the camp had completed most of the work. The new arrivals had only to add a roof and fireproof the flue. The final disposition of their predecessors was the subject of much conjecture and conversation.

On this particular day most of the men were outside in the sunshine of the afternoon, attempting to glean every bit of warmth and comfort they could from sun's life-giving rays. James had a bit of a chill that the sunlight could not dispel so he went back inside to stoke the fire. He sat quietly as one of the Marylanders slept soundly against the back wall.

James was enjoying the moment of peace when, right on cue, Joel Moffat burst into the room.

"Good news! Good news! Good news! Jamie boy, I done heerd us some good news!"

"What is it this time, Joel? Are the Redcoats serving us steak and eggs for Christmas?"

"Nope!" He paused stiffly. "I ain't heerd that one, Jamie. Where did you pick up on that? You reckon we'll really see beef-critter and eggs for Christmas?"

"I was kidding, Joel. They call it sarcasm."

Joel shrugged his shoulders and raised his eyebrows.

"I never heerd of that. But do you want to hear this good news, or not?"

James sniffed the air. He smelled something different ... something really good.

"What's that smell?"

"That's my good news!" he exclaimed.

The Marylander sleeping in the back of the room let loose a loud snore and then grunted.

Joel stopped talking, glanced over James' shoulder, and eyed the sleeping soldier suspiciously. He raised his finger to his lips to form the universal "shhh" signal.

He whispered excitedly, "That's my good news ... part of it, anyways. You see, I was skulkin' around the west fence ... you know, down yonder behind the buryin' trench ... just a mindin' my own business."

"What were you doin' over there? You ain't got no reason to be over there."

"Will you let me tell my story, you dumb fartleberry?"

James exhaled, "Go on."

"Like I was sayin', I was just over there by the west fence, just a surveyin' for some weak spots in the wire ... mindin' my own business, ya know ... when somebody up and throwed a pebble at me and then hissed at me out of that thicket of trees."

"Really?" James commented doubtfully. "Who was it?"

"It was a purty young thang named Louise Martin. At least she sounded purty. I never did get a good gander at her."

"What did she say?" inquired James, intrigued.

"Well, she whispered to me that she was a lady of the Patriot persuasion, and then she offered to help me get word home about us bein' here."

James' thoughts raced. Surely Joel had lost his mind. There's no way that could have happened. This couldn't possibly be true. But he had to find out more.

"What did you say to her?"

"Well, I twern't worried about nobody but me and you, so I told her my name and your name. I told her my paw's name and about your little brother, Johnny and your maw, Mrs. Farr. I told her we was from the county of Mecklenburg near Charlotte town and that folks there would know our folks. She up and recited it all right back to me. Then she promised she was headin' right back to her house and that she was goin' to write letters to our families to let 'em know where we is."

"You're lyin'! Ain't no way that happened.! You ain't talked to no girl through a fence."

"So you're gonna be like that, then?" challenged Joel. "Well, I reckon then I'll just keep all these here vittles to myself."

James' eyes grew wide as Joel took off his hat and produced a small rectangle wrapped in linen cloth and tied in a bow with a piece of dirty string. James smelled the sharp bite of hickory smoke and pork. His mouth began to water. Slobber actually drained from his lips and dribbled onto his breeches.

Joel pulled the loose end of the bow and dropped the string into his coat pocket. Then he carefully and ever-so-slowly opened the flaps of cloth to reveal two large squares of cornbread and two half-inch thick slabs of smoked middlin' meat.

"God, Almighty!" James exclaimed in a shrill whisper. "Where did you get that?"

"Well, my darlin' Louise never left the cover of the thicket. But she pushed that little bundle with a cane fishin' pole about ten foot across open ground and slipped it right under the fence wire. I snatched it right up and stuffed it under my hat."

Joel handed a strip of the smoked pork to James and grabbed the other for himself. They tore into the smoky, greasy meat like ravenous wolves. James had never tasted anything so good in all his life.

"What else did she tell you?" James asked through the thickness of the pork grease that coated his mouth and tongue.

"She told me to wait three days and then come back to the same spot mid-mornin'. She promised she'd be there and have some more food me. So my idee is to split one pone of this cornbread tomorrow, and one the day after that."

"That sounds good to me!" responded James.

Both men stared into the fire as they pondered the turn of events and savored the remnants of the tasty fat still lingering in their mouths. It seemed that their fortunes had, indeed, turned. First they got off of that God-forsaken ship. And then they discovered an angel of mercy on the other side of their prison walls.

"Why in the world did she pick you, Joel Moffat?"

"Well, that's funny, now. I asked her the exact same question. And she told me she's been visitin' that same spot every day for over a week now, and that I was the first soldier who ever came close 'nuff to talk to her."

"And you're sure she's writin' to our folks?"

"That's what she promised! She said that she would get the letter out in a wagon north in a day or two. Seems that the Patriot locals have 'em a spy and letter system all set up. They get news in from up north right regular and send out sometimes, too."

James wrapped his arm around his friend's shoulder, drawing their foreheads together. "Well, Joel, old pal, that is most definitely good news!"

Christmas was shaping up to be a joyous time for John and William. There would be little in the way of gifts, but the time among family and friends was sure to be sweet, indeed. John had his entire holiday season planned out. He would, of course, spend Christmas day at home with William, his mother, and half siblings. Christmas Eve was on Sunday. The church leaders already had plans to forego regular morning services that day and, instead, have a candlelight service at sundown. These yearly Christmas Eve services at the Poplar Tent Presbyterian Church always drew a large crowd. John looked forward to it immensely.

Since morning services were cancelled John decided to spend the entire day with Mary and her family. The Skillingtons had a long family tradition of exchanging gifts on Christmas Eve. They reassured John that he was under no obligations to provide gifts for anyone, but he still resolved to have something special for Mary and something unique to share with her family.

The household feasted throughout the day and finally settled down to exchange gifts mid-afternoon. Their exchange was simple, meaningful, and beautiful. The Skillingtons blessed their children with all handmade items. There were garments of clothing, hand-sewn dolls for the younger girls, and hand-carved soldier figurines for the lads. John was thoroughly embarrassed when they presented him with a stunning green-checkered homespun shirt. He couldn't imagine where Mrs. Skillington had found the cloth. Textiles were almost impossible to find and most local men had reverted back to using deerskin garments.

Finally, the moment came for John to share his gifts. He gave cloth sacks full of dried fruit and nuts to the children, a beautifully scrimshawed horn of gunpowder to Mr. Skillington, and a five-pound sack of salt and a tiny paper package containing ten brand new sewing needles to Mrs. Skillington.

But he saved his best for last. He reached into his grain sack and pulled out a small rectangular package covered with brown paper and a red ribbon bow. Mary opened it with trembling hands. Inside she found an exquisite silver-handled looking glass, a silver and mother-of pearl hair comb, and package of writing paper. The paper itself was so rare that it was unimaginable, and must have cost a small fortune.

Mary was beside herself with awe and joy. She jumped and ran to John, throwing her arms around his neck.

She whispered into his ear, "Oh, Johnny Hamilton! Paper! And such a beautiful silver glass and comb! Where in heaven's name did you find such unspeakable treasures?"

He looked into her eyes and smiled mischievously.

"A man's gotta have a secret or two."

The candlelight service was beautiful, indeed. Each of the participants brought their own candle from home. They lit the candles, bathing the tent in their soft glow, and they sang hymns. The people shared openly about the trials of the past year and the blessings that they enjoyed now that the British were gone. The congregation responded with hearty "Amens" and "Hallelujahs." It was a heartwarming gathering. Elder William Scott finally read the story of the Nativity from the Scriptures, the typical ending to their gathering. The church people began to gather their belongings and await the closing prayer.

The Elder spoke to the crowd, "Friends, before we dismiss in prayer and return to our homes to celebrate the birth of our Lord among our families, I have one last thing to share."

He reached into his pocket and took out a small, worn square of paper. It had a dirty string wrapped around it and the fold of the paper was sealed with a daub of yellow wax. It was a letter.

"Yesterday, I received this letter from a courier who was passing through Charlotte town on his way north with dispatches to Hillsboro. He actually had two letters. After learning that I was a minister of the Gospel, he asked if I knew the individuals to whom these letters were addressed. When I informed him that I did, indeed, know the addressees for both letters, he entrusted them to me for delivery. He stressed that these letters were confidential and that they were recently smuggled out of Charlestown."

A gasp of excitement traveled through the crowd. A general chatter broke out among the congregation. "Charlestown! Who would be sending letters from Charlestown?" An air of tension descended upon the church.

The Elder continued, "I delivered the first letter yesterday afternoon. The man to whom it was addressed is not a part of our church. Some of you probably know him ... Silas Moffat."

More excited chatter erupted. John's heart climbed into his throat. He knew full well that Silas' son, Joel Moffat, was James' best friend in the entire world. The Elder held up his hands to calm the crowd.

He spoke over the murmur of their voices, "The other letter … this letter … is addressed to one of our very own."

He turned his head to John Hamilton. John's heart throbbed in his chest. He felt light-headed. He thought he might pass out.

"John Hamilton, will you please come and claim your correspondence? And if you feel led and sense the freedom to do so, once you have read the letter, please consider sharing the news from Charlestown with our brethren."

John rose from his bench. His legs didn't want to move, but somehow he ambled methodically and deliberately to the end of the row and made his way down the aisle. Every eye was upon him. The tension was palpable.

John finally reached the platform and joined the Elder who placed the crumpled letter in his hand. He folded the letter slightly and slid the string off and then used his fingernail to break the wax seal. He looked out into the congregation and locked eyes with his mother. Tears were streaming down her cheeks. William, sitting beside her, wept also. He could almost swear that he saw a tear in Ephraim Farr's eye. It was obvious that they all assumed the letter was a source of bad news. John smiled at his mother and then handed the letter back to the Elder.

"Sir, I don't read so good. And I'm a bit too excited to even try."

The congregation laughed nervously. His mother smiled through her tears.

John continued, "I would be honored if you would just go ahead and read the letter to all the folk. Mama deserves to hear what it says, too."

"Are you sure, John?"

"Yes, sir. Please just get on with it."

"Very well."

The Elder handed his candle to John and took the letter in his hands. John held up both candles to give the elderly gentleman more illumination.

The old man cleared his throat and began reading,

> *"Dear Mr. John Hamilton,*
> *"I have not had the pleasure to make your acquaintance. I cannot share my name at this time for fear of reprisal from our British occupiers. Suffice it to say that I am a woman and a Patriot and that I long for the day when our oppressors will be run back into the sea. It is my sincere hope that the news I bear in this correspondence will lift your spirits as the Christmas season draws nigh.*
> *"By means that I cannot disclose I have made contact with a gentleman now housed in the prison barracks in Charlestown. His name is Joel Moffat, captured during Gates' defeat at Camden. He asked that I endeavor to inform you that your brother, James Hamilton, is alive and well and living with him in the barracks housing."*

A huge cheer erupted from the congregation. John wept openly, as did his mother. She wrapped William in her arms. Even Elder Scott wiped a tear of joy from his face as he basked in the celebration ongoing in what was ordinarily a very quiet, reserved, and conservative church body.

He waved his hands in a hopeless effort to try and calm the crowd. It was several minutes before he was able to resume reading the letter. Finally, the rowdy din dulled to an excited murmur.

"Folks, if I might continue … "

He cleared his throat again.

> *"Mr. Moffat has informed me that there are several dozen men from your county's regiment who were captured on the same day as he. Many have perished from the pox, the bloody flux, and starvation, but some remain alive. Please know that their situation is dire and that the British are most harsh in their treatment. But also know that they are more*

determined than ever to remain alive and defiant in the face of their cruel captors.

"Please know also that I and others like me are attempting to send food and supplies to the men inside the camp. I will also endeavor to forward further correspondence and information to you as I have the opportunity.

"Please give my regards to Mrs. Farr, and let her know that her son loves her and misses her dearly. I am your humble servant, a lady and Patriot of South Carolina. God save the United States of America!"

Elder Scott placed his arm around John's shoulders and in a very uncharacteristic fashion shouted, "Now, folks, that is good news!"

The men picked up and waved their hats and broke out in cheers of, "Huzzah!"

20

FEVER AND BLOOD

A wet snow fell in early January, and then the temperature dropped precipitously. John came down with the fever three days later. It was a Wednesday. It didn't seem very serious early on, just a horribly sore throat and a mild fever. But it grew worse. William took care of him at first, but two days later William took sick as well. Their little brother, Hugh, discovered them in their sweat-soaked beds when they failed to show up for dinner on Friday. William was still lucid, but John seemed almost outside his mind. He was ranting and hallucinating.

Their frantic mother had both of them brought into the main house. She had her younger sons place corn shuck mattresses in front of the fireplace and placed the boys there. Ephraim headed into town to fetch the doctor. Hugh mounted his horse and went to the Skillington farm to get Mary. John's mother knew that Mary would want to join her in taking care of her boys.

Mary was there within the hour. The doctor arrived around nightfall. The condition of the boys was grave. Their fevers waxed and waned. One moment their bodies were on fire, almost too hot to touch, and they poured forth sweat that soaked their mattresses. Moments later they were racked with chills and had to be pulled closer to the fire and covered with multiple layers of quilts.

Mary and Margaret hovered over them incessantly, and they prayed for them constantly. The doctor remained to supervise their condition overnight, but declared the following morning that there was nothing he could do. The boys had to sweat out the fever. They would either survive, or they wouldn't

He declared, "It is all in God's hands now."

The burning fever and alternating rigor of chills continued for four more days before it finally broke. Both of the women had fallen asleep in their chairs beside the fire. The stark silence and lack of movement from the mattresses in the floor was what snatched Mary from her sleep.

She wailed, "On, God, no!" Diving to the floor she placed her ear to John's chest. She wept when she felt it rise slowly and heard the strong, steady thumping of his heart. She reached up and felt of his head. His fever had broken, as had William's. Both of them were sleeping peacefully.

Ten hours later Mary heard the rustling of the mattresses. She looked to see John no longer flat on his back, but instead lying on his side and facing her direction. He smiled softly at her and then closed his eyes again.

Both boys slept almost without interruption for two more days. Mary and Margaret took every opportunity to spoon water into their mouths. They tried to give them warm chicken broth on the second day after the fever broke, but both boys gagged. So they continued to keep them hydrated and they waited patiently.

It was Sunday morning and eleven full days after John took sick when he finally emerged from his body's protective cocoon of sleep. The women didn't even know that he was awake. Mary jumped like she had been shot when John groaned from the floor, "I'm hungry."

She ran and dropped to the floor beside him, showering him with kisses.

"You rest easy, Johnny, and I'll get you something. Do you feel like sitting up?"

"My back is sore and my neck feels stiff as a board, but I think so."

Mary helped John sit up and lean against a pillow to cushion his back against the stone hearth.

"Where is everybody?" he asked.

"They've all gone to church. It's Sunday morning, John. They'll be back in a couple of hours."

Mary fixed him a small bowl of hot broth. He drank it down quickly and requested more … and something a little more solid. She brought him another bowl of broth and two slices of bread coated with butter. He wolfed down the bread, wincing as it grated across his raw throat. He washed down the deliciousness with the hot broth.

"Is there any chance a man could get some coffee in this house?"

Mary smiled and winked at him. "I'll see what I can do."

Fifteen minutes later John was sipping a delicious cup of coffee flavored with creamy milk and lots of sugar.

John looked at Mary, and then reached out and took her hand.

"How long have I been down, Mary?"

"Eleven days now."

John spewed some of his coffee from his mouth.

"Eleven days? How? There's no way!"

Mary shrugged and pursed her lips. "I'm telling you the truth. Your mama said you started feeling bad a week ago Wednesday, and then by Friday you and William were both down hard with the fever. You're not the only ones. There's at least three dozen other folk took sick, as well. Seven have died that I know of, six of those small children."

John looked over at his brother. "Is William all right?"

"He's fine. His fever broke the same night that yours did. He's still sleeping hard, though. But I think he'll come out of it soon."

"How long have you been here, Mary?"

"They came and got me on Friday … the day that Hugh found you two in the bed. Nine days ago."

John's eyes swelled with emotion. "I love you, Mary"

She leaned forward and kissed him on the cheek. She whispered into his ear, "I've always loved you, Johnny."

William awakened an hour later, ravenous just like his older brother. Mary fed him, as well. The Farr family arrived back home shortly after noon, accompanied by the Skillington clan. The boys' mother screamed and wept with joy at the sight of her sons sitting up against the hearth. She smothered both of them with her hugs and kisses and then set about cooking a Sunday feast. William requested a bed. He wanted to sleep some more. So they made him put on a fresh sleeping shirt and then placed him in a bed in the far corner of the cabin. He fell back to sleep almost immediately.

They relocated John to a comfortable chair by the window, freeing up the space around the fireplace for cooking. Ephraim Farr and John Skillington pulled up their own chairs and joined him.

"You missed a lot while you were sick, John," stated Ephraim. He smiled. "We won us a big 'un on Wednesday."

John's eyes lit up. "Where? What happened?"

"It was at a placed called Hannah's Cowpens, about sixty miles west from here in South Carolina. It was that giant of a general, Daniel Morgan. He outfoxed Tarleton and wiped out his command. It was a rout, they say."

"Tarleton?" inquired John. "It was the British Legion?"

"There's not much left of the British Legion, John," confirmed Mr. Skillington. "Morgan killed or captured pretty much all of them. Over three hundred killed or wounded, and over eight hundred captured. They say it's the biggest victory of the war."

"What about Tarleton?"

"Word is he got away, somehow," answered Ephraim.

"But the war's turned," added John Skillington. "First it was King's Mountain, and then Hannah's Cowpens. People's thinking has changed. Our new country's going to win this war and everybody seems to know it. We know it. The French know it. The Spaniards know it. It's just Cornwallis that hasn't quite figured it out yet."

"So we keep pressin' the fight to the end," stated John.

"To the end," affirmed the two men sitting with him.

William bounced back from the fever pretty quickly, but John's recovery was slow. It seemed clear that, whatever the disease was, he had endured a more serious case. John had neither the inclination nor the strength to leave the house throughout the months of January and February.

News of the war varied from week to week during those months. After the humiliating loss by Tarleton at Cowpens, Cornwallis mobilized his army and headed north in pursuit the army of General Greene. He crossed into North Carolina to the west of Charlotte. During the pursuit there were skirmishes in January and February just to the northwest and north at places like Beattie's Ford, Tarrant's Tavern, Grant's Creek, and Reedy Creek. Greene managed to stay one step ahead of Cornwallis and made his escape across the flooded Dan River into the safety of Virginia on February 13 and 14.

Cornwallis occupied Hillsborough and set about recruiting Tories to increase the ranks of his army. He also implemented a new strategy of freeing slaves and drafting thousands of them, as well. But on February 5 an event occurred that brought the recruitment of local Tories to a screeching halt. Known as Pyle's Massacre, it was a pitched battle between the forces of Colonel "Light Horse Harry" Lee and four hundred Loyalist militia under the command of Dr. John Pyle. It was a total rout, with ninety-three Loyalists killed and about two hundred and fifty wounded. Still, General Lord Cornwallis fought on.

Meanwhile, back in Mecklenburg County, warm weather broke in early March. John joined William back in their old cave house. Life returned to more of a routine. William was already back into the normal flow of his life. He hunted daily, skinned and butchered his kills, and continued tanning hides. John slowly began to return to accomplishing light chores, though he tended to run out of strength pretty quickly. He had to take a nap every afternoon, something very uncharacteristic of him. But his strength was definitely coming back a little more with each passing day.

John was sitting in the warm sun one afternoon in the second week of March when an unexpected visitor came to call. It was Captain Jonathan Potts of the local militia. John knew who the man was, but didn't really know him. The captain rode in and tied his horse to a post.

"Good afternoon, John."

"Good afternoon to you, Cap'n Potts. What brings you out this way?"

"Well, John, General Greene has issued a call for militia companies to join his army. He's expecting a major engagement with Cornwallis in the coming days. Colonel Locke has sent us out in search of recruits. I was hoping that I might entice you to come with my company as a wagon driver and rifleman."

"Cap'n, nothin' would make me happier than to join your company and get back in this fight, but I just can't do it right now. Maybe I can in a month or so. I just don't know. I still ain't over the fever I caught back in the winter. I liked to have died from it, and I still don't have my strength back."

"I heard in town that you got sick this winter. I reckon I didn't know you were that bad off."

"Yes, sir. I was out for eleven days they tell me. I'm still tryin' to put it behind me. I don't have the strength to make it through a whole day. I find myself havin' to sleep every afternoon. There ain't no way I could hold out to drive a team."

The Captain seemed disappointed. "Well, I hate to hear it, John. Word is you're a good man to have in a fight. You just get yourself better and we'll talk again before the next campaign."

"You can count on that, sir. Trust me, I'm ready to get out of this chair and get back to the war."

The captain tipped his hat to John, "Until next time, then." He quickly mounted his horse and rode away.

John climbed slowly from his chair and headed inside for some desperately needed sleep.

The engagement that General Greene anticipated came to fruition on March 15 when two massive armies clashed on the hilltop at Guilford Courthouse, seventy-five miles northeast of John's home. Cornwallis took the ground, but at a terrible price. He lost a full one fourth of all of his men dead or wounded. The British general moved his army back to Hillsborough, but soon realized that it was too decimated, too under equipped, and too poorly supplied to maintain its hold on the center of the state. He began to march his men toward the coastal town of Wilmington to recruit new soldiers and refit his struggling army.

Andrew and Robert Jackson were on the run. The night before they had attended a meeting of the local militia at the Waxhaws Church. The gathering had been a trap. About forty men were gathered at the church when a company of British dragoons and several dozen Tories attacked them. Eleven men were captured, but the rest managed to slip away into the woods. Robert and Andrew watched a bright orange glow illuminate the sky as the British burned the church in reprisal.

The brothers were hiding out in the trees about a mile away. It had rained during the night and they were freezing. Andy was turning blue with cold. They hadn't eaten anything since the previous morning. They desperately needed to find shelter. The boys huddled together to make a plan.

"What are we going to do now, Robert? We can't go back home. We can't lead them back to Mama."

"No, we can't do that. We have to find someplace else to hide out."

"Let's go to Uncle Thomas. He'll feed us and hide us, for sure. After things settle down a bit we can make our way north in a day or two and join up with the Greene's army."

"That sounds good to me. I'm halfway froze. Let's go!"

They mounted their horses and cut through the woods toward Thomas Crawford's home. A half-hour later they crept up to the thicket beside their uncle's house, dismounted, and tied their horses to a small tree. They left their rifles in the protection of their oiled leather wraps. They watched for several minutes before Robert ventured out in the open and approached the back door. He knocked and waited. His uncle opened the door, wide-eyed.

"Robert! I was worried sick! What happened to Andrew?"

"He's right behind me."

Robert signaled to his brother over his shoulder and then Andy came scurrying out of the woods.

"Get in here and get warm. We must get you out of those wet clothes."

"Uncle Thomas, it was horrible! They burned our church!" exclaimed Robert.

"Them sorry, murdering sumbitches," muttered Andy.

Their uncle took their coats. "I know, boys. I got word during the night. The Tories have already been through here looking for both of you. They know your names. You must not go back home."

"That's why we're here. We were hoping that we could get dried off and fed and then make our way north in a day or two," explained Robert.

Crawford responded, "I believe that's a sound plan. Now hurry up and get those clothes off. There are extras in Junior's bedroom. I'll get you some porridge and eggs and a cup of hot tea."

Ten minutes later the boys were wolfing down the delicious, hot food and savoring the warmth of the rich, dark tea. It appeared that they were well on their way to making their escape. Moments later both doors to the house crashed inward, the wood of their facings splintering and exploding as they were kicked in by a swarm of British dragoons.

The first soldier to enher the dining room exclaimed, "They're in here, Captain! It's the two lads that we've been looking for!"

A pompous captain soon entered the room. He removed his helmet and gloves as he examined the room in disgust. He barked at one of his sergeants in the hallway, "There may be more rebels in the house. Search it thoroughly! Tear this place apart!"

For the next several minutes the soldiers attacked the Crawford home. They ripped curtains off of the walls, bayoneted the mattresses on the beds, tore all of the clothing from the closets and drawers, and smashed every window and dish in the house. The officer leered at the boys and Thomas Crawford while the destruction went on all around them.

The captain reached for one of the dining table chairs and started to sit. When he looked down he noticed that his boots were covered with mud from the nearby swamps. He bent over and wrestled his boots off of his feet and then unceremoniously tossed them onto the table in the middle of the food and drink.

He stared at Andrew Jackson and then ordered, "You, boy. You're the reason for this mess. Fetch a rag and polish my boots."

Andy pushed his chair back from the table and rose to his feet, stretching as tall as his fourteen-year-old frame would allow him to stretch.

He retorted, "Sir, I am now a prisoner of war, and I expect I'll be treated as such."

The officer slammed his hand down on the table. "Boy, you will obey me this instant! Now clean and shine my boots!"

Andy Jackson seethed. He chewed his lip and tried to restrain his words, but he could not manage such restraint. He spoke, despite his desire not to.

"Sir, you may take those muddy, stinking boots and stuff them up your pompous, murdering, thieving British arse!"

The Captain jumped to his feet and drew his sword in a single, swift movement.

Thomas Crawford exclaimed, "Captain, no!"

The British captain swung his sword in a high arc and slashed at Andy's neck. Andy instinctively raised his hand in front of his face and fell backward. The razor sharp blade of the sword sliced across the palm of his hand and across his forehead just below the hairline. Blood gushed from both wounds. He cursed the captain with words that shocked his uncle.

The captain spun around and faced the elder Jackson brother, brandishing his bloody sword.

"I suppose the responsibility falls to you now, young man. You clean my boots!"

Robert stood tall and thrust out his chest. "I'm not touching your bloody boots you Redcoat bastard!"

The officer screamed hysterically and slashed with his sword again. Robert's skull took the force of the blade as it sliced a gaping gash across the right side of his head. The top of his ear simply fell off into the floor. The boy fell unconscious from the blow of the steel, bleeding profusely from the wound.

The captain spit on the boy and howled, "Throw some water on the little bugger and wake him up. Get these two ready to march to Camden. We'll see how tough they are in the King's prison!"

One of the Redcoats doused Robert with a bucket of cold water from the well. It mixed with the blood and ran all over the floor of the dining room and into the hallway, staining the pine floors. Robert awakened and grabbed at his stinging ear. He wailed in humiliation and pain.

The boys' uncle covered and bound their wounds as best he could, but the Redcoats were in no mood to wait. They jerked the boys to their feet and kicked them out the door. The Jackson brothers joined a group of twenty other captives waiting outside in the cold rain, and then the march began. Three days and forty torturous miles later the group arrived at the squalid prison camp in Camden.

21

OLD FRIENDS

John drove his wagon hard southward toward Camden. He was not hauling goods on this trip. This time he carried men. He drove one of three wagons out of Charlotte carrying forty men in a small, fast-moving convoy headed for the British-occupied South Carolina town. They were determined to get to Camden in time for the fight. Captain William Nesbitt was in command of this detachment. Most of the men were from his company of Mecklenburg County militia. Some, like John, volunteered as minutemen in answer to the call to action.

The Patriot forces were on the offensive in South Carolina. After Cornwallis' departure for the port at Wilmington, General Greene turned his army south, hoping to break the British stranglehold upon that state. The town of Camden was too well fortified with redoubts and trenches, so Greene hoped to lure the Redcoats out to fight. He was encamped in plain sight on a small hill about a mile and a half north of Camden. His force blocked the road north into the Waxhaws.

It was April 25. Over seven weeks had passed since John had received the visit from the militia captain right before the battle at the Guilford Courthouse. His health had improved dramatically during those weeks. The warm air of spring and the generous care provided by his loved ones were like a healing balm for both his body and soul. He was completely healed, completely rested, and anxious to fight.

John snapped the reins and yelled out a mighty, "Hyah!" to encourage his team. He was the middle wagon in the formation, and he was determined not to fall behind the driver who was in the lead. He heard a rattle at his feet. He glanced down to make sure that his rifle was still secure. He certainly did not want to lose his papa's precious Fowler gun.

The gun remained safely in its place, tied off and secure. John had a sudden flash of memory of hunting in the woods near home. Deep in his mind he saw a very clear picture of his father's face ... a face that he thought he had long since forgotten. He tried to capture the image in his memory and in his heart. He smiled.

"What in tarnation are you grinning about, Johnny?"

It was the shouting voice of his faithful companion Daniel Pippin, riding beside him on the seat of the wagon. Daniel reached up and grabbed his cocked hat just as it bounced into the air in response to a hard bump in the rough road.

"I was just thinkin' about Papa. I remembered a time when we was rabbit huntin' together. I saw his face in my mind ... it's been a while since I could remember his face."

"And now we're off hunting Redcoats together!" responded Daniel.

"Maybe so, if we can get there in time."

Daniel held his hat in place and strained to look ahead. "I ain't heard any shooting or cannon fire."

"We're still a ways off, yet. We might not be able to hear it from way up here."

"I reckon," Daniel responded. "How much farther you think we've got?"

"About ten or twelve miles. Won't be long. You need to set still, I keep thinkin' you're gonna get throwed out."

Daniel retorted, "Good Lord! It's like I'm riding off to war with my mama, or something."

"Yeah … or somethin' …"
John smiled at his pal.

"Look, Robert! The Redcoats are headed out. I think there's going to be a big fight. We'll be out of here soon."

Andrew Jackson watched the lines of Redcoats and Tory militiamen marching between the pits and redoubts that ringed the slopes of the hill upon which sat the town of Camden. There looked to be almost one thousand men. They were all headed to the woods to the east. No doubt, they were making their way around the right flank for an attack upon the Patriot encampment on Hobkirk's Hill. Andy just hoped that the Continentals could see where they were heading.

He looked down at his immobile brother. Robert was unresponsive. He merely stared upward toward the cloudy sky, his gaze locked upon some distant sight deep within his subconscious mind. Andy wasn't sure why he kept talking to Robert as if he might respond. He hadn't spoken in days. Maybe it was because he still needed a brother to talk to.

The boys had been in the squalid British prison yard for almost two weeks. Over two hundred and fifty men were crammed into a tiny animal pen inside a low stone wall and kept under constant armed guard. There had been no food or medical care since the boys' arrival. Their only source of water was a large trough in the southwest corner of the pen. Each day the Redcoats refilled it with muddy, foul water from a nearby creek.

Several of the men erupted with the bloody flucks, so there was rancid human excrement all over the pen. So far Andy had been spared the flux, but Robert was not so lucky. He came down with the bloody diarrhea on their third day in the camp and deteriorated rapidly. Then the smallpox hit. Neither Robert nor Andy had ever been exposed to the disease. One week ago about half of the men in the compound began to experience high fever, splitting headaches, and pain down their backs. Three days ago the pox pustules erupted all over the infected men.

Those who were suffering the flucks fared the worst when the pox placed its grip on their already-diminished bodies. Eight men had died. The other prisoners unceremoniously dumped their bodies over the wall and then the British, anxious to avoid touching their infected carcasses, looped nooses around their ankles and dragged them off with horses. They burned the bodies along with the ropes that they used to drag them.

John sat down on the ground and cradled Robert's head in his lap. The boy was a mere shell of the vibrant youth that he once was. The wound across his skull was swelled in a bulbous, angry, red mass. It poured forth putrid pus and stench. Andy couldn't keep the flies off of it. His bowels emptied themselves without encouragement, and though Andy tried to move him as often as he could, Robert was always laying in a puddle of his own waste. Andy surmised that his brother had lost at least forty pounds ... almost a third of his prior body weight.

Robert was dying and Andy knew it. He shuddered at the thought of seeing his own brother tossed out of the animal pen and roasted on a British bonfire. His only hope was the one thousand Patriot soldiers that he saw encamped on the hill to the north. Perhaps they could defeat the British garrison and Andy might somehow find care for his brother.

The three wagons careened into the encampment during the late morning. It was a typical army camp. The small knoll was covered with neatly-spaced two-man shelters. The wispy smoke of small cooking fires trailed into the sky and formed a dull haze that hovered over the hilltop. Men lounged around the camp, some of them washing their laundry in large pots, others cooking in smaller pots. None of them seemed overly-concerned about the proximity of the British garrison in Camden.

A sentry directed the wagons to the North Carolina militia sector of the camp. There were already groups on the hill from Burke, Lincoln, and Rowan Counties. John recognized the faces of a couple of the Rowan boys who had been in the fight in Charlotte.

A militiaman with something of an air of authority approached the wagons. "Where are you gentlemen from? Who is in command?"

Captain Nesbitt hopped down from his seat in the first wagon. "Mecklenburg County. I'm William Nesbitt, Captain of this detachment."

The other fellow extended his hand. "Welcome, Captain Nesbitt. I'm Captain John Bickerstaff out of Burke County. You boys are welcome to unload and pitch camp right here with us. We'll be eating dinner soon. One of the Lincoln County boys got a deer yesterday afternoon. We've put together a fine, large pot of stew. There's plenty for you fellows to join us."

Captain Nesbitt surveyed the camp. "We got word that a fight was about to commence so we got down here fast. But this almost looks like a garrison camp. I haven't see so much laundry drying on lines since last summer!"

Captain Bickerstaff chuckled, "That's about right. We've been camped here for three days. General Greene was hoping that parking out here in the open might gall the British enough to draw them out into a fight. But so far they're staying up there in town behind the safety of those redoubts. There's no way that we can run 'em out of there, so I really don't know what's going to happen next. For now we're just waiting."

"I reckon we'll join you then," commented Nesbitt. He turned to the men milling about the wagons. "Boys, it looks like we're camping for a while. Secure the wagons and we'll set up right here."

The men began to settle in for their stay. They gathered their belongings and pitched their tents. John didn't bother with a tent.

He prepared sleeping quarters for himself and Daniel in the back of his wagon. They stretched the canvas cover over the head rails. John pulled two tied up bundles of straw from underneath the wagon seat. He brought the soft grass from home for wagon bedding. He and Daniel spread the straw evenly in the back of the wagon and then rolled out their blankets.

"This is the best bedroom on the hill!" remarked Daniel.

John joked, "Nothin' but the best for you, Danny boy."

They decided to forego the invitation to join in the community dinner of venison stew. Both boys had packed plenty of rations from home. They lay down in the back of the wagon and snacked on dried beef and biscuits washed down with fresh, cool milk. They chatted about home and family, and even shared some of their dreams about what they might do after the war.

Both boys were just drifting off to sleep when the first shots went off over on the left flank. The Patriot pickets were firing in a heavy volume. John and Daniel jumped from the wagon. They grabbed their bags and guns and followed the rush of men running in the direction of the gunfire. The cluster of militiamen reached the crest of the hill to the southwest.

The sight of the colorful British and Tory armies stole John's breath. He had never seen anything so beautiful and yet so dreadful and deadly.

"How did them Redcoats get so close without anybody seein' 'em?" demanded one of the North Carolina militiamen standing near John. "Didn't we have any sentries out on watch?"

Another man remarked, "They must've slipped in through that swamp down yonder and formed up before the lookouts knew what was happenin'."

The Redcoats were tearing into the first line of Continentals near the base of the hill. The Patriots fought valiantly with muskets and bayonets, but in a matter of minutes the first line was overwhelmed and breeched. The wave of Redcoats and Irishmen in green poured through the gap and into the second line of Continentals. Another flanking force was moving around the hill to the left. The British were trying to surround them. If the British flanking movement succeeded then the entire force would be cut off from retreat. It appeared, at least for the moment, that the second battle of Camden might possibly end in the same result as the first.

The prisoners who were able to stand rose to their feet and rushed to the northern wall of their enclosure when they heard the first shots on the distant hill. Their British guards didn't appreciate the sudden movement. A line of ten soldiers formed quickly between the prisoners and their view of the ongoing battle.

The sergeant of the guard screamed, "Back off, you rebel scum! If just one of you tries to top that wall, we'll be shooting the whole lot of you!"

Andy exclaimed in his shrill, adolescent voice, "We're just trying to see the fight, you ignorant Redcoat arse! Move out of the way and get back to buggerin' one another!"

A hearty laugh erupted through the sickly, pox-covered mass of men. None of them had laughed in a long time. And none of them had the courage to unleash such an egregious insult upon their captors. Several of the men slapped Andy in affirmation on the back.

"That's tellin' 'em, laddie!" one imprisoned Irishman hissed.

The sergeant shot a glance at Andy, and then pronounced, "I'll deal with you later, Squire Jackson."

Andy winced a bit. The sergeant actually knew his name, which was definitely not a good thing. Soon, however, the guards disengaged and returned to their regular posts, giving the prisoners a clear view of the battlefield.

Andy and several others of the helpless prisoners cheered their Patriot comrades as the slugfest on the hillside played itself out.

"What do we do?" screamed one of the militiamen.

"Yeah! What are our orders?" yelled another.

A Continental colonel appeared rather suddenly and took charge of the gathering of men at the crest of the hill.

He yelled, "Militia with muskets will hold in reserve on the hilltop. Men with rifles, follow me. I need sharpshooters on the left flank!"

John and Daniel joined a cluster of about thirty men trotting to the far left side of the hill in pursuit of the energetic colonel. Once they reached the far left side the colonel pointed out their targets.

"Men, those infantry and light cavalry are attempting to get around behind us. Their range is much too far for muskets, but I'm counting on you farmer boys to stretch those long rifles out there and find me a few Redcoats! Can you do that men?"

"Yes, sir!" barked the newly initiated sharpshooters.

"Excellent! Extend a line from my position to the left. Space yourselves one yard apart. Get comfortable and choose your targets. Make every shot count. Men, I want you to kill the enemy!"

They barked again, "Yes, sir!"

"Fire at will, gentlemen!"

John and Daniel dropped to one knee and prepared to fire.

"I wish I had a shootin' stick," Daniel complained.

"Yep, we should have thought of that sooner," agree John. "Just do the best you can."

Shots began to erupt from the corps of snipers. Not many of the first rounds found their marks, but a few did. John's first shot fell well short of his target. He discovered that he would have to shoot high and try to drop the rounds in on them. There was no other way. They were well over four hundred yards down range. John put seven or eight shots down range, but had absolutely no idea if he actually hit any targets. There was simply too much distance and too much smoke.

Despite the overall inaccuracy of their shooting, the volume of lead descending upon the flanking attackers began to slow their momentum. Then, moments later, the thunder of a small cannon erupted from behind the militiamen. A round from a second cannon quickly followed the first shot. The sound of the cannon fire further slowed the end-run assault. In a matter of minutes the end was turned. The flank attack turned back, and the militiamen rose and cheered.

John and Daniel jumped to their feet and ran back toward the crest to observe the main line of attack by the British. They hoped to, once again, bring their sharpshooting skills to bear. The small cannons continued to rain down their death upon the British attackers, but still they continued up the hill. Something was wrong among the Marylanders on the right side. They appeared stalled. Then suddenly and unexpectedly the Irish volunteers ran them over and poured through the second line. The green-clad Irishmen swarmed behind the Continentals.

John knew that the battle was lost. Even though the Patriots had more men and artillery in their support, the British still somehow managed to take the field.

Suddenly the call erupted, followed by the cadence on the drums, "Retreat! Full retreat! General Greene has called the retreat!"

"Let's skedaddle, Daniel!" yelled John.

"Right behind you, Johnny!"

The two boys took off running for the Hamilton wagon. John was shocked to see another militiaman sitting in the seat of his personal wagon and fumbling for the reins. He ran full-speed at the driver and jumped into the air with the butt of his rifle aimed at the man's head. The man turned in wide-eyed surprise at the airborne lad flying toward him.

The last thing the frantic wagon thief saw was the brass butt plate of John's Fowler as it smacked him in the bridge of the nose. The man tumbled backward limply over the back of the seat. Daniel climbed up on the other side, untangled the unconscious man's feet, and then rolled him into the back of the wagon.

John slapped the leather reins and screamed, "Hyah!" at his team. He turned them sharp to the left and began to head north back up the rutted road that he had traveled earlier that morning. As he encouraged the team he yelled to running men all around him, "Get in! Jump in the back!"

By the time he reached the base of Hobkirk's Hill, John had a wagon load of twenty-three men stacked and wiggling on top of one another, holding on for dear life. He pushed the struggling team hard and didn't stop for two miles. He had to stop at that point because his horses were played out. He pulled off of the road and ordered the men out of his wagon. Daniel helped him find a small pond nearby to water the animals and allow them to rest. Then the boys sat down and waited for the rest of Greene's retreating army. They waited for most of the day. Their stopping point soon became a rally and collection point for the Patriot forces.

John thought that all was, indeed, lost. But their retreat didn't last very long. William Washington's Continental cavalry had been out on their own flanking maneuver. They captured almost two hundred British prisoners in the rear area of the enemy position. The sheer number of prisoners slowed them down significantly and the cavalry missed the main part of the battle. They were, however, able to come onto the field near the end and save the artillery from capture.

For some unknown reason, the British pulled back into Camden and left only a single company of dragoons on Hobkirk's Hill. Later that afternoon Washington's cavalry drove out the dragoons and re-occupied the position. By nightfall John Hamilton and the other men of Nathanael Greene's army were back on top of Hobkirk's Hill. Even thought the British technically took the field in the battle, the Patriots were back in their own tents before sundown.

"Sir, I beseech you! Release my sons to my custody and care. I can assure you that they pose no threat to you or your army."

The major looked condescendingly over the top of his glasses at the annoying woman standing before him.

He exhaled, "Madam, you have my sympathy, but the exchange has already been arranged. Seven men have been selected. It is the agreed-upon amount with General Greene. I will make no exceptions. Now if you will please excuse me!"

"But, Major! Surely you can see that my two little boys are not men of any army! They are being held unjustly and without cause. Please just give them back to me. They are all I have left in this world!"

"Madam ... excuse me, but I do not know your name ..."

"Mrs. Elizabeth Jackson, of Lancaster."

"Yes ... Mrs. Jackson, surely you can understand ...wait ... Jackson did you say?"

"Yes, my lord."

"And you are the mother of one Andrew Jackson?" The man acted as if the boy's very name tasted bitter to his tongue.

"Yes, he is my youngest child. You hold my son, Robert, as well."

The major's countenance changed from annoyance to rage. He stood and leaned forward toward the woman, balancing himself with his fists on his desk. He growled ... an actual, guttural growl of disgust.

"Madam, you have my deepest sympathy. That boy, Andrew, is an incorrigible, unruly, unbearable, foul-mouthed twit! He has been a bane to my existence from the moment he marched barefoot into this camp!"

"He is only barefoot, sir, because your soldiers took his shoes!" she shrieked.

"Be that as it may, I doubt that the presence or absence of footwear has little affect upon the demeanor of your uncouth child. I have wanted him out of here for days, but had no idea of what to do with him. I count it is a blessing that you have come to claim the little twit! Take him and be gone. If I ever lay eyes upon him again I will run him through, myself. Now, on your way!"

The major shouted, "Sergeant!"

"Sir!"

"Inform Captain Davis that the Jackson boys are to be released to their mother's recognizance. They will depart immediately."

"Yes, sir!"

The sergeant turned to Elizabeth Jackson and extended his left hand toward the door of the study. He nodded and spoke courteously, "Madam, after you, please."

Elizabeth Jackson turned and exited the British major's office, not quite believing what had just transpired.

Three days after the battle at Hobkirk's Hill Captain Nesbitt sought out John Hamilton. He soon located John and Daniel lounging in the back of their wagon.

"Wake up, Johnny Hamilton!" The captain kicked the side of the rig.

John stuck his head out of the back of the wagon. Seeing the captain he jumped out and came to a state of semi-attention.

John inquired, "Is something wrong, sir?"

"No, John. I just need you to do a little bit of running for the officers' corps."

"Sir?" John was confused.

"General Greene has dispatches to deliver north. He doesn't want to commit any of the regulars to the task, so he asked among the militia for the most reliable wagon man that we have. I volunteered you for the job."

John's ears perked up a bit. "Really, sir?"

"Absolutely. You're the best we've got. And this bag is full of important correspondence. I need you to make sure it gets to Charlotte and then forwarded on by courier to Hillsborough. Can you handle that?"

"Yes, sir. Definitely, sir."

"I thought so. And you'll need a rider for security. I don't suppose Private Pippin would be willing to take that job, would he?"

A muffled response emanated from the wagon, "Yes, sir!" Daniel's smiling face popped out from under the canvas.

The Captain grinned and shook his head. "I figured as much. That's why I have these papers all drawn up for the two of you. They show you on detached duty with the company for the defense of Charlotte through the end of July. That'll give you three months credit for this service in the militia. But you're basically on your own to mind your own business between now and then. Maybe someday we'll all get paid for this, huh?"

"I'll believe it when I see it, sir," commented John.

"I quite agree. Anyhow, you're free to go right now. Secure this satchel and travel safely."

He handed the heavy bag to John.

"Yes, sir. And thank you, sir."

The captain shook John's hand. "I'll see you back in Charlotte town one of these days, Johnny. Maybe it'll be better times."

"Let's hope so, sir."

The captain turned and walked back toward officer country. Daniel was already climbing into his seat, ready to head back home.

"You plannin' to ride this rig back with no team?" teased John.

"Oh, yeah … that."

Daniel and John both laughed as Daniel jumped down to help hitch the horses. They were rolling toward home fifteen minutes later. They were less than a mile up the road when the rain started.

"How much further do think we have, Andrew?"

Andy Jackson didn't respond. He stared ahead in a trance-like state. He was raging with a smallpox fever. His back was killing him. He was soaked to the bone by the rain, his teeth chattering from the cold. His bare feet left a bloody trail mixed with the water and mud. He barely heard his mother's voice.

Elizabeth Jackson struggled to keep Robert on the horse. The boy was basically comatose. The British soldiers had laid him belly down across the bare back of the animal. They really did not want to touch the infected boy, but their captain stood watch and forced them to obey his commands to load him on the horse. They tossed a short length of rope to Elizabeth and took off running to find soap and water to wash the pus and blood from their hands.

Elizabeth tied the rope to Robert's hands and feet beneath the horse's belly, but she was weak and unable to tie him securely. His limp body kept sliding off of one side of the horse. So throughout most of their journey she struggled to walk, lead the horse, and keep Robert balanced on top of the animal. She was thoroughly exhausted and completely heartbroken, not sure if she could carry on.

"Andy! Wake up! I asked you a question! How much further?"

"Mama, I don't know! How could I know? I've been looking at the same road that you have!"

Elizabeth wept and trudged along. For the longest time she heard nothing but the sound of the rain pouring down. Then another sound broke through the tapping of the rain. She heard horses and the squeaky wheels of a wagon.

Elizabeth prayed, "Heavenly Father, I cannot handle one more travail. Please make it be Godly men in this wagon who will pass without doing harm to a helpless woman and her children. I beg you in Jesus' name ..."

She walked on and kept her head low, determined not to make eye contact with whoever was in the approaching wagon.

The boys topped a hill about five miles below the cutoff to the road that ran through Lancaster and led on to Charlotte. The rain was pouring down in sheets.

"I sure hope we can find a dry place in Lancaster for the night," remarked Daniel. "I don't have no desire to keep on driving through this monsoon."

"I reckon we can find a spot. There's a tavern or two with rooms to rent. I also know a few folks down that way. We can at least find a barn to sleep in tonight."

"I'd settle for a barn," affirmed Daniel.

John saw shadows along the road on the left side. He strained to see what was in the road and discern if there might be any kind of threat.

"We got people on foot up ahead, Daniel. Get in the back and keep 'em covered. We don't need any trouble."

Daniel didn't even respond. He was already clamoring over the back of the seat and taking a position in the bed of the wagon. As they neared the people along the road John saw that there was no threat. It was a woman in a mud soaked dress struggling to hold a body on the back of a horse. A barefoot boy walked slowly along on the far side of the horse.

John spoke over his shoulder, "It's all right, Daniel. It's a woman and a kid haulin' a body. Prob'ly a mama or wife takin' a soldier home for buryin'."

John covered the hundred yards to the pedestrians quickly and pulled up alongside the woman. She was obviously afraid as she quickened her pace and refused to look at John.

John's heart broke for the woman. He called out to her, "Ma'am, can we be of assistance? You look like you're havin' a rough time."

The woman proudly threw back her shoulders and marched on through her fear. She shrieked, "We'll be fine! Now leave us be! We have nothing to take!"

"Ma'am, we don't want nothin' but to help you. We're soldiers from up Charlotte way just released from General Greene's army and headed home. Please, let us help you."

The barefoot boy on the other side of the horse suddenly stopped walking. His mother continued on. The boy slowly turned and faced the wagon, lifting his hand over his eyes to shield them from the pouring rain. The boy staring at John had a face that was swelled beyond description. The boy almost looked inhuman. And then he spoke.

"Johnny Hamilton? Is that you?"

John's heart leapt. He didn't know the face, but he knew that sing-song little voice.

"Andy? Andy Jackson?"

John jumped from the wagon and ran to the boy. He was just about to pick him up in an embrace.

"Don't touch me, John. I've got the pox. So does Robert … worse than I do."

John looked in disbelief at the body tied on the horse.

"That's Robert? Is he still alive?"

"The last time I checked."

John responded, "Well come on then, let's get you folks in the wagon and get you home."

Elizabeth Jackson's voice interrupted the reunion, "Andrew, who is this boy, and how do you know him?"

"Mama, this is John Hamilton. He's one of the Hamilton brothers I stayed with at the McClelland farm last year. We fought off the British Legion together."

A look of realization washed across Mrs. Jackson's face, and then she burst into tears. She tumbled into John's arms.

Daniel jumped down from the wagon seat and helped Mrs. Jackson into the shelter of the covered wagon. John grabbed a blanket from the wagon and placed it under the horse's belly. He then cut the rope that tied Robert's hands and feet together and carefully released the boy onto the blanket. He and Daniel wrapped him into a roll within the blanket and loaded him into the wagon, as well. After Andy climbed in they tied the Jacksons' horse to the rear of the rig and set off at a trot toward Lancaster. Andy passed out from exhaustion before they were even moving. Elizabeth napped lightly, waking often to check the boys.

Two hours later, with a little direction from Elizabeth, they arrived at the Jackson home. Daniel and John helped get Robert and Andy into the house. Daniel took the team into the barn and got them some grain while Andy took their belongings inside the home.

Mrs. Jackson stripped the nasty clothes off of her boys and put fresh shirts on them. Soon they were sleeping soundly in their own beds. John and Daniel built a fire in the huge stone fireplace and set about drying their clothes and warming themselves. Minutes later Daniel was asleep on the floor in front of the fire. John took a seat at the table. Mrs. Jackson soon joined him.

"Mr. Hamilton, I don't know how I can ever repay you. When I heard your wagon I feared for our safety and prayed that God you let you pass us by and leave us alone. Little did I know that His very angels of mercy and deliverance were in that wagon."

John smiled, "Well, we ain't no angels, ma'am. But we was glad to help some old friends."

Mrs. Jackson nodded humbly and then asked, "Are you the young man who fell in love with that dear, sweet Margaret McClelland?"

"No ma'am, that was my older brother, James. He was captured at Camden last year and is in the Redcoat prison down at Charlestown."

"Ah ... I see."

There was an uncomfortable moment of silence.

"Well, Mr. Hamilton, how can I repay you for the kindness that you have bestowed upon my family and home?"

"Ma'am we don't need a thing 'cept a roof over our heads tonight. If you would let us bed down here by the fire tonight we'll be on our way before you even wake up in the mornin'."

"Oh, John, that will be just fine. You are most welcome here to stay as long as you like. There's no need to be running off in the dark tomorrow."

"Well, ma'am, we have army dispatches that we need to get to Charlotte. So we do need to light out early. I hope you understand."

"Yes, John, of course. I can see that you are a man of honor and one who takes his duty very seriously."

"I like to think so, ma'am."

"Well then, John, I will let you get some rest. I am exhausted myself after this ordeal and I will have much work to do nursing these boys back to health in the coming days."

"Yes ma'am. I'm sure you will."

"Good night then, John Hamilton."

"Good night to you, Mrs. Jackson."

John dropped down next to Daniel by the warm, glowing fire and soon fell fast asleep.

It seemed like only moments had passed when he felt Daniel shaking him awake in the darkness. The boys quietly gathered their gear and made a silent exit. They hooked up the team and headed north out of Lancaster just as the sun was beginning to rise.

Four hours later they rounded the bend to their familiar hometown of Charlotte.

Two days later Robert Jackson died in his bed.

22

BROTHERS

J ohn settled back into normal life after returning home from the battle at Hobkirk's Hill. It was mid-May and the boys should have been in the middle of planting and farming season, but there was no seed to be found in Mecklenburg County in the spring of 1781. Since their farm was non-producing and dormant, they stayed on the Farr property and helped Ephraim whenever they could. They would have to hold on and make do until the war was over and James came home. They hoped beyond hope that life would return to normal sometime soon.

John and William counted their blessings that their property was paid for free and clear. Even without a crop they did not fear the loss of their land. Plus, James had tucked away just enough to pay a couple of years' taxes. All the Hamilton boys had to do was find food and stay alive. Being surrounded by family and friends and seemingly out from under the yoke of the British and their Tory lapdogs made those tasks relatively simple.

Another letter made it through from Charlestown and broke the monotony of their day-to-day existence. It arrived on June 5, but it was dated May 22. The letter read:

"Dear Mr. John Hamilton,

"It is with great joy that I write to you again to send you news of your dear brother. I apologize sincerely for the lack of correspondence over these past months. Our courier system was compromised during the winter and discovered by our common enemy. It has taken several months to re-establish a dependable network by which to forward correspondence northward.

"James is doing as well as can be expected. I have had regular contact with him through Mr. Moffat. I even spoke to him personally on two occasions when he ventured close enough to our normal place of rendezvous. Both men have fared well during their stay in the prisoner barracks. There is less disease and privation in the camp than on board the deathly ships in our harbor.

"I have managed to smuggle modest amounts of food and supplies through the fence to them. We cannot exchange much in the way of goods, though, as we do not want to betray your brother and his friend through the appearance of health that is better than that of their comrades. It is a difficult balance to find.

"We hold hope that there will soon be a general exchange of prisoners. Rumors abound in Charlestown regarding such a possibility, but I have no way to confirm those rumors.

"There is also another rumor that the camp will soon be shut down and all men moved on board prison ships. We pray that this is not the case. I trust that you will join us in that prayer.

"Please rest assured that if there is any change in your brother's status that I will endeavor to forward information to you at the first possible opportunity.

"Please give my regards to James' mother, and let her know that her son still loves her and misses her dearly. I remain

your humble servant, a lady and Patriot of the free state of South Carolina. God save the United States of America."

So John and his mother and all of their family and friends prayed fervently that his brother would not have to serve any more time on a British prison ship.

James and Joel were crestfallen. The dreaded day finally arrived. They were headed back to a prison ship. Rumors had been circulating through the camp for weeks that the men were headed back to the floating dungeons. The British apparently felt that there was no need for the camps since they had such ample space aboard their floating cities of death.

Sadly, the prisoner population had dropped by one-half during the winter. Most of the men perished from disease and exposure. Many others gave in to the constant pressure of the British to switch allegiances in the conflict and join the English cause. Still others were simply pressed into a service of enslavement in the Royal Navy. The end result of the yearlong attrition was the consolidation of the prison population on board the prison ships.

James and Joel were among the lucky few who made it through the cold months. But their luck had finally run out. Now they sat in the bottom of a crowded skiff among a group of twelve men shackled together at the ankles. The one thing that added serious insult to their current injury was the fact that one of their captives had, only months ago, been one of their own.

Linus Ellman, formerly of the Burke County, North Carolina militia, was on one of the oars that propelled the captives toward their new home. He wore the dingy, baggy clothes of a British seaman. Back in February he was one of the turncoats who had finally given in, sworn his allegiance to King George, and enlisted in the British

Royal Navy. And he had the gall to actually speak to Joel Moffat from Mecklenburg County.

"C'mon over to the winnin' side, Joel. We gets a brand new hammock and two solid meals a day in the King's navy! And these nice new duds, to boot! We could always use a few more good workers, even scrawny, loud-mouthed scarecrows like you."

Joel crooned over his shoulder to James, "Jamie, did you hear something? I thought I heard an old bull drop its load ... sounded like it landed right here in this canoe."

"I didn't hear nuthin', Joel, 'cept maybe a squawkin' she-male seagull. Or was it one of them dodo birds? I can't hardly tell the difference."

The other prisoners broke out into laughter and joined in deriding the traitor.

The oarsman's neck and head flushed in embarrassment and rage. "Ha ha! Go ahead and laugh you dimwits. I'll crack your dumb skulls with this here paddle. We'll see who's laughin' then."

Joel plunged the knife of insult deeper. "Wowee, Jamie! It talks! Now that's a good one. I dee-clare, I t'aint never heerd a big, talkin' turd before! Somebody ought to sign up that talkin' turd for one of them travelin' shows. Oh, wait. That ain't a talkin' turd! He just looks like one 'cause he's been crawled up so deep into a British arse!"

The prisoners began to double over with loud, uncontrollable laughter. Even the other British oarsmen couldn't hide their grins.

This time the traitor Ellman jumped to his feet and wielded the oar high over his head, threatening to strike Joel Moffat. Joel never blinked. He just stared the man directly in the eye.

The man grinned a wicked smile at Joel and then mocked, "You won't have such a smart mouth, I'm thinkin', when your skinny arse is throwed down in that ship's hold."

"You're prob'ly right," Joel admitted. "But I won't be down in that hold forever. One day soon this war'll be over, and I'll go back home to my farm. Alls you got to go home to is your little limey pals here, you traitor bastard. You sure can't go back to Carolina. Because iff'n you ever do, I'll kill you dead. And that's a promise."

The sailor thought for a moment. His countenance fell as his mind ventured back home to North Carolina. He dropped his oar back into its cradle and began rowing once again, staring at the water.

James reached up and squeezed his friend's shoulder.

James became ill three weeks after returning to the ship. It started as a mild fever and headache. In three days it progressed into a raging fever accompanied by a horribly sore throat. Joel feared that it might be ship's fever … cholera. He did the best that he could to care for his friend, but his abilities were limited. There was no regular supply of food and no medicine. The best that he could do was keep giving him water and take him outside in the sunshine as much as possible. He was fearful that his friend might perish.

On Monday, June 25, as soon as their captors opened the hatch, the men clamored up the ladder into the warmth of the summer morning. Once they were all on the main deck the sergeant of the guard made a most amazing announcement.

"Listen up, you rebels! You lucky bastards are having Christmas in the middle of summer on this fine day. The commandant of prisoners has graciously granted permission for a contingent of nurse women to come on board with food, medicine, and supplies. For some mysterious reason that eludes me, he seems to think that your sickly arses are worth the trouble. So be on your best behavior. If I hear that any of you say or do anything ungentlemanly, I'll see you hanging from the mast this very day!"

At first the men thought that the announcement was some sort of cruel joke. But, sure enough, just before mid-day a small boat approached from the Charlestown docks. Almost one hundred men lined the rail of the ship to watch it come in. The rest of the men, sixty or more, were too sick to stand. James Hamilton was in that group. He hadn't stood in days. Poor Joel pulled and dragged him everywhere he went.

Minutes later Joel ran over to his friend. "Jamie, it's true. There's a boat comin' that has twelve or fifteen women in it! I see big iron pots and all manner of parcels. You just hang on, buddy, I'm gonna get you some help."

A half-hour later Joel returned, dragging an older woman with him.

"Ma'am, this here's my friend I was tellin' you about. He's mighty sick with a fever. Has been for a few days now."

The kindly-looking woman knelt beside James and checked his temperature.

"Oh, my! This boys is burning up!" she exclaimed. "Has he had the flucks or been throwin' food up from his mouth?"

"No ma'am, just a fever and headache and powerful sore throat. We ain't had no food in a week now, anyways."

"No food in a week! Well, I will see that we get that little problem taken care of. We brought plenty of broth soup with rice for you men today. Son ... what is your name?"

"Joel Moffat, ma'am." He extended his hand humbly to the woman.

"Mr. Moffat, can you go over and tell the ladies that I need a hearty cup of soup for this sick man? Bring a chunk of that bread, as well. And be sure to get you some for yourself while you're over there. You look a might bit peckish."

"Yes ma'am. Don't mind if I do."

Joel scurried off to fetch some soup. The woman turned her attention to James. James stared at her with hollow, tired eyes. She smiled at him and stroked his hair away from his face.

"Well, young man, I don't think you have ship's fever. You don't have all of the symptoms of that. You have another fever of some sort that has nothing to do with your bowels. So we are going to feed you and get lots of good clean water in you and get you cleaned up a bit on the outside, too. Is that all right?"

James nodded his affirmation. The woman dipped a clean linen cloth into a bucket of soapy water and began to wash James' face, chest, and arms.

"I declare, son, you are a dirty one! I'm going to need a fresh bucket of water when I get done with you! And you look a fright with that shaggy hair all over your face. I must admit that I cannot get used to seeing such furry faces as I see on board these ships. It's just not civilized."

James smiled at her honesty. He whispered through aching lips, "It's not my fault ma'am. I would love to have my wash tub and razor from back home."

"I bet you would at that. Where is your home, laddie?"

"I'm from Mecklenburg County up in North Carolina.

The woman laughed out loud and slapped both hands on her legs. She cackled, "Is that so, now? I come from Lancaster, just south of you down in the Waxhaws. We're neighbors! Now, isn't that something?"

Her laughter melted into a smile as she continued her hospital bath for her sickly patient.

"What is your name, laddie?"

James whispered, "I'm James Hamilton, ma'am. And I am most pleased to make your acquaintance."

The woman stopped her bathing activities and stared at James wide-eyed.

"Did you say James Hamilton?"

"Yes' ma'am."

"Have you ever been down to the Waxhaws?"

"Yes ma'am. Last year I visited for a while."

The woman paused. She glanced around to see if anyone was listening.

"Do you have a brother named John?"

James' heart began to thump in his chest. How could she know that? How could a stranger know that? He answered, "Yes ma'am. I have brother named John."

The woman's eyes began to swell and a tear formed in her right eye. It quickly gained enough mass to dislodge itself and run down the length of her cheek.

She asked excitedly, "And do you know two boys named Andrew and Robert Jackson?"

James began to cry when he heard those two familiar names.

"Yes ma'am. I worked with them on the McClelland farm last year. We fought the Tories together."

The woman leaned forward and placed her hand beneath James' neck. She brought her face low, hovering just inches above his. Her stone gray eyes stared into his deep blue eyes.

She whispered, "James Hamilton. I am *very* pleased to make *your* acquaintance. My name is Elizabeth Jackson. I am Andy and Robert's mother."

"You're kiddin' me!" exclaimed Joel, his shrill voice reverberating through the hold of the dark ship.

Several of the prisoners cursed in protest.

James whispered, "I swear, Joel! Mrs. Jackson told me all about it. John's been fightin' in the militia. She met him when he was headin' back home after another fight at Camden. He helped her get her two boys sick with the pox back home after she got 'em out of a British prison."

"And little Johnny's just fine, then?"

"He's just fine and he's fightin'!"

"And she told you we're winnin' this war?"

"She told me things have turned. We fought the Redcoats to a draw up at Guilford Courthouse, and then whupped 'em at King's Mountain and at another place called Cowpens. Now' they've lit out to the coast up at Virginia around Jamestown. Our army's moved into South Carolina. The British have even been run out of Augusta, Georgia!"

"I can't hardly believe it," Joel muttered. "Jamie, we might actually get off of this boat one of these days!"

"And soon," added James.

The notice arrived unexpectedly on July 4. It came by courier from Camden and points south. The sheriff posted it at the courthouse. It was the best that he could do to get the information disseminated into the community. His method worked very quickly, especially with the patriotic fervor and celebrations surrounding the fifth anniversary of the Declaration of Independence from Great Britain. Word of mouth spread quickly throughout the county and region.

The notice read:

> "By Order of General Sir Henry Clinton, Commander of His Majesty's Forces in the Americas –
>
> "A most amicable agreement for the exchange of prisoners has been attained between His Majesty's forces and the armies and naval forces currently in rebellion against Great Britain. All rebel prisoners taken in the colonies of Georgia, North Carolina, South Carolina, and Virginia and being held in facilities in and around Charlestown will be exchanged forthwith on the island of Jamestown, Virginia. Such exchange to commence on July 15 and will continue until all agreed terms are met. Families wishing to redeem their family members are instructed to proceed to the point of exchange at their own leisure and expense.
>
> "God save King George III."

Daniel Pippin was breathless when he rode up to the Farr cabin in search of Johnny late that evening. The younger Farr children directed him to the cave house. He ran up to the front of the shack and rapped on the door. John answered the knock in his nightshirt.

He yawned, "What's wrong, Daniel?"

"They're being released right away! Our brothers are being released!"

"What? How do you know? Where?"

"There's a letter posted at the courthouse, just sent north from Charlestown. It says that Clinton has ordered an exchange to commence on the fifteenth of this month."

"That's less than two weeks!" exclaimed John.

"I know! That's why I came right over. We've to go get 'em."

"Where?"

"Jamestown."

"Virginia?" John exclaimed. "Why Virginia? Why not just let 'em go at Charlestown?"

"I don't rightly know. Maybe because it's an exchange. Our prisoner camps are all up north. Maybe its half-way in betwixt the two of 'em, or somethin'."

John nodded, "That makes sense."

"We need to get goin' as quick as we can. I say we light out tomorrow."

"You're prob'ly right," John affirmed. "No tellin' how long it'll take to get there. But we need to plan a bit, though."

"What's to plan? We take plenty of food, extra clothes, and some powder 'n lead. We'll sort the rest out as we go."

John smiled at his friend and placed his hand on his shoulder, "Dan, you know we've not heard a word about Henry."

Daniel looked down at the floor, "I know, Johnny, but I can still hope. I got to, for Ma and Pa's sake, at least. But even if Henry's dead, I gotta help you get James back home. That's what friends do."

John hugged his best friend.

"I'll see you in the mornin', Daniel. I need to go tell Mary and her family what's goin' on. Mama, too. Let's plan on leavin' around dinner or so."

"Sounds good. I'll see you at dinner." Daniel grinned mischievously. "Tell your mama to save me a plate."

John awakened early the next morning and made his preparations. He went to the main house at breakfast and told his mother the good news. She wept, of course, as she always did whether news was good or bad. The entire house was thrown into an uproar. After the initial emotional outburst subsided she immediately set about cooking breakfast and packing food for his journey. She poured John a cup of milk and invited him to sit down at the table.

John was floored when Ephraim sat down with him and stated his personal intentions.

"John, I am to go to Jamestown with you."

"Me, too!" injected William.

Ephraim looked at William and started to object, but then nodded his head in agreement.

"William deserves to go, as well. James is his brother, too."

John objected, "But Mr. Farr, Daniel Pippin is already goin' with me. We were figurin' on doin' this ourselves."

Ephraim shook his head in disagreement, "I don't think that's a good idea, John. It's a long way to Jamestown … every bit of three hundred miles. There will be river crossings along the way. There might be Tories still on the loose up that way. You need more hands and guns. Four will be better than two."

"What about the horses? That'll be a heavy load for one team, especially bringin' men back with us. It might be more than James and Joel Moffat that need a ride home."

"We'll take extra horses. We'll tie on my team as a spare, and William and I will ride our own mounts."

John smiled, "Sounds like you've thought this all through."

Ephraim nodded, "Truth is, I thought this out a long time ago. I've just been waitin' on the time and place to go and get James."

"I'm grateful, Mr. Farr."

"John, I know that you'll never call me Pa. I don't deserve that, at all, after the way I acted toward you boys through the years. But can you at least call me Ephraim?"

"I can do that, Ephraim."

Ephraim smiled and smacked John on the knee. "Good! Now let's eat some of your Mama's fine cooking and pack us a wagon."

"I gotta go see Mary after breakfast before I do anything else."

"I figured as much. No rush. Jamestown ain't going nowhere, I don't reckon."

❧

Mary ran out of the door of the cabin when she saw John approaching on horseback. She laughed and babbled as she ran.

"Oh, Johnny, I heard the news! Isn't it wonderful? How will James get back home from Jamestown?"

"I'm leavin' to go get him in a couple of hours, Mary."

Her excited talking ceased, and her demeanor changed.

"You are? So soon?"

John jumped down from his horse. She was in his arms before his second foot hit the ground.

"Yes, sweetheart. Jamestown is many days' ride away. I want to be there when he comes off of the boat."

"You're not going alone, are you?"

"No, Mary. Ephraim and William are going. Daniel Pippin is going as well."

"That's good. And I am so glad Ephraim is going with you."

"Me, too."

Mary smiled wryly, "I never thought I'd hear you say that."

"I never though I would, either!" he laughed.

"Please be careful, Johnny. Come back home to me. I have big plans for you."

He took her in his arms. "I have big plans for us."

They embraced and kissed.

It was twelve days later, July 17, when the wagon and four weary riders from Mecklenburg County arrived at Swanns Point on the James River opposite Jamestown. It was a torturous journey. Because it was an unfamiliar land and terrain for them, they lost their way several times and twice had to cut cross-country in an effort to find suitable roads to reach their destination. But at long last the village was in view. There were two large ships anchored off the point and military encampments littered the far shore.

John left the other men to set up camp and hired a small boat to take him across the wide, slow-moving river. He soon found a very polite British major who had the dubious responsibility of disseminating information to people in search of their loved ones. The officer informed him that, thus far, only four ships bearing prisoners had arrived from Charlestown. A quick survey of the passenger manifests showed that James Hamilton was not on any of those vessels. Furthermore, the British government could not give any assurances of how many ships were coming or the schedules of any possible arrivals. John returned downcast to their camp across the river.

For the next three days the men amused themselves as best they could. During the daytime they alternately took the time for taking naps in the shade or for fishing in the brackish water. They talked, ate, and smoked their pipes. They played cards and told stories. They sought out and talked to other families waiting diligently for their sons and husbands to arrive.

The nights were miserable, for it was in the darkness that hordes of buzzing mosquitoes descended upon them. They tried everything to keep them at bay. They lit heavily smoking fires throughout their camp and covered their exposed skin with mud and ash. Still, the blood-sucking pests fought their way through and left all four of them covered with hundreds of itchy welts. Poor Daniel Pippin seemed to have excessive numbers of the bites and appeared especially sensitive to the insect's venom. The others appropriately dubbed him, "Sweet meat."

Early on the morning of the fifth day, July 21, William shocked the others from their boredom when he literally shrieked, "Boat comin'!"

Sure enough, there was a schooner downriver. It had just rounded the point four miles to the southeast and was slowly making its way toward Jamestown.

John shot Ephraim a hopeful look.

"You boys go on over," Ephraim instructed. "I'll wait here and keep an eye on camp."

John grabbed a silver coin from his bag to pay the oarsman and the boys joined the small flotilla of tiny fishing vessels making its way northeast across the river. They pulled up on the muddy shore about ten minutes before the ship docked. People began to crowd around the point of debarkation.

A loud British captain bellowed, "Civilians will kindly stay behind the fence! Please allow us to do our work. If your family member is aboard this vessel, you will know shortly! Do not make me tell you again!"

A small detail of Redcoats pushed its way through the crowd and stationed themselves as a barrier between the family members and the dock. The crowd backed up several steps.

Moments later the ship came into clear view. Well over one hundred men crowded the rail around the deck and peered into the waiting crowd. Each man, most assuredly, prayed and hoped that they had at least one loved one in the mass of people.

John strained to see the faces of the men, but they all looked the same to him. They were all bearded and filthy and dressed in little more than rags. They were a pitiful sight, indeed.

The ship soon bumped and groaned to a stop against the timbers along the dock. It rode low in the water, so the level of descent from the deck of the boat to the small wooden dock was only about eight feet. A British soldier on board kicked a rope ladder over the side. The ladder dropped and the bottom end landed on the wood platform with a loud thump. Then, one by one, the skinny, pitiful men began to come down the ladder.

The Redcoat major standing at the base of the ladder shouted, "Prisoners! As you disembark you will state your name for checking against the ship's official manifest. You will be informed whether you are dismissed or if you must wait in the holding area for further documentation or interrogation. First prisoner!"

The pitiful man at the front of the line stated plainly, "Michael Overby."

The officer marked an "x" on his paper and then stated, "Michael Overby, you are dismissed."

This ritual was repeated over and over again. Only two of the men so far had family waiting for their return. The look of want and disappointment on all the other men's faces was almost unbearable. John fought the urge of his heart to cry. He simply could not believe the emaciated state of the men. His hatred for the British burned. He wanted to kill every Redcoat on that dock.

Over thirty men had descended the ladder, but so far no familiar names had sounded off. John's disappointment grew.

He thought dejectedly, "James must be on another boat."

Suddenly the officer in charged blurted out, "Well, state your name, you ignorant rebel arse!"

"My name's Joel Moffat, you wig-wearin' fairy!"

"Watch your mouth, boy, or I'll have you run through!"

"Well you shite-lickers have been tryin' to kill me for thirteen months now and ain't figgered out how to do it, yet! You might as well give it a go."

The crowd held it's collective breath, not believing the insolence of this skinny, wooly mountain man. John fought his way toward the front of the crowd to try and see Joel. The officer hesitated with his response, and then marked an "x" on his paper.

"The rebel Joel Moffat is dismissed ... and good riddance! Next!"

The next emaciated man spoke, "James Hamilton."

"James Hamilton, you are dismissed."

John finally plowed his way through the crowd. His eyes met his brother's eyes. He screamed from the depths of his lungs and his soul, "Jamie!"

James didn't run to him. He couldn't. He could barely shuffle his feet. But he finally made his way past the Redcoat guards. John reached out to him and picked his big brother up in his arms in a tremendous bear hug. Unbelievably, John Hamilton now outweighed his elder brother by at least fifty pounds.

The crowd cheered at their emotional reunion. They parted to allow William and Daniel through, as well. William took hold of his big brother and wept.

"What about me, you fat turds?" ask the smiling Joel Moffat who stood nearby watching the entire spectacle.

The Hamilton boys pulled him into their huddle, as well. Only Daniel Pippin stood alone. He peered anxiously at the men who continued to climb slowly down the ladder from the prison ship.

James reached over and took Daniel by the arm, pulling him near. He grabbed the boy behind the back of his neck and pulled him close, looking him directly in the eyes.

"Daniel, he ain't comin'."

Daniel nodded, tears welling in his eyes. "I figgered he wasn't. We ain't heard from nobody but you and Joel these past months."

"Daniel, your brother was mine and Joel's best good friend. He took sick right after we got on the first prison ship and died a few weeks later. He died peaceful in his sleep. He just went to sleep one night and didn't wake up. Truth is, me and Joel prayed for that to happen to us most nights in that hellhole."

"That's the honest truth, Daniel," affirmed Joel.

James continued, "We volunteered for the burial detail that day. Joel and me buried him ourselves. We picked a pretty spot on the beach and we marked it in our minds. We know where he lays. Maybe we can take you there one of these days. Would you like to do that, maybe?"

Daniel nodded in silent response. James pulled the boy close and hugged him.

After a few more minutes of celebration, John spoke up, "Why don't we get on back across the river. I don't care nothin' 'bout bein' round all these Lobsterbacks."

"Amen to that, Johnny!" exclaimed Joel as the group made their way to their small hired boat.

William and John helped support James as they walked across the hard rock and shells. Daniel helped Joel, but the sharp surface didn't seem to bother him as much.

William told James as they walked, "Ephraim is waitin' for us across the river."

James stopped in his tracks and looked at John. He exclaimed, "Ephraim Farr?"

John smiled and kept walking. "I'll tell you all about it, brother. Right now we need to get you two on over to the other side and get hold of some soap and razors. You both smell like a skunk died and willed you his arse."

"Two skunks, at least!" chirped William. "I ain't never gonna get the stench of your armpits off'n my shirt."

The young men howled with laughter.

One hour later James and Joel bathed in the brackish water of the James River. Ephraim boiled some fresh water and gave them both a much-needed shave. He had to sharpen his razor three times to cut through their matted beards. James watched the man closely as he patiently shaved his face. It was hard to believe that the man who had been so mean to him for so many years, and was the object of his hatred for so long, was now showing him such mercy and kindness.

While Ephraim took care of their hair problems and helped make them more socially presentable, the other boys burned their nasty clothes and laid out fresh breeches, socks, shirts, and weskits for them both. William provided them each with a beautiful set of moccasins that he made from elk hide.

Then they ate. They tried to eat too much at first, but Ephraim insisted that they proceed carefully in order to not become sick from overstuffing their shrunken stomachs. The men paced themselves, eating small meals and snacks, almost without ceasing. They ate and relaxed for two whole days along the river as their strength slowly found its way back into their members.

On the third morning Ephraim and the boys awakened to find James and Joel breaking camp and loading their gear into the wagon.

James stated plainly and simply, "Let's go home."

"The Redcoats burned our cabin and barn, James. We don't have a home, anymore," replied William.

James walked over to his little brother. "William, my home is where you are. It's where Johnny is. My brothers are my home."

William smiled and responded, "I'm ready. Let's go home ... together."

And they did. James and Johnny Hamilton's war was over.

Three months later George Washington slipped down from the north and the French fleet sailed into Chesapeake Bay and cornered Cornwallis just twenty miles to the east of Jamestown at a place called Yorktown, Virginia.

The American Revolution was over. The United States of America won its freedom and independence. The Hamilton boys went back to Mecklenburg County, rebuilt their cabin, and finally found peace.

THE REAL HAMILTON BROTHERS

Though some of the characters in this story are fictional, most were real, historical individuals. James, John, William, and Hugh Hamilton were all the sons of Hugh Hamilton of Mecklenburg County. Their descendants are legion and were once described in a 1921 book by James Alexander Hamilton entitled *A Genealogy of the Descendants of Hugh Hamilton.* Both the Sons and Daughters of the American Revolution recognize James and John Hamilton as Patriots of the Revolution.

James Hamilton served in the militia in Mecklenburg County. His service is described in detail in his federal pension file in the National Archives. In that record he offered testimony regarding his actual battles and his capture at Camden. All of these events are described with dramatic fictional license in this work.

James left North Carolina after the Revolution and returned to York County, Pennsylvania to live near extended family. The reason for his departure from the south is unknown. James took up the art of gunsmithing, a career common to that area of Pennsylvania. In 1799, at the ripe old age of thirty-eight, he finally married a woman named Martha Wallace. They had four sons and two daughters and lived in York County until James' mother passed away in 1814. He inherited a portion of the Farr farm and moved his family to Cabarrus County (formed from Mecklenburg). He received a pension for his

Revolutionary War service while residing there and lived in North Carolina until his death in 1842. His wife remained on the farm until her death in 1866.

John Hamilton served the Patriot cause, as well. He received payment for providing supplies to the cause and for actual service in the militia. The records for those transactions are located in the North Carolina archives. He received reimbursement payments in 1782 and 1783, after the cessation of hostilities. However, the details of his actual service during the war are lost in time. Suffice it to say that he was, indeed, a Patriot and a soldier in the American Revolution.

After the war John Hamilton married his beloved Mary Skillington. They had four sons and six daughters. Mary died before the 1830 census was taken. In the 1830's John and some of his children moved west across the mountains to McMinn County, Tennessee, where John died around 1839. Both of their burial sites have been lost.

I descend from their oldest son, Hugh Skillington Hamilton. John Hamilton is my fifth great-grandfather. It has been a joy to explore his history and share what could have been his story.

Geoff Baggett

ABOUT THE AUTHOR

Geoff Baggett is a small town pastor in rural Kentucky. Though his formal education and degrees are in the fields of chemistry, biology, and Christian theology, his hobbies and obsessions (according to his wife) are genealogy and Revolutionary War history. He is an active member of the Sons of the American Revolution and has discovered over twenty Patriot ancestors in his family tree from the states of Virginia, North and South Carolina, and Georgia.

Geoff is an avid living historian, appearing regularly in period uniform in classrooms, reenactments, and other Revolutionary War commemorative events throughout the southeastern United States. He lives on a small piece of land in rural Trigg County, Kentucky, with his amazing wife, a daughter and grandson, and a yard full of fruit trees and perpetually hungry chickens and goats.

Made in the USA
Charleston, SC
13 April 2016